Books by Donna S. Frelick

The Interstellar Rescue Series:
Unchained Memory
Trouble in Mind
Fools Rush In

FOOLS RUSH IN

By

Donna S. Frelick

First INK'd Press edition.

ISBN-13: 978-0692752692
ISBN-10: 0692752692

The meek shall inherit the earth; the rest of us are going to the stars.

 --Old Earth Proverb

To kick some alien butt!

 --Rayna Carver, Field Agent,
 Interstellar Council for Abolition and Rescue

CHAPTER ONE

The starship's hold was as dark and humid as a womb, as hot as blood. But Rayna hated the crowding most of all, the slaves packed inside the space like multiple embryos, filling metal scaffolding three levels high. On the lowest level, shoulder to hip with the others, she had to grit her teeth to keep from lashing out at those around her.

Rayna had lost track of how many in the hold had died, though it was one of her duties to estimate a number. She was too busy trying not to be one of them. Ten ship-days out from the processing center at Del Origa, judging from the tiny blisters that had been reabsorbed into the skin of her belly to help her keep track of time, and they'd been given no solid food and precious little water to cut down on waste. Still the squat toilets overflowed, and the air was a fetid swamp. Illness was common. Misery was universal. The strong preyed on the weak. The weakest died.

She stood to allow the blood to flow into her cramped legs, careful of her head in the restricted space. Pins and needles greeted the arrival of renewed circulation to her limbs, and she stamped her numb feet on the slimy decking. Her neighbors growled in protest.

"Yeah? And fuck you, too." Without appearing to give a centimeter, she shifted to allow them more room. Territory was defended or lost in this place, but she wasn't a complete asshole. At least one woman next to her was not long for this plane of existence.

Rayna was in the middle of a much-needed stretch when she froze. She lifted her head, reaching for a fading fragment of sound. She turned to the people at her feet.

"Did you hear that?"

They stared at her, eyes dull.

There it is again!

"Red alert. We're under attack." She could just catch a whisper of the alarms behind the heavy plasteel of the hold, but there was no mistaking that sound. She'd dodged phased energy bursts on enough fighting ships to know.

No one around her seemed to care. A more immediate threat loomed. Three meters away a girl no more than fourteen was being pinned against the bulkhead by a male twice her size. The girl fought him, but she had no skills, and he had all the advantages. He slapped her, snapping her head back against the unforgiving metal behind her, and ground into her, hip to hip. The girl sobbed.

"Aw, *hell*, no." Rayna ignored her own internal

warnings that the man was too big for her—shit, they were all too big for her—and waded through the bodies to get to him. She didn't bother with a sucker punch, though he was too distracted to see her coming. Instead, she put her boot in the side of the big man's knee and crumpled his leg. He went down with a howl. Then she dropped her knee on his chest and punched him in the throat. His eyes went wide, realizing he would never draw another breath through that crushed trachea.

Rayna lifted herself off him as he began to thrash, and started back toward her place against the bulkhead. People stepped all over each other to give her room to pass. She paused to see that the girl was okay. Someone had wrapped her in a hug, an older woman. *Good. That's good.*

Abruptly the ship lurched and slewed to starboard. A startled cry went up from the hold as people were knocked off their feet. Rayna barely managed to stay upright as the deck rolled and pitched beneath her. A series of concussions shook the air around them—deep, thudding, rhythmic. The ship was firing back—plasma cannon, it sounded like. Her briefing hadn't included the weapons load of her transport.

Another bone-crushing impact and the lights went out. People screamed, out of fear rather than injury— the bulkheads remained intact. Red emergency lights came on to light the doorways and the lines where the hull walls met the deck. Yet another blast and the artificial gravity faltered, lifting bodies off the deck, then slamming them back in place. People vomited.

In any other circumstances, now would be a good time to get out of this hellhole. Even on a slave transport in the black of space there were places to conceal yourself if you were trained for it and didn't have to hide too long. But Rayna Carver had worked her ass off to get inside this hold and, by God, she was going to stay.

"We've got 'em on the run now, Cap." The Pataran glanced up from the touchscreen set into the console under his hands. "Their shields are down to 30 percent aft."

The helm officer grinned. "Confirmed. Heading away from us at 148 mark 22. Full ion speed."

Sam Murphy, captain of the *Shadowhawk*, rolled his shoulders in anticipation. "Well, what are you waiting for, ladies and gentlemen? After them! Pursuit course, helm. Bring us alongside."

"Aye, Cap! Pursuit course and speed."

"Patel, hail that ship."

"Aye, Cap. Hailing . . . go ahead, sir."

Captain Murphy stood at his post and watched the visual come up on the main viewscreen. He composed his features, but he didn't try to hide the hatred and disgust he felt for the captain of the defeated ship.

The other man, a bloated Ninoctin well past his prime, leapt at the screen. "What is the meaning of this attack?"

"Well, Captain, I would have thought that was clear enough when we hailed you the first time." Murphy scratched at his jaw. "We asked you nicely to prepare to be boarded, but you fired on us and look what it got you. My sensors tell me you've got no shields. The next time we fire on you, you'll lose your engines."

"Who are you that you dare to interfere with legitimate trade on a protected route in Minertsan space? I'll have your hide tacked to the bar in the nearest spacers' hole before this circuit is out!"

Murphy met the threat with a sly grin. "Well, shall I take each of those issues in order, Captain? You are a slave ship. I hate slavers beyond all reason. I don't consider slaving legitimate trade—not like hauling malerium crystals or slipping stolen artwork from Ztera Prime. As for this being a protected route in Gray space, I guess not. I'm Captain Solomon Armstrong Murphy of the *Shadowhawk*, and I don't think you'll be in position to tack my hide up anytime soon."

The Ninoctin's neck flanges abruptly tightened, and he slumped back in his seat. "The *Shadowhawk*. We, uh, we seem to have misidentified you."

Murphy shrugged. "We are pirates, after all. False ID beam."

The Ninoctin seemed to recover himself with a little smile. "Now, Captain Murphy, perhaps you'll forgive my . . . belligerence. After all, you have done considerable damage to my ship. I'm not even certain I can make it to my destination now. I suppose I'll just have to limp back to my home base with my cargo and forego my entire profit from this ill-considered voyage."

Murphy exchanged glances with his crew and erupted into laughter. "Well, Captain, I have to give it to you, you are the best groveler I've had in a while! Go back to home base—no, no, *limp* back to home base. That's a good one! With your *cargo*!" He slapped his helm officer on the back so hard she pitched forward. She was laughing so hard she didn't seem to notice.

"No, but you're right about one thing." He swiped at his eyes. "You will be foregoing your profit. I'm confiscating your ship and cargo—profits of war. You'll be glad to know I'm sparing your miserable life for the time being. That could change. You may want to consider a new career."

He signaled to Patel to cut the connection and left the Ninoctin gaping at the screen. His Pataran Executive Officer glided to his side. Murphy stood head and shoulders over most of his crew, but he had to look *up* to see the scowl on Mo Maatik's dark face.

"You're going to remind me the nearest Rescue relocation center is ten ship-days from here in the opposite direction from our planned itinerary," Murphy said.

Maatik stared down at him without a word.

"Then you're going to say towing that hulk will put undue strain on my engines. And that there's not enough room between the two ships to house the slaves comfortably. My own crew will be put out. They'll be unhappy."

Mo stared some more. He crossed his arms over a chest the size of a water storage canister.

Murphy glanced at him. "You're already unhappy."

"Where is the profit in this, Sam?" The Pataran's voice was pitched for his captain's ears alone. "Drew Vort is waiting for us in the Norian Sector."

Old anger flared in Murphy's chest. "Vort will still be there when we're done."

"If we don't make that rendezvous, he'll come after us. And this time he'll be out for blood."

"Vort owes *me* blood." Murphy clenched a hand at his side. "It's the only reason I agreed to the meet."

"That and the credits. Our reserves are low. We can't afford to do this."

Murphy emitted a low growl meant only for the two of them. A quick check of the members of his bridge crew confirmed they were playing deaf and blind.

"We can't afford *not* to do this. Ever. Have you forgotten what it was like in the hold of one of those ships? I haven't." He turned toward his helm officer. "Put a tractor on them, Dartha. Patel, get me a boarding party. Full security team." He glanced back at his XO, who stood without emotion in the center of the bridge. "I think I'll go with them. Mo, you've got the conn."

As his data stream collected into flesh and blood in the landing bay of the slave ship, Sam Murphy asked himself what the hell he was doing here. He had crew chiefs fully capable of leading the boarding party. Even now they were doing their jobs just fine without him, spreading the teams out to disarm the ship's security in the bay and secure the passageways into the interior of the slaver. He strode through the efficient operation, grim and silent, intent on getting to the bridge and the Ninoctin bloatfish who ran this ship.

He and his crew passed unopposed through the corridors of the massive transport on their way to the ship's nerve centers—engineering, communications, security, bridge. A large team took the lift down into the belly of the ship, to the hold where Sam knew the slaves would be packed as thick as rock in a fragment swarm. He didn't go with them. He could imagine well enough what they'd find.

The ship stank. All slavers had the same stink, a stench their owners couldn't scrub away no matter how many filters or circulation vents they used. Sam knew if they were to tear this ship apart and rebuild her in spacedock from hull to bridge they could never get rid of that reek.

They reached the bridge and discovered the captain of the slaver had decided to make a stand after all. The hatch was dogged and sensors showed the Ninoctin holed up with an armed security team and his bridge crew on the other side.

Sam hit the emergency comm on the bulkhead outside the hatch. "Open up, you *shalssiti* coward! If I have to blast this hatch, I'll be beating your fat ass next!"

"I have several items I wish to negotiate first." The captain's voice seemed calm enough.

Ice replaced the heat under Sam's skin. "Negotiation is not my strongpoint." He waved at the men beside him. Laser rifles were brought to bear on the hinges of the plasteel hatch. Blue-white light arced; the area of contact glowed red. Within seconds, the hatch groaned and fell askew with a clang.

His men stood off to the sides, wary of fire from the bridge, but none came. Sam could see the men on the other side of the hatch were positioned likewise.

"Throw your weapons out the hatch or we burn you out. You have nowhere to go."

"I just want to talk, Captain."

"Weapons. Now."

The defeated captain gave his orders, and an irregular collection of laser rifles, stunners, electric prods, whipsticks, even a knife or two clattered and slid along the deck through the hatch. Sam raised an eyebrow at the crew chief at his side. The man searched his scanner for any additional powered weapons that might be inside, then gave a nod. Finally, Sam waved his people through. They wasted no time patting down the bridge crew and putting them in restraints.

Sam inclined his head toward the hatch. "Take them below." He stopped them before they could leave with the Ninoctin. "Except for him."

Like all the males of his race, the captain of the

slaver was tall—over seven feet in height—with the elongated skull that gave the Ninoctins an almost comical hangdog look. In this man's case, the expression was accentuated by the fear that his life was about to end in the most gruesome manner—gutted by a pirate with a known reputation for brutality when it came to certain tradesmen.

It was a reputation that Sam Murphy cultivated with fervor. And the look he was seeing in the Ninoctin's yellow eyes was one he lived for.

"I ought to shoot you out the nearest airlock."

The captain's neck flanges quivered. "But you promised you would spare my life!"

"That was before you tried your little Xandoran standoff. Now I'm unhappy. People could've been killed."

"But Captain Murphy,"—the Ninoctin spread his hands in supplication—"no one was hurt. I had no intention of letting things go that far. I simply wanted to make certain my crew was taken care of."

"Your crew." Sam made no secret of his skepticism.

"Of course. I need to know your intentions for us— uh, them."

Sam barked out a laugh. "My intentions? Captain, believe me, I have the worst of intentions. I intend to dry-fuck you all and never call you again."

Since the Ninoctin looked thoroughly confused, Sam elaborated in clear Galactic Standard. "I am towing your ship to the Fontax spaceport on Madras III, a journey of ten ship-days. There you and your crew will be delivered to local authorities for prosecution under sector penalties against trafficking in sentient species. The people aboard your ship—those you refer to as your cargo—will be placed in the care of representatives of the Interstellar Council for Abolition and Rescue to be repatriated or resettled. Oh, and your ship will be sold on the open market for my trouble. Should be worth a good deal of trouble—she looks like a trim ship, even if she is a stinking slaver."

The Ninoctin's normally pasty skin went even paler under this assault. Sam understood. Death was one thing. The end of one's livelihood was something else, especially to a Ninoctin of a certain age. Throw imprisonment into the mix and things could get volatile. Sam watched as the captain of the slave ship began to fall apart.

"You . . . you—" He fell into a string of unintelligible Ninoctin curses. "It's true what they say about you. Son of a whore-mongering *ptark*! I'll cut your balls off and have them for dinner!"

The Ninoctin rushed him then, something glinting in his right hand. Sam dodged to the left, placing his body on the outside of the man's thrust just in time. He grabbed the wrist with both hands and twisted, but his opponent was meaty and had a firm grip on the slim knife. Sam pivoted before the bigger man could use his other hand to brain him and drove a knee into the side of the Ninoctin's leg, hoping to hit the joint, a release point, anything, though gods knew where those things were on a *mulaak* Ninoctin.

The captain began to buckle. Sam came over the top of his arm with his elbow, cranked some more on the wrist and sat down, forcing the Ninoctin to the deck. There was an audible crack, something giving way on the man, and his grip on the knife slipped at last. Sam slammed his elbow up and back into the captain's chin. He spun and straddled the man, the knife in his own hand now and at the Ninoctin's throat.

He wanted to kill the sonofabitch. "Give me one reason why I shouldn't, you fucking bastard."

"Captain?"

The word sifted past the red haze in his mind. The urge to drive the knife in his hand into the pulsing flesh of the Ninoctin's throat was a compulsion as fundamental as his heartbeat. Blood welled around the blade.

"Captain Murphy! Sir!"

He held. Focus returned, and he saw the terror in the captain's eyes below him, the gritty gray deck, the lights of the bridge. He looked up to see his crew chief—Blindar—watching him. Waiting.

He took a breath. Backed off and stood up. Gave Blindar the knife.

"Get this slave-trading piece of shit out of my sight. And the crewman who missed that knife in the body search is confined to quarters for the night."

Blindar motioned to the two crew members standing closest to him. "Take him down to the hold with the others." As they scraped the blubbering slaver off the deck and hauled him away, Blindar turned to his captain. "Sir, we have an unusual problem belowdecks."

Sam pushed a shaky hand through his hair. He hadn't lost control like that since . . . not for a while. *Fucking slavers*. He looked at his crew chief.

"What kind of problem?"

"A woman down there is giving us holy hell. Says she wants to see you."

"One of these bastards wants to see me?" He laughed. "Spacer's luck with that! Tell her she can talk to me from a cell on Madras."

"No, Cap, not one of the crew. One of the, uh . . ."

Murphy's gaze grew dangerous. "Don't say it. They're people, not slaves. And on my ship they're the lucky ones."

Blindar swallowed. "Aye, sir. One of the LO's, sir. She's threatening to kick serious ass if she doesn't speak with you directly." He shook his head. "She don't look like much, Cap, but some of the folks with her say she's perfectly capable of doing like she says."

The captain of the *Shadowhawk* gave up an exasperated laugh and lifted his hands in surrender. "Fine. I'll see her. We've had enough mayhem for today. Tell Patel to assign her a berth on board the *'hawk*, and I'll meet her in my command room in two hours."

No, no, no, no, NO! This was *not* how this mission was supposed to go down. Rayna couldn't help seeing it as a disaster, though, of course, she couldn't ignore the implications for the people around her. They were all going home now. Or going on to new lives, if they could not be sent back home.

The impact hadn't hit them yet. When she'd been called out of the hold to her berth assignment, her fellow captives had still been milling around in confusion and a muted sort of fear. Their blunted response was an effect of their programming, the mindwipe that took their higher emotions, their identities and their memories of home before they were assigned to labor throughout the Minertsan Consortium. The Rescue relocation center would do their best to restore these things—and eliminate the memories of their abduction into slavery. The level of success of this process would determine whether the former slaves went back home to Earth or were relocated on Terrene or another colony planet.

So, yes, this hijacking by space pirates was just freaking great for them! But for Rayna and the Interstellar Council for Abolition and Rescue it meant half a circuit of meticulous planning out the thruster tubes. Finding a way to salvage her mission had just become her top priority.

She'd been allowed to shower before being shown to her bunk in a closet-size, six-person cabin that now slept twelve in two shifts. Her bunkmate was not in evidence, so Rayna supposed she was expected to be sleeping now. But her appointment with the captain of this hunk of junk was coming up in a few minutes. Now was not the time for a nap.

She glanced across the narrow space between the rows of bunks to see a member of the crew practicing an intricate sleight-of-hand with what appeared to be a razor-sharp blade. "Nice *slith*."

The girl, who couldn't have been more than 17, glanced up at her but didn't speak. The blade disappeared up her sleeve.

"Must be a real pain in the ass to have all these extra people crowding your space, huh?"

The girl considered her from under a fringe of dark hair. "We're used to it. Cap does it all the time."

"What do you mean?"

She shrugged. "We take the slavers, LO's gotta go somewhere 'til we get to the nearest relo center."

"LO's?"

"Lucky ones. That's you, I guess."

"Yeah. I guess." Rayna swallowed a swirl of resentment. She had to separate her own situation from that of the rest of the people in that hold. "So, what, your captain got some kind of crusade going?"

The girl's blue eyes flashed. "He need a crusade to save your ass?"

Rayna's lips twitched. The kid had a point—and an attitude.

"No, but there's not much profit in it, either. Aren't pirates all about the loot?"

The kid drew herself up with a frown. "The *'hawk*

ain't no pirate ship! We're legitimate traders! The slavers are the criminals in this sector!"

Hawk? What kind of name was that for a ship? "I won't argue that point with you, uh . . ."

"Lainie." The girl gave the information up like it was a carefully-guarded secret known to a select few.

"How did you get to be a member of the crew, Lainie?"

The girl was pissed off now, Rayna saw. Or maybe that was her default setting. She sprawled in her bunk and pulled the blade out again, making it appear and disappear in her hands.

"You ask a lot of questions for an LO."

Rayna shrugged. "Just naturally curious."

Lainie's gaze hit her like a laser. "And the mindwipe? Doesn't affect you, huh?"

"No. I'm resistant."

"Huh."

Rayna was beginning to think Lainie wouldn't answer her question when the girl said, "Cap saw me one day on Barelius at a slave auction. I was just a kid. If he hadn't scooped me up I'd have been headed for a partyhouse. Guess that makes me an LO, too." Lainie's lips lifted at one corner.

"Guess it does."

Lainie wasn't finished. "Don't ask me why Cap stops every slaver he comes across. I don't give a fuck. I'd do anything he asked me to do. Everyone on this ship would do the same thing."

Before Rayna could respond, a crewman with a

body like a spacedock tug and "Security" in yellow across his chest appeared in the hatch and motioned in her direction.

"You. Follow me."

She nodded at Lainie, hopped down off the bunk and did as the crewman had ordered. Time to meet the great man at last.

A crowded ship's corridor and a lift ride later, Rayna and her escort arrived at a cabin just off the bridge. The Security man banged on the hatch.

"The, uh, woman . . ." The man stumbled to a halt, unsure exactly why he'd been asked to bring her. "Sir."

A voice from inside, one that captured your attention. "All right, Zefron. Dismissed."

"But, Cap, she . . . um . . ." The guard glanced down at her and frowned.

Rayna lifted her chin and drew herself up to her maximum height. That put her eyes level with the "S" in "Security" on her guard's chest. Then the captain was there in the open hatch. Sweet Jesus, was he something to look at! He filled the doorway with smooth muscle, and he was trimmed out more like a Confederated Systems Fleet officer than a pirate. His black hair was cut short, the stubble on his strong jaw was no more than a shadow and his bright green eyes were untroubled by the haze of habitual drug or alcohol abuse.

Nope, not your typical pirate. At. All.

Captain Murphy grinned when he saw her. "What's the matter, Zeph, 'fraid she's gonna murder me and hijack the ship?"

Zephron swallowed awkwardly.

Rayna bristled. "Not today. I just want to talk."

His grin widened. "I'm relieved." He looked at his Security man again. "Dismissed, crewman."

"Yes, sir." The man slung a sideways glance at Rayna and left.

The captain retreated back into the tiny cabin and waited for her to follow him. Inside the cabin, narrow benches lined the two short walls across and to the left of the hatch. The desk—with the captain, one hip cocked on its edge—filled the rest of the space. There was a datapad thrown among the clutter on the desk, a desk screen and a holo-projector for meetings. The captain's command room, such as it was.

"Captain Sam Murphy of the *Shadowhawk*." He held out a hand.

Holy shit! Not *Hawk*—*Shadowhawk*! The ship's captain was known to her organization. The mention of his name could be guaranteed to induce screaming fits of frustration in Rescue officials, no matter how much they admired him. Rayna guessed she was about to find out why.

She took his hand and tried to ignore the warmth flowing from his big palm. "Rayna Carver. Thank you for seeing me."

Murphy radiated amusement. What did he think was so damn funny?

"My people said you seemed to think it was pretty important."

"You might say that. May I ask where the *Shadowhawk* is bound, Captain?"

"Bound?" A frown drew his dark brows together. "It's no secret that I plan to release you and the rest of the LO's on Madras—that's the nearest Rescue relocation center."

Madras—that wouldn't do. "I need you to make a stop on the way."

Murphy laughed, the rich sound rolling up out of his chest. "Did somebody give you the impression the *'hawk* is a taxi?"

Rayna flushed, suddenly feeling like an idiot. Her next words were out of her mouth before she could call them back.

"Better a taxi than a blackjack."

The captain rose slowly to his feet, his casual demeanor gone. He towered over her, glowering down into her eyes with a green gaze as hard and cold as a frozen sea.

"This blackjack just kept you from a short lifetime of back-breaking labor, of rape and humiliation and cold and hunger." His hands curled into fists at his side. His voice lowered into a growl. "I would think a little gratitude would be in order."

Her own emotion flared to meet his. "You think I don't know what we were headed for? What all those poor souls in that stinking hold were destined to go through? Jesus, the belly of that slaver was just the beginning."

His eyes narrowed, and he leaned forward. "Who

are you? You're no slave."

"You found me in the hold of a slave ship. What else would I be?" She struggled to hold her ground against his size, his *presence*. The urge to take a step backward was overwhelming.

"Your mind is intact. Even people who are resistant to the mindwipe take some time to come back to themselves after programming. Who the hell are you?"

"Maybe I'm luckier than most."

"And maybe you're ConSys Intel undercover, looking for a way to turn me in."

It was Rayna's turn to laugh. "Those clowns? They couldn't find their own asses with both hands."

Murphy seemed to appreciate the joke, but he didn't join in the laugh. "A common bounty hunter, then, though I admit hiding out on a slaver is a long way to go to get to me. I wasn't aware my capture price was that high."

The last she'd heard the price on the *Shadowhawk* was more than enough to mean retirement for the bounty hunter lucky enough to claim it. "I wouldn't know. But trolling for you on a slave ship seems like a plan with pretty low odds of success. Who knew you were going to pick my ship in all of space to rescue?"

His face relaxed into a smile. "Right. And now I'm certain you're no slave. No one resents having their shit pulled out of the fire." He considered. "So, if you aren't here for me, maybe ConSys sent you to LinHo to spy on the Minertsans. I hear the factory those slaves were bound for is making weapons for the rebels in the

Grays' nasty little civil war. Is that it?"

"I told you before, I don't work for ConSys."

"Ah, but you do work for someone. Who's left? The Minertsans themselves? The rebels? Some criminal element hoping to make a profit off the weapons trade? Now if that's the case I might be in a position to help for a split."

The son-of-a-bitch! "No! What I'm doing on LinHo has nothing to do with profit and everything to do with saving lives. But it's *my* business. You don't need the details to know whether you can drop me off at the spaceport."

"That's where you're wrong. I need all the details or I won't consider helping you. I told you before, the *'hawk* is no taxi, and I'm certainly no brainless transport hauler."

"Well, we just seem to be repeating ourselves, don't we?" She crossed her arms over her chest. The man was infuriating. "What part of 'I can't tell you the details' don't you understand?"

"Fuck!" The captain moved as if he wanted to pace—or strangle her, Rayna couldn't be sure. "Suppose I let you rest in the brig until we get to Madras? Because not only will I not help you, but I don't even trust you to have the run of my ship until you tell me what the hell is going on." He reached for the comm.

Rayna struggled to regain control of her temper. "No, wait!"

He looked back at her. "You have ten seconds."

She weighed her options. The plans that had taken half a circuit to develop were in ruins, thanks to this freaking Good Samaritan. Getting to LinHo and the weapons factory via her original plan would be nearly impossible from Madras, a planet with strict anti-slavery regulations. If she allowed him to take her there, she'd have to find passage back to MgT25 where she'd started her journey and begin again. That would take time she didn't have. She had to bring him into this and find a way to convince him to drop her on LinHo.

"I need to trust you, Captain."

He scowled. "I wouldn't if I were you. I'm a blackjack, after all."

She closed her eyes and took a deep breath. "I'm sorry. That was . . . I shouldn't have said that."

"I may be a pirate, Ms. Carver, but I don't rape, I don't murder, I don't set ships afire just to watch them burn."

She found his gaze. "I believe you."

His frown softened into a more neutral expression of curiosity. He settled his hip back onto his desk.

"Why don't you start over?"

"Right." She rubbed the back of her neck. "I'm an agent for the Interstellar Council for Abolition and Rescue, working with a cell on MgT25. I'm a conductor—do you know what that is?"

"No. Enlighten me."

"We infiltrate the Minertsan work camps, the factories, the mines. Set up communications with the outside to pass information back and forth. Identify candidates for extraction—those who are resistant to programming—and help get them out. Organize smuggling and protection. Commit sabotage."

Murphy looked at her and laughed. "Well, you're just a regular death-defying little concussion torpedo, aren't ya?"

She wasn't sure quite how to take that. "Beg pardon?"

"The Kinz facility on LinHo is no ordinary work camp. It's an *ultimate-security* prison factory, and you're telling me you were planning to slip inside with the people in that hold?" His expression communicated open disbelief. "You were going in there to set up an undercover operation among the unlucky ones. All by your lonesome. Little bitty thing that you are."

All right, that's it! Temper rose like floodwaters and broke the dam of her fragile control.

"Just takes a *little bit* of plasmion to blow you to hell, Captain Snark. And guess what, I've done this before. Once on Riza, where I helped thirty escape before I took the factory to the ground; once on Apparion where a team of us blasted a dam to flood the *orm* fields and commandeered a freighter to take 400 slaves off-planet."

"And how many were killed in those operations?" The captain was on his feet again, no longer laughing. "I heard nearly 50 on Riza; no one would give a number on Apparion. There were locals there, you know, living near the dam."

"What you heard were lies." She shook as she stood toe-to-toe with him, arching her neck to glare up at him. "We made certain no one else was hurt." *Please, God, let it be so. We did everything we could.*

The corners of his mouth ticked upwards. "Maybe. But LinHo is not Riza or Apparion. The factory itself is a para-military installation."

She cut him off. "Rumor exaggerates. Can you get me there or not?"

"Not. It's suicide. And not just for you. The spaceport requires special permissions for berthing. Without them, automated orbital defenses would blow us apart."

"There must be a way to get those permissions."

"If there is, I don't know it. I've never had business on that godsforsaken dirtball."

"But you have connections. Friends who've been there. Chips you can call in." She was fishing.

And hooked something. The amusement returned to Murphy's eyes.

"I might have. I would have to be convinced it was worthwhile to call them in. You're asking me to spend huge amounts of political capital, to risk my ship and crew, just to drop you on that planet so you can put your pretty ass in a world of danger. And without a plan of any kind, so far as I can see."

God! She balled up her fists to keep from throttling him. "What makes you think I don't have a plan?"

He spread his hands. "Please. Share."

"I can't. Do you think I'd get very far in my business if I 'shared' every time someone asked?"

"I'm not just anyone. You're asking for my help. That makes me a partner."

"No, it doesn't. I've already told you too much."

Murphy shrugged. "Madras it is, then."

"I have contacts on LinHo. They'll be able to find me a way into Kinz. I just need to get on-planet."

He studied her face for a long moment, weighing the odds, all humor gone from his eyes. Then, "It's too dangerous."

This couldn't be the end of it. So much was at stake. Rayna glared at him, words on the tip of her tongue that she knew she shouldn't say: *Coward! Credit-grubbing fireworm!*

His hand was suddenly under her chin, lifting it. "Cheer up, little torpedo." There was a crinkle of— sympathy?—at the corners of his green, green eyes. "You'll live to fight another day."

The heat that surged into her chest was equal parts anger and arousal. The moment she recognized that unacceptable fact, Rayna turned on her heel and stalked out, Captain Murphy's soft laughter caressing her ears.

CHAPTER TWO

Sam watched Rayna Carver's retreat down the corridor of his ship with a curious mixture of emotions roiling in his chest. Or not properly his chest, because, gods knew, just her presence made his blood boil, his stomach do strange, unsettling things and everything that made him male stand to attention. Maybe it was those dark eyes flashing fire. Or her smooth skin blushing red under his stare. But the idea of that tiny woman—*perai*, she barely reached to his shoulder!—stuffed in the hold of a slaver, choosing to throw herself into the worst hellholes in the galaxy. And for what? Some misguided heroic impulse?

He shook his head as if that would free him of the hold Rayna had on him and turned toward his bridge. He strode through the hatch and saw all eyes turn in his direction.

"Cap." The chorus of voices greeted him in unison.

"Crew." He sat at his station in the center of the open semi-circle of consoles that constituted the heart of the bridge. "Give me a report, Mo."

From a station a step down and to starboard, the big Pataran turned and spoke. "All hostiles are secured in the hold of the *Fleeflek*, a total of 41, including the captain. Eight hundred LO's are stowed aboard their ship and ours. We've doubled up in the crew cabins, got some in the cargo bay and the rec lounge. Morale is plummeting."

"How is the grog supply?"

Mo exhaled slowly. "Newly replenished on Taxos."

"Break it out when things settle down, say two, three days. Mash time."

Barely suppressed cheers and a few whoops greeted this announcement.

Mo was not among the celebrants. "And where would you suggest this drunken slog take place, Captain?"

"PT deck. Put Marinda in charge. She always does the best drunken slogs. Right, crew?"

"Aye, Cap!" Enthusiastic grins all around.

His second-in-command was not amused. His second-in-command was never amused. It was a wonder Mo had stayed with him all these years.

"Using the Physical Training deck will require reconfiguring the exercise modules."

Sam simply looked at him.

With a sigh, the Pataran acknowledged the inevitability of things. "Aye, Cap."

"Navigation, we'll need a course for Madras III. I believe that takes us through the C4 jump node?"

His navigator turned to raise an eyebrow at him. At least, that's how Sam had come to interpret the expression. Sipritz was Mper and as wrinkled as a prune, though she assured everyone she was considered young and beautiful on her home planet.

"We'll have to make two jumps, Cap." The

whispery voice was disapproving. "To summarize: the first at C4 comes up in seven ship-days. The second is at C5 in nine. Then we have another day to Madras. All very approximate. I'll have exact times and distances in a few minutes, sir."

"Efficient as always, Sipritz. Thank you."

"I live to serve, sir."

The Mper had served aboard the 'hawk for two years now and Sam still didn't know whether sarcasm was completely unknown or a sport of nu-Olympic caliber on her planet.

Sam rubbed a hand across the stubble on his chin. Jump Node C4 was within a ship-day of LinHo, but it was an interstellar transfer station, nothing more. Linzer-Holmatuziskru 1423, named for the Tularian who had first mapped the jump nodes and the human who had translated, wasn't even a planet, with a decent solar system to call its own. It was just the largest of the broken fragments of rock slowly circling the disturbance in the fabric of space caused by the portal into hyperspace. Like many other enterprising business owners, the founders of the Kinz works had taken advantage of its location to build a quiet little operation away from the prying eyes of any sort of authority. And they guarded their privacy with cannons blazing.

Getting into LinHo spacedock would be a bitch. *No, forget it, it's crazy. We have absolutely no reason for being there.* He rubbed a hand through his hair in frustration. *What the hell is she thinking?*

Sam deliberately put the beautiful Ms. Carver and her insane schemes out of his mind and called up the energy conversion data from Engineering on his compscreen. He wasn't surprised to see the strain put on his engines by stabilizing the slaver in tow.

He hit a connection on his console. "Engineering. Kwan, you there?"

"Aye, Cap. I figured you'd be calling me."

"How bad is it?"

"Bad enough. The 'hawk wasn't built as a tug, you know. Do you have any idea how many adjustments per hour have to be made just to keep that damn thing from drifting up our asses? My comps are overloaded, the thrusters are in constant play, I've had to assign extra crew and my conversion ratios are fucked!"

"Yeah, I know. You're doing a great job. We're planning a mash to take the edge off."

"Yeah? All *right*, then! When?"

"Couple days. When we get squared away."

"Ah, incentive. That'll get the boys and girls fired up!"

Sam grinned. "Carry on. I'm out."

He glanced around, saw his crew was doing what it was trained to do, then, restless, he got up and climbed the step to what everyone else referred to as the "Cap walk" above the control cockpit. He paced until Mo came up to see what was wrong.

"What did the woman have to say?" The Pataran was ever economical with words.

"Oh, not much. Just that she needs to be dropped

off on LinHo so she can infiltrate the Kinz facility."

To the casual observer, Mo's expression would not have appeared to change. But Sam saw his pale eyes flare with shock.

"That's insane."

"My thoughts exactly." He smiled. "She's a determined little thing, though."

Mo turned toward him and crossed his arms over his chest, a gesture that Sam knew well. "No."

Sam held his hands out in surrender. "Don't worry! Even I'm not that crazy!" He started pacing again. "There are all those *mulaak* permissions to go through to get to the 'docks. And I can't think of a single reason for us to be there, can you?"

Mo placed himself in Sam's path, forcing his captain to look up at him. "Stop thinking with your dick. Drop her on Madras with the others and be done with it. Unless you're *trying* to get her killed? You could do that yourself without putting the rest of us at risk."

Perai! Was he seriously thinking of doing this? No. *Hell, no!*

"You're right. Of course, you're right, Mo. She . . . I . . . has it been that long since I've had a woman?"

"Too long to be healthy, if you ask me." The Pataran grunted. "The last two shore leaves you were too drunk to follow through. I know because I had to rescue you from some very torqued-off women."

The last two shore leaves he'd been trying to forget his last two voyages, which had been near-disasters before they barely broke even. The pressure was beginning to wear on him. He needed this deal with Drew Vort. Why else get in bed with a fang-eel?

He ran a hand through his hair, leaving it in dark, unruly spikes. "Do *not* let me get drunk on Madras."

"Don't suppose the lady would be willing . . ."

Sam exhaled. "Not a freaking chance in Portal's Hell." Though *gods*, he wished he could make it happen. Her skin was just the color of coffee with cream, her eyes like dark chocolate. He was suddenly starving.

Mo leaned in close. "We can't go to LinHo, Cap. We have to make that rendezvous."

Sam saw the warning in his friend's gaze before he turned to stare out at the starry field of the viewscreen. His course was set for Madras. He had no intention of changing it. But Rayna Carver had that lightning spark of destiny about her. The captain of the *Shadowhawk* was well aware one ignored fate at one's peril.

Rayna had given up trying to rest in the cramped crew quarters, now stacked to the overhead with her talkative cabinmates. The conversation with Captain Murphy had circled her brain in an endless, maddening loop until it forced her out into the corridor, anger and frustration propelling her on an agitated prowl in search of distraction.

Two hours into second watch, the ship's corridors

were still lively, members of the crew going about their business with an equal sense of purpose whether they were on-duty or off. Rayna could see that they were well-fed, healthy and disciplined; that the ship was trim and locked-down, if a bit Spartan in the furnishings. By reputation, the *Shadowhawk*'s captain spared no expense in the outfitting of her engines or weapons, but Rayna'd had no chance to confirm that.

Lainie was fiercely loyal to her captain, and Rayna's walkaround was only adding to the impression that this was a happy ship. But, my God, her captain was a stubborn, arrogant, self-serving bastard! It was no wonder her colleagues in Rescue wanted to tear their hair out every time his name came up. He practically defined the term "loose cannon."

What kind of pirate was he, anyway? If the *Fleeflek* was typical of his "conquests," profit could hardly be his motive. He planned to turn the slaves over to Rescue to be repatriated. Sure, he could sell the ship and claim the bounty on her captain, but his own crew knew that wouldn't pay enough to make up for the jobs they'd miss going out of their way to Madras. Lainie and the others in her cabin had defended their captain on that point with a shrug and "Cap has the conn."

Rayna's mouth twisted in disgust. It was like a freaking mantra around here.

"Does that frown mean you're lost, *Agent* Carver?" Captain Murphy had somehow materialized in the corridor beside her. "Or don't tell me we've got *veers* again."

Oh, God, she hated a *veer* worse than any rat. Maybe it was the lack of fur. Or the twin tails. The snaky twin tails.

"Don't call me agent. Someone might hear." But her voice shook despite her effort to control it.

The bastard laughed. "Finally something that strikes fear in that tritantium heart. Don't worry, I wouldn't use the term in public. And, no, we don't have *veers*. I let a few of the crew keep pets. The cats and the Jack Russells cleaned out the ship within a twentydays. Now they're working on each other."

Rayna couldn't help a smile of relief. "Where are all the pets? I haven't seen them. In fact"—God, she hated herself for saying this—" you keep a very trim ship, Captain."

"For a pirate, you mean?" His lips barely curved, but his green eyes were bright with mischief. "Everyone is under orders to crate the animals while we've got so much other chaos going on. The dogs submitted to orders. The cats, well, they're better pirates than we are and refused to be taken. They're in hiding."

This glimpse of life onboard his ship was starting to make her feel just a little too warm in the chest. Rayna moved on. Murphy trailed along beside her.

"So you have a pretty big crew to worry about, I guess, Captain. What's she carry—about sixty?"

"Seventy-five."

She stopped mid-stride to stare at him. "That's as big as a ConSys frigate."

"And armed like one, too. In my line of work it pays to carry a big stick."

Her heart stuttered, and the warmth she'd been feeling went cold.

"You're thinking it would take a lot of firepower to bring me down." His eyes glittered now with something hard and unyielding. "You'd be right about that. Mostly the ConSys patrols leave me alone. Not just because I'd be a lot of trouble to get rid of—because I do their job for them. Like today."

Rayna snorted. "We weren't in a ConSys patrol area today." She and her Rescue cohort had made certain of it when they chose the ship she'd be on. "This was Minertsan space all the way."

Murphy rounded on her. "All the more reason to do what I did. No one else was going to save those people. Do you think I give a fuck that it's the *shalssiti* Grays' space?"

"You should. The Grays would be happy to blow your ass through the nearest jump node."

The Captain's mouth lifted into a grim smile. "Might be fun to see them try."

Rayna cocked her head at him. "This is personal for you."

"Oh, and it's all business for you, I suppose. Just another day at the office." He moved, slow and smooth as a stalking *targa*, and suddenly she found herself backed up against the plasteel wall of the companionway, her pulse pounding. "Tell me, Agent Carver, just how does a little bit like you end up in the hold of a slave ship bound for hell? Why would you volunteer for this job—the one most likely to get you tortured or raped or just worked to death?"

His face had hardened into sharp, grim lines; his eyes showed no more warmth than bits of cold, green glass. Where his anger came from Rayna had no idea, but it had turned him into a mountain of ice. The wrong word from her could bring that avalanche crashing down in the next moment.

But all that cold created only heat in her. Who was he to question her motivation? She stood her ground.

"I never said it wasn't personal for me. I've got a debt to pay." She tugged at the zipper on her jumpsuit and bared the upper part of her chest. There on the left was the small tattooed heart with the initials T and S that she'd worn since the day her mother died, fifty-four days after her father. "My parents were slaves— taken from Earth when they were just teenagers. Rescue saved them, but they couldn't return them. Too much time was lost; too much was lost to the mindwipe. Still, if it hadn't been for Rescue, I wouldn't be here. So I owe Rescue my life and my parents' lives. But I also owe the Grays some payback."

At last Murphy stepped back, the anger gone from his expression. "Revenge is a lonely game, Little Bit. And it rarely works out like you think it will. Trust me on that one." His gaze met hers for half a second. Then he spun on his heel and strode off down the corridor.

What the hell did he call me? She took a few steps after him, but he was gone, not even glancing back.

Damn, arrogant son of a ptark!

But she didn't waste any more time thinking about Captain Snark's lack of manners. She wanted to know why he had appointed himself the single-handed savior of shipboard slaves throughout the galaxy. It was definitely personal, this slaver-hunt of his. The profit just wasn't big enough to justify the risks he was taking with a ship and a crew he so obviously cared about. What she wouldn't give right now for access to—well, no one had said she couldn't use the library computers; they must have Z-net access. She moved off with new purpose, determined to learn as much as she could about this man who was well on his way to driving her crazy.

Perai, but she was a nosy, pushy, *irritating* little thing! Shit, yes, it was personal. It didn't get any more personal than his history with the Grays, but Sam wasn't about to spill it all out for this woman he'd known for a matter of hours. Only one other person on the *Shadowhawk* knew that history. His crew depended on him. They needed him to be strong—hell, *infallible*, when you came down to it. He couldn't afford to have the kind of past he had. A past he'd escaped at the age of 17 in a stasis crate full of vegetables fresh-picked off the plantation where he'd worked since his family had been Taken.

Sam paced the corridors of his ship, watching for

trouble. It was crowded in the crew cabins, in the mess and on the PT deck. No surprise. But everyone gave him a smile and a nod. No scowls, no averted faces. The lucky ones looked dazed and blank as always. They would until Rescue got hold of them and reversed the Grays' mind programming. Until then, his people would look out for them.

He took the lift down and stood on the catwalk looking over the vast, open cargo deck. Cots had been arranged into rows in one section of the deck, with smaller portable latrine and shower sections marked off with partitions. Tables at the other end of the rows of beds gave the LO's a place to eat. Everything was neat and clean and organized. A warm pride in his people tugged at his chest.

His cargo chief, Ramirez, hustled up the ladder from below. "Hey, Cap. Need something?"

"No, Chief. Looks like you have everything under control."

The chief beamed. "Yes, sir. We've got about a hundred down there, but everyone's behaving."

"A hundred, huh? You make it look easy." He slapped a hand on Ramirez's shoulder. "Need anything from me?"

"Well, uh, even with the mindwipe, folks get kinda bored with nothing to do. Think maybe we could get some media units down here or something?"

That great aching emptiness. Something lost in the darkness. Despite all efforts to control it, the memories made his heartbeat accelerate. He'd been just a child when he'd been Taken, but he remembered. The mindwipe had had little effect on him.

Ramirez had asked him a question. "I'll put Truong on it."

"Oh, yeah, great. She'll know what to do."

Sam took another look around the transformed cargo bay and forced himself to see, not a vision of a much blacker hold thirty years earlier, but what was actually there. He was in control now, and things would be as they should be.

CHAPTER THREE

"So you're not goin'?" Lainie gaped at her in obvious disbelief. "A mash is almost as good as shore leave. Something we get maybe twice a year—well, okay, maybe it's more often than that, but it's not nearly often enough in my opinion. And you're gonna sit it out like some old lady."

Rayna shook her head. "If everybody's going to this shindig, I might just be able to get some decent sleep."

"There's grog."

"Not thirsty." Though that bordered on a lie. A little grog would go down very nicely right now. "And besides, alcohol and the mindwipe don't mix. I don't think it's a great idea to let a bunch of drunken lucky ones loose on the ship with nothing but basic emotions and no memory of what counts for polite behavior."

"They're not invited. Cap made that very clear. LO's still suffering from programming are to stay in quarters."

Rayna thrust her arms from her sides in exasperation. "Then why are you trying to drag me to a crew function in direct contradiction of his orders?"

Lainie snorted. "You're obviously not wiped. Grog would do you good."

Amen to that, but it wasn't the point.

"There's music, too."

"Hurts my ears." *Really? Music? Why am I being so stubborn?*

"Oh, for *maak's* sake." The girl heaved a huge sigh. "Do not make me say it."

"Say what?"

"Cap will be there." She practically sang it.

Heat flared in Rayna's belly. "And what makes you think that's of any interest to me?"

Lainie laughed, a rough bark of sound. It occurred to Rayna that it was the first time she'd even seen the kid smile.

"Are you kidding me? The way you look at him? Not that I blame you. Not that anyone of the female persuasion blames you."

"Bullshit." If there had been anywhere in the tight cabin to go, Rayna would have jumped up to pace. "The man might have a nice-looking wrapper, but as for what's inside, I'm not so impressed."

Lainie's mouth fell slightly open, anger replacing the smile that had been on her face seconds before. "You can't be serious. After what I told you? You've been on this ship three days. You must have seen what Cap does for people. Shit, he scooped your ass up on the way to hell. That should count for something."

"I'm grateful for that, truly." *Interfering moron!* "Without him all the people on that ship would be headed for a short, miserable life." *I have to remember that!* "And I can tell that you and lots of others on this ship owe him a debt of gratitude. But he's human, Lainie, and he has his faults, like anyone else. Maybe more than anyone else. I'm not ready to overlook them."

Lainie's expression hardened. "Maybe you can't see beyond the fact that he's an independent operator, huh? No matter the good he's done? He doesn't wear a uniform or follow some admiral's orders, so he's scum." Her youthful enthusiasm was gone, replaced by the cynicism more typical of someone who'd grown up on the streets.

"I didn't say that."

"You didn't have to." The girl shot up from her bunk and bolted for the hatch. But she turned back and took a stand. "You know what, just forget it. I got you pegged now. You're no more a slave than I am. I don't know what you were doing on that slaver, but Cap put an end to it, and I say good for him." She shot Rayna a look that could've curdled milk and disappeared out the hatch.

Rayna was even more determined not to go to the party that Lainie had referred to as a mash, but the return of her bunkmate signaling a change in shift had meant she had few other options. The PT deck had been requisitioned for the event. She couldn't hang out in the darkened rec lounge where others were trying to sleep. She could walk the corridors, but she'd just look pathetic should she run into Captain Snark. She had already put in enough fruitless hours on the library comps where she'd learned only that Solomon Armstrong Murphy had been born on the agricultural planet of Ixta IV 35 years ago. A farmer.

That was about as far away from where she'd grown up as you could get. Life in the domes and tunnels of Terrene had been raucous, stimulating, a daily lesson in trade, communications and cultural and interspecies diversity, but also robbery, theft, coercion and worse. It was urban, proudly so, a place built by returned slaves to welcome their own. The only agriculture on her planet was conducted in hydroponic tanks in the surface domes. She'd toured them once on a school field trip.

Okay, so Murphy had started out with dirt on his boots. After that the record was silent until six years ago when he showed up in command of the *Shadowhawk*, previously captained by one Marlena McCoy. He was wanted throughout Confederated space for numerous crimes of piracy, and God only knew what the Grays wanted him for. According to the computer he was single, childless and unattached, though why she should find that of any interest, she refused to consider.

There was nothing more to be learned about him from searching the files. So maybe, eyes and ears open, she might learn something at this "mash" thing. She joined the throng in the corridor outside the PT deck and shuffled through the hatch into the converted exercise space. There she was assaulted by a wave of pounding sound so dense she immediately looked for somewhere to hide. The press of humanity in the dark left nowhere to run. Someone nudged her in the back, and she was forced to move forward though she had no destination and no sense of her bearings. Christ, they didn't call it a mash for nothing.

The flow of people took her past a table where a line of crew members staffed a bank of dispensers. The eager hands reaching for mugs of grog across the table told her this was the place to start. No one challenged her right to drink, so she grabbed a mug and fought to hold it steady against the jostling crowd. Then she shuffled and dodged her way around to a relatively underpopulated section of the room where she could observe the fracas without being crushed.

Damn it, she couldn't see in this crowd! She took a step up on one of the exercise modules folded back into place against the wall. Mug held high, she could survey the scene from a normal man's height, at least. And what she saw was sheer, piratical chaos. Either Murphy's crew had been drinking a while or they'd been drinking fast, because the dancing, boasting, shoving, sparring, and thinly disguised lovemaking were well under way. Rayna took a deep draught of the bittersweet grog; though she intended to stay mostly sober, she had some catching up to do just to fit in.

She found herself scanning the crowd for a certain tall, dark and handsome and blew out a breath in disgust. *Give it a break, Carver! He's probably drunk on his ass screwing a pretty little engine room tech in a corner somewhere. Setting a great example for his lovely crew.*

A scuffle broke out at the edge of the crowd nearest her—two burly crewmen too far gone to land a hard punch where it would do much damage. People pulled back to make room for Security, who arrived within seconds and scraped them up off the floor.

"Come on, Frang, do you have to do this every time?" The Security man was the same one who'd taken her to the captain her first day. He had a firm grip on his man as he marched him past Rayna. "You know Cap will have your ass for this."

"Yeah, yeah. No fightin' at th' mash. Tol' me."

"He started it." This from his opponent who was next in line with his own escort.

"We know. You get to go to bed anyway."

Rayna had to give them credit. Murphy's Security boys knew their business. The party had absorbed the incident without a ripple and was still going full bore. She looked over the crowd again, seeking out the enforcers in the milling, murky dark. There were a lot of the crewmen with the yellow letters across their chests and the vigilant expressions on their faces stationed throughout the room. They weren't drinking or talking, unless it was into earcoms. Organized, trained security. On a pirate ship. *Stars and wonders.*

"I'm telling you, Arden, these are *pirates*. Their captain is one of the worst ones in the galaxy."

Rayna lifted her head at the snatch of conversation. She searched people nearby for the source, but could not make it out.

"He's . . . to take us and sell us . . . open market."

"I don't . . . Murphy seems okay."

The crowd shifted and surged around her. Other conversations drowned out part of the words. She craned her neck, trying to see past the bodies surrounding her to find what had to be slaves from the *Fleeflek*, slaves who weren't supposed to be here. She'd been hoping to pick up a juicy tidbit or two from Captain Snark's own crew, but something about these particular morsels attracted her interest.

The voices drifted to the right with the movement of the crowd. "Sure, that's what he wants us to think. You and me . . . others who are resistant. He wants . . . think he's this great hero . . . let us go. That's bullshit. He's just like all the rest of them. He'll sell us . . . bidder."

Rayna still couldn't get a good look at who was talking. She gave up her perch on the machine and dove into the crowd after the voices.

A small, wiry human just in front of her guffawed. "So what are we supposed to do about it? Steal a shuttle or something?"

"No, you *mulaak* dumbass." Someone in front of him, moving, fast now, through the pack. *Damn it! Where is he?* "There are more of us than them. It's like the engineer said. We make him give us the freakin' ship."

The guy in front of her pulled up, and Rayna nearly plowed into his back. She sheared off just in time, but found herself in front of a massive crewman who seemed to want to dance with her.

". . . fucking nuts? Most of us . . . barely remember our names." The little man was hissing in agitation. "You expect . . . some *mulaak* big plan?"

The giant in front of her was insistent. "Come on, baby! Just one dance. This is my favorite song!"

Fuck! She was desperate to see the other man's face, if only for a second. "Okay, but on one condition."

The big crewman grinned in anticipation. "Sure, sweetheart, anything."

She smiled sweetly at him. "Lift me up in those big, strong arms for a minute. I just have to have a look around from up there."

The crewman's grin widened as he hoisted her up on one enormous bicep. She squealed with what she hoped was appropriate girlish enthusiasm. And just as she spotted the lanky, fox-faced human she was looking for, she heard him say:

"Anyway, don't worry. The big man gave us a plan for tonight, didn't he?"

What the hell? Sam stared across a heaving sea of partying crew to see Javin Darto deadlifting the troublesome subject of his thoughts up on one beefy shoulder above the crowd. Though he was too far away to be certain, Rayna seemed to be enjoying the experience, giggling like a marketplace wh . . . well, like she'd been paid. *Shalssit!*

"Security report, Cap."

Sam turned to Lieutenant Chen and nodded.

Chen was efficiency in a slim, compact package. She wasted no time with preliminaries.

"You were right about the LO's, sir. We've got at least a dozen in the crowd. The Sec crew is rounding them up now."

"How the hell did they get in here in the first place, Mei? I thought I was clear."

"You were, sir, and I believe things held up for the first hour or so. We had the main entrance well covered." Chen shook her head. "Right now I don't have enough information to give you a good explanation, but I think someone must have let them in a side door. And by this time, one or two could have just walked in the front."

Sam surveyed the feverish scene from his post on the climbing scaffold overlooking the main deck and conceded the point. Managing this throng of wildly-diverse, deeply-intoxicated beings was a mighty challenge, but this wasn't the first time he'd asked Chen to rise to the occasion. She always handled the task well and without complaint. He started to dismiss her to do her job when he spotted a scuffle in one section of the crowd as the Sec crew struggled to subdue a drunk-and-resisting LO. As he watched, someone standing nearby started a shoving match and fists shot out in multiple directions. Rumbles erupted all across the deck, merging into a huge, malignant pattern.

"Shit, Mei, your people are in trouble. We have to

close this thing down."   But his Security Chief had already seen what he'd seen and was calling for backup.

Sam swung down through the bars of the climbing structure, headed for the sound system and lights, Chen right behind him on the stairs, barking instructions into her comm unit.   His crew could generally hold its liquor—and its temper—but LO's coming out of the mindwipe and captivity were volatile and often violent. It would be easy for them to serve as the catalyst for something dark and dangerous in the grog-soaked mob.

And worse, Rayna was in the middle of it.

Brawlers blocked his way at the base of the unit, and he waded in, tossing lighter combatants aside to get to the heart of the conflict. Sam took a few random hits before the fighters realized their captain was in the fray. He barely felt the blows. He was angry. Furious. Someone had started this mess on his ship, and they would pay, the sonsofbitches!

He finally reached the center of the floor and found a crazed LO and two crewmen, with one beleaguered Security man trying to pull them apart.   The LO's broken nose was streaming blood in a bright red flood, and he swayed with every punch he threw, but he refused to give up. The two crewmen were just as battered—eyes blackened, cheeks bruised, lips split— but still they circled, looking for an opportunity to attack. The exhausted Security officer stood between them, unable to do anything but take a blow meant for one or the other of the combatants.

"All right, that's enough!"   Sam put all of his authority as captain behind the words.

His crewmen and the Sec officer froze, eyes wide. One of the crewmen opened his mouth to explain.

Sam held up a hand.   "Don't."   He turned to consider the LO—and caught a sucker punch in the jaw. Staggered, his next move was pure instinct. He blocked the second broad swing coming at his head and let fly with his own right. With Sam's weight behind it, the punch lifted the scrawny little guy off his feet and back onto the deck, where he remained in a crumpled, unconscious heap.

Sam stared down at the man in surprise. "Huh."

"We must have softened him up for you, Cap." The two bloodied crewmen and the Security officer grinned at him.

He would have returned the grin, but the scene around him had become a riot. He had to regain control fast.

Sam gestured at the Security man. "Get this guy back to Sickbay. And you two are confined to quarters. Get out of here. Now."

All around him men and women pushed, shoved, shouted and screamed. Punches flew, bodies slammed to the deck. He smelled blood and sweat and the bittersweet of grog. This was worse than any bar brawl he'd ever fought on any dusty, backwater planet in the galaxy. Worse, because it was on his own, sweet ship and, damn it, he couldn't seem to stop it.

"Captain, we have a new problem."   Chen was

suddenly at his side again.

"What now?"

"All the exits have been sealed from the outside. The computer locking mechanisms were engaged, then the programs were fritzed somehow. We're stuck in here until Engineering can cut us out."

"Come on, we have to get you out of here."

"Uh, no, that's okay, big guy. I really need to stay for a minute." Rayna struggled to extract herself from her protector's grip, but the man wouldn't let her go. She had to admit the roiling crowd around her was intimidating, but it was imperative she follow the two slaves from the *Fleeflek*, especially now that their plan seemed to be taking effect.

The big crewman kept walking, pushing his way through the throng toward an exit. "You're not even supposed to be in here. Cap said so—no LO's. Must admit you're cute, though. If I'd been working the door, I'd have let you in, too."

"Yeah, thanks." Seems like that policy hadn't worked so well tonight. But Security had tipped to the large number of visitors crashing the party. Their efforts to scoop them up were causing a ruckus. No, make that a riot. And it was spreading. Fights erupting everywhere, fueled by too much grog and encouraged by a few choice words or pushes from *Fleeflek* conspirators. The Sec crew was overwhelmed.

But Rayna's brawny dance partner knew how to make his way through a bar brawl. He never stopped moving, and his size guaranteed that no one dared to stand in his way. He kept her in front of his massive body, framing her in a protective cage of muscle as they moved through the crowd. Scrappers careened into them, and he shoved them sprawling back into the fray. Rayna would have pitched in with a punch or two, but he wouldn't allow it, steering her aside and taking out any offenders with a simple one-handed push to the face.

"Damn, sweets. I have to say I'm impressed." She tilted her head back to look up at him once they'd reached the exit. "You've got skills."

He gave her a goofy grin. "I played professional bloodball back home on Argent for a while."

"And you still have teeth?" She grinned back at him. She glanced at the exit, where Security officers led a steady stream of injured and restrained through the open double hatch. People were making their way out and back to their quarters, but not nearly as quickly as the situation warranted. They lingered inside, hoping for more fun, or in the companionway, waiting to see how it all turned out.

There! The two she'd been looking for just slipped through the hatch. She turned to her rescuer. "Hey. Thanks for getting me through that. I better go."

Just before things got awkward, a Security officer grabbed the big man's arm. "Hey, Javin. We need you in there. Give us a hand?"

He nodded at the man. "Sure." Then he looked at Rayna. "See you."

She was already a step away, keeping her guys in sight. "Watch your back in there."

He grinned and turned to make his way back through the crowd.

The two from the *Fleeflek* were loitering in the corridor like the others, the taller one wearing an expression of secret amusement, the shorter one looking worried. Rayna gave a moment's thought to approaching them openly. They'd all been on the slaver together, hadn't they? But there was little to be gained from showing her hand at this stage of the game. She resolved to watch and wait a while longer.

Outraged shouts and a sudden tattoo of heavy pounding broke out at the entrance to the PT deck. Rayna jerked around to see crew members and Security officers throwing themselves uselessly against the closed hatch doors, pulling at the handles, trying the emergency releases at the sides and giving every indication that the hatch doors were locked.

Rayna turned to the woman next to her. "What the hell happened?"

The woman blinked at the scene in front of the locked hatch. "You got me. One minute the hatch was open, the next it slammed shut. Now they can't get it open again." She pointed down the companionway. "Looks like the same thing happened with the B exit."

"Holy shit! You mean they're locked in there?"

The woman, who reeked of grog, swayed slightly as

she goggled at Rayna. "Yeah. Damn."

Rayna spun around, scanning the milling crowd for her quarry. They were already headed down the corridor, nearly at the turn in the passageway that would take them out of sight. She spared a glance back toward the barred hatch and found her big crewman still on this side.

"Javin!" When she saw his head swivel in her direction, she waved at him. "I need your help. With me. Now!" Then she started pushing through the crowd.

She could only pray that Javin had heard her and was following somewhere in her wake. She couldn't spare another look over her shoulder; she had to see which direction the men from the *Fleeflek* turned at the junction of the corridors. *Left!* And they were picking up speed, as if they had a destination in mind. Her blood chilled as she realized what was down that passage—Engineering, the heart of the ship. She began to wish not only for Javin but for a whole squad of Security at her back.

She saw the pair turn right at the next corridor—definitely heading for Engineering now—and took it up to a light-footed run. She slowed at the turn, thinking to take a cautious peek before she followed her prey. As she eased around the corner, she was met with a hard punch to the head. Stunned, she fell back, but she recovered quickly, tribute to her training and the fact that her attacker had misjudged her height and struck her in the forehead rather than the nose. He cursed and bent over his right hand. She took advantage by delivering a savage kick to the inside of his knee. He went to the deck with a howl.

His taller companion came at her with the skills and focus of a street fighter, and within seconds she was pinned against the bulkhead, trying without hope to block a hailstorm of blows with her forearms and elbows and knees. She felt her rib crack, then her cheekbone; she put an elbow in his sternum, but it only angered him. She got in a knee to his groin and smiled in grim satisfaction, figuring it would be the last time she smiled, with all her teeth, anyway. The taste of blood was thick in her mouth. *Jesus Chris! That hurt, you fucker!* She knew if she didn't get away from this bulkhead, she'd be unconscious soon, but there was no room to duck or step or even breathe.

Her vision was starting to flash black, and she could barely hold her arms up when the rain of abuse abruptly ended. "Javin . . ." she mumbled and slumped to the deck, vaguely aware that the big man had pulled her attacker off her and was busy beating him to a pulp. Just before the blackness swept up to carry her away, she managed to say one word.

"Engineering."

CHAPTER FOUR

"Shalssiti pulak! What the fucking hell is happening on my ship!"

Captain Murphy seldom lost his temper, but things seldom spiraled out of control the way they were spinning toward the horizon right now. His Security Chief responded with stoic silence. She hadn't had any answers in some time.

He strode toward the small stage that had been erected in the converted exercise space, looking for a voice amplification system to make his feelings known to his crew. The young crew chief in charge there made it happen fast.

Murphy wasted no time trying to get his crew's attention. He whistled into the mic, an action that was first met with whoops of protest, then a fall into silence as people began to realize who had shattered their eardrums. Those who were not actively involved in fighting turned to face their leader on the stage. And gradually, as Murphy waited, Security began to get a handle on the remaining knots of scuffling crew.

"What the living *hell* is going on here?" He paused, letting his question sink in. "This is the *Shadowhawk*, the biggest, the *proudest* independent trader in the galaxy. We fight slavers. We fight *mulaak* Thrane thugs and Gray slimedogs and assholes wherever we find them. We don't fight each other. Ever."

He walked from one end of the little stage to the other, staring each of his crew members in the face. None of them could meet his gaze. His comm unit buzzed at his waist, but he ignored it. He was on a roll.

"People call us blackjacks, pirates, worse than murderers or thieves. They imagine our lives are just like the brawls I saw in here tonight. I know different. I expect different. And because of that there will be consequences for this." The young girl directly in front of him—*Laurie? No, Lainie*—grew visibly paler.

"Now we have another problem." He looked toward a disturbance at one side of the room. "Shut the fuck up back there!" Whoever it was got quiet in a hurry. "There's been a malfunction with the main exit hatches. It's going to take Engineering a minute to get it fixed. Until that happens you're going to sit quietly like nice boys and girls and wait. When the hatches open you're going to get up and go back to your bunks and sleep this off. Give me any reason to notice your ass individually except for exceptional bravery or willingness to help in this emergency, and you will be scrubbing out the filter tanks for a month. Am I clear?"

Several dozen voices answered, "Aye, Cap!" Most of them sat down where they were, too disheartened to speak with their neighbors. Lainie scowled at her fellow crew members like she would be the one to enforce his orders.

He threw the mic at the startled crew chief and jumped down off the stage, where Chen met him with more bad news. "Engineering reports an attempt to take over the engine control room a few minutes ago. Kwan was there, says they were amateurs and he has it under control. I sent what I had left of my auxiliaries over anyway."

Murphy scrubbed a hand down his face. "Shit, what a night. Remind me never to allow a mash again."

"You said that last time."

"And did you remind me?" He suddenly had an urgent need to know the rest of his ship was in one piece. He pulled out his comm unit and called Mo on the bridge to demand a status report.

"Cap. I've been trying to reach you. Chen tells me you're trapped on the PT deck with most of the crew."

"Don't sound so smug. And, yes, I ignored your buzz while I was dragging the crew over the thrusters for their rowdy behavior. Tell me my ship is intact."

"So far. But we do seem to be the target of a coordinated, if inept, attack by a faction of lucky ones from the *Fleeflek*. We have half a dozen in the brig from a genuinely comical assault on Engineering and two more that Javin Darto put in Sickbay after they had a run-in with your friend Rayna Carver. She apparently had been following them from the mash toward Engineering when they caught her. They, uh, they beat her up pretty badly before Javin stepped in."

"Bleeding gods!" A hole opened up in his chest, making it hard for him to breathe. "Is she okay?"

"Doc says she's got her under the light; you should be able to talk to her in a couple of hours."

Interviewing her hadn't been his first concern, but he added it to the list. "You say these *veers* were going from here to Engineering? Then what was going on here at the mash could have been a staged distraction. Someone let at least a dozen LO's in here despite my orders to the contrary. Any of those guys in the brig seem resistant to the mindwipe?"

"Most, if not all of them. I don't think the others are capable of following a plan."

"Agreed. Let's start with the ones in the brig, see if we can identify a leader." He suspected they'd end up in Sickbay, though. The man who came up with a plan usually liked to see how it was coming together. The men Rayna had been following had been positioned to see both aspects of the plan come to fruition. The question that soured in his gut like a batch of home brewed 'shroom ale was how Rayna could have known that. He intended to find out how this snippet of a female with an attitude the size of Malenga's second moon could know more about what was going on around his ship than he did.

Doc Berta was busy patching up half of his crew, but she spared a few minutes to give Sam a status report. "The light's out of her face, so you can talk to her now *for a minute*. She's tough, but she took a beating before Javin got there—hairline fractures in the ribs, cheekbone, forearms, multiple contusions. I don't see any internal injuries. That was just plain lucky."

Heat rose in Sam's chest, accelerating his heartbeat, strangling his breath. What kind of animal beat a female—beat *anyone*—so badly with so little provocation? He knew Rayna wouldn't welcome his protectiveness, but he couldn't help the images that came to mind, of the tiny woman trying to fend off the vicious blows from a much bigger attacker, and he wanted to finish the job Javin Darto had begun.

"Cap? You okay?" His Chief MO laid a hand on his arm. The expression on her face said she saw too much.

He scraped up a smile. "Yeah. It's been a rough night. You said she's under the healing light. She's not going to need the regen tank?"

"There's someone with a broken leg and another with a cracked skull ahead of her." Sam opened his mouth to ask for the details, but Berta, ever efficient, beat him to it. "Bentor and Axl. They'll be fine. By the time they get done, she won't need it."

"How long until she's up and around?"

Again, there was understanding behind Berta's smile. "A few days. She's in great shape; she'll heal fast."

Sam nodded, breathed. He took the few steps to Rayna's cubicle and peeked around the curtain. Seeing her there, shrunken and lost in the Sickbay bunk, her vibrant lifeforce reduced to a subdued rhythmic beeping of the monitors, would have been a shock in any case. But her face still showed the marks of her fight, the swelling and purplish-black bruising along one cheekbone, the cuts over the eyes, the blackened, puffed-up eyelids, the split lips. Within hours the swelling would be gone, the bruising beginning to fade, the result of the therapeutic action of the healing light. At this moment, though . . . looking at her made Sam tremble with the need to hold her, or to kill somebody, he wasn't sure which.

"That bad, huh?" The papery whisper emerged with some effort between lips that barely moved.

Sam found a smile. "You look like one of us now. Very piratical." He came all the way inside the cubicle and stood close by the bed.

Rayna grunted. "Be popular . . . with the crew."

"You're already popular with me. Thanks to you I have someone to question about what happened tonight. I won't forget that."

Her eyes closed in denial. "Thank Javin."

"I did." Out of sight below the healing bed, his fists clenched. "If he hadn't already put those guys in Sickbay, I'd be looking to do it myself."

The eyes opened again and something crossed her face like sunshine on troubled water. "Why, Captain. I didn't know you cared."

His chest tightened, equal parts irritation and embarrassment and . . . *damn it!* "My ship. My responsibility."

The teasing light went out of her eyes. "Ah."

He shook his head. "What made you follow those two anyway?"

"Caught some talk . . . at the mash. Some crazy plan." She moved as if to sit up, but got no further than the hunching of her shoulders before she fell back against her pillows with a grimace.

Sam put a hand on her arm to hold her in place. "Not on your life, Little Bit. Doc just got you put back together. If you behave you might get out of here in a day or two."

Rayna shot him a glare. "Keep calling me that . . . you'll be trading places with me."

"See? You're feeling better already." He didn't want to, but he removed his hand from her arm.

"Did . . . *shit* . . . did you talk to them?"

"Not yet. So what was the plan? Besides inciting a riot among my crew?"

"Dumbasses expected you to give them the *Fleeflek*." Rayna closed her eyes, sighing with pain and exhaustion. "Don't think they know you very well."

Sam gave in to the urge to touch her, knowing she was so close to unconscious she wouldn't be aware of it. He reached out and covered her small, bruised hand with his large, calloused one.

"No, honey, they don't. But trust me, they're about to find out."

"I'm Captain Murphy, and you're going to be very sorry you met me." Sam took every bit of the anger he felt as a man and the authority he held as ship's captain and threw it at the man glaring up at him from the Sickbay bunk. "Who the fuck are you?"

The man shrugged one narrow shoulder at him. "You have the *Fleeflek*'s cargo manifest. You figure it out."

Sam placed a hand on the man's other shoulder— the one bound in a sling—and squeezed ever so gently. "Your attitude is admirable, but misplaced. I'm an impatient man, and you might want to save the resistance for the important stuff. Tell me your name."

"Fuck! Okay! Falla. Ven Falla."

"Tell me why you tried to take over my ship, Ven Falla."

"What? What the hell are you talking about?"

"I'm talking about the riot your people started at the mash tonight. And the attack in my engine room. All part of a coordinated plan to take over my ship. Not a very competent plan, mind you, but a plan nonetheless. Masterminded by you, Ven Falla."

Sweat beaded on Falla's forehead and began to roll down his temples. "You've gone space-happy. I snuck into the *mulaak* party, sure. I hadn't had a drink in months, that's why. Maybe I got a little carried away with that sweet piece of ass, but she was willing enough until her boyfriend showed up—"

Sam snapped, his hand coming up to close on Falla's throat before he'd even thought about it. "Stop right there. I ought to cut your lying tongue out of your mouth." His fingers tightened, and Falla struggled for breath until his face darkened. "You see, you've got it all wrong, Ven. That wasn't the lady's boyfriend who came to her rescue. She's a particular friend of *mine*. Yeah. And I happen to know she was fighting for her life before my man Javin showed up."

The idea that he had a personal stake in the outcome of the conversation had the desired effect on Falla, who was staring at him in horror out of a face now purple from lack of oxygen. Sam released his hold on the man's throat.

Falla's retching and coughing brought Doc Berta over to raise a disapproving eyebrow, but Sam waved her off. The doctor retreated, holding up a hand with fingers spread as she left. He nodded. Five minutes would be plenty for what he had in mind.

"How can you even know her?" Falla sputtered at last. "She was on the slaver with us."

"I work fast. And what's more important is that she was under my protection when you beat the crap out of her. Like my ship is under my protection, *ptark*. *My* protection—the guy who wants to rip your throat out. So, again. Tell me why you were trying to take over my ship."

Falla wouldn't meet his eyes now; his gaze jittered from one side of the treatment cubicle to the other, seeking escape. "Not your ship we wanted."

"If not my ship, then what?"

"The *Fleeflek*."

Sam held back a laugh. "One, if you wanted the *mulaak* wreck, it would have been a helluva lot easier to take her than the *'hawk*. And, two, why would you want a broken-down old slaver in the first place?"

"Most of us who were resistant to the mindwipe ended up here on the *Shadowhawk*. We needed to negotiate for what we wanted. As for why . . ." Falla looked up in defiance. "We deserve to set our own course."

"Oh. A freedom fighter, huh?" Sam sat back and considered his prisoner in silence. Falla's expression had turned sullen, but there was something of a performance about it. There was more to this story, Sam could feel it.

Before he could pursue it, his comm unit beeped at his waist with an urgent code from Engineering. "Kwan?"

"Hey, Cap. Need you down here as soon as you can make it."

"What's the problem?"

"Your ears only, Cap."

"Be there in five." He replaced the unit at his waist with a curse and turned on Falla. "We're not done. You still owe me for what you did to my friend, and if you've so much as scratched a bulkhead on my ship you can plan on spending the rest of your life in the penal colony on Braga."

CHAPTER FIVE

"One little processing unit. This whole fucking engine room and they picked the one that sabotages our jump drive."

The captain and his chief engineer stood staring at the offending unit, a cube of crystal nanoplex no bigger than a newbie's locker. Acid had eaten away one side of the delicate matrix.

"They knew what they were after, all right," Kwan agreed. "And they were discreet about it. I might not have even noticed it if we hadn't scheduled a maintenance check for today."

The unit did only one thing: It monitored and controlled the wild fluxes in power that overtook the engines during travel through the jump nodes. Without it, the ship risked violent explosion or endless limbo between nodes. Without it, attempting jump was suicide.

Sam tried in vain to rub the tension out of his neck. "How long to regrow the matrix?"

Kwan shrugged. "We might get lucky and be ready by the time we get to C4."

"So five days."

"I said *might*. More likely we'll have to hang out there a day or two until it firms up."

Sam refused to say out loud what was on his mind

and instead sent a silent prayer to the universe to keep the Grays off his trail until his crippled ship got her wings back. "Okay. Coddle it. Sing to it. Feed it chocolate. I don't care what you have to do, but get us back in shape to move, Engineer."

"Aye, Cap. I'm on it."

Sam left the engine room, blood in his eye for Ven Falla.

Everything hurt. No. Every *fucking* thing hurt. And what didn't hurt so much also itched, a function of the healing brought on by the light that was currently focused on Rayna's battered torso. Where the light had already passed, over her face and neck, the itching was maddening as the cells regenerated and the circulatory and lymphatic systems operated at an accelerated pace. Rayna thought again of pressing the button near her hand for another shot of sedative, but denied herself a little longer. There was something on her mind.

Captain Solomon Armstrong Murphy. She hadn't imagined his visit earlier, though she was pretty sure she'd fallen asleep in the middle of it. And—she couldn't really be remembering this right—he'd had a look in his eyes. Something . . . soft . . . and hard at the same time. One minute like she was a little broken bird that he wanted to pick up and hold in his hand, the next like she was down on some battlefield and he was fending off all attackers. What the hell? Twelve hours ago he wouldn't have spit on her if her hair was on fire.

Unwelcome warmth crept into her chest at the thought of Murphy's protectiveness, making her squirm. Damn that *mulaak* slave anyway for putting her flat on her back in this Sickbay, where the hardass captain could play the magnanimous guardian. The only thing she wanted to owe Murphy for was a trip to LinHo.

The life signs monitor beside her bunk noted the rise in her heartbeat and blood pressure with an alert tone and a change in the color of its display from green to yellow. Rayna took a deep breath and used her biofeedback training to calm herself, hoping to fend off an unnecessary visit from the medics. She'd had enough of their fussing already. By the time the monitor display had gone back to green she realized she was exhausted. She fumbled for the sedative button in the tangle of the blankets.

A shadow moving in the bay outside her cubicle made her glance up. She thought at first it was a medic coming to check the monitor after all, but the shadow slipped past the open side of her enclosure without stopping. Something about the way the man moved told her he wasn't a medic; he wasn't a visitor or a patient. He didn't look like someone on a charitable mission at all. *Shit!* Murphy had said those two she'd been following had ended up in Sickbay.

She sat up and stripped the monitor sensor from her wrist. That would bring the medics running in a minute or two, so backup would be on the way.

Certainly *she* had no more than the element of surprise to stop what the man intended to do a couple of cubicles over.

Rayna swung her feet over the side of the bunk and tried to ignore the dizziness swamping her as she struggled to stand. Her legs threatened to give way beneath her, so she shuffled slowly from the top of the bunk to the bottom, from there to the corner of the cubicle, keeping a hand on something solid for support. Her ribs screamed at her, refusing to let her stand up straight.

"Freaking light still has some work to do," she muttered through clenched teeth.

She had begun to realize what she was planning was impossible when she saw a middle-aged woman in blue scrubs and a younger male in no discernible uniform hurrying through the bay in her direction.

"Please don't tell me you're looking for the bathroom," the woman said.

"Call Security. You have an intruder trying to get to a couple of your patients."

The male assistant looked at the woman, who seemed to be the one in charge. Rayna squinted at her nametag: Doc Berta. The doctor pulled them all back into Rayna's cubicle and reached for the comm unit at her waist.

"Chen, we have a problem in Sickbay." As she talked she gestured to the medic to get her patient back in bed. Rayna was only too happy to comply. "Somebody's trying to get to those two Cap's got under guard down here. No, I don't see your boy. Whoever it is must've already taken him out and is in there with the prisoners. Well, hurry it up, damn it."

The doctor keyed off the comm and jabbed a finger at Rayna. "Stay in that bed. Am I clear?"

"Not a problem." Rayna could barely find the energy to speak the words.

The doctor pulled at her orderly. "With me, hon. On the double." Rayna sat up, though the agony that flared through her ribs nearly sent her right back down again. "No! Let Security handle it. He'll kill you."

The doctor was already moving, her lanky assistant close behind. "Honey, this is my sickbay. Nobody messes with my patients but me." Rayna tried to get up. She really did. She knew the kind of man Doc Berta was going up against—a skilled agent, an assassin for hire. He wasn't the kind to listen to unarmed argument, no matter how courageous. He would kill the woman if she got in his way. He would kill her if she annoyed him. And, chances were, he would kill her just for the fun of it.

So Rayna tried to get out of that bunk and help the woman. But her battered body would not cooperate. Her limbs felt like they were encased in tritanium shielding, and every breath drew in pain. She was glued to the bunk, like it or not. She waited, expecting raised voices, scuffling, the eventual whine of a laser pistol or the brief, shocked gasp of pain if he used a knife. But all she heard was the low murmur of Doc Berta's calm voice. What was she doing, talking him into joining her for milk and cookies?

Security arrived on the double, led by a sturdy, no-nonsense Terrene with the genetic markers of Earth's Asia. The team disappeared in the direction of the prisoners' cubicle, but no firefight broke out. The fact that more talking ensued could only mean that the prisoners were dead and the assassin had somehow escaped.

Rayna was dead beat, but she forced her heavy eyelids to stay open. She knew it wouldn't be long, and, sure enough, within minutes Captain Murphy's determined stride took him past her cubicle toward the crime scene. Then, at last, she heard those raised voices she'd been expecting.

"How the hell did this happen, Chen? You're telling me he waltzed through Sickbay, got through an armed guard, killed two men and disappeared without anyone seeing him?"

Both Berta and Chen started to answer, but the captain's bark shut them up. "One at a time!"

"Only partially correct, Cap," Chen said. "Doc here got a glimpse of him."

"On his way out. But I wouldn't have if Rayna hadn't seen him first and limped out of bed to follow him."

"What?" Throughout Sickbay, sensitive monitoring equipment responded to the roar with alarm. "Where is she now?"

"She's fine. She didn't get more than about three steps before I found her and sent her back to bed. But she's the one who saw the man in the first place. Without her we wouldn't have had a clue what happened here. I would have just diagnosed death by post-traumatic seizure. Rare, but it happens."

"Twice?" Murphy sounded skeptical.

"No, that's the beauty of it. The other fellow— Arden?—his was a standard heart attack. Had a genetic basis for it. This guy was good."

"Well, let's give him the Assassin of the Year Award, shall we? Chen, what's the plan?"

"I've got people working an expanding grid from this point, checking for all unauthorized personnel in the air ducts, engineering access points and service tubes as well as companionways and lifts. It would help if we had a description."

A description. Rayna thought back to her glimpse of the man as he passed through Sickbay, but she could recall few details. He'd been little more than a darker shape against the unlit background of the outer bay. She could say he'd been of average height and wiry. Beyond that, she had nothing to offer. She hadn't seen his face or his hair. She tried to picture the shadowy figure, but kept drifting.

"Rayna? You awake?"

"What?" She blinked at him, confused. He was so close, sitting at the head of the bunk. She'd been alone just a moment ago. Her heartbeat sped up, alerting the monitor again. "I was waiting for you. I must have fallen asleep."

"I'm sorry to have to wake you. I have to ask you a

few questions." His brow wrinkled. "Did you say you were waiting for me?"

"You want to know about the assassin. You need a description."

"Um, yeah. Did you see him?"

"No. I'm sorry. All I saw was a shadow—medium height, kinda thin. I didn't see his face." There was something about the way he moved, though. Her mind just wouldn't process it.

Murphy nodded as if he'd suspected as much. "Doc Berta said about the same thing. The man was a pro."

"Did you learn anything from your prisoners before he got to them?"

"No." His jaw clenched hard. "Something about this stinks."

"If you mean there's more to it than a few slaves taking a notion to steal a ship and strike out on their own, then, yeah, I agree. Too much trouble to protect such a hare-brained scheme."

"Thank you, Agent. Or is it Detective now?" He smiled and tugged a little at her covers. "How about you think about staying in bed? You need your rest."

Ruthless, she pressed her advantage. "How about you think about taking me to LinHo? You owe me now."

She expected a scowl, but instead he grinned. "You're right, Little Bit, I do owe you. Maybe dinner in my cabin once you're feeling better. But LinHo? Not only no, but *hell* no. Especially not now. I'm getting these people off my ship double-quick before the Grays find me and blow me out of space." He stood up and paused to touch her cheek ever so gently. "Sleep. Feel better. I'll see you tomorrow."

Of course the monitor beeped to alert everyone in range that her heartbeat had surged once more. She saw Murphy glance at it and smile as he left the cubicle, the damn, cocky sonofabitch! Rayna couldn't tell which was more infuriating, the insufferable captain or her uncontrollable reaction to him. Only two things were certain: everything fucking hurt, and she was tired of thinking. She gave in at last and pushed the button at her side. Within seconds the patch attached to the skin of her arm delivered the medication that brought both relief from pain and blessed unconsciousness. She sighed and knew no more.

Chen shook her head. "I'm sorry, Cap. He's gone. Short of locking up every LO on this ship and the *Fleeflek*, I don't see what else I can do."

Sam took a deep breath and scanned his crowded command room. Both Chen and his ceiling-scraping Executive Officer were too much for the space. He had to get out.

He ducked through the hatch. "Walk with me."

The two officers flanked him as he stalked the corridors toward the PT deck, scattering crew along the way. "The LO's stay on lockdown. Confine them to quarters except for eating, and rec and shower rotations."

"Cap, we don't have time to babysit these people." Mo's protest was just loud enough for Sam to hear. "We've got a ship to run. Do you realize we'll have to escort them everywhere? How we gonna do that?"

"Mo, you know damn well while we're running deep space there's nothing to do on shift but run systems checks and swab the decks. This'll give the crew something new to do."

His XO stared at him. "'Swab the decks'? What the hell does that mean?"

"Old pirate term. Look it up." He paused, pulling his officers to the side of the corridor to let two crew members pass by. "The more time we spend with these people the greater the chance we'll uncover something. The assassin is still out there, which means the conspirators that tried to take my ship are still out there. I want them. Make it happen."

Chen stepped up. "How about I coordinate an effort to put together a master schedule with all the sections that are housing LO's? If I sit on the section heads they can make assignments by the end of the day. I'll run it by Mo when I'm done, and he can brief you when we've got a final?"

Sam raised an eyebrow at Mo, waiting for him to approve the plan. Chen was taking on a bit much, but Mo had the rest of the ship to worry about, and he usually chose efficiency over territoriality. When the Pataran inclined his head, the captain gave his orders.

"All right, Mei. I'll expect a report by the middle of

the second watch."

"You'll have it, Cap." The Security officer turned and headed off in the opposite direction just as the two men pulled up at the PT deck. The hatches stood open and a cleaning crew was still working on transforming the space back to its intended use.

Sam surveyed the disruption with weary resignation.

"Tell me you weren't planning to work out." Mo frowned at his captain.

"I had hoped to work off some of this frustration, yes."

"What you are feeling, my friend, is exhaustion." Mo took him by the arm and led him down the corridor toward the lift. "You haven't slept in . . . even I don't know how long. I'll wager you haven't eaten in at least a day. Don't make me quote the regs to force you to rest."

"Pirate ships don't have regs."

"This one does. You wrote them yourself."

By the time they reached his cabin, Sam was crumbling. Just the mention of how long he'd been on his feet had been enough to make him stumble; now all he could think about was stretching out in his bunk in sweet oblivion. He managed to kick off his boots and drag a blanket over his shoulders before his eyelids drifted shut.

Mo's voice reached him from a long way off. "Should I call up for some food . . . never mind. I'll buzz you at 1800. Sleep well."

He registered the time—1130—heaved a deep sigh and slept.

CHAPTER SIX

Doc Berta shook her head and frowned at the readings on the panel behind Rayna's head. "I can't find a reason to keep you here any longer, Carver." She sighed. "But if I let you out of my sight Cap will have my ass."

Rayna's brows came together in the center of her forehead. "What does Murphy have to do with it?" She had an ugly suspicion she knew the answer.

When the doctor wouldn't meet her gaze, that guess was confirmed. "This is my Sickbay, but it's Captain Murphy's ship. He gives the orders. We follow them."

Outrage propelled her forward in her sickbed, but the pain from her abused ribs immediately put a leash on her anger. "Am I ready to be discharged or not? I feel fine!" That last wasn't exactly the truth—she still felt like the discards from making an omelet—but if she didn't get out of bed this minute she just might lose what was left of her sanity.

The doctor drew herself up to her full height, which was only impressive if you were flat on your back in a hospital bed. "The captain has the last say about every damn thing on his ship. And in this case, I have to agree with him. Security is at stake. We have an assassin on the loose—an assassin *you* saw, need I remind you? Cap says you aren't going anywhere until he clears it."

The monitors still attached to Rayna's body went crazy. "To hell with that! The assassin doesn't know I saw him!" She swung her legs to the floor, ignoring the dizziness that followed the action. She began stripping the patches from her skin and the alarms fell silent. "Where are my clothes?"

"What the hell is going on here?"

Rayna didn't have to see him to know who belonged to the voice. The commanding baritone was enough to freeze her in place and put her heart in overdrive. She turned to see Sam Murphy standing in the opening to her cubicle, his expression dark.

She lifted her chin. "The doctor says I'm well enough to leave."

The captain glared at Doc Berta, who gave an exasperated sigh and raised her arms in surrender. "I gave orders she should be kept here under guard until I said otherwise." Murphy's voice was a growl now, low and primal.

"I can't justify keeping her here on medical reasons," the doctor argued.

Rayna found a set of clean clothes in the cabinet next to her bed and stuck her legs into the jumpsuit. She turned to the wall to avoid Murphy's stare as she slipped her upper body into the suit, responding to the hunger in his gaze with a blush that spread heat over every inch of her skin.

"She needs protection."

Dressed, she turned to confront him. "I can take

care of myself, Captain." She fought the light-headeness the turn had caused her.

He smirked. "You're weak as a day-old *targa*."

"*Targas* are born with claws and teeth. And you can't keep me in a cage." She stood facing him, waiting for him to step aside.

A muscle twitched in his jaw. Fire smoldered deep in his eyes. If he had stood across a sparring mat from her, she would have had no idea how to anticipate the strike. Was he angry? Was he frustrated? Was he attracted? Did he want to protect her, or kill her himself? Maybe what she saw in his eyes was only a reflection of what she felt. The man drove her crazy.

"At least let me walk you back to your cabin." The words were bitten off and spit out.

"That won't be necessary."

"You don't have a choice."

She bent to put on the soft, Vibram-soled boots most everyone wore onboard ship and had to swallow a groan. It still hurt so damn much! She stood, hiding her pain, concealing any sign of weakness. She couldn't afford to let him see; she refused to give him the advantage. Despite all her care, he reached out to help steady her. She shrugged him off and pushed past him to the cubicle entrance.

Rayna glanced at Doc Berta. "Am I good to go?"

It infuriated her that the doctor looked to the captain. "Cap?"

"If she passes out in the corridor, what should I do?"

Berta grinned. "Guess you'll have to pick her up and haul her ass back here."

"Right." He met Rayna's narrowed gaze and inclined his head in the direction of the exit. "After you."

As they left Sickbay, the two Security guards who'd been stationed at the entrance to the med facility fell in behind them. Rayna let out an exasperated breath.

"Is that really necessary?"

"What? Are you suggesting you're in shape to fight off another attacker—or two—even with my help?"

She had to admit the thought of hand-to-hand combat right now made her sick to her stomach.

Murphy caught her expression and took a breath. "Let's just say I'm feeling lazy today. Any trouble and we'll let the boys handle it."

They reached the lift and took it to Deck Five, where she shared the cabin with Lainie and the others. As they took to the corridor again, she noticed his usual conquering stride had slowed to a moseying stroll. In deference to her? Truthfully she didn't feel like moving with any kind of catlike grace, either. Damn it!

She needed a distraction. "How goes the search for the assassin?"

His face turned stormy. "We've eliminated several possibilities."

"That well, huh?"

"The murders had a sobering effect on the men we had in the brig."

"They're not talking."

"No. And without a description or any evidence left at the scene, searching two ships and 800 LO's is a near-impossible task."

"It could be anyone."

"In effect. I don't suppose you noticed anyone suspicious in that hold with you before we captured the *Fleeflek*?"

She laughed. "Besides myself, you mean?"

He turned to stare at her. "Funny that this particular slaver should harbor not just one, but two . . . shall we say, trained agents undercover?"

She hadn't thought of it that way. It was, in fact, damned strange. Had the operation been blown? In that case, why not just go after her? Why all the craziness with an attempted takeover of Murphy's ship, unless it was to regain the slaves?

Rayna shook her head. She had no answers for him. When she looked away from his interrogation, she saw they had arrived at her cabin. Her bunk, thank God, was empty.

"I've found another place for your bunkmates." He swallowed—embarrassed? "For a couple of days, anyway. I thought you could use the extra rest."

She found she was genuinely grateful. "Thank you." Her throat closed up then, taking any more words, as she looked up into a stare that had become much too intimate.

It seemed as if he stopped breathing at the same time, equally robbed of speech. Instead, one corner of his mouth lifted, and he nodded. Then he turned away and strode off down the corridor, leaving the guards behind at the hatch of her cabin.

And Rayna, of course, watching him and wondering what the hell was wrong with her.

"What the hell is wrong with you?" Mo towered over the desk in his command room, a frown worrying his dark face.

Sam refused to do more than glance up from the datapad he'd been staring at—and not seeing—for the last half-hour. "Why should anything be wrong? I've got an assassin on the loose, 800 LO's crowding two ships, a gimpy jump drive and a pain-in-the-ass XO to deal with. And this is a good day."

"Customarily, the captain of a ship is found on the bridge. With his crew." The Pataran crossed his arms over his chest, his usual sign of displeasure. "You stomped in here over an hour ago without a word to anyone, and you've been in here ever since."

"Is there an emergency on the bridge that requires my attention?"

Mo glared, but said nothing.

"Then I have work to do. Here. In my command room." He waved a hand. "Which is why I have a desk and everything in here."

"You're not in the habit of working in your command room. At your . . . desk and everything. Makes me think you're hiding."

Sam abandoned the futile effort to go over the fuel reports. "If you've got something to say, Mo, spit it out. I don't have time to trade riddles with you."

"Okay." The big man dropped his arms and took a step toward the desk. "You haven't been yourself since that woman came aboard."

Irritation flamed into anger. "What woman are you referring to, Mo? The one who got herself beat to shit trying to protect my ship? The same one, by the way, who might be an assassin's target because she's the only one who got a look at him?"

"The one who seems to know more about this shit than anyone else and has you tied in knots," Mo shot back. "That one."

Sam jumped to his feet, all the wrong words on the tip of his tongue, but thankfully he didn't have a chance to say them. His desk comm interrupted with an urgent buzz before he could take the argument to a darker place.

He took a breath and answered. "Murphy here."

"Patel, Cap. I have Captain Manneh onscreen from the *Fleeflek*. She says it's important."

He'd put Manneh in charge of the slaver not only because she was smart, but because she handled just about any emergency with calm and efficiency. If she said it was important, things had gone to Portal's Hell.

"Fatou? What's going on?"

"Cap. Not urgent, but I thought I'd give you a heads up so you'd have time to prepare. We're losing power in the Environmental Control system—down 18 percent now and falling. Cause unknown so far. I've already closed off nonessential areas, but soon I'm going to have to start shutting down sections where we've got people living. That means we'll have to shift some more bodies over to you unless we get the problem fixed."

Sam swallowed a curse. "I'll have Kwan send a team to look at it. What's the rate of loss?"

"Currently at about one percent every ninety minutes. But it seems to be accelerating."

"Not good. Let's hope Kwan can do something quick."

"Aye, sir."

Sam signed off with Manneh and called Engineering to explain the situation to Stephen Kwan. The Chief Engineer said he would go himself at the head of the duty team.

By the time Sam had finished, his XO was standing poised to leave his command room. "Was there anything else, Mister Maatik?"

The Pataran shook his head slowly. "No, Cap. I'm done for now." The big man ducked out the hatch and went back to the bridge.

But Sam hadn't missed the questions that remained in his friend's dark eyes. Questions he himself had yet to answer.

Rayna spent the better part of a day and night close

to her bunk in the crowded crew cabin. She got up, walked the corridors, ate in the mess hall, took a shower, collapsed again. On the second day, she braved a limited workout on the treadmill in the PT deck, but the ribs couldn't hack much pounding. She cut it short, showered up and headed back to the cabin. At the open cabin hatch, she pulled up when she saw the teenager sprawled on the bunk across from hers, scowling over a datapadd.

At least the knife is sheathed this time.

The kid looked up. Sat up. The expression on her face was . . . not hateful. "Oh. Hi."

Rayna came all the way into the cabin, greeting and stepping around two others who filled the space until she reached her own bunk. "Hi, back."

Lainie considered the deck between them, her dark hair falling across her face. Then she hit Rayna with a bright blue gaze. "I heard you beat the crap out of a couple of guys trying to sabotage the ship last week."

Rayna's lips quirked. "More like they beat the crap out of me. If it hadn't been for Javin Darto, I'd have been dead meat."

"Yeah, Javin's a good one to have at your back."

"None better." *Where is she going with this?*

The girl looked her over. "You had to go under the light in Sickbay?"

"Yeah. But I'm getting around okay now."

"Good. That's good." The deck again. After a long moment, she looked up. "I, uh, I just wanted to say I might have been wrong about you. You might be okay."

She tried out a smile. "At least Cap seems to think so."

So she had worked around to an apology of sorts. Rayna smiled. The kid had more edges than a Scithian throwing star, but maybe there was something solid at her center, something that guided her and held her up straight. If Lainie judged others by that internal yardstick, apparently Rayna had measured up.

She kept it short and to the point. "Thanks."

Still, she wasn't so sure the girl had it right about Sam Murphy's opinion. The guards still hovered outside the cabin and followed her wherever she went. The captain might say he was protecting her, but the constant surveillance made her feel like she was the criminal. That was going to have to stop.

Sixteen hours later the Captain's command room was full to capacity, everyone talking at once. Sam held up a hand and blessed silence fell.

"Kwan, you first. How bad is the EC on the *Fleeflek*?"

"That *mulaak* Ninoctin let his ship fall to pieces under his ass. Environmental Control is limping along at about 50 percent. I can't do any better, but at least I stopped the slide. Damn system is missing so many parts it's a freaking miracle it's working at all."

"Impact, Mo?"

"Manneh's doubled up all she can over there," the Pataran said. "We've got to take on at least another 75 people here."

A groan ran through the room; Sam ignored it. "Make it a hundred and find a way. Do it today."

Mo stared at him. "Cap!"

He raised his hands. "What do you want me to do? Leave them gasping for air in the companionways over there? We can put a few more in the cargo hold; clear out the PT deck."

Kwan moaned. "Seriously? The PT deck? I can't get a TREX machine as it is."

"Double-time the stairs in Engineering. That should get the blood pumping." Sam gave him a wry grin. "Come to think of it, maybe I'll join you." He turned to his Security Chief. "What about you, Chen? Any luck with our prisoners in the brig?"

"No, sir, they're still refusing to talk. But I do have some new information." Despite the good news, Chen's face gave away nothing. "We've had reports of unauthorized activity all along the starboard side of hull space over the last 24 hours. I waited to confirm that it wasn't the cats or just crew being spooked, but it looks like these are for real. Somebody's in there."

Sam's pulse accelerated. "Not a bad place to hide—it's where I'd go if I had to, even with the zero G. Pull in all your people and set up search teams. We'll go over hull space with a flea comb. And if we don't find that *shalssiti pultafa* today I'm going to start ejecting those assholes in the brig out an airlock one by one until they tell me something."

CHAPTER SEVEN

Rayna stood staring at a body-sized access hatch to Gravity Lock 7a in a quiet section of Auxiliary Maintenance, preparing to violate the regulations posted in bright yellow. She certainly wasn't "authorized." She wasn't even "personnel." She was, however, the "only" person planning to use the access—at least, she hoped she was.

She was sore, but nearly three days after leaving Sickbay, the broken ribs had knitted and any sign of bruising was gone. Still, her core muscles and those damaged ribs needed a workout, but she wasn't ready to do it with the added pull of gravity.

For some reason she couldn't fathom, Captain Murphy in his infinite wisdom must have also determined it was time for her to stand on her own two feet. Her guards had disappeared from outside her cabin an hour ago, leaving her on her own without a word of explanation. Either he'd found the assassin from Sickbay, or he'd finally come to the conclusion she could take care of herself. Suited her purposes, so she wouldn't complain.

According to the schematics she'd found behind several layers of security in the ship's computer, GL 7a would take her between the inner and outer hulls of the ship. This space between hulls was a zero-G dead zone of mechanicals and equipment back doors, of coolant panels and plasma tubing and nano-matrix cells that only showed their faces on the inner hull. The place she had chosen, through this pressure lock, was in the waste-processing area of the ship, a big, interconnecting series of tanks that relied on interior pressure and was best serviced in zero-G.

Rayna took a last look around the deserted maintenance room and opened the hatch. She was fully prepared to ignore the red sign above her head that shouted "Warning! Low light conditions, confined space, egress at zero G!" But below that some pirate comedian had scribbled, "Weight limit 150kg. This means you, Darto." She recognized the name of the big man who had saved her ass. If she'd had a pen she would have added an appropriate response on his behalf. Instead she grabbed the handle on the hatch and yanked it a quarter turn at a time until it swung open. Shit, that *hurt*, the pain like rivets in the contracting muscles of her torso. She paused at the open hatch, breathing until the pain faded, then she stepped inside and pulled the hatch shut.

It occurred to her that if she got in real trouble in here, there would be no one to help her. No one knew where she was; even the sardonic Lainie had been out of the cabin when she'd left. Rayna laughed a little and scanned the inside of the chamber for controls. Doc Berta had pronounced her "completely recovered" when she'd left Sickbay, right? So she had to be even better today. Not like she was going to pass out from the pain of a few zero-G exercises.

It was a tight squeeze inside the chamber, dim and confining and nearly airless; whoever had scratched that graffiti about Darto wasn't so funny after all. Rayna focused on initiating the sequence. She didn't want to spend any more time in GL 7a than she had to.

The pads on the panel by the hatch were backlit in white: Sequence A: One G to Zero G; Sequence B: Zero G to One G. Current Status: One G. The letters "One G" were lit in green. Minimal instructions below the pads told her to grab a handle before she made her selection, then press a pad. There was just enough light in the tiny square of space to find the grab bar. Then she hit the pad for Sequence A, and the computer counted her down. She felt her feet slowly lift off the deck. Her stomach lurched as her inner ear tried to adjust to the lack of gravity. Within seconds she was floating free and the computer informed her the sequence was complete.

She grabbed the release for the exterior hatch and turned, trying to ignore the catch in her ribs. As the hatch came open, she pushed through into the empty space on the other side. Rayna wasn't an engineer. She wasn't sure exactly how you zoned AG for one part of the ship and turned it off in another. She knew doing so saved you a shipload of energy, though, and made some things easier—like repairs on equipment that backed up into hull space. And she'd been on enough ships to know hull space was a fine place for certain kinds of workouts—physical and, uh, otherwise.

Like that time she and her ex-partner had found

their own zero-G paradise on a transport home from Sector Nine. A fond little smile crossed her lips. She missed Daniel sometimes, though God knew there was no reason to deny herself. He was still there for the taking anytime. She blew out a breath and cut off that line of thought before it could sprout branches and tangle her up in distracting emotions. She was here in this hull space so she could test herself where no one would bother her.

She pushed herself all the way out of the hatch and hooked her legs around one of the many grab bars bolted into the metal skin of the hull. She dogged the hatch shut and turned to survey the space, floating as she took note of how much room she had to move, of where the sharp edges were (clearly marked in red), of the sensitive equipment (in orange). Sam Murphy's pirate ship would pass a Confederated Systems Fleet standard inspection, which was more than Rayna could say for quite a few Fleet cruisers she'd been aboard. How could a man who had chosen a life outside the law—stealing, hijacking, smuggling, God knows what else—captain a ship with such discipline and order? Damn, the man was such a mystery!

Okay, that's it! Her mind had called up two men in as many minutes. She really needed this workout. She exerted the barest pressure against the wall to move into the open center of the hull space and began with simple starfish movements, pulling her arms and legs in and tucking into a tight ball, then extending everything out wide. She adjusted to account for her drift and managed to stay roughly in place while she repeated the exercise until the sweat was rolling and her ribs were screaming.

It didn't take long.   Dozens of tiny stabilizing muscles came into play in zero G that had little to do under normal conditions.   Those little muscles had been battered and bruised, too. Not to mention the fact that her body had been relatively immobile for days and, well . . . *shit*. Gasping for air, she was forced to stop and just hang for a minute. Her pulse pounded in her temples and joined the symphony of whoosh and hum from the waste processors that shared the space with her. The breathing of her lungs, the breathing of the ship, the stuff of life in space.

But as she lifted her head to begin again, something cut through that background noise—the clang of metal against metal, like a tool being dropped. Rayna curled in on herself and oriented her body so she could get a look around at the cleanout cages on the filter tanks. She didn't see anyone; the cages were clear, as were the maintenance and repair stations for the massive recyclers. The hair rose on the back of her neck. She was exposed here in the open. Anyone in the section could see her and remain hidden. She stretched out and "swam" back to one side of the central space where there was some chance of cover. Then she listened.

Nothing came back but the whoosh and hum and the thump of her heartbeat, louder than ever. *Fuck it*, she told herself. Imagination. Or one of the crew's secretive cats.

She eyed a spot on the opposite hull wall and launched herself toward it, tucked and rolled in the middle of her trajectory, and came out of the roll in time to extend, grab the bar on the other side and land gracefully. But, God, it hurt! Something she could have done in her sleep two weeks ago had become awkward, slow and painful. *Christ!*

Though every muscle protested, she turned and gathered herself to do it again. This time as she pushed off, she felt the pressure of compaction from her thighs to her collarbone. As she extended out across the open hull space, the stiff, scarred connective tissue between her ribs stretched and twisted, sending agony through her torso. The tuck-and-roll was like folding herself in on broken glass—she barely came out of it with enough consciousness to reach for the grab bar in front of her face.

She wrapped arms around the bar, aware now that uncontrolled drift was a serious possibility. Black spots were stealing big parts of her vision, and her head was throbbing.

"Okay," she admitted out loud to herself. "Maybe this wasn't your best idea."

"You think?"

Well, shit. Didn't that just put the icing on the cake.

"Captain." Her greeting didn't come out with the smartass twang she was hoping to put in it. Not enough breath.

He was suddenly very close. How had he gotten so close, so fast? He had an arm around her to keep her attached to the grab bar, and he felt . . . warm.

"What the hell do you think you're doing? This is a restricted area."

She shrugged off his arm—she was fine now, thank you very much—and glanced up at his face. His expression didn't match the censure in his words. The furrows between his brows didn't look like anger, but she couldn't quite interpret their true meaning.

"For a pirate ship, you sure have a lot of rules."

"Discipline is necessary no matter what kind of ship it is." His lips curved upwards. "Now answer my question."

Sam Murphy really was a fine-looking man, a dangerously fine-looking man, with those green eyes and a face that belonged in holovids rather than on the deck of a real ship. But damned if he was going to back her up, even in zero G.

"You saw what I was doing; I was working out. On most of the ships I've been on, that's been okay unofficially. I didn't think I'd have to ask for permission, especially since I was back here in the sewer."

Murphy leaned in closer. In spite of herself, Rayna inhaled and took him in. God, he smelled good—like . . . the first breath of fresh air dirtside after months on a ship. For a second she was lost, drifting as surely as if she had let go of her mooring on the hull.

"This is my ship, Little Bit." His voice was a seductive purr. "You need permission for everything."

Heat flashed from the top of her head to the

bottoms of her feet. She meant to shout, but her voice came out in a matching sultry whisper. "Why you puffed up, self-righteous, arrogant—"

The beep of his comm interrupted her tirade. He held up a finger to put her on pause. "Chen? Anything in your sections?"

He listened. She couldn't hear what was being said.

"Roger that. I've got a little complication here in Section 4. I'll take care of it and meet you in the aft quarter."

Rayna got her hormones in check and started over. "Control seems to be your middle name, Murphy. Well, let me tell you something: I joined Rescue because Independence is mine."

"Do I have to remind you you're a guest on my ship?" His expression had tightened into a smoky scowl. "The one place I have plenty of room onboard is the brig—maybe you'd like accommodations there." His eyes held hers like he meant it, but a muscle jumped in his jaw. His tell, she realized. He wanted something quite different for her. That heat flashed through her once again, and this time she was certain it had nothing to do with anger.

Damn it.

"All right, yeah, I saw the big 'Keep Out' signs. But every other square centimeter of space on this tug is occupied. I needed a workout, and zero G is a good place to get started. I didn't think anyone would be back here."

His expressive face changed yet again, the hard

lines around his mouth and eyes going soft as the tension drained from him. "Any day but today you'd have been right."

"What's different about today?"

He scanned the empty hull space before he answered. "The ship's on lockdown; we still haven't found the Sickbay assassin. We've had reports of unauthorized activity in the hull space, starboard side. I've ordered a full security sweep."

Understanding dawned. All that bluster was because Murphy was feeling protective. She looked up at him and, yep, there it was, shining from those green eyes, despite his stern refusal to smile.

But just because her body responded instantly with warm anticipation didn't mean her mind should be onboard with this program. Seriously, how would it ever work between them? He was a pirate, for chrissake. According to him, she was an interfering bleeding heart. The only thing they had in common was a disregard for authority, and they would never even agree on the reasons for that.

Oh, but, damn, he smelled so good. He kept floating closer, and she was so tired. She wanted to let go and settle into those arms.

"You miscalculated." His arm was around her shoulders again, his lips against her ear.

"What do you mean?" Her protest came out in a breathy murmur.

"You're exhausted. You weren't ready for this much exertion." He was so close, so warm, encouraging her to let go. "I bet you didn't ask Doc Berta for permission either."

She finally gave up and transferred her hold to him, arms and legs wrapping around his hard body. He hooked both feet around the handholds below them, anchored one hand and used the other to clasp her to him; she was so small in comparison, his arm stretched all the way across her lower back.

She looked up at him, lips inches from his. "I don't ask for permission for anything."

He made a low sound of amusement, then he gave her what she wanted, just a brief, warm touch at first, a brush of his firm lips across hers, but it was enough to send a thrill of electric sensation through her chest. She gasped, even as he pulled her closer and stroked into her mouth, his tongue tangling with hers. The way he felt, so smooth and hot, the way he tasted, like dark cherries, the way his arm curled around her back like he would never let her go, every detail was clear in her mind. Still she was gone, as if he had somehow turned off her rational mind and allowed her access only to the more primitive part of her brain, the part that wanted to take this kiss to a place where they were both naked and straining toward climax.

She knew it couldn't happen—could it? A moment ago they'd been arguing. But, God, the way he held her, the way he was kissing her, set every nerve-ending on fire. She tilted her hips and settled herself over the hard ridge of his erection. With a groan, he pressed her closer, sending a spike of need straight through to her core.

In desperation she broke off the kiss. "What is it about you?" As she spoke his lips were at her throat, nuzzling his way down to her shoulder. "You drive me crazy."

"The feeling's mutual. And I'm damned if I understand it." He turned and backed her gently against the hull wall, caging her in with arms on either side of her. His gaze captured hers. "We shouldn't be doing this."

Her hands fisted in the heavy fabric of his deck jacket. "Stop, then."

His eyes went suddenly dark, and he bent to take her lips again. But this was no tentative tasting, no gentle exploration. His hands framed her head as his tongue plunged into her mouth, insistent, demanding, fiery and sweet.

Need grew and throbbed deep in her belly. Heat flared and swelled between her legs. Somewhere in the rational part of her brain, she knew this had gone too far, but she never wanted it to stop. She wanted him to use that talented tongue to make her come. She wanted to ride what she felt pressing against her thigh until they both lost their minds. She wanted to forget everything except what existed between them, here in this weightless space, in this timeless moment.

One level up, clinging like a cliff-gripper to the side

of a recycling tank, Zetana Be-Kor watched the lovers and cursed her bad luck. There, but for the turn of fortune, but for the merest glance of a god's eye, was her own sweet plan in action. She should have been the one seducing the handsome captain of the ship, whispering in his ear that LinHo was worth a stop. Instead the human bitch was twined around his muscular body like a *mer* vine, while she'd been forced to hide behind the stinking slop tanks for days, dodging Security to meet with her team, to communicate with the outside, even to eat or use the facilities.

Her bondmate was a comforting presence in her mind. *Don't worry, k'taama. The little slut is probably whispering nothing more interesting than "Fuck me!" in the captain's ear.*

She glanced at Rexus Kor, grinning darkly at her from his position just above. He was a handsome man, from one of the most powerful houses on Thrane, but he was not the most intelligent partner in their pairing. This thought she shielded from him.

--The point is, my love, she's gotten there first. She's attracted the captain's interest, and she's managed to be in the right place at the wrong time more than once.

He shrugged. *She may have led to Falla's capture, but he said nothing before you ended him. His death ensures the others' silence. How can she be a threat to us?*

--You can't see that she's closing off another avenue of escape for us as we watch? We have no

alternative now but to contact the Tifan *for pickup.*

--The Minertsans will not be pleased.

--And we will have to find another way in to the Kinz factory. Zetana returned her regard to the couple below. *But this scrap of trouble—who is she?*

--ConSys Intel, perhaps? Her mate was bored with the discussion. His disinterest came through clearly.

--Possibly. If she was onboard the Fleeflek *with us she could have had the same goal: to infiltrate the Kinz facility. I imagine the Confederated Systems could use their own information from inside that factory.*

Rex smirked. *They will find the inside is a dangerous place to be soon enough. Once we've done what we've come to do, our employers can go back to ruling their Empire without looking over their bony little Gray shoulders, and we, my* k'taama, *can take a long vacation on the tourmaline islands of Pinon with our well-earned credits.*

--I have every confidence in your special skills, k'taam, *but they do us no good if we can't get ourselves and the team to LinHo as planned. Our "rescue" by the hero down below*—she gestured impatiently at Murphy, still fascinated with his little slut's lips—*has put a starfreighter-sized hole in our plans, and all our work has not patched the tear.*

Her mate sent a wave of warmth and encouragement along their bond. *So send the message to the* Tifan, *and we can be on LinHo well within our parameters. And besides*—the touch of his mind became sensual, erotic, nearly physical—*our interfering agent has found a distraction that may serve us well. Why don't we just enjoy the show?*

It was true that Captain Murphy was a legitimate target in his own right, with a price on his head that would make it worth the agent's trouble. Did Murphy know he was climbing into bed with a fang-eel?

Zetana watched Murphy's hips move as he pressed the woman up against the wall. No, he didn't seem to care who she was, and judging from the look of bliss on her face, the seductress had forgotten what she had come to do.

Zetana huffed out a silent laugh. *Not very professional. First rule of the game, little agent: don't let your opponent distract you.*

Rex joined her in silent laughter while they watched and made their calculations.

Sweet Jesus, we have to stop! Rayna couldn't find the breath to speak, but she managed to break off the kiss and shift a small distance away from Sam. This . . . this . . . *whatever* was between them was too much too fast—and in the wrong place.

Sam looked at her, eyes glazed with desire. He swallowed and seemed to come back to himself.

He gave her a grin. (*Did it seem a little shaky?*) "Sorry. I seem to have taken what you said as a challenge."

Rayna pulled back even further. "Let's consider

this skirmish a draw then. Surely you have better things to do."

He tore his gaze away from hers and scanned the open space around them. "The search . . ."

"You really think he's here?" She fought her body for focus, trying hard to ignore the throbbing in her veins. "Wouldn't it have been safer for him to stay hidden in the general population?"

"Lockdown doesn't suit his agenda. He needs freedom of movement."

"His agenda?"

But the captain wasn't sharing that information. "Come on. I'll take you back to the access hatch."

"I can help with the search." Though she felt like a week-old kitten.

"No! This bastard has already killed two men." He muttered a curse. "Come on, we've been here too long."

Rayna saw his point—their moment of vulnerability could have cost them in more ways than one. She pushed off from the wall in the direction of the bright yellow-and-black-striped access hatch where she'd come in. Sam followed at her four o'clock, head swiveling to catch any movement in the open space between the hulls.

Then she heard it. A scrabble of something—cloth? boots?—against metal between the recycling tanks on the level above them. Evidence of life where there was normally only the hum of machinery and the spark of artificial power. She grabbed a handhold and turned to snag Sam in a close embrace.

"What the hell?" He floundered a second, but he didn't pull away.

"I heard something." From underneath his shoulder she scanned the long, unbroken vista of gunmetal gray, black and white. Nothing moved.

Sam slowly turned their bodies so he could look. "What do you see?"

She shook her head. "Nothing. But I could have sworn I heard something up there." She gathered herself to push off. "I think we should go take a look."

"Hold on there, Little Bit." He caught her around the waist. "Think about it," he said into her ear, as if he had any number of things in mind other than the security of his ship. "He's watching us. By the time we get up there, he'll be long gone. I'll call in a search team from the gravity lock."

While he spoke he'd been moving them toward the access hatch in a leisurely float. They got inside and dogged the hatch shut at last. The captain hit the button at his throat to call in a Security team.

Gravity yanked at Rayna's bones as the pressure rose in the tiny chamber to match that of the AG-conditioned ship. She ignored the pain racking her body while she picked at the puzzle in her mind. She put a hand on Sam's arm as he was speaking to his Security chief.

He paused and raised an eyebrow at her.

"She's a woman."

He frowned. "What?"

"The one you're looking for. The assassin—she's

female. I knew there was something about the way she'd moved that night in Sickbay. She's tall and muscular—maybe Thrane or Ninoctin—but definitely female. She didn't move like a guy."

"If she's a trained fighter she'd have moved like a fighter. And you weren't at your best that night."

She scowled at him. "Maybe. But I'm a trained observer. I know what I'm looking at. The hips are different. The shoulders are different. I'm telling you, you're looking for a woman, not a man."

"And this came to you how?"

"Call it intuition—and sometimes I have to move around a little before I can think."

Sam didn't laugh or roll his eyes—the usual reactions when she said that—he just nodded and spoke. "Chen. Be aware you may be looking for a female on advice of our witness from that night in Sickbay. Yeah. I'll check in later."

He closed the comm and considered Rayna with narrowed eyes, but he said nothing.

The pull of gravity in the chamber now was almost at one G and moving seemed an insurmountable trial. Every muscle felt the strain of her workout, every organ, every nerve, every blood cell. She was dripping with sweat and shaking with fatigue. Her ribs protested with a bright flare of pain, evidence that she'd overestimated her recovery by days, if not a full week.

The light over the exit hatch went green at last. She opened the hatch and tumbled out onto the Auxiliary

Maintenance deck in a boneless heap.

Sam followed her with somewhat more grace and squatted down beside her. "Are you okay?"

"I'm whipped." She couldn't deny it, so she gave him a thin smile.

Without another word he slipped his arms beneath her and began to lift.

"What?" She struggled, freeing herself from his grip. "Oh, hell no. You are not going to carry me through this ship." She stood up, wobbling on legs that didn't seem to agree with her decision. "I can walk."

The captain stifled a grin. "Suit yourself. But if you fall on your ass, I'm taking you to Sickbay."

She retrieved a waterpak from the deep side pocket of her jumpsuit and popped the top. She drained it without a pause, grateful for the slide of cool liquid down her throat.

"Probably should've done that about half-an-hour ago." She tossed the container in the nearest recycle bin and turned to see Sam watching her, that grin still threatening to break out on his face.

"Got any more of those?"

She started to reach for another pak. "You thirsty?"

He stopped her with a warm hand on hers, the teasing smile still playing around his lips. "No. I just wanted to watch you drink some more."

"Hm. Smartass." How is it she could be pissed at him and amused by him at the same time?

"You need rest. Promise me you'll go back to your cabin and get some."

"Right." She held back a sigh.

"What's wrong?" His face fell as comprehension dawned. "The new consignment of LO's from the *Fleeflek*."

"Not my sleep shift for another four hours." She felt like she could drop right where she was. "You wouldn't know where there's a nice, quiet piece of decking would you?" *Or I could lash myself to the bulkhead in hull space and just float.*

He considered her for a second longer. "I know just the place for you." He led the way through the echoing Aux. Main. Section to the lift and, once inside, hit the pad for Level Two.

She waved a hand at the controls. "I'm on Five."

He nodded. "That's right, you were."

She started to reach for the pad. He intercepted her hand. *What the hell?*

She tried again. "I need to get to Five."

"We're going to Two. My cabin."

Her heart started a slow, heavy thudding. "Just because we got a little carried away back there doesn't mean I'm ready to go to your cabin, *Captain*. I mean, you could at least ask."

He turned to her, his grin widening. "Just because we're going to my cabin doesn't mean I intend to get carried away once we get there, *Ms. Carver*. And I'll ask when I'm good and ready."

The chime sounded for Level Two and the doors opened to let them off, but Rayna wasn't going anywhere with Captain HighandMighty. "Ask all you want, Captain, the answer will be no. I'm going to *my* cabin on Level Five."

Sam stopped the doors and looked down at her. "Rayna. You don't have a place to sleep—that's all I'm offering. I won't even be here for the next few hours; I have to finish the security sweep of hull space and work off the rest of my duty shift. It's quiet; it's comfortable. You need the rest. I don't mean to imply anything else."

Rayna felt a hot flush of embarrassment creep from her chest up her throat to her face. Her gaze dropped to his lips, and she couldn't keep from thinking of how they had felt against hers, how she wanted to taste them again. Maybe she hadn't been ready for everything sleeping in his cabin implied, but she had been ready for something. She had been more than ready for something. And he wasn't.

"I'm sorry. I, uh, I shouldn't have assumed."

He cocked his head at her. "Maybe you should have. What happened in the Maintenance Bay was . . . out of line. I'm sorry. You don't have to worry. Come on."

She followed him off the lift. "Actually, I could really use a little peace and quiet." She looked up at him. "Thank you."

He grinned—no, his face lit up like she'd told him he just won a pardon from the ConSys Administrator—and he slid a hand under her elbow to guide her down the corridor. She started to call him on it, but decided to let it go. Her legs had gone wobbly on her again, and she needed the help. They reached his cabin and got inside before anyone saw them—a plus in her book—then it was time to feel awkward.

"I'll order you some food." He was looking at her again, eyes full of another kind of hunger.

"No, you don't have to." At the mention of food, though, her stomach immediately set up a clamor of need.

"You need to eat. Save some for me. I'll eat when I get back."

He was on the comm before she could stop him. Making assumptions—about what she wanted, about whether she'd be here when he got back. She frowned. Damn him anyway. Was she really so tired that she couldn't bring herself to care?

She glanced around. His cabin was clean and tidy, the harsh ship's metal softened with splashes of color from his travels throughout the galaxy: fabrics in red and ochre from Taxos, artwork from Terrene, pottery from Illis. Rayna had visited those places, too, had lived in them. But she had come away with nothing but what she could carry in a bag across her shoulders.

Sam cleared his throat. "You can, uh, you can use the shower if you want." He nodded at a bank of drawers in the wall. "Tee-shirts there should be big enough to cover you, um, all the way."

Rayna glanced down at her clothes. Yeah, they needed to be tossed in the recycler. She just hated to use the replicator. The sizes almost never came out right.

"Thanks. I'll be fine." She didn't want to tell him she wouldn't be here when he got back. She didn't want to get into it. "Don't you have an assassin to chase?"

He smiled, making her want to change her mind about being here when he got back. "Yeah. A female assassin, apparently. The deadliest kind." He took a step closer and reached out to touch her hair. "Sleep well."

Damn it, she wanted to kiss him so badly.

But he was gone.

CHAPTER EIGHT

What the hell are you thinking, Murphy?
As the lift took him back to Engineering, Sam tried to remember the last time he'd had a woman in his cabin. He came up blank. No surprise, there; he'd had a rule against bringing a woman to his cabin since he'd taken command of the *Shadowhawk*, seven years ago. Before that, he'd been sleeping with the *Shadowhawk*'s captain, so it was a moot point. Gods' eyes, he was in trouble.

It was only a matter of time. He knew it. The way she looked at him made him think she knew it, too. Rayna Carver might act like she thought he was lower than deck plating, but her heart beat fast under his hands, her mouth opened hungrily for his, her hips stroked him until he nearly came. She would be his—soon. The only question was, what came after? That he even thought to ask meant . . .

Trouble! It means trouble! Sam cursed and ran a hand through his hair, leaving it in angry spikes. He vowed to send her back down to Level Five as soon as he got back from his shift. It was the only safe move.

The resolution left him feeling better as he left the lift and headed for the access tube to rejoin the search in hull space. Security Chief Chen and her search team intercepted him before he reached the tube entrance.

Chen gave him a weary nod. "Cap." She handed him a pad.

The screen showed a schematic of the hull space, Sections 3 and 4. Several small surfaces on the recycling tanks, the hull walls and the access hatches were marked in red.

"What am I looking at?"

"DNA traces, very faint, not very definitive."

"Can you make a guess?"

Chen glanced at one of her techs, who nodded. "It's Thrane." She looked back at the captain. "Mostly. Whoever it was tried to be very careful. But our equipment is sensitive."

"Dozens of people have been through here," Sam protested. "We even have a few Thranes in the crew— Bant, and the engine room tech, Agar."

Chen shook her head. "No match. And no match with any of the LO's on board."

"You sampled all the LO's?" Sam grinned at his Security Chief. "Chen, you obsessive little creature!"

"I will admit to a tendency to obsessive-compulsive disorder, sir." Her smile was nearly imperceptible.

"But it's such a useful trait in a Security Chief." Sam handed the pad back to Chen. "This is it? That's all we came up with—just the DNA? No clothing, no trash, nothing else."

Chen shook her head. "Like I said. Careful."

"Okay. The ship's manifest from the *Fleeflek* should have the marker we're looking for, wouldn't you think, Chief?"

"The Grays get the pertinent info from every slave and list it in the manifest for the ship's captain, yes, sir. I'll get on that right away."

"So what do you think of the theory that our assassin is a woman?"

Chen exchanged a look with her tech, then turned dark eyes on him. "What makes your witness think so?"

"Ray says it was something about the way the person moved. She said the assassin might have been Thrane—looks like she got that right."

Chen stood for a long moment, no expression on her face at all. Sam thought maybe he'd revealed more about himself than about the assassin, and Chen didn't like what she saw. But at last his Security Chief looked up at him and nodded.

"It's possible. The attacks on the two men in Sickbay used finesse, not strength. Thranes are generally taller and more muscular than humans at any rate. There's no reason to believe it's not a woman. Of course, the DNA will confirm."

He exhaled. "Okay, we're done here. Let me know when you have something. I need to see Kwan."

Chen nodded in acknowledgment and stepped off to do what had to be done. Sam turned in the other direction, toward the heart of Engineering and the Chief Engineer's office. He could have taken the lift down two levels and over three sections, but he preferred to see his ship up close, to feel her engines thrumming and her ventilation system pumping, to know she was running happily. And the thought that a smart, sabotaging killer with an unknown agenda had free run of his ship made him even more anxious to see to the *Shadowhawk*'s well-being personally. He stalked the narrow maintenance bays on his way to Main Engineering with his ears open and his fists clenched, hoping his enemy would make one little mistake. A bit of hand-to-hand would go a long way toward easing the tension in his body and mind right now.

But it wasn't to be. The Engineering sections remained quiet and undisturbed as Captain Murphy strode through them, and he arrived at Chief Kwan's office just as tense as when he'd started out.

The Chief Engineer saw him coming and shook his head. "That matrix is not going to grow any faster by you watching it, you know."

Sam smiled without humor. "Matrix? What matrix?"

Kwan came out from behind his desk in the transwall-enclosed office and joined his captain on the engine room deck. "You'd think the little nano-darlings were your children or something."

"No, I acknowledge they call you Daddy. But surely you're starving them."

Kwan's jaw dropped in mock offense. "Take that back."

The two men pulled to a stop beside the frame housing the incomplete nano-matrix. The liquid rare earth-silica bath fell from a spigot at the top and washed over the frame in a constant stream, feeding the hungry microscopic machines hard at work on reconstructing the crucial piece of equipment.

Sam's chest tightened as he noted how much of the matrix still remained to be filled. "Steve, we make the C4 jump node in less than 36 hours. We can't afford to have to hang out there while this thing rebuilds. For all I know we could have a Gray warbird on our tail now, just waiting to take us."

Kwan looked like he'd swallowed a phase blaster. "If I enrich the RES bath, they'll grow faster, but the matrix will be brittle. We might only get a couple of uses out of it before I'll have to grow it all over again."

"Do it." The extra RES fluid would cost him three months' profit, but better to spend the credits than wind up dead. "We need a working matrix in 36 hours, you get me?"

"Aye, Cap." Kwan met his gaze. "You'll have it."

Rayna held the piece of soft fabric to her nose and inhaled. The tee-shirt was clean, but somehow it still smelled like him, like fresh air and warm earth. Some primal, human part of her responded to that scent as if she were conditioned to it, muscles relaxing, skin warming, breath deepening. But the part of her born and raised in the artificial environment of Terrene found that sensual reminder of open spaces disturbing. Or maybe it was just Sam Murphy himself that put her on edge.

She frowned and slipped the shirt over her head. He'd been right; his shirt covered her to the knees. But its worn fabric caressed her skin, his scent filled her senses. As tired as she was, she couldn't help a little shiver of pleasure.

Rayna was contemplating the bunk, wondering if Sam's scent would make her dream of open grassland, when a knock came at the cabin door. Before she had a chance to answer, the door banged open and a huge, dark Pataran male entered carrying a tray of food. When he saw her he drew to a halt and stared with eyes so pale a blue they seemed to glow in the low light of the cabin.

From a defensive crouch behind a desk chair, Rayna challenged the invader. "Aren't you Murphy's XO? What the hell are you doing here?"

The Pataran gestured at the piece of pottery in her hand. "I don't think you'll need that, and the captain would be very unhappy if you busted it over my, uh, knee."

She glanced at the item in question and put it back where it belonged. "Well, it was meant for your head, where it would have done more good, but you do have a point. Couldn't reach you even if I jumped off this desk."

"And the captain—"

"Would be pissed, yeah, I get it. So, uh, Commander?"

"Just Mo."

"Mo. Since the XO doesn't usually deliver dinner, I assume you're looking for the Captain. He's not here."

"So I see. What are you doing here?"

Rayna felt the blood rush to her face. "It's not what it looks like."

Mo allowed a small smile while he put the tray on the desk. "I would hope not. Cap called down for food less than twenty minutes ago. He's already gone. And I happen to know he was in hull space conducting a search before that." He *tsked*.

"Really." Her answering smile was wry. "I wouldn't have been impressed either, not that the occasional quickie doesn't have its place."

Mo straightened to his full, very intimidating height, crossed his arms across his chest and waited for an explanation.

"Oh. Captain Murphy found me working out in hull space. My first time doing anything physical since. . ." She couldn't find the words. She stumbled over the concept. For the first time it really came to her: She hadn't just lost a fight; in another time and place, the beating she had taken could have killed her.

Mo waited some more while Rayna swallowed the hard lump that had formed in her throat. ". . . the fight. Since the fight. I guess I overdid the workout a little. I was exhausted, and I couldn't go back to my assigned space for few hours. He offered his cabin to let me rest. I'll be gone before he gets back."

The XO raised an eyebrow. Then he sat in one of the chairs near the desk and waved her to the other one.

"He ordered the food for you, then. Sit and eat."

The smell of the food had been wafting up from the tray and driving her mad since he'd placed it on the desk. Rayna didn't hesitate. She sat and lifted the cover from the closest dish—some sort of stew—and dug in.

After a while she began to get self-conscious. "Are you hungry?" She gestured at the other bowl. "You want some?"

"No. And, no." The Pataran continued to watch her, his expression unreadable.

She cleaned up the stew with a crust of bread and settled back into her chair with the second of four paks of flavored water that had come with the tray. "Are you afraid I'll hack into Murphy's comp and steal all your ship's secrets while he's out? Is that why you're still here?"

Mo pulled back his lips to show white teeth in a feral grin. "I'd like to see you try."

"Oh, so you're responsible for net security?" When he said nothing, she went on. "You probably think I'd like to slap a pair of sensor-cuffs on your boss; claim that bounty I keep hearing about."

The grin turned into a laugh. "This is *his* ship, *his* crew. You're just a lone female. Don't think you'd have much of a chance. Unless he gave himself up."

Her heart tripped, stopped, started beating at a different pace. "So *that's* what you're worried about. Doesn't matter who I'm working for. If I'm working for anyone at all." She leaned forward to stare at the XO. "You're afraid I'll seduce him, then betray him somehow."

"It's an old story. Wouldn't be the first time a good man was brought low by a bad woman."

"Why would it be your business if he was?"

Mo's pale eyes glittered with warning. "Cap is always my business."

"And if the seduction was mutual and betrayal wasn't part of the equation?"

"Doesn't mean pain isn't part of the equation. Maybe on both sides."

Rayna flinched like she'd been slapped. She got up and moved to the other side of the cabin, spent a long, silent moment staring at some pottery lined up on a shelf.

She didn't look at him as she spoke. "You always this cheerful?"

"I've known Sam Murphy since I found him stowed away in a vegetable stasis container we stole off an ag freighter. He was a skinny, 17-year-old growling *targa* cub. We've been together on this ship ever since. In all those years I've found Sam to be resourceful, courageous, determined, compassionate, even kind. But rarely has he given me any reason to be cheerful."

Rayna turned to stare at the Pataran with mouth hanging agape. If she had plied the man with liquor and questioned him for a week, she couldn't have learned more about Sam Murphy than she had just heard in one sentence.

"He was a stowaway? On a pirate ship?" What could he have been running from?

Mo raised that eyebrow again. "Not originally. It wasn't in his plan for the ag freighter to get waylaid by the *Shadowhawk*. Just as it wasn't in yours."

She allowed a short laugh. "Right. He just got lucky." *Oh, hell! He got lucky!* "Sam Murphy was an escaped slave."

Mo's expression closed up. "I didn't come here to talk about the captain."

Didn't you? "Why did you come here, Mo?"

The XO stood and moved to the hatch. "I came to deliver the food."

Rayna grinned. "Oh? Not to assess the threat to your captain from a lone female?"

The Pataran inclined his head. "All right then. I've made my assessment. You may be tiny, Ms. Carver, but you are extremely dangerous. And there's not a damn thing I can do about it."

Rayna watched the hatch close behind Mo's broad back and stood wondering what to do. "He thinks I'm dangerous?" She paced two steps in the cramped space. "What about his 'kind and courageous and determined and compassionate' boss? Think that's not dangerous?" She paced three steps in the other direction. "Man looks like some kind of sex holo actor or something, tastes like bourbon and cherry candy and . . . and . . . *shit*!" She couldn't say out loud what she was thinking about the way he felt holding her, his body hard against hers, the proof of his arousal pressed hot and heavy into her hip.

"I should go. I should definitely go." If she stayed she wouldn't be able to resist taking that hard length deep inside, letting Sam Murphy get through the walls she'd spent a lifetime building. And then, as Mo had so perceptively put it, pain would be inevitable.

She looked with longing at Sam's bunk. God, she was so tired. Her ribs ached. If she left now, she still wouldn't have access to her own bunk for two hours or more. She took a deep breath, drawing all that open-air-and-deep-earth into her lungs. She longed to wrap herself in that scent, if only for while.

She pulled back the covers and slipped into the bunk. She stretched out with a sigh, letting the soft, soft sheets and feather-light blanket drift down, bringing Sam with them. *Just for an hour*, she told herself. She could dream just for an hour. Then she would go back to the real world.

He was sprawled in the chair across from the bunk, his eyes closed as if in sleep, and for a moment, Rayna thought she was still dreaming. His hair was tousled and wet—he must have just come from the shower—and he was wearing nothing but a pair of loose, black workout pants. For the first time she got a good look at his bare shoulders and chest—the sharply-defined muscles, the fine spray of dark hair across the broad span of chest, the scars that broke the smooth perfection of his lightly-tanned skin. She wanted to trace each one with a fingertip, to tease the story of each wound from him with kisses and licks. She didn't know if it was the mystery of this man or simply his presence that drew her, like a comet to the sun.

"You're awake."

She was mildly startled to hear him speak, and said the first thing that came to mind. "I meant to be gone before you came back."

Eyes the color of sea-gems flashed below dark brows. "I meant to stay gone until you had left."

"I'll go." She sat up in the bunk, started to swing her legs down to the floor.

He stood up. "No." He came closer, pulled her up until she was standing on the mattress. They were face-to-face now; she didn't have to look up to see his need. "Stay. Please."

Rayna didn't know, she couldn't remember, when she had decided to take a chance on Sam Murphy. Maybe she hadn't. Maybe she just had to have him. Just once. She slipped her arms around his neck and drew his mouth to hers. She opened her lips to let him in, and his kiss was hot, sweet, stealing her breath as his tongue tangled with hers.

He broke the kiss for the seconds it would take to slip his tee-shirt off over her head. He exhaled as he stared at her.

"Gods, you're perfect."

He ducked his head, seeking her lips again, but she held him off, wanting the same pleasure of looking at him, touching him. She ran her hands over the smooth expanse of his chest and down over the tight muscles of his belly. She smiled to hear him gasp as she skimmed his nipples and made a note to use that later. Right now she had a more immediate goal.

She slipped her hands inside his waistband and worked his pants down so he could step out of them. And, oh, God, there he was at last, long and thick and jutting up out of a nest of dark curls at the juncture of his strong thighs. She reached for him, but he swept her up into his arms before she could touch him, wrapping her legs around him, trapping his erection between their naked bodies.

"Not now," he growled into her ear. "I swear if you touch me now, I'll explode. I want you too much."

The ache in his voice tugged at something below her ribs, something that had been buried deep and long protected. In self-defense she kissed him, seeking the firm answer of his lips, the silky touch of his tongue, the heady taste of intoxication.

He lowered her to the bunk, stretching her out beneath him, and she groaned with the pleasure of it—the slide of his skin on hers, the heated spike of his erection pressing into the groove of her hip, his breath matching hers. His freshly-shaved cheek was smooth against her skin, and his lips were soft, so soft, as he lifted them from her mouth to nibble at her ear, her neck, her throat.

His mouth found her breast, and his tongue circled the sensitive peak. He suckled, drawing just hard enough on her nipple to cause a sharp twinge of pain, a sizzle that ended in a warmth she felt in her deepest core. She lifted her hips, wanting more. His hand slipped down her belly, across her hip, down the outside of her thigh and up the inside to the intimate folds between her legs. His fingers began to explore the slick flesh.

His name escaped her on a sigh.

He switched his attentions to her other breast while one finger massaged the swollen pearl of her desire, slowly, maddeningly.

He stopped. Looked at her. "Tell me you want this."

She could barely find the breath to answer him. "God, yes, I want this!"

He nipped gently at her nipple. "Tell me you want *me*."

She grabbed his hair and made him look at her. "I want *you*, Murphy. Nobody else."

He looked back at her with a slow, seductive smile, and, God help her, she nearly came. His hand between her legs had set up an unbearable ache, one only he could satisfy. At last she insisted on the pleasure of touching him, wrapping her hand around his thick shaft, feeling his pulse in her palm. He closed his eyes and shuddered as she stroked him, and her chest expanded in delight to hold him in her hand.

When he spoke again his voice was a whisper of sand. "Tell me . . . how . . . you want it."

"Now, baby." She couldn't believe she was saying this to him, but it was what she wanted and she wouldn't wait any longer. She needed this from him. "Hard and fast and don't even let me breathe until I come."

She saw his eyes darken with understanding. He rose over her and centered himself between her legs. His broad tip waited at her entrance—hot and blunt and ready. She pulsed against him, eager, needy. She held her breath as he guided himself in and lingered to caress her just above the place where they were joined. For some seconds he didn't move. He simply filled her and stroked her while she adjusted to his length and his thickness. He stretched her enough to sting, but Jesus God she ached for him! She burned in a fire of longing.

She squirmed under him. "Sam! Goddammit!"

"Shh. I'll give you what you want." His voice was a low, soothing baritone. "I'll give you everything you want."

He began to move in her slick channel and soon swung into the rhythm she needed—long strokes, hard ones, enough to shake her where she lay beneath him. He held his weight on his hands on either side of her; she reached up to grab his forearms, roped with taut muscle, and held on while he drove her relentlessly up to a steep, airless peak. She looked down her body at him, at the sight of his flat abdomen rippling as he pistoned in and out of her, the column of his shaft starkly pale between her dark thighs. His muscles gleamed under a sheen of sweat. And his face—the way he watched her, as if her every reaction fed the hunger in him.

But then she closed her eyes because it was good, *so damn good*, and she couldn't do anything but feel. Her blood was molten metal; her lungs were on fire. Every stroke into her core sent electric shocks deep into her belly, into her chest. The pleasure drove her higher. And tighter. She couldn't think. She couldn't breathe. She could only scream as she fell apart under his sweet assault.

Rayna came, her hips arching up off the mattress into his, her sheath clamping down on his shaft in rolling spasms, and it was everything Sam could do to hold back his own climax in the storm of her release. Gods, she was so beautiful, her face flushed with color, her full lips parted to pull in breath, her breasts rising as her back bowed in ecstasy. He gritted his teeth and fought for control as waves of scalding need swept up through his groin when she squeezed him, fought for breath as his chest constricted when she gasped his name. He thrust deeper and she only flew higher, soaring for the next peak.

She pulled him down into her arms and moaned a command: "Don't stop, Sam. Just don't stop."

He growled in response, shifted his hips to make sure she felt him in all the right spots and kept on. He refused to stop, refused to slow his pounding rhythm, though every move brought him closer to losing control. He held on. He had promised her, and he would deliver.

She writhed under him, clinging to his shoulders as a second orgasm took her, her breath coming in keening gasps, as if she was unable to pull in enough air to scream or call his name. Tiny muscles spasmed and clutched at him, her climax bathing him in hot cream. Her hips moved greedily beneath his, milking him of every possible pleasure, igniting a wave of answering fire in him.

Near his limit, he waited for the frantic seizing of her intimate muscles to subside, for her breath to stop its desperate rasping. Then at last he slowed, drawing out his strokes to his full length and reseating himself high and tight. The pressure in his balls eased from now! to merely urgent. She trembled in his arms, her core pulsed around him, and he knew she wasn't done yet. She needed more. His swollen shaft jerked in response, ready to provide it.

He took her mouth as he took her body—a hot, deep, lazy plundering of the treasure of her kiss while he moved slow and deep inside her. Her honeyed taste and the silky slide of her tongue distracted him for a moment from the blazing need in his groin. She moaned into his kiss, and he felt it all the way to the base of his spine. Liquid fire gathered there, a pressure building that would not long be denied.

He broke off the kiss with a groan. On his elbows now, his body covering hers, he ground into her in unrelenting circles. Every stroke was fire, her channel answering with flame, their bodies moving together, their hearts beating in unison as they strained towards paradise. She began to whisper in his ear, words of encouragement, words of undeniable passion, words that made him crazy with the need to fill her, to claim her, to *own* her.

And when she said, "Now, baby. Give it to me," he couldn't hold on any longer. Every muscle clenched as the climax took him, and he drove deep into her welcoming warmth, again and again. He felt her close around him as she cried out his name, joining him as he went up in flames, and for a moment there was only that heat, that delicious, mindless heat.

Then, when it was over, there was Rayna, looking up at him with a slightly dazed, disbelieving smile. Rayna, her eyes liquid, black and glazed with pleasure, her lips swollen from his kisses and her hands still tracing warm circles on his back. His heart expanded in his chest, surprising him so that his breath hitched.

She reached up to touch his face. "You know, you are sweeter than *luta* nectar when you want to be. You could definitely spoil a girl's appetite for anything else."

Her tone was light, teasing, but her smile didn't reach her dark eyes. He realized with a fierce rush of possessiveness that he *wanted* to spoil her for anyone else. He wouldn't share. She was his.

The unaccustomed emotion made his chest tighten around his thudding heart, but he kept his tone light, just as she had. "I could get used to spoiling your appetite, Little Bit. Breakfast—" he kissed her ear— "lunch—" he nuzzled her neck—"and dinner." He dropped tiny kisses along her jaw until he reached her lips. There he lingered, teasing, nibbling, suckling, eventually plunging deep into the warm cavern of her mouth to entice her tongue to play. After a while he grew hard again inside her, and the sweet ache encouraged him to move.

She sighed into his ear. "God, yes, Murphy. You could make a woman lose her mind."

Sam smiled and took his time, knowing now just how to please her. First her mind, then her heart—that had to be the plan. It was the only way to even the score between them. Because somewhere between "My name is Rayna Carver" and "oh, God, Sam!" she had stolen what belonged to him. He doubted he would ever get his heart back in one piece.

CHAPTER NINE

Zetana Be-Kor sent instructions to her team in half-second microbursts over an infrared frequency so low as to be nearly part of the background noise of the ship. They had less than 30 hours until the C4 jump, and she had been assured by their allies that assistance would arrive before then. When the moment came her people needed to be ready, at their posts with a complete understanding of what they were to do.

If she'd had a handful of professional Thrane soldiers to accomplish her tasks, she would be confident of success. But she had been forced to recruit amateurs in the hold of that slaver—resistant slaves barely out of the grip of the mindwipe. They were unpredictable, as Falla had so clearly shown.

--*You set an excellent example with Falla, my love*. Rex cupped her cheek with one large hand. In the confined space of the access tube they could touch, they could share the intimacies of their bond, but speech was still forbidden lest the sound give them away. *Discipline is easy to maintain now. Besides, the task we have given them is not complicated.*

Zetana allowed a humorless smile. She supposed assaulting the crew member nearest you was not too complicated. In fact, it was ridiculously simple, and it usually met with a high degree of success, especially on a pirate vessel.

--You have to admit, however, their success is not guaranteed on the Shadowhawk.

Rex rubbed at the stubble on the sharp planes of his face. *Agreed. Captain Murphy runs a very disciplined ship for a blackjack.* He grinned as his natural optimism resurfaced. *But no matter. My work is done. When my darlings start going off all over the ship, no one will be concerned with the fighting in the corridors.*

She placed a hand on his chest and looked up at him in delight. *You have been busy!*

--Did you think I spend my days lying around thinking only of new ways to please you in bed, k'taama?

--I had hoped so. Her hand moved from his chest to his thigh and squeezed.

He pulled her head down to his and savaged her lips in a long, brutal taking of her mouth. Her body responded instantly, heat flaring all along their bond. Whatever their problems, they were well-matched in the art of love. She wanted him, as she always had. He knew it, as he always had. Zetana allowed her bondmate to press his advantage now while they had time.

And even as she surrendered, she acknowledged the responses from her team members, one by one. When the ship reached the rendezvous point they would be ready.

Rayna drew her hand across the captain's broad chest, followed the line of fine, dark hair down his tight stomach to his navel and stroked across to his hip. She petted him, her captain, knowing it was an indulgence she shouldn't allow herself. Like the night she'd just spent with him. A temptation she should never have given into—a rich dessert before dinner, a treat all the sweeter for having been stolen.

Who'd have thought a pirate would have been such a talented and sensitive lover? Oh, he'd been a machine when she wanted it, too—the thought of that made her flush with heat—but it was the subtlety of his lovemaking that surprised her. The way he seemed to know what she needed—fast or slow, deep or shallow, tongue or hands or teeth or . . . Jesus, she had to stop or she would wake him up and start all over again.

Maybe she had surprised him a little, too. That look in his eyes seemed to say so. Like he'd suddenly discovered who she really was. No. *Like he'd discovered a treasure.* Now what was she supposed to do with that? What were they supposed to do with that and the way it made her feel?

Nothing. The answer was nothing. He was who he was. She was who she was, and that wasn't going to change. He was taking her to Madras, *goddamn it!* And it would set her mission back multiple twentydays and there was nothing she could do about it. She wasn't fool enough to think one night in the captain's bunk would be enough to change things, no matter how much she—or he—had enjoyed it.

Frustrated and riding an edge of anger now, she pulled back from Sam's warm body and rolled out of bed. She reached for her clothes.

Instantly awake, Sam came up on an elbow to look at her. "What's wrong?"

"Nothing." She got her clothes on as quickly as she could. "Third watch is almost over. I should go back to my cabin now."

"You don't have to. Stay here with me for a while."

She faltered, part of her wanting *so much* just to crawl back into bed with him. The other part of her, the part most people saw when they looked at her, stiffened her spine.

"Wouldn't look so good, Captain, you sleeping with someone like me."

He got out of bed and came to put his hands on her shoulders. "My ship. My rules."

She lifted her chin. "Let's just say I'm not ready for the attention, then."

"Discretion is my middle name." He smiled, but there was defiance in his eyes, blocking her withdrawal.

Damn it. Something ached deep in her chest. She slipped both arms around his neck, stood on tiptoe and put her lips to his. He still tasted like bourbon and cherries.

She whispered in his ear, "Thank you for last night." It was all she would allow herself.

He pulled back, left a hand on her cheek. "'Thank you' is much too weak a term for what I'm feeling right now. Besides, the night's not over yet." He hit her with that intense green gaze of his, and she couldn't hold on to her resolve. She knew she had to get out of there or be lost. She started to protest, but he kissed her again, stopping the words. Her traitorous body responded with shortened breath and pounding heart and an ache of desire that betrayed every argument of her logical mind.

He nipped at her ear. "Come back to bed."

She took a step back. "I can't, baby. I have to do my job now, and you're going to have to be the captain."

"*Perai*, are you going to pull a stunner on me and take over my ship?" He didn't look particularly worried about that scenario. "Can I at least put my pants on?"

In spite of everything, a smile broke through Rayna's guard. "Yes and no."

Sam folded his arms across his chest and waited, eyebrows raised.

"Yes, you can put your pants on. No, I'm not going to pull a stunner on you and take over your ship."

Sam's expression cleared, but lightning flashed in his eyes. "You, my vicious Little Bit, are taking a fast run through an asteroid field. What is it you're after?"

"You still refuse to take me to LinHo?"

He took a step toward her, a dark, dangerous smile spreading across his face. "Are you trying to tell me last night was a *bribe*? Because I wouldn't believe that,

Agent Carver, no matter what you tell me now."

"Jesus, no!" It was the last thing she wanted him to think. Her feelings for him had been real—*were* real—which only made what came next harder. "I didn't plan what happened last night. I did it because I wanted you. I should regret it, but I don't." She touched his face. "Last night was you and me, Sam and Rayna. I wasn't thinking about anything else."

Sam took her hand from his cheek, held it for the briefest second, then released it. "Let's say I believe you. What about today?"

"Today, if I'm not going to make LinHo, I need to contact my people and let them know. We need to get started on a Plan B."

Sam was silent for a long moment, his expression stony, but at last he relented. "All right. I'll set it up with Communications. You can use my comp right here."

She reached out to touch him again, but found he'd retreated somehow. He was the captain of the *Shadowhawk* now, not Sam, the man who'd been inside her such a short time ago. She had only herself to blame, though. She had set aside his warm lover for the cold-blooded Rescue agent that woke him up this morning.

Still, he could just as well have said no to her request; that deserved some acknowledgment. "Thank you, Captain."

His jaw clenched, but he said nothing to her. He turned and punched the deskpad to connect him with the bridge.

A face appeared on the inclined reading surface of his desk. "Patel, here, Cap."

"Morning, Patel. Agent Rayna Carver of the Interstellar Council for Abolition and Rescue needs access to the next comm packet. Patch her through from my cabin and give her whatever she needs, okay?"

"Aye, Cap. No problem."

"When's the next transmission to Madras?"

"I'll be sending it out in the next hour. Even with two relays, it should reach there by 1100 hours."

"Good. Stand by for Carver's message."

"Acknowledged. Standing by."

Sam stepped away from the desk and waved her over. "It's all yours." She might have been a complete stranger.

Anger flared. "Thanks for announcing my presence to the whole ship."

"Why do you always assume my ship is run like some sleazy Ninoctin orejacker?" he said with a scowl. "Patel knows to keep his mouth shut."

Rayna reddened. Sam Murphy wasn't a blackjack or a slaver or a sleazy Ninoctin orejacker. He barely qualified as a pirate.

"Sorry. I should know better by now."

Sam stared at her for a moment. Then he smiled, but there was no amusement in his wolf's eyes.

"Why, Little Bit! Was that an apology?" He didn't wait for an answer, but headed straight for the shower, leaving Rayna alone.

Sent Via photon packet from M.S. Shadowhawk
GSD   2.05.213/0846   hrs.   Enhanced   encryption.
Verification 4279166G/SAM/sp
Fm.: Carver, R., Field Agent
    To: Oksana, S., ICAR Station Supervisor,
Madras
    Subject: Request for Assistance
Forced to change current travel plan (ref. 6157).
Expect arrival on Madras in 72 hours (approx.).
Request you inform D. at destination of change in
plan. Will formulate Plan B on arrival Madras. Guess
that means I'll owe you one.

When she had finished composing her message,
Rayna encrypted it and uploaded it to Patel's station on
the bridge. Then she took a last look around the cabin
where she'd spent a few happy hours with the infamous
captain of the *Shadowhawk* and let herself out. She
didn't expect to see the inside of that cabin again—or to
spend that kind of time with Sam Murphy again, either.

CHAPTER TEN

"Will you stop worrying?" His chief engineer shook his head in exasperation. "The enhanced solution is working. The matrix is growing like crazy. Tomorrow this time we'll be good to go."

Sam frowned at the delicate frame, now nearly covered by the growing nanomatrix. "Yes, but will it hold up?"

Kwan shrugged. "That was the risk we agreed to take, remember? We needed it fast. It should be enough to make the two jumps to Madras if we're lucky."

There was only one place to go if the matrix collapsed after one jump—and wouldn't his single-minded Rescue agent love that! Sam wouldn't allow himself to think what would happen if the matrix collapsed mid-jump.

"We've had spacer's luck so far, Stephen. Something tells me it won't get much better." Sam moved on to something else. "Weapons status. You get those port laser cannons loosened up?"

"Slick as sex in the shower. We're still going to have most of our firepower aft, though. The forward transducer coils need replacing. You'll remember I've had that on the list."

"And you'll remember I've told you I can't afford

them right now."

Kwan grunted. "Better run, then, and show them our ass in a fight."

"Believe me, brother, I plan to." Sam rubbed at the back of his neck, where the weight of keeping his ship and crew in one piece had suddenly landed with a familiar *thump*. He squared his shoulders to distribute the burden and clapped Kwan on the back. "All right, Stephen. I know you've been working hard. If pirate ships had commendations, I would write you up for one."

"Guess that means you owe me a grog on Madras." Kwan's expression showed it was only his due.

"Guess it means I owe you a few."

He'd promised himself not to get drunk on Madras. But as he left Engineering and headed for the bridge it occurred to him that his reason for staying sober dirtside was no longer valid—and he had a damn good reason for getting drunk. He'd made love to her all night, had felt her unmistakable response to him, not just once, but over and over again. He had seen the sweet smile on her lips, the tenderness in her eyes. And the way it made him feel . . .

Damn it! What the hell happened? How could she go to sleep so warm and willing in his arms and wake up so cold and unyielding just a few hours later?

Sam felt just the slightest twinge of guilt, thinking of some of his own sexual adventures. Hadn't he exited just as efficiently in the morning—sometimes not even waiting that long—from nights just as pleasurable?

Well, yes, but at least he'd left the girls smiling. That could not be said for the way Rayna had left him this morning.

And, besides, this was different somehow. From the beginning he had been drawn to this woman in a way he'd never experienced before. From the first time he'd seen her, he hadn't been able to get her off his mind or make his body stop responding to the thought of her. He thought once he'd had her it would end this unbearable craving, but he wanted her even more now. Last night had been the most erotic experience of his life, and his body insisted on reliving every moment of it at the most inconvenient times. Sharp and inexplicable need made him want to find her and pick up where they left off, to break through that wall she'd erected between them this morning. To bury himself deep and thrust hard until she screamed for him again.

Sam adjusted himself with some difficulty, staring all the while at the touch pad where the Number Five for Rayna's deck seemed to stand out with painful clarity. No! He was captain of this ship, after all. He had *important duties* to attend to. Damned if he was going to chase that woman a mere hour after she had slipped out of his cabin without a word. The day was long. He'd have her before it was over. She couldn't have forgotten how he'd made her feel any more than he'd forgotten her.

Could she?

The lift arrived at the bridge level at last, and he strode toward the command room, thinking to give himself a minute to reorient before he hit the primary stage of his life. *Read the reports, look over the comm logs . . .*

Mo caught him before he reached sanctuary. "Cap."

He sighed. "Mo. Tell me everything's running smoothly on my ship."

"I'd be lying."

"What kind of XO are you?"

"The kind that ought to be kicking your ass right now." They pulled up outside the tiny cabin that served as Sam's office. Mo waited for his captain to enter first then came in and shut the hatch behind him.

Sam hit the well-worn button for [coffee, light/sweet] on the dispenser behind his desk. "If you mean what I think you mean, Commander, you should reconsider what you're about to say."

"Really?" Mo folded his arms over his chest. "What exactly do you pay me for?"

"Pretty sure the duties of 'Executive Officer' don't cover monitoring the private life of the captain of the ship." He retrieved his coffee from the dispenser and sat, propping his feet up on the desk. He refused to show how angry the whole subject of how he'd spent his last hours was making him.

"Whether you and Rayna Carver spent the night fucking each other's limited brains out is of no concern to me." Mo held up a hand when Sam tensed. "The bigger problem—and the one I *am* concerned with—is how that makes you feel about the woman. Might we be feeling a little tender this morning? Protective, maybe? Or, I don't know, more inclined to take a detour to LinHo?"

Sam brought his feet to the floor with a thump. Scalding hot coffee sloshed over his hand and the desk. The anger and frustration of the morning came to a rapid boil and erupted in a blast of temper.

"Son of a *mulaak* bitch! You're going to cut me open and read my emotions like I'm some kind of sacrifice on a Pataran altar? We've known each other a long time, *azhtar*, but that's *way* out of line."

"Is it, *war brother*?" The big man remained as stolid and relentless as a moon in its orbit. "When your feelings affect every person on this ship?"

"You don't have to school me on my duty to this ship. When have I ever failed it? Tell me." He grabbed his XO's gaze and wouldn't let go.

Mo refused to look away. "Never."

"Never." Sam nodded, and his rage began to ease. "I'm not going to start now. I have no intention of going to LinHo. Rayna informed her people on Madras this morning that LinHo was off. It's official. We're going to Madras. Happy, now?"

Mo inclined his head, and after a moment he smiled. "And if I said that Rayna Carver was a manipulating, cold-hearted, evil bitch who's only going to break your heart?"

Sam ignored a stab of unreasonable fear and grinned. "Well, then I'd have to gut you where you stand, my friend. You wouldn't say something like that, would you?"

"No." Mo's expression turned somber. "I actually believe quite the opposite."

"You think I'm going to break *her* heart?"

Mo grunted with something that was not quite amusement. "I think you're both skipping toward disaster, hand-in-hand." He opened the hatch and ducked through it. "What fools these mortals be."

"Oh, so it's Shakespeare now?" The captain came out from behind his desk and called after his retreating officer. "That was from a comedy, you know, not a tragedy."

Mo sat at his station on the bridge, ignoring him. The other members of his crew reacted to their captain's outburst with smiles and raised eyebrows. An argument of this sort between the captain and his XO was nothing new.

Sam suppressed a sigh and took up a position on the narrow walk overlooking the horseshoe containing navigation, helm and the conn. "Where are we, Sipritz?"

"Course heading 257 mark 13, speed point 87 of ion drive. Approximately 20 hours estimated time of arrival at Jump Node C4. Of course, 'where' is a relative question. I can only guess at an answer."

Sam held up a hand to forestall the Mper's lecture. "That'll do."

He stared at the viewscreen, empty except for the too-distant stars. Something cold crawled up his spine. His ship was humming along through clear space; the matrix was growing to replace what was needed to make the jump at C4; there wasn't a threat within a hundred parsecs. But his intuition was telling him the threat existed just the same—and his gut was always right.

Mo slipped into place at his side. "What's wrong?"

"There's something out there."

"There's nothing on the sensors for as far as they can scan."

"I know." Sam ran a hand through his hair, thinking. Then he looked up at his XO. "Put on an extra body per shift to monitor the long-range sensors. Boost the power on those sensors—you'll probably have to steal it from Communications or Medical temporarily. Patel and Berta will squawk; just tell 'em it'll be over by tomorrow."

Mo nodded. Sam knew the XO might not trust him to guide his own personal life, but Mo had long ago decided he could be trusted to lead the *Shadowhawk*. The Pataran moved off to go to work.

Sam continued to pace his bridge for another half-hour, but it was clear there was nothing for him to do there. The bridge in deep space is a dull place unless the ship is under attack, when boredom is replaced by sheer terror. Despite the tension at the back of his neck, Sam had to admit such an attack didn't seem imminent. And only one other subject dominated his mind.

"Take the conn, Mo. I've got reports to get through in my command room." Then he was going to take a turn around the ship, though he didn't say so. He and

Rayna Carver were due for a talk, but that was nobody's business but their own.

Rayna wanted to scream in frustration. Was there no place to get a little peace and quiet on this freakin' trash hauler? She desperately needed some time to herself—to think, to just . . . sort out her feelings. She had been to the PT deck for a brief, very painful run through the cardio module and a shower in the crowded locker room. She had managed to grab a bite to eat in the packed mess hall—standing up. She had tried the tiny library, the raucous cargo deck, even a back corner of the shuttle deck, where Security had nearly thrown her in the brig.

Now all she wanted to do was curl up somewhere and lick her wounds. She hurt—not the ribs so much, though they were still sore, but what was behind them, someplace closer to her heart. What had she been thinking when she kissed Sam Murphy? When she let him make love to her? Beyond that point there was no sense in asking about what she'd been thinking. She hadn't been thinking at all. She'd only been feeling—so many unexpected, transforming feelings, and not just physical ones. She'd felt safe and warm and *loved* in his arms. How could that be? They hardly knew each other. Christ, she'd even felt happy, maybe for the first time in her life.

All of which, now that she was away from the

source of these unfamiliar emotions, terrified her. She was standing at the edge of a yawning precipice, the ground crumbling beneath her feet. She would fall; it was inevitable. And since she couldn't fly there was nothing to keep her from being smashed to pieces on the jagged rocks below.

She wandered past her cabin in the vain hope one of the bunks might be unoccupied, but found it noisy and full, as always. She turned back into the corridor, but not before Lainie looked up from a game of cards and saw her.

The kid ran out into the passageway to catch her. "Hey! Hi."

"Hi." Their truce had expanded into a tentative friendship. At least, Rayna didn't fear for her life around the girl now.

Lainie cocked an eyebrow. "Ribs bothering you?"

"Not really."

"You look like shit."

Rayna just folded her arms over her chest and glared at the girl until she backed off.

"Okay. Sorry." She gestured back toward the cabin. "You, uh, want something from inside?"

Rayna sighed. "No, I was just looking for some peace and quiet."

"Try Sickbay. Always quiet in there." Lainie actually grinned. "My favorite hiding place." She turned and ducked back into the cabin before Rayna could thank her.

With new purpose, Rayna moved through the ship

toward Sickbay, determined now to find her peace. As she neared her goal someone entered the corridor from a hatch on the right just ahead of her, startling them both. He recovered quickly enough, turning to stride off in the other direction, but not before she'd caught a glimpse of a frown on dark, handsome features. He was Thrane, she was sure of that, and the better look she got of the tall, broad-shouldered figure turning a corner at the far end of the corridor confirmed it. Captain Murphy had several Thranes among his crew, but Rayna hadn't seen this one before.

The thought of the *Shadowhawk*'s captain brought her back to her quest. She smiled when she realized the Thrane had emerged from one of the auxiliary entrances to Sickbay. *Finally! Doc Berta won't begrudge me a spot to sit and think this through.*

Before she could take a step, warm hands encircled her waist, warm breath tickled her ear. "You've been avoiding me."

"Jesus H. Christ, Sam!" Her heart crashed against her ribs as she spun in the arms of the man who'd leapt from her thoughts to this empty corridor. "Don't do that!"

He tightened his grip. "Or what?"

She pushed a thumb slowly, but firmly into the base of his throat. "Or this."

He let go, coughing, and she turned to escape into the nearest Sickbay entrance. The ward she found herself in was familiar—and currently unoccupied. The only life in the unit was at the far end, near Doc Berta's office and the exam rooms. Rayna turned right instead, toward another exit at the opposite end of the ward.

Sam came in the way she had and caught up with her. "Nice trick." His voice was only a little huskier than usual.

"You didn't seem to get the message."

"We need to talk."

She pulled up at the hatch and turned to face him. "I've been searching all over this damn ship all day for some privacy. I don't feel like talking."

"Fine." He bent and scooped her up, parting her thighs so her legs twined around his hips.

His hands were warm on her butt and lower back and without thinking she slipped her arms around his neck to complete the circle. "You are such a *veer's* ass."

He hummed in satisfaction and pushed through into the next room where it was close and dark, the only illumination coming from an emergency lightcell in a corner.

She buried her face into the hollow of his neck and inhaled his exhilirating smell of open skies and grassy plains. His lips nibbled at her throat, her jawline, her ear. The hard ridge of his erection pulsed at the juncture of her thighs, arched up into her belly. Damn it, just his smell and his heat made her ache. She wanted to rub on him like a cat in heat.

But she did have her pride, even if it was in shreds. "We have to stop this."

He backed her up against the only bed—a tall gurney, this was the surgery recovery room, she realized now—and set her down. He stood between her legs and leaned in to kiss her, teasing at the seam of her mouth until she opened to his exploration, then breaking off with a tender tug at her lower lip.

He brought his lips to her ear. "If you really want to stop, we will. But I want you, Little Bit—I haven't been able to think of anything else since you left me this morning. And you want me—I can read it in your breath, in your heartbeat." He cupped her mound and squeezed gently. "If I were to touch you, Rayna, would you be wet for me?"

She arched her back in pleasure—and met his lips again as he took her mouth, his tongue sweet with the taste of drunken cherries, hot with need. Every stroke of his tongue, every squeeze of his hand chipped away at her resolve. God, she wanted him so bad, she almost didn't care what the consequences would be.

"Sam." She had meant it to be a command; his name came out on a sigh.

He unzipped the top half of her jumpsuit and lifted her undershirt to caress her breasts. "Yeah, honey." He bent his head to one tight nipple, took it in his mouth and sucked hard. Rayna groaned as sensation arrowed straight to her core.

"Oh, Jesus. Do that again." When he complied, she writhed against him on the edge of the gurney, her hands gripping his shoulders. Then she remembered what she had been about to say. "We need to talk."

He moved to the other breast and licked delicately at its dark peak. "Later." He took her into his mouth and sucked hard until the flesh between her legs swelled and wept for him.

Later. Yeah, later for everything, because she couldn't think now. He was insisting she strip out of her clothes, and she couldn't get out of them fast enough. She wanted him naked, too, and the black jacket, pants and boots that he wore as a uniform were gone in seconds. They took a minute just to hold each other, skin to skin, breath to breath, her legs wrapped intimately around his hips. Then he was kissing her, deep, insistent kisses full of fire and sinful promise. His erection was a length of hot iron between them; she moved, wanting to feel him in her most intimate places, desperate to have him inside her. He groaned, pressing closer, sliding along the slick groove between her thighs until she bathed them both in the hot liquid of her arousal.

Sam hadn't allowed her to explore nearly enough in their first encounter and now she ached to touch him. She reached for him, and pressed the base of his shaft against her, making them both moan. She used both hands to stroke him up and back down again, to trace the veins that twined around the arching column, to squeeze the helmeted tip until the muscles of Sam's thighs were quivering with the strain of holding back his release.

"*Perai*, woman, you have to stop!" He captured her hands in both of his and shuddered with pleasure. Then he stood for so long without moving that Rayna feared he would turn and leave her here, alone, burning for him. The thought made her heart pound.

He lifted a hand to her face, a universe of emotion in his eyes. The words hung between them, unsaid.

He pushed her back onto the gurney and ran his fingertips down her body from collarbone to hip. Once. And again. She shivered under his touch, wanting more. Wanting the warmth of his hands, the smooth heat of his tongue, the hard length of his shaft. When he lifted her calves to his shoulders and bent to taste her, she whimpered in anticipation. At the first flick of his tongue, she bucked into his mouth in an agony of sensation. He splayed his hands across her hips to hold her in place as he tasted and teased, driving her straight up and over the screaming peak of a climax so intense she thrashed under him like a wild thing.

And just when she thought she couldn't take any more, he lifted his head and flipped her so only her upper body rested on the gurney and her backside and thighs came snugly up against his hips. *Oh, God, yes!* She pushed back against the ridge of his erection, making sure he knew she approved. He didn't waste time, only gave that rumble of satisfaction she was beginning to recognize, and joined them in one fluid motion.

God, with every stroke he went deeper and she burned hotter. The flames spread from her melting core to her clenching belly, from her gasping lungs to her hands clutching the gurney sheets and her legs shaking to hold steady against his strength. For a long delirious time she just reveled in that heat, letting him fill her up with it, feeling his thick steel stoke the fire until it flared white-hot. Then he reached around to press rhythmic circles into the sensitive flesh above where they were joined. Need flared deep in her core.

"Now, baby," he whispered into her ear. "Come for me."

He quickened the pace, and she shot right over the edge of a precipice she hadn't even known was there. Every muscle clenched as she moaned his name into the mattress, ecstasy rolling through her in waves from her core and her belly to her fingers and toes. On some other level of consciousness she was aware he wrapped her up in both his arms and held her tight, pounding into her with heavy, filling strength to meet the demands of her greedy body as the climax rolled on and on.

At last the sharp edges of orgasm began to soften into the sweet slopes of satisfaction. She turned her attention to Sam now, growing impossibly harder deep inside her as he neared his own release. She arched her back and pushed back against him. He pulled in a breath and let it out in a growl of pure male delight. She smiled as his strokes grew faster, deeper, as both hands went to her hips to pull her in closer. She had thought she would just enjoy feeling him come, but the way he was moving inside her slick channel was . . . *Jesus God, that feels good!*

And still he stroked in and out of her, so hot, so demanding, until the climax rose up to overwhelm her. She gave in to it, lost in her body's response to him, while he let himself go at last, his seed emptying into her in furious jets.

Then, as if she were waking from some kind of erotic dream, it was over. They lay together in a boneless heap, unable, unwilling to move. Her heart raced like she had been running a marathon, and the blood thrummed in her core where he still rested, warm and semi-hard. God, no one had ever loved her like that before. Sam Murphy was beyond her experience. And somehow she knew it was not just about the sex.

She felt the loss when he slid out of her and backed away to search the shelves of the room for a towel. But he flashed her a smile when he came back that slipped past her guard and touched her heart. She accepted the towel from him and cleaned up, feeling a little shy now that it was all over. She reached for her clothes, but he put a hand on her arm to stop her.

"Not yet." He gestured at the gurney. "It won't be very comfortable, but . . ." He shrugged and offered up a grin. "We never did have that talk."

She stifled her own grin. The pirate captain feared throughout the galaxy wanted to *cuddle*? Well, who was she to complain? He'd just given her three mind-blowing orgasms, the least she could do was spend some time scrunched together on a narrow medical cot.

But in truth, as she settled in under his arm, her head resting in the crook of his shoulder, her hand tracing circles on his smooth, broad chest and hard belly, there was no place she'd rather be. This felt natural. And right. She slid a leg over his thigh, and when she heard him rumble in satisfaction, she sighed.

His hand smoothed her dark curls, traced the line of her jaw and finally tipped her chin up to meet his gaze. "So tell me, Little Bit. That wasn't just my imagination. It was good for you, right?"

She flushed hot and a grin took over her face. "You couldn't tell by the way I was screaming your name? Yes, God, it was good, baby."

"And last night? That was good, too?"

"It was incredible." She raised up on one elbow to look at him. "And I never said so, did I. Jesus, I'm sorry, I –"

"Not my point." He grinned. "Well, not exactly. A man always likes to hear that he's done a good job." The smile faded. "What I want to know is why you ran, Rayna. We had something last night, and then you ran. Now we're here, and I want to know if you plan on running again."

She was caught, and her heart started a slow thud in her chest. "Running is the only safe thing to do with you, Murphy." She tried to keep her tone light, but failed.

"Safe? You want safe? The woman who was willing to hide away on a slave ship to sneak into the most secure arms factory in the galaxy?" He teased her with a warm light in his eyes and a smile playing around his lips, but she knew he could be hurt by her answer. She knew because the truth of it was already causing her pain.

She touched his cheek. "You're a lot more dangerous than any job."

His hand covered hers. "I won't hurt you, Rayna."

"How can you not?" She pulled away and sat up. "You're a *pirate*, for chrissake."

"Yes. A pirate who loves you."

She gaped at him. "What?"

He stared back. "You heard me."

"You can't possibly love me. We've only known each other a few days!" But she looked at him and knew it was true. Worse, she knew the edge of the cliff she'd been teetering on had finally given way under her feet. She was falling, too, and unless Sam caught her, there was no hope for her.

In Sam's eyes was a swirl of emotion—elation, apprehension, determination. "I knew it the minute I saw you, Little Bit. You're all I've been thinking about ever since."

"You're crazy." But her heart was triple-timing in her chest. For him.

"Then why are you smiling at me like that?" He sat up and gathered her in his arms. He held her close, the muscles of his chest hard under her cheek, his skin warm and smooth. "Say you love me, too. You know you do."

"You think I'm as crazy as you are?" She'd tried so hard not to love him, but from the first he'd stolen her heart and nothing would persuade it to leave him. His pulse beat wild and strong under her ear as he waited for her answer. "All right, then, yes, I admit it. I love you. Are you happy now?"

He held her tighter. "Ecstatic."

She went hot from her head to her toes, and all her smart-ass attitude melted in the glow. "Me, too."

He brought her lips up to meet his kiss and she was lost again, in his taste, in his tongue's slow exploration of her mouth, in the heat building between them once more. He broke it off, only to murmur, "I need to be inside you," sending a thrill of need straight through her from her core to her heart. She straddled him and took him in, joining them in one, smooth glide. He caressed her with his gaze as much as with his hands as she rode him, and she abandoned herself to the feel of him deep inside. They took their time, a slow, steamy push all the way to the top. And when she came, her whole body gave in to him, responding with a depth and power and emotion she'd never felt before.

Sam wrapped Rayna in his arms and held her while his heartbeat evened out and his breath returned to normal. Gods, she'd been magnificent, her perfect body arched in pleasure over his, her face a portrait of beauty lost to sensation. But then she had looked at him, and everything he felt for her had been reflected in her eyes. His heart had swelled in his chest, sending an arrow of fresh desire through him. And when she'd come, he'd followed her into paradise with a shout of joy.

Now he knew he was in trouble, but he couldn't bring himself to care. She was warm and soft and *here* in his arms. He'd worry about the broken heart—and Mo was right, there was sure to be one—later.

"Damn, sweets, what am I supposed to do now?" Rayna's whisper blew a gentle breath across his chest. He supposed she was trying for her usual smart-ass tone, but she sounded sad, so sad. "I'm gonna need a regular fix of that . . . And it's a big, freakin' galaxy."

He pushed a stray hair back out of her face. "We'll find each other. And, trust me, if you try to ditch me, I'll come looking for you."

She smiled up at him. "You know, I believe you would." The smile dissolved, and she looked away. "So. We'll just have to get used to a long time between dates, I guess."

She didn't believe they were capable of maintaining even that much; he could read it in the slight trembling of her tiny body. He held her tighter.

"We'll do whatever we have to. I won't be without you."

She kissed his chest and snuggled closer with a sigh.

Seeing her once every few fiftydays would never be enough for him; he knew that deep down. He needed her in some fundamental way, needed to go to sleep beside her every night, wake up beside her every morning. She answered some growling primal call in him, and without her whatever it was that called out would grow wild and unmanageable. But Sam knew better than to try and swallow this problem in one gulp. He would gnaw at it until it was bite-size.

"If your crew ever discovers how soft you are on the inside, you might have a mutiny on your hands." Rayna was smiling up at him as she said this, teasing. "I don't know what you've done with Captain Snark. I'm beginning to worry about him."

Sam grunted in amusement. "I suspect my crew is already on to me. And 'Captain Snark'? That's just . . . a little too close to the truth. But it does remind me: I have a ship to run." He gave her a last, lingering kiss and disengaged, rolling off the gurney to land on his feet with the grace of a cat. He cast about in the dim light, looking for the towel he'd found earlier.

Rayna watched him from the gurney, propped up on one elbow in a pose so seductive his cock twitched in appreciation. "Did you lose something?"

"Yes. My resolve if I don't find that towel so I can get cleaned up and dressed in about ten seconds."

"Should we turn on the lights?"

He squatted down on his haunches to peek under the gurney and enjoyed a brief boost of triumph as his hand closed on the square of terry cloth. But something else caught his eye—a tiny blink of red light in the far corner on the underside of a shelf. He couldn't see what was generating the light, a modest rhythm of low-emission winks that would have been hidden from anywhere else in the room. *What the hell?* Maybe just a power indicator, but . . .

"Sam?"

He stood and used the towel, then found a clean one for Rayna. "Sorry. I saw something under there that I need to check out. We'll have to move this." He put a hand on the gurney.

"Something? What kind of something?"

"Not sure. Maybe nothing." He had a bad feeling about it all the same.

Rayna was cleaned up and dressed in less than a minute. They hit the lights and saw that the gurney was pushed up close to the storage unit that extended along the far wall of the small room. There was a monitoring station on the left wall closer to the center of the room that indicated the gurney should more properly have been placed there.

Rayna blushed. "Did we move that gurney? I mean, I know we—"

"I don't think so. It felt solid to me. It's not quite up against the cabinets, so the wheels must be locked."

"So somebody else moved it."

"Come on." He reached underneath the gurney to release the wheels, then the two of them moved the bed away from the storage unit and back to the center of the room where it belonged. Sam made a mental note to strip the sheets. He turned back to the cabinets, where Rayna was already crouched in the corner.

She'd opened a sliding door in the bottom unit. Now she looked up at him, her lips set in a thin, hard line.

"Captain, we have a problem."

Fully revealed, the red light blinked even brighter,

sitting on top of a handmade plasmion bomb big enough to blast a hole the size of a small asteroid through the deck of Sam Murphy's ship.

CHAPTER ELEVEN

Security Chief Chen, the ship's XO, Sam and Rayna stood to one side while a crew member who normally worked the cargo deck examined the bomb. As Sam had explained it, Chule Fl'x had grown up fighting Thrane occupation on her home planet of Oxtra—and had the most munitions expertise of anyone onboard.

"I doubt this is the only one of these on the ship, Cap," Chen said. "Sure, this one is big enough to take out this section, but Sickbay is hardly crucial to continued functioning of the ship."

Sam nodded. "All right, we're gonna give this ship a tongue bath. Institute a search, everybody working in their own section, cabin and workspace. As soon as Chule figures out what we're dealing with we'll put together a squad to take care of what we find."

Rayna couldn't help it; she grinned—but she kept her voice low. "A tongue bath, really?" She ignored Sam when he scowled at her. "What about the bastards who planted these things?"

His scowl deepened as he turned to his Security head. "What about it, Mei?"

"I've got two-person patrols in the corridors, in Engineering, in the auxiliary control rooms, guarding the bridge and searching cargo, the shuttle bay and hull space. Any other ideas, Cap?"

"Oh, shit!" Rayna turned and looked at Sam with her mouth open in astonishment. *A tall Thrane, dark hair, broad shoulders—*"I think I saw him!"

"What?" Sam grabbed her elbow and squeezed. "What are you talking about?"

"Just before we, uh, saw each other in the corridor, someone came out that door." She pointed at the door leading to the outside from the room next door. "He was Thrane, and I got a good look at him. I just assumed he was crew, coming from Doc Berta's office. Do you have images of your Thrane crew members?"

Chen moved to her side and punched up the images on her pad. "Sure. Take a look."

Rayna studied the faces, then shook her head. "Nope. This guy was better looking—the kind that makes you look twice. Tall. Big shoulders. Sharp angles to his face. Dark, dark eyes."

Sam growled. "Great. Our bomber is also a multimix star."

Rayna frowned at the newly-returned Captain Snark. "Just trying to give a description here. What else do you need, Chief?"

"That should be enough to start with. I'll send the description to all the teams." Chen's gaze shot back and forth between Rayna and Sam. "And thanks, Agent Carver."

"Hope it helps." Rayna made sure to make eye contact with Murphy as she spoke. Now that the *veer* was out of the air vent about her job title, she wasn't going to be shy about using her training.

A glint of amusement in his eyes was his only acknowledgement—and apology. "Chule—anything?"

The munitions tech rocked back on her heels. "Looks pretty simple, Cap. Whoever put it here didn't figure on it being found or he would've made it harder to disarm. Clear the area and give me a suit and I'll have it done in a couple of minutes."

Sam and Rayna both spat a curse at the same time. Chen and Mo looked grim.

Chule looked up at them in confusion. "Uh, sir? Isn't that good news?"

"It would be if there was any hope this was the only bomb on board." Sam ran a hand through his hair. "Simple and slapdash only confirms he's hidden these things all over the ship."

The towering XO nodded. "And we're due at C4 in a little over eight hours. We hit jump with even one of these things onboard—"

"—and we'll come out the other side in bite-size pieces. We need to find the bombs—all of them. And we need to find the *mulaak* bastards who planted them. Now." His voice was soft, so soft, but there was no mistaking the steel behind it. "Go."

"I'll, uh, go get the disposal equipment, Cap," Chule said, and left the room with the others.

Rayna put a hand on Sam's arm, found it rock hard with tension. "I want your permission to join the search teams in hull space."

"No." He started to pull away, but she held on tight and he was forced to answer. "This isn't your business,

Ray. Let us take care of it."

"Your business is my business, now, Sam, and I can help. I'm sure that bomber and his girlfriend are hiding in hull space."

Sam's eyebrows lifted. "His girlfriend?"

"The assassin is female; we'd already figured that out. This is a team. The Thranes often used bonded pairs for undercover work."

"How do you know that?"

She grinned up at him. "Undercover agent, remember? It's my job to know."

"Your job." He touched her face. Frowned. "You know, it's my job to protect my ship—and everybody aboard her. Not yours."

Sweet, so sweet—but she couldn't allow it. "So I'm supposed to sit on my protected ass in your cabin while everyone else on the ship works to solve this life-threatening problem."

At last the muscles of his jaw relaxed, and he almost allowed a smile. "Not going for it, huh?"

"Not while I'm drawing breath."

He held her gaze. "Figures. I don't suppose you'd like to search the living quarters with a squad of Security instead?"

"Well, I could join the disposal team. I have munitions training. Would that be better?"

"Hell, no! It's just . . . you're still recovering, you know."

"I'm fine. We tested out the equipment just a little while ago, remember?" She let her fingers slip down his arm, stroking. A warm little thrill of remembered pleasure shot through her core.

He squeezed her hand—the only touch he would allow himself. "Then remember what I told you a while ago. I don't say those kinds of things often. So be careful." He turned and was gone.

"How could this have happened, Rexus?" Zetana didn't bother to limit the venom in her hiss. She was tired of hiding in this cramped service tube, tired of waiting, tired of his excuses. "We are so close—we should have had a signal from the *shalssiti* Grays already—and now the crew is crawling all over this ship looking for your explosives. They're on high alert. What in the name of Portal's balls happened?"

She could smell her mate's sweat in the hot, enclosed space. Then she saw in his mind an image of the dark-skinned human female—the ConSys Intel agent. One word seared across their linked minds. *Her?*

Rex dared not use their link to answer. "She saw me coming out of Sickbay, but I swear at the time she raised no alarm; she had no suspicion. I hid the package in an unused emergency surgery. Why would she have reason to be there?"

Zetana cursed. "What does it matter? She found it, the *mulaak* bitch, and all it took was one discovery. Now the captain has ordered a ship-wide search. I will kill her with my own hands."

"Don't worry, beloved." Rex's voice was both smug and cajoling. At this moment she hated the sound of it. "They can't possibly find every one. And even one is enough to destroy this ship if it goes off while they are in jump."

That was a comforting thought. Still—"The explosives had another purpose, and you know it. Our slimy little friends will need the distraction to allow our escape. And besides, you fool, this search is just as likely to find us!"

"We've managed to avoid them so far, *k'taama*." He didn't sound quite so confident now.

"Come, we can't stay here." She uncoiled from her place in the tube and began crawling toward the exit. "There's more freedom of movement in hull space." *And pray to the gods that signal comes soon.*

Rayna floated in the semi-dark of hull space and waited. The others in her search party criss-crossed the space in pairs at wide intervals, hoping to flush out their quarry, but Rayna thought the Thranes were too smart for that. They'd hidden in plain sight for days already, avoiding any sighting by or suspicion from Murphy's crew. They wouldn't panic and make a mistake now. But they couldn't stay in one place forever, either, hunkering down in a service tube or an empty storage locker. With the search in its sixth hour now, they'd have to give themselves some maneuvering room. From a shadowed spot between the hulking backsides of the ship's air filtration pumps, Rayna looked down on the empty space between hulls and watched for them to make their move.

At the far end of her line of vision, where the band of hull space narrowed at the fore of the ship, something caught her eye. Had someone found something down there?

The Security team leader's voice came through the commpiece in her ear. "Dawson-Pak, is that you up at the fore? What's going on?"

The response came back. "Yes, sir. We're checking in a new team."

A new team? "What new team? Let me hear 'em."

There was a pause, long enough to make Rayna twitchy. "Sir? This is I'x and Taylor checking in. Chief Chen sent us up from the living quarters detail." Light static underlay the voice.

At that moment Rayna would have given a lot for a crew manifest and the means to use it. Her instincts tugged at her sleeve, warning her that something was off. Still, logic dictated that on a ship this small, crew would recognize crew.

"All right. Fall in the pattern at the end of the line, side-to-side sweep. Keep your eyes open. And adjust your comm; you're breaking up."

"Aye, sir. We're on it."

The two new crew members pushed off from the inner hull, separating from the others and forming yet another weave in the net that was meant to catch their fleeing fish. They were too far from her position for Rayna to see their faces, but she could identify them as one male and one female, both tall and dark-haired. As they floated closer, she could discern the muscular build on both of them, hers lithe and tight, his lean and broad-shouldered.

Damn it, they have to be Thrane! Why didn't— wait, of course. They'd been close enough to touch the others, close enough to use the mind control techniques for which the Thranes were feared throughout the galaxy. And now they were making their way to another hiding place, one that had already passed inspection and had egress to other parts of the ship.

Rayna didn't bother with the comm; the Thranes were listening in and no one was close enough to grab them before they could disappear again. The criss-crossing pattern of the search made it impossible to predict where they might break out of the grid—port side or starboard side—and go to ground. She could only watch, muscles clenched, sweat trickling down her spine, and wait for them to make their move.

At last they slowed and drifted away from the tight formation of searchers. There was no order to re-form from the Security team leader. The pair pulled up next to a hull space access hatch on the port side just aft of Rayna's position, opened the hatch and swung in, one after the other. Before Rayna could scramble out of her hiding place, they had dogged the hatch shut behind them and vanished.

Rayna launched herself across the expanse of space toward the hatch, using the seconds it took to hurtle through the empty air to put two fingers to her mouth and blow a shrill whistle. Startled faces turned in her direction from all over hull space. She reached the hatch and waved an arm, pointing inside. Then she put a hand over her mouth and shook her head, hoping they'd understand not to use the comms. It was the best she could do; she'd already wasted too much time. She opened the hatch and ducked inside, turned and dogged it shut, waited impatiently for the pressure to equalize in the antechamber.

The go-light went green, but still she stood flattened against the inside of the hatch, peering through the porthole for a glimpse of her quarry. Either they'd gone, or they were well out of sight. She gripped the stun gun they'd issued her as part of the search detail, opened the hatch and slipped out into a square of light surrounded by an unknown quantity of darkness—filled with containers. *Fuck!* Finding those two in a cargo hold would take more time than they had, even with half the crew looking.

Rayna was out of her depth now, she knew it, but watching an opportunity float out of reach just wasn't part of her personality. She lifted the gun into ready position and stepped off into the darkness, trusting that her eyes would adjust to the lower light in a few seconds. She passed the first few meters without incident and started breathing again.

*You should have been waiting for me right there,
you* mulaak *idiots. I wouldn't have been able to see
you.*

As it was, alarms were blaring from every nerve in
her body. She was a house cat stalking two tigers, and
from what she'd read of the fierce Earth predators, the
puddy tat didn't have a chance. *Don't engage them,
Ray, you hear me? Just shoot 'em dead and ask
questions later.* Like most lectures, this one rolled
right off her back. When she was on the hunt, she
listened to no one, not even herself.

She tried without success to call up her location
from what she could remember of the ship's layout.
The main cargo deck was crowded with LO's; this must
be a secondary hold for storing water, foodstuffs, raw
materials for the replicator and other bulky goods
necessary for life onboard.

Rayna crept down a wide aisle, the containers
stacked high on either side limiting her view to a few
meters just before and behind her. The constant hum
of ventilation fans filled the unplumbable darkness
beyond that tiny circle of awareness. The back of her
neck prickled with nerves—she refused to acknowledge
the feeling as fear—waiting for an attack that could
come from anywhere. Why should they run when she
made such an easy target?

Rayna came to the end of the row and pressed
herself against the last container. Wary of exposing
herself, she peeked around the end of the big crate,
only to jump back as a thin white line of laze fire shot

past her face and burned a hole in the polymer container next to her. The angle had put the shooter up on a catwalk about six meters above her and to her left.

Her stunner wasn't made for distance, but the Max Level would at least make them duck and cover. She shifted right and fired in the direction of the laze gun, saw the tracer line splash against the metal decking of the catwalk and outline the shadow of movement there. She fired again, leading a pair of fleeing shadows, then ran after them. Laze fire whizzed by her head and kicked sparks off an electrical panel. *Shit, did that just fry the gravity lock hatch?*

She zig-zagged across the floor to the stack of containers opposite and shot upwards again, but she'd lost sight of her quarry now. The catwalk circled the cargo hold, allowing access to the stacks with ramps above the main aisles. At the end of each ramp was an exit to the deck above. There was no way to determine which way they'd gone.

Where the hell is my backup? Rayna's hand slipped to the comm at her throat. She had little to lose now; the Thranes already knew she was on to them. But . . . *shit!* She turned a corner and saw their goal at the aft end of the hold—the freaking dematerialization pad! They were trying to get off the ship!

Her quarry ran for the pad. She fired, but the range was too great for her little stunner. The Thrane male actually laughed before he launched a round of laze fire in her direction. Rayna dove for cover and hit her comm at the same time.

She heard the D-mat sequence start up. "Security, this is Carver. Shut down—" But that's all she had time to say before a roar of fire and flame erupted at her back and the world flipped upside down.

CHAPTER TWELVE

Voices and alarms assailed him from every direction, demanding attention. The captain held up a hand and commanded silence. Hands slapped down on consoles, jaws slammed shut and the bridge fell eerily quiet.

"Mo, can we pinpoint that explosion?"

"Aye, Cap. Deck Six, Cargo Hold Four A, near the D-mat pad."

Sam turned to a pale crew member monitoring equipment on the other side of the deck. "Is that the same D-mat pad you were trying to tell me just went active without authorization?"

The kid looked at him and swallowed. "Aye, Cap."

"Destination coordinates?"

The crewman read them off, and faces turned toward an empty viewscreen.

But Sam knew what they were seeing was a lie. "Shields up! Now! Battlestations!"

Alarms began to blare anew all over the ship as the call went out to man battlestations.

"Arnett, get me Captain Manneh on the *Fleeflek*." Manneh had been with him almost as long as he'd been captain of the *'hawk*, and she wouldn't panic if they were under attack by a whole fleet of Gray cruisers. When her face appeared on the screen, he didn't waste time with greetings. "Fatou, get your shields up, if that pile of shit has any. I expect a Gray attack any second. Stay in my shadow if you can. I'll do my best to protect you."

A grin creased Manneh's smooth face, but didn't reach her dark eyes. "Don't worry, Cap. We're not completely defenseless. I think there's a working ion cannon onboard, at least."

"Good. You can watch my back, then."

"Will do. Good hunting, Cap."

He nodded back to her and signed off. He turned, meaning to get a quick damage report from Mo, but the grim expression on his XO's face stopped his heart.

"What? Tell me."

"The bomb caused automatic fire control systems to shut down the hatches to Cargo Hold Four. We're having a little trouble getting inside to see the actual damage." The Pataran didn't seem to know how to go on.

"Okay. And?"

Mo straightened. "At last report, Agent Carver had tracked the Thranes into that hold. Security received a partial transmission from her just before the bomb went off. They haven't heard from her since."

Sam's vision blanked as the blood rushed from his head to the center of his body in a futile effort to protect his heart. He swayed.

Mo grabbed his arm. "Sam?"

He forced himself to breathe. "Find a way into that hold. I don't care how you do it. Find her."

"We're on it, Cap." Mo dropped his arm, recognizing the steel in his captain's voice.

"What's the status of the sweep for explosives in the rest of the ship? We can't miss any more of them."

Mo shook his head. "Ninety percent complete."

"Not good enough. Once we're in place at battlestations, have each person inspect his or her area—"

Deep, rolling booms shook the *Shadowhawk* at her core. The deck rattled under Sam's feet. New alarms blared on the bridge. On the viewscreen, their attackers remained hidden.

The captain's voice went quiet as he stepped to the center of the bridge. "Talk to me, crew."

"Two more explosions, Cap." It was the young crewman at his internal sensors, even paler and shakier than before. "Uh, mess hall and shuttle bay. Damage control teams are on it."

"Thank you, Ordman. Let me know as soon as they have a damage estimate." He motioned his XO closer. "Run down the results of our search for me again. How many packages did we find?"

The Pataran matched his low tone. "Nine. They were all over the ship."

"Yes. Living quarters, cargo, hull space, Sickbay, now the mess hall and shuttle bay. But not Engineering, not Weapons, not Environmental Control, not the bridge. If they'd wanted to really hurt us, they'd have planted the things where they could do some good."

"That's an easy one, Cap. No access. Security's not that tight on the 'hawk, but we do watch some things. How was an outsider going to walk onto the bridge and stick a plasmion strip under your conn?"

Sam turned the air blue with a string of curses in three languages. "He wasn't. He was going to go through the crawl space between decks. Send someone between decks to check Engineering and Environmental Control; that should cover Weapons, too."

"Aye, Cap. What about the bridge?"

"I'll do it my—"

"Captain! I have a vessel approaching at 184 point 45 mark 7. Distance 56,000 kilometers. Identification as Minertsan battle cruiser, class D." Sipritz looked up to meet his gaze. "Weapons read hot."

"Shit, they're right on top of us. All hands brace for incoming fire. Ot, fire starboard cannons as we bear."

A duet of "Aye, Caps" met his orders just as bright white light flared out from the enemy ship and splashed against the *Shadowhawk*'s forward shields. The bridge shuddered and rocked under the impact. The 'hawk's cannons stuttered out an answer, but the fire glanced harmlessly off the Gray's shields amidships.

"Keep at him, Ot, just a few degrees to port and you'll have his engines!" Sam stalked the narrow walk above the control console like the Angel of Death. "Dartha, keep that slaver behind us as much as you can."

182 | Donna S. Frelick

But the Gray ship was dodging fire now and lifting for an attempt at coming up and over to attack them from aft, leaving the *Fleeflek* vulnerable. "Belay that! Come about to port and let Manneh take them."

The *'hawk*'s stabilizers screamed as Dartha pulled her into a tight turn out of the way of the *Fleeflek*'s cannons. Manneh saw what was coming at her and fired as soon as her companion cleared the way. The bigger enemy cruiser was hit again amidships, but shrugged off the blows and kept coming, bearing down on the slaver.

"Aft cannons now, Ot! Aim for his shuttle bays. The shielding is weaker there."

"Aye, Cap. Firing aft!"

The cruiser sheared off to the starboard side of the *Fleeflek*, raking the battered hulk with laze fire. Sam saw the shields along the ship's flank flicker and spark under the assault before the Grays pulled up and came about to bear down on the *'hawk*.

"The slaver's down to 40 percent of her shields on the starboard side, Cap." Mo straightened from his sensors. "She's losing maneuverability, too."

"Draw us away from her, Dartha. Give us some fighting room. Sip, how far are we from jump?"

The Mper shook her head. "Too far to do us any good. Thirty-two minutes at tow speed."

Sam swallowed. He'd never hold the Grays off that long. As if to prove the point, laze fire bloomed across the *'hawk*'s bow, knocking him into the rail at his gut.

"Shields!" he demanded when he could get his

breath back.

"Still holding at 80 percent, Cap." Mo glanced up from his sensors. "But not for long."

"Damage reports, sir!" Ordman tried his best to keep his game face on. "Fire teams working on Decks One, Two, Three, uh, well, on all decks now, sir. Assistant Engineer Ang reports some concern over ventilation system overload, but she's working on it. Major structural damage reported in Cargo Hold Four and hull space Section Seven; the rest is minor. Sickbay reports minor casualties so far. But there's rioting in the main cargo bay among the LO's, sir. Security Chief Chen had to send in a squad."

"What!" Sam grabbed the handrail and held on as another blast of laze fire shook the ship. "Damn it, Dartha, can't you lose this sonofabitch?"

"Trying, Cap."

There was no time to process what was going on in the cargo bay. Chen would have to take care of it. Sam put off analyzing it until later.

What he saw on the viewscreen took precedence. "Ot, he's making another try at the slaver. Hit him as he comes in."

"Aye, Cap."

Sam stepped closer to Ordman and put a hand on his shoulder. "Any word on Agent Carver?"

"Sir?"

"In Cargo Hold Four? Have they found her?"

"Oh. Uh, no, Cap. There wasn't any report from Sickbay." The kid bit his lip. "That should be good news, though, right?"

Sam's heart twisted in his chest. He turned back to the viewscreen without answering.

And cursed—the enemy ship was taking the bait, pursuing them at maximum ion thrust just aft of the *Shadowhawk*'s tailfeathers. But Manneh had taken his "order" to watch his back literally. She had come about to follow, wounded as she was.

"Arnett, warn Manneh off. Tell her I said to stand down. She's done enough."

He heard his Comm Officer hail the *Fleeflek* and relay his orders, but the slaver kept coming, spitting weak fire from two forward ion cannons. Then twin lines of white laze fire arced from the aft weapons of the Gray ship and converged on the *Fleeflek*'s battered hull. Her shields collapsed.

"Ot, fire aft cannons! Now!"

"Aye, Cap. Firing"

Laze fire blazed against the Gray's forward shields. For a split-second they wavered, then firmed again as more power was directed to them. Answering fire came at the *'hawk* from their forward cannons. The bridge heaved as the shields took the hit, knocking Sam to his knees. Consoles sparked, stabilizers screamed, and the smoke that was overloading the ventilation system throughout the ship now began to leak onto the bridge.

But the worst damage was done in a blinding flare of light that filled the viewscreen. Sam struggled to his feet, staring at the expanding cloud of gas and debris that was all that was left of the *Fleeflek* and those aboard her. His chest constricted around his breath as grief and disbelief held him frozen. His stunned mind kept repeating *The Grays take prisoners. The Grays* always *take prisoners. What the hell happened?*

Deep within the bones of his own ship, two thudding booms rolled like thunder. He turned to Ordman.

The kid nodded. "Aye, sir, that's two more. I'm locating them now."

"Helm, get us the hell out of here. Maximum ion drive. We've got to make that jump node *now*."

"Aye, Cap, Max ID. We might actually be a little faster than those *mulaak* SOB's."

"We better hope so." He stepped down to his own console and punched the comm pad for Engineering. "Kwan, you there?"

"Little busy, here, Cap!"

"Yeah, we all are. You locate any packages between decks?"

"Aye, sir. One sitting just below the ion thruster controls, another under the jump matrix. Would have made a nice mess."

"You know we have to hit jump before you're ready."

"How soon?"

"Depends on how much ID you can give me."

An exhale. "I can give you maximum for as long as you need it."

"That'll put us there in fourteen minutes."

Now a heartbeat of silence at Kwan's end. "We'll do

what we can, Cap. The matrix will hold through the jump, anyway."

"That's all we can ask, Engineer. See you on the other side."

"Aye, Cap."

Laze fire from the Gray ship grazed the 'hawk's shields to port, rocking the bridge. The *Shadowhawk* slewed and skittered just in front of her pursuer, trying to avoid another hit. Sam knew his shields were weakening, and the division of power between shields and weapons would soon become critical. In minutes he wouldn't have anything to throw back at the cruiser but rancid protein mash from the galley.

Mo appeared at his side and grabbed the railing just as the ship absorbed another glancing blow. "You know we can't put it off much longer. We have to check under this bridge for a bomb."

"My disposal unit is running all over this ship. And in case you hadn't noticed, we're in the middle of a battle here."

"I can go."

Sam laughed. "You? You couldn't get your big toe between decks."

"Mo *is* as big as a damn freighter, but you've picked an odd time to trade insults."

The voice, full of familiar snappish humor and a newer smoky rasp, sent an electric jolt through his chest. He whirled in the direction of the hatch and gods! there she was, all in one piece, offering up a tired grin as she waited on the threshold of his bridge.

"Gods' eyes, Rayna." Her name left him on a sigh. *I thought you were dead*, he thought, but he didn't say it.

"Permission, Captain?" She nodded at his bridge.

He took the few steps to where she stood and wrapped his arms around her. His crew gave a muted cheer, but he ignored them. Her body was warm and solid and *breathing* against his; that was all that mattered.

"Are you okay?"

"A little woozy. It'll pass. Doc says I'm fine."

Laze fire slammed into the aft shields, pitching them toward the bulkhead. His arm shot out to fend them off.

She turned to study the cruiser on the viewscreen. "So that's where they escaped to." She looked back at him. "Where's the *Fleeflek*?"

"Destroyed." His fists clenched as he stood away from her.

She looked as if she would say something, but the Pataran joined them and nodded in Rayna's direction. "Glad to see you well, Agent Carver. I hear it was a close thing."

She shrugged. "Close enough."

"Cap. The package? We're ten minutes from jump—we can't afford to wait any longer."

"You're right. Arnett, have Chule Fl'x and her team leave whatever they're doing and report to the bridge on the double."

The laze fire was relentless now, beating at the

'hawk without letup. The bridge tossed and rolled like the deck of some ancient pirate frigate in a storybook. Sam couldn't say it was the least bit romantic.

Mo had returned to his station and was studying his scanners with a scowl. "Shields are down to 50 percent aft."

"Weapons Control reports overheating on the aft laze cannon, too, Cap," Ot added.

"And they're gaining on us, 13,000 klicks and closing." Sipritz grabbed her console as her partner at the helm threw them into a complicated maneuver to avoid the worst of the fire from the oncoming ship. "Recommend Plan B tactic to allow us to take advantage of port and starboard shields and weapons."

Sam hated Plan B. It played hell with his stabilizers and his artificial gravity systems, not to mention his stomach and his mental processes. But he'd come up with the spiraling maneuver to get out of a tight spot years ago, and it had saved his ship and his crew more than a few times since then. They would have to slow their headlong flight to perform the "barrel roll" around the enemy ship, spraying it with fire from all weapons as they went, but the ploy might keep the Grays off them long enough to find any explosives under his bridge before they hit jump.

"Agreed. Sip, prepare the approach. Dartha, try to keep them off us until Navigation is ready. Ot, stand by all weapons."

He heard the enthusiasm in their acknowledgement. His crew was tired of being pounded. As the bridge shook once more from enemy fire, he couldn't blame them.

"Cap!" Ordman again, and could the kid look any worse? "They finally located the munitions team. Dead, sir, all of them! The bomb went off just as they got to it. Between decks under Weapons."

Sam took the news like a physical blow, muscles clenching, breath catching in his chest. Damn it, this was costing too much. And the payoff, if there was any, was too far in the future.

"Damage." *If the weapons were gone . . .*

"Minimal, Cap. The forward transducer coils took most of it."

"They were already worthless." He breathed again. He took a step, knowing it was imperative he move before the wave of disaster caught him and pulled him under.

He felt a hand on his arm. "Why did you need the munitions team?"

All his horror, his stubborn resistance, his protectiveness must have shown on his face before he ever said a word, because Rayna just shook her head without the hint of a smile. "You don't get to say no, Captain. You need me for this job, I can tell. I've got the expertise, and right now I'm the only one available. So what is it?"

Mo was staring at him. The Pataran gave him a slow nod. Sam's heart stopped beating.

He faced her and spoke just loud enough to be heard above the noise of the bridge. "We suspect there's another explosives package between decks in the space just below the bridge. We have to check it out before we hit jump."

"So let's see if I've got this straight. You need someone small to crawl around between decks and find a bomb—someone smart enough to disarm it once it's found." One corner of her mouth kicked up. "See? I told you I was perfect for the job."

CHAPTER THIRTEEN

Rayna had volunteered to do what was needed, but the truth was the dark, close, meter-high gap between decks, crisscrossed with a latticework of reinforcing durasteel, made her sweat and shake. *Damn all tight spaces to Portal's Hell!* She surveyed the vast area to be searched with despair, feeling the press of time like flames on her back.

She started off on her hands and knees, thanking God for her one advantage—her size. She slipped in and out of the reinforcing beams with relative ease, splashing a broad swath of bright light from side to side with her headlamp as she moved. A bigger woman or a man would be crawling at a snail's pace, and the instant she realized it, she knew she could speed up her search.

The commpiece in her ear crackled. "Rayna, can you hear me?"

"I'm here, Sa—Captain."

"Any progress?"

"I think I've figured out the route he took through here. He's bigger, so he would have avoided the sides where the beams come together. I'll go where the gaps are bigger, see what I can find."

"Good. You've got about sixty seconds before we execute Plan B. When that happens you'll have to find a place to strap in for a few minutes."

She squeezed through a cross-spar and banged an elbow. "Fuck!" She rubbed at the sore spot and moved on. "What the hell is Plan B anyway?"

"Offensive maneuver. You don't want to know beyond that. When I give you the word, find a corner, curl up in a ball and wait it out."

"Sounds like loads of fun." She crawled out through the latticework onto a narrow catwalk running beside several lengths of conduit. Her hands and kneecaps ached, so she got up and duck-walked, hunched and huffing, until she could hear the muffled sounds of the bridge above her. "Hey, I'm right under you!"

His voice was warm and intimate in her ear. "I'd tell you what I think of that, but this is not a secure channel. What do you see?"

"Oh, shit, there it is." The red light blinked at her from an overhead durasteel support a meter to starboard. "You're sitting on it."

"Thought things were a little uncomfortable. Don't you dare touch it. Find a place to hang on. The ride is gonna get ugly for a while."

"What? No, wait! Let me disarm this thing first."

"Belay that! We're going in now. We can't exactly turn around and try again later!"

"And we don't know how these things have been rigged to blow! Timers, radio signals from that ship, too much jiggling?"

"They've saved this one for jump. It's their failsafe."

"You don't know that. Damn it, Sam!" She wanted to shout at him; maybe she was shouting at him. The ship was shuddering under another hail of laze fire and she couldn't tell.

The voice in her ear was calm and soothing. "Trust me, Ray. You'll have time after we do this. Strap down. Now. Tell me you're ready."

Guts twisting, Rayna gave up the argument. It was his ship, and there came a time when everyone aboard followed his orders. She scrambled back toward the framework of reinforcing metal and ducked under the nearest crossbeam. Bracing her back against the cold durasteel, she locked her legs against the beam across from her. If she stretched her arms out to her sides she could grab on to the neighboring beams. It wasn't ideal, but it was better than nothing.

She glanced up at the decking as though she could see the man who held all their fates in his hands. "Ready when you are, Captain."

"See you on the other side, Little Bit," Sam said, and closed off his communication with Rayna. Then he shut down that part of his mind, because to think of her trapped down below with enough plasmion to blow her to bits while he spun his ship like a beer token on a bartop was enough to make him crazy.

"Dartha, what's our distance?"

"Fifteen hundred kilometers and closing." The

helm officer shook her head and Sam heard the tiny jingle from multiple piercings in the dead quiet of the bridge.

Sipritz spoke from Navigation. "You'll need at least a thousand to make the turn. Course is already laid in."

"Do it now, helm. Full about turn. All hands prepare for extreme turbulence and possible loss of AG." He stepped down to his own seat at the center of the control console and strapped in.

He registered the acknowledgements, heard the warnings go out over the ship's loudspeakers. His body took the strain as the ship came about far faster than she was meant to, stabilizers screaming in protest. But his focus was on the Gray cruiser growing ever larger on his viewscreen.

I'm going to gut you, you fucker. "Fire forward cannons as we bear, Ot."

"But the transducers—"

"Just do it. We'll have a couple of shots anyway. That's all we'll need."

"Aye, Cap. Firing forward cannons."

Actinic white light splashed against the cruiser's forward shields until they wavered and shimmered under the assault. The Gray commander brought more power to bear on his shields. They held, but the brutal assault kept up. The *Shadowhawk* swept closer and closer, the forward cannons spitting fire, while the cruiser was nearly silent, confused by this switch in tactics.

Within seconds Ot looked up at him from a panel

awash in red light. "The transducers, Cap."

Kwan's voice shouted in his commpiece. "Damn it, Sam! Those things are gonna blow any second! I warned you!"

"Keep your breather on. We're there." Sam turned to Arnett. "All hands brace for Plan B. Stand by on weapons. Okay, helm, your show."

"Aye, Cap." Dartha set her shoulders and moved her fingers over the screen at her station. The *Shadowhawk* shot over the enemy cruiser, so close Sam imagined he could see the startled faces of the Gray crew in the bridge bubble topside. Aft of the Gray ship, the helm officer pulled the 'hawk into another tight full about turn and came back at the cruiser from behind, matching her speed and readying for the maneuver that would send the 'hawk in a tight corkscrew around the enemy ship from aft to fore, firing all weapons as she went.

The Mper spoke into a near-silent bridge. "Here we go."

The *Shadowhawk* lifted and canted to starboard, the real-time view on the viewscreen replaced with a graphic of their projected spiraling course around the cruiser. Sam's stomach lurched as his inner ear registered the change in orientation, and he heard Ordman discreetly lose his breakfast at his station as the ship flipped over and around. He held on tight and fought for control of his own insides.

"Fire as we bear, Ot! Give 'em everything, starboard and port!"

"Aye, Cap, I'm on it." The response was crisp. His weapons officer was Tendik; he had an iron gut.

New alarms blared as the AG struggled to compensate for the ship's slow roll onto its back and over again not just once, but continuously as she hurtled forward along the course of the Gray cruiser. The *Shadowhawk*'s crew was thrown against decks and bulkheads, lifted and dropped, battered and bounced while the ship groaned as if she'd come apart under the strain. Sparks flew as circuits overloaded and backups couldn't be brought online fast enough; smoke thickened on the bridge until Sam's eyes stung and his lungs burned. The air stank of singed plasform and ozone—never a good smell on a starship.

"Mo, tell me we're doing some good here."

"Their shields are down 40 percent starboard, 50 percent port. Pull out and we might have a shot at their engines."

Pull out? Is he fucking crazy? Sam glanced at Sipritz, who was giving him the Mper equivalent of the same expression.

"What do you think, Sip? Flatten out the spiral to their fore, come about to port and take a shot?"

She appeared to consider it. "Your ship, Cap. Think she'll take the strain?"

"She'll have to. Lay it in."

"Acknowledged. Ready at your mark."

"Ot, ready port cannons."

"Aye, Cap. Ready."

He watched the graphic on the screen, trying to

ignore the corresponding dizziness in his head, and waited. The green spiral traced by the *Shadowhawk* approached the fore of the Gray ship. Just before his ship would have turned into another barrel roll, he gave his order.

"Turn her out, helm. Go new course."

"Aye, Cap, new course."

The 'hawk on the screen left its tight spiral and pulled hard to port, circling back on its prey. The ship shuddered and groaned under the load of forces generated by its own momentum, stabilizers overloaded and howling. More of the crew hit the deck.

Sam watched the screen as his ship came around. "Now, Ot, target their engines as we bear. Fire port cannons!"

"With pleasure, Cap!"

"Let's see it in real time, Arnett."

As the deck below their feet thudded with cannon fire, the viewscreen flickered and changed to show the enemy ship against a background of black space. Laze fire bloomed against the cruiser's weak port side. The Grays' shields frizzed and collapsed.

"Now, Ot! Hit 'em again!"

"Oh, yeah!"

The cannons bucked again. The white light flared, as bright as any sun, and this time the cruiser sustained a crippling wound. An angry red gash opened in her side, near her port engines, flames jetting as she lost oxygen from the hole in her outer hull.

But like a wounded animal, she would be even more

dangerous. Sam wouldn't stay to gloat, despite the cheers of his crew.

"Let's get out of here. Sipritz, set course for C4 as fast as we can go." He stood and put a hand on the shoulders of his helm and weapons officer. "Excellent work, you two. Extra shares on the next job. You, too, Sip. Good job, everyone. Forget what I said about canceling mashes. You deserve a little fun."

Another round of cheers went up at that. Sam used the distraction to call Rayna.

There was no answer.

Rayna thought she was wedged solidly between the metal reinforcing beams under the bridge, but how could she know her diabolically insane lover would turn his ship upside down—over and over again? She managed to hold on through the first revolution and half of the second. But when the AG stuttered—making her first weightless, then as heavy as a waste recycler— she lost her grip and was tossed between the crossbeams like a lotto ball in its cage.

She slapped her hands and feet outward to gain some stability and slowed her tumbling for the moment, but she needed a permanent fix. She had no utility belt—*for God's sake, why not?*—so in a brief half-second of quiet she unzipped the top half of her jumpsuit, wriggled out of the arms and tied them to the nearest beam behind her. The metal was ice-cold on her bare back, but she was secure. At least until the ship skewed violently to port, her head jerked into the beam on the opposite side and the lights went out.

"Rayna, wake up, baby. Come on. Open your eyes. Look at me."

"No. Absolutely not. First of all, there's something warm and sticky dripping into one of them. And that light you're waving around will hurt. A lot." Despite what she said, she struggled to do as he asked. It was Sam, after all. She had a bone to pick with him.

A cold, wet cloth dabbed at her brow. It smelled like bad synthohol and stung like a buzz gun, but when she opened her eyes, she could see.

She frowned at him. "Don't you have a ship to run?"

He only smiled back. "It seemed more important to make sure you were still among the living."

His tone was as light as hers, but Rayna caught the lingering worry in his eyes. That he would leave his bridge to find her both warmed and disturbed her. She sat up and fought the dizzy nausea that came with being vertical.

His hand was warm on her back. "Take it easy. You've got a nasty bump. I'm not sure how long you were out."

"How long since you took that hard a-port?" She probed the goose-egg over her right eye and winced.

"And, by the way, what the hell was going on up there?"

"Offensive maneuver. I told you to hang on." He grinned and waved at the sleeves of her jumpsuit, still tied loosely to the beam. "This was your solution? Where's your utility belt?"

She scowled at him. "I never wear one. I'm a spy not a plumber. Wouldn't have done my head much good anyway."

He kissed her gently on the forehead. "I'm sorry. But the maneuver worked. We're on our way to C4 without the Grays on our tail. Come on, Doc Berta needs to have a look at you."

"Aren't you forgetting something?" She pointed up and to starboard. The red light winked like a malevolent eye.

Sam shook his head. "There must be someone else on this ship who can disarm that thing. You've just had your brains scrambled."

"Are you saying you don't trust me to handle it?" Even as she argued her head threatened to float off her shoulders. He had a point, but there wasn't anyone else, and he knew it.

He tried again. "Any other time—"

"There is no other time, Sam." There was only one way to do this. She stood, ignoring the wave of pain and weakness that washed over her, and made her way toward the blinking light.

"Rayna—"

"How long until jump?"

"We can take as long as you need now. We don't

have anyone behind us."

She stared at him. "Bullshit. We can't wait around at the jump node while they catch up to us. How long 'til we get there?"

He glanced at his chrono. "Four minutes."

She took a deep breath and looked up at the device mounted vertically on the beam just above her head. Her head swam.

Okay, remove cover: four screws. Visually confirm components: explosive (plasmion strip), accelerant/catalyst capsules, timer/receiver chip(s), nanoprocessor links, color-coded. The units Chule Fl'x and her team had found had three NPLs, red, yellow, green. *Use the laser knife to deactivate the green one first, then the yellow, then the red. Easy.*

She took the screwdriver from her pocket and removed the cover. The light continued to blink without a sound. But inside all was not as it should be. The links were not red, green and yellow. They were black, gray and white. And they were attached to enough plasmion to blow the *Shadowhawk* to kingdom come.

"Holy fuck." Sam stared at the guts of the device from her elbow.

They doubled the charge, changed the pattern. "They wanted to make sure we didn't survive the jump." Her voice drifted out of her mouth as if she had no control over it.

His hand went to her shoulder and squeezed in silent gratitude.

Yeah, well, I may have found it, but I haven't disarmed it. She was surprised he couldn't feel her heart under his palm; it was pounding hard enough to shake her whole body. Her sweat was already rolling, and she hadn't even touched the cover yet. All she could see were those twisting threads of living nanos—white, gray and black.

Mo's voice broke over their commpieces. "Cap, it looks like that Gray cruiser has put itself back together somehow. They're on our tail and fast enough to catch up to us just before we hit jump—Sip says three minutes."

Sam ran a hand through his hair. "What the fuck did I do to piss these people off so damn bad? It was just one freaking slave ship, for hell's sake!"

"Must be your charming personality, Cap." Mo's voice indicated complete sincerity.

Rayna snorted. "To know you is to love you."

He told his XO, "I'm on my way." Then he turned to Rayna and cupped her cheek with one large hand. "Are you all right?"

"Go. I've got this. Just see if you can fly this bucket straight for a minute or two, would ya?"

"I'll try." He bent to kiss her, a kiss warm enough to drive off the chill that iced her bones every time she looked up. "For what it's worth, I think black equals red. I love you, Little Bit."

Sam moved off down the catwalk in a fast crouch. Rayna whispered, "Love you, too," at his back and took a deep breath. She wanted to be angry at him for tossing off an "easy" solution to the link conundrum, but his was as good as any. She probably would have agreed with him if left to her own devices: white first, then gray, then black. Lightest to darkest, just as the green, yellow, red had a sort of logic. Of course, the Thrane could have chosen to reverse the logic, or to use none at all. But he had been consistent so far—after all, he had to remember which link to connect in which order himself. Rayna prayed he kept within his own parameters.

As Rayna looked closer at the package design, she saw the nanolinks would not be her only problem. She would also have to remove the two delicate glass catalyst capsules connected to the links and keep them intact. The strips of plasmion at the bottom of the box were mostly inert without the catalyst, but let even a drop of that chemical touch the explosive and the *Shadowhawk* and all aboard her were history. The heat of the completed circuit was all that was required to break the tiny vials in the bomb's design; handling them was very tricky work.

Okay, you can do this. She'd gotten through her training with a minimum of smoke and fire. She knew what she was doing. Still her heart wanted to break her ribs from the inside. *Just breathe, Rayna.*

Rayna wiped her sweaty palms on her thighs and grabbed the laser knife from her pocket. The heat of the knife itself presented a danger; a slip could set off the mechanism. Even the electronics in her commpiece were a threat. She turned it off, took it out of her ear and set it aside. She settled herself directly under the package. Then she reached up and laid sure hands on the white link. She sliced it, destroying a section of the nanocolony that maintained the link.

The red light continued to blink. One of the catalyst capsules, no bigger than the vitamin supplements she called breakfast, lost some of its support and relaxed toward the mass of plasmion. Rayna's heart sped up. She cradled the capsules ever so gently with the fingers of her left hand as she cut the gray link. The vials slipped under her touch, but stayed in place. When she sliced through the last link, the vials would swing free; she held them in her palm like two fragile newborns to make certain there was no chance they would drop downward toward the explosive, come together and fracture, or otherwise ruin her day. She took another deep breath.

Then she severed the final link, the black one. The red light stopped blinking. The glass capsules nestled into her palm as the dead stumps of the links pulled slightly away from the box. She exhaled, a grin spreading over her face.

"Damn, I'm good!" She didn't mind that no one was there to hear it. She had to say it.

She swiped at the sweat on her face with her free arm, then brought up the knife to cut all the deactivated NPL threads away. But above her head, alarms broke the relative peace. She couldn't quite make it out, but she could have sworn she heard the call to "Battlestations!"

"Shit!" She just had time to brace her feet and one hand before the first attack came, rocking the 'hawk and throwing Rayna roughly against the beam that held the disemboweled bomb. She fought to hold the vials without crushing them, to stand upright so she could burn the links free, but the ship was skewing and pitching, bucking and yawing like a demon from Portal's Hell. The wild gyrations threatened to send her flying until she wrapped an arm and a leg around the beam and clamped on tight. Still the vials were at risk, the whipsawing G-forces pulling at her unsecured arm. The glass clinked in her palm as she struggled not to smash it.

"Fuck, Murphy, will you please keep this beast steady?" The worst of the fishtailing seemed to ease. With a surge of effort she brought the knife up in front of her face and stripped the links from their attachments. The vials and a snarl of tiny threads came loose in her hand. She dropped away from the beam, staggering as a shot from the Gray cruiser made contact and shook the 'hawk from stem to stern.

She fell to her knees beside the commpiece, jammed it in her ear and slapped the button at her throat. "Sam, you there?"

"Rayna!"

"We're good to go. Package is disarmed. I'm coming out."

"Good job, Little Bit." There was no mistaking the relief in his voice—and the pride. "Get out of there as quick as you can. Security will meet you to take the components.   We're hitting jump as soon as you're clear."

"Roger that, baby. See you on the other side."

CHAPTER FOURTEEN

"J minus thirty seconds, Cap."

Sam acknowledged the data from his helm officer and opened the comm to Engineering. "Kwan, you ready?"

"Ready as we'll ever be, Cap. Just say the word."

Mo looked up from his sensors. "They're backing off."

The corner of Sam's mouth lifted. "They think that bomb will take care of us in jump."

Mo's expression darkened. "We might have missed something."

"We know this ship. We've covered her, bridge to waste scuttles. We didn't miss anything." He ignored the voice deep inside that told him they hadn't had enough time. There was no other choice. They had to believe they'd found everything that Thrane bastard had left behind.

"All hands prepare for jump." Sam heard the order go out, saw the bridge crew settle down. He took his own seat and buckled in, ready for the disorientation that always accompanied jump. Once they'd gone through that door in space they called the jump node, the chronos on board would indicate no time had passed, but their bodies would protest their "instantaneous" appearance in another sector of space with dizziness, nausea and a sense of dislocation. The engines, too, would show the strain if they weren't optimal, and gods knew they weren't. The young matrix, which was supposed to hold everything together, might even collapse altogether under the furious pressure of that nanosecond of jump time.

Time passed in jump, all right. Enough to manipulate with complicated formulas and intricate entry timing, if you were the freakin' Interstellar Council for Abolition and Rescue, Rayna's outfit. But mostly enough to blow you to bits if you weren't careful. Sam swallowed as he heard Dartha count them down.

"Jump in three, two, one!"

One second the viewscreen was full of angry Gray cruiser; the next it showed nothing but black space. Sam's head swirled with a sick buzz, and reddish spots swam in front of his eyes. He ignored the signals from his stomach that insisted throwing up was an excellent idea.

"Jump complete, Cap. Screens show all clear."

"Thank you, helm." He took a breath. "Stand by for course setting."

"Aye, Cap. Standing by."

He hit the comm button for Engineering. "Kwan. What's the news?"

"The worst, Cap. Matrix is fried."

Sam raked a hand through his hair. "Engines?"

"Oh, no problems there. We can tool around the galaxy at ion speed all you want while we grow *another* jump matrix. My poor babies. I shouldn't even be talking to you."

"You're blaming *me* for this?"

"You're the captain. Who else should I blame?"

Sam could hear the grin in Kwan's voice, but the truth stung just the same. "You should thank me for making sure that Gray ship didn't blow your ass out of space."

"Well, there is that." Kwan sighed. "At least I can collect on that drink you owe me. They do have a bar or two on LinHo, don't they?"

"Yeah. One or two." *The dump.* An armpit of a place, and now they would be stuck there for days while Rayna . . . *damn it!* "Finding RES fluid is going to be the trick."

"Leave that to me, Cap. Every rock in space has its black market."

"Roger that." He switched off and turned back to Sipritz. "Set course for LinHo station, Navigation. Full ID."

"Setting course for LinHo station, full ion drive, Captain. Estimating arrival in . . . 12 hours, 42 minutes."

"Go when ready, helm."

"Aye, Cap. New course now."

"Okay. Mo, I want damage reports from all sections and the casualty list from Doc Berta as soon as you can get them to me. Arnett, stand down from battlestations."

The next few hours passed in a blur of orders given

and decisions made, some of them difficult; of questions asked and answers returned, some of which he didn't want to hear; of reports and responses and proposed workarounds for impossible disasters. His ship was cut and bleeding in a dozen places, not to mention the serious limp represented by the lost jump matrix. Worst of all, Sam had lost family—three of his crew dead on the *Shadowhawk* alone, five more seriously injured, a couple dozen banged up enough to need attention in Sickbay. And the *Fleeflek* . . .

What they needed was a long rest in a decent watering hole, not a forced layover in a garbage pit like LinHo. But it was the middle of the third watch, and Sam was too tired to think about that now. He rose from his seat on the bridge and stretched.

He put a hand on Mo's broad shoulder. "I'm hitting the rack."

Mo straightened from his data screen. "I'll be here." He had the next watch, but Sam knew the XO wasn't referring to his location. "How long until they come after us?"

"Hell, I don't know why they came after us the first time. Maybe they'll let us go."

Mo shrugged. "Maybe. Or maybe we're carrying something they want to get rid of."

Sam stared at him. "Rayna? Kind of a lot of trouble just to kill one agent, don't you think?" *No matter how tough she is.*

"Maybe you're right. Maybe she's just bad luck."

Anger flared, bright and hot. A sailor's luck was a

touchy subject; Rayna was a touchy subject.

"Not for me. Or for the 'hawk either. If it hadn't been for her we'd have been blown into a thousand pieces today, and don't you forget it."

Mo's dark jaw clenched. "Oh, it's like that, then."

"Yeah, it is most definitely like that." He waited.

The Pataran shook his head, giving up, and returned to the original question. "I expect to see that Gray ship at LinHo. For some reason, I think they'll have business there."

"The same business Rayna has?" Something twisted in his gut.

Mo's gaze drilled into him. "Only you and she know what that is."

"Ha. Well, I can tell you that plan went to hell when the *Fleeflek* was lost." Hot pain slashed through his chest at the thought of the people he'd lost along with the doomed ship—not only Manneh, one of his best and brightest, but 15 others, along with 560 lucky ones, now not so lucky, and ten of the ship's original crew. *So many.*

"Cap?"

He stared at the viewscreen, but it showed nothing but a few pinpricks of light. "Did you say something?"

"The partingways. For Manneh and the others. I thought it best to get it done before we hit LinHo. Say 0930 tomorrow morning?"

"Yeah. Put the word out." He swallowed, but couldn't seem to get past a lump in his throat. "You know I've got to contact Drew Vort to get the permissions to dock on LinHo."

"*Shalssit.*   That   bastard   wouldn't   give   you directions to the sunrise."

Sam grunted with something less than amusement. "No kidding.   But if he wants me to make that rendezvous in the Norian Sector, he'll have to agree to it. We need repairs."

"Expensive repairs. In a closed port. How do you know Vort can even get you onto LinHo?"

"He's got the contracts to supply synthohol to what passes for drinking establishments on that rock."

Mo laughed. "What? All three of them? What kind of profit can there be in that?"

"None.   It's the smuggling trade that brings the profit—off-the-books slaves, real liquor, drugs, both recreational and medicinal."

His XO scowled, and Sam nodded. "Yeah. Vort's a real sweetheart."

"He   wouldn't   stop   at   bounty   hunting,   then,   I imagine."

"No." Sam suddenly felt very weary. "I just have to get in and out of LinHo before he makes a move."

Mo watched him with his ebony jaw clenched tight.

"I know, I know."   Sam shook his head.   The last place he'd wanted to go and he would be there in less than eight hours. "I have to go send that message, then I'm done.   I'll see you at the service."   With a final glance at his crew, the captain of the *Shadowhawk* left the bridge, thinking only of how soon he could put his arms around his woman and sink into oblivion.

The Gray captain was in a howling rage, though there was no judging it from his placid, moon-like face. His large, liquid black eyes blinked with seeming calm over his tiny, upturned mouth, and he stood nearly motionless as he addressed the two Thranes towering above his desk.

Ah, but his aura! Zetana thought. The captain of the Minertsan cruiser *Tifan* was not bothering to hide his emotions; the energy around his small body was awash in the colors of blood and deepest nightmares.

--My ship is damaged! I have lost many crewmen! Not only have you failed in your mission to infiltrate the Kinz factory, but we have lost a shipload of valuable slaves. My superiors will no doubt insist that I bind you in chains and deliver you for trial for your part in this. Then they will have my head!

--Captain, the loss of the Fleeflek *is indeed regrettable, but the ship was an enemy combatant. And Captain Murphy has been terrorizing your space trade for years.* Zetana refused to be intimidated by this slimehole. *You have won a brave and difficult battle, and eliminated this threat to your profits! He will steal your slaves no more. Your crewmen died in a glorious cause. They are heroes to the Consortium, are they not?*

The captain considered this, his aura lightening to a mere thunderous gray. *Perhaps it could be made to seem so.*

--Of course. The Shadowhawk *has been destroyed—by the* Tifan! *There is no reason to think the mission is a failure. The slaves bound for Kinz must be replaced—and quickly. We'll be among that shipment.*

--But where will we get such a shipment? And repairs to my ship? And my superiors—

Rex's confidence bordered on arrogance. *I can arrange a trade with some allies on Paradon, near the C3 jump. It will mean a few days' delay, but I believe you'll find my friends reasonable.*

The captain's aura flashed dark again, but Zetana didn't miss the tinge of green that indicated fear. She suppressed her own smirk.

--Paradon! Murderers and thieves! You expect me to trust them?

--Engineers, mechanics and traders! Rex spread his hands. *And you can trust us. While your ship is being repaired I will negotiate the purchase of a small shipment of slaves for delivery to Kinz. It won't replace what was aboard the* Fleeflek, *but it will be welcome under the circumstances. The profit will be all yours, and Zetana and I will be able to infiltrate the new shipment as before.*

An unreadable mix of murky color swirled about the Minertsan's body. Zetana reined in an urge to reach out and grab the creature's limp little gray arm and snatch his thoughts from his bulbous head.

--You expect me to believe your 'friends' can

produce a shipment of slaves out of the mud—not to mention the parts and expertise I need to repair my engines?

Zetana's bondmate was unperturbed. *Captain. My friends can produce virtually anything out of the 'mud,' as you say, of Paradon.* He grinned. *For a price.*

The worm drew himself up. *And if I don't wish to pay their price?*

Zetana lost patience. *Then they will kill you. It's either deal with Paradon or crawl back to the Consortium at half-ion speed, your mission a failure and with no proof of your great triumph over the* Shadowhawk. *I suspect things would not go well for you under those circumstances, Captain.*

Angry red boiled through the midnight black of the captain's aura once more. *Very well. We set course for Paradon. But I warn you I have my own skills in negotiation. If the price of repairs is too steep, I will sell you to the highest bidder on that piece of stinking rock and take my chances back home.*

Zetana smiled. Of course the little algae-eater had no chance of following through on his threat. But she liked him for having the tiny balls to make it.

Rayna woke in the semi-dark of the cabin, cocooned in the heavy warmth of Sam's arms. He slept on, undisturbed, curled at her back, but though it had only been a few hours since they had fallen exhausted into bed together, Rayna's worries had pulled her out of sleep.

They were going to LinHo after all. Daniel was still in place dirtside; he had the contacts that could get her into the Kinz facility. The mission could go on. She'd be able to do the job she'd come here to do. She should feel great about that; she should be jumping for joy.

Instead she was miserable.

Rayna would gladly stay in this bunk with Sam Murphy for the next twentydays and Rescue be damned. Let Daniel go inside that freaking weapons factory and work 18 hours a day; let him sleep in the stinking, cold slave barracks, piled up with a couple dozen other lice-infested bodies just to keep warm. Let *him* fight for food and a place in the pecking order until the others began to respect him, in the long, dragging time before the work could even begin. *Shit!*

All she wanted was Sam. The one thing she could never have.

She'd been a fool to think—well, what was the use? She had a job to do, an important job, one that mattered. People depended on her to do it, lives depended on it. She couldn't just quit.

And Sam—he may have been a pirate, but his crew depended on him just as much as her partners depended on her. Their lives were tied to his; they respected him, even loved him. Rescue was wrong about him; he did as much good in his own maverick way as they did. She couldn't ask him to give up his world for hers any more than she could for him.

So they were stuck. And LinHo would be goodbye, probably forever. God, that *hurt*.

"What's wrong, Little Bit?" Sam's breath was warm in her ear. "Can't sleep?"

She turned in his arms and reached up to touch his face. "Sorry if I woke you."

"No." He took a breath. "I have my own reasons for lying awake tonight."

His lost crew. His damaged ship. A ceremony to send his shipmates and friends on their way to the next world in a few hours. Rayna could feel the hurt squeezing his chest with every beat of his heart beneath her hand.

"I know. I'm sorry, sweets."

His fingers stroked down her cheek to lift her chin. "A few days ago I didn't even know you. Now I can't imagine . . . " His gaze held hers. "Tell me you're not going to do something crazy on LinHo."

She shook free of him. "I don't want to talk about LinHo."

He pulled away and sat up. "We'll hit orbit in less than six hours. When exactly did you plan to talk about it?"

"When I no longer have a choice."

"Consider that now, Rayna. We've got things to settle."

There was no trace of humor in the set of Sam's features. There was only raw emotion—anger and determination and something that looked too much like fear. Her heart stumbled in response.

"There's nothing to talk about, Sam. I won't know what will happen until I get to LinHo and make contact with my partner."

"So you're going through with this."

Tell him you don't want to. "You know I have to."

"Damn it, Rayna!" Sam threw off the covers and launched himself from the bunk. He began a clenched pacing in the confined space between the bunk and the hatch leading to the head. "This mission was a suicide run from the get-go; it's brought nothing but disaster onto my ship, and you think you can just carry on with it like nothing's happened? The sabotage, the Thrane assassin, the Gray ship—none of that's coincidence, you know. It's connected to you and LinHo. Your cover's blown, Rayna! The mission's over!"

"My cover?" She'd been running through this argument in her head for the last hour. He wouldn't win it. "First of all, everyone on that Gray ship thinks I'm dead. Secondly, they all work for the Minertsan military. The LinHo factory is producing weapons for the Gray rebels—the *other side*. Those slaves were bound for a rebel factory, so the Thranes onboard the *Fleeflek* were working undercover, like me. Who's going to tell?"

"We don't know that, Ray. All we know is that we've been beat to shit and barely survived to tell the tale. You're walking into a deathtrap on LinHo, and you're walking into it blind."

"I'll know more when I talk to Daniel." She stood

up and blocked Sam's restless pacing. "I know what I'm doing, Sam. It's my job, like being captain of this ship is yours. You have to trust me."

"I do!" He gripped her arms, fought for control. Then, more quietly, "I do. You saved my ship yesterday. You've shown more guts and brains in the few days I've known you than some men I've known for ten circuits." He stopped, swallowed hard. "But you can't control everything, Ray. No matter what you do, sometimes things go wrong. Sometimes people die."

She knew it was true, but she had to convince him otherwise. "Not this time. Not me. And not you."

He took her face between his large hands and brought her mouth to his. His kiss was warm and soft, his breath sighing across her lips. "Rayna . . ."

She put her arms around his neck and nestled near to him, needing these last moments of closeness with him. He bent and lifted her into his embrace, her legs circling his waist, as though she weighed nothing. He deepened his kiss, and it was as if she could taste his longing and desperation. She answered him back with her own as the heat rose between them. The ache between her legs became a molten throb. She moved, seeking relief. He groaned, and pressed her against the hard ridge of flesh that marked his arousal.

Yes, there! God, again! She attacked his mouth, spearing deep while she moved against him and was vaguely aware of Sam staggering under the assault. But, no, he was just maneuvering closer to the bunk, and now she was standing, ripping at his clothes and hers until they were naked and falling into the bunk.

Then he was hovering over her, his eyes asking permission, and *God, yes, don't waste time!* She was wet and ready and when he joined them, *Jesus!* he felt like heaven inside her. He thrust deep, setting every nerve ending alight. Again and again, bringing her to the edge of pain. Fire swept through her and she came, a wordless scream torn from her throat.

She clung to him, urging him deeper, harder as the first orgasm rolled through her and blossomed into the second with hardly a breath between them. She sobbed his name, lost now in the sweet oblivion of connection, her body to his, her heart to his. They moved together and with every stroke she could feel his barely-held control, the quivering tension in the muscles of his thighs under her hands as she pulled him into her, the sweat slicking the skin of his back. His heart hammered; she could feel it against her ribs. He groaned, close, so close to his own heaven, and the vibrations filled her chest.

Her body responded with a fresh surge of desire, the blood running hot in her veins. His strokes were coming faster, harder as he came to the end of his control, and she couldn't speak, she couldn't breathe. She could only hold on as the beautiful, blinding pleasure blasted through her once more. Sam moaned and drove forward, every muscle tensing as he found his own release.

For several long moments neither of them moved. Rayna hardly felt capable of it. And to speak would only break the spell they had woven with their bodies and their sweat and their passion. She didn't want this moment to end.

Sam lifted his head at last and shifted his body to her side. He kissed her, a tender brushing of his warm lips against hers.

"I love you, Little Bit. No matter what happens tomorrow, that won't change."

She looked up at him, at his strong jaw and his earnest green eyes, and tried to memorize every detail. She told him she loved him too, but she was all too aware that wouldn't be enough. They might love each other, but after tomorrow, they would likely never see each other again.

CHAPTER FIFTEEN

"Haven't seen much of you lately." Lainie caught Rayna in the corridor not far from the D-mat room. She didn't look happy. "Is it true what everyone's been saying?"

Rayna swallowed a curse. Could it really be all over the ship already? She would have thought with all that had been going on, people would have more to worry about than who was in the captain's cabin and what they were doing there.

She stalled. "What do you mean?"

"You're leaving the ship today?" Lainie saw her expression—relief, Rayna guessed—and scowled. "You could have told somebody."

"This is my stop."

"LinHo? You've got to be kidding! It's the worst ass-dump in the galaxy!" Lainie's gaze sharpened to a knife-edge. "What the hell kind of business could anyone have here?"

Rayna grabbed her arm and pulled her into the bulkhead, out of the path of several crew members coming down the corridor. "Whatever business would be mine, don't you think?"

Lainie's mobile face was set in stone. "There are only two reasons anyone comes to LinHo. They're brought here as slaves. Or they have something to do with Kinz. I don't see any chains on you."

"Your whole ship is here, Lainie!" Rayna was backpedaling, trying to distract the kid from the truth.

"My captain is trying to get us away from here as fast as he can. Why would you want to stay?"

God, the kid is as stubborn as a Meringean stumppuller. "I can't tell you. This wasn't my plan, but it's the best I can do under the circumstances."

"And what about Cap?"

Rayna's eyebrows shot up. "What about him?"

"You're going to tell me he's happy about this?"

"You don't even know what 'this' is!" Her frustration with this conversation had hit its limit. "I'm going. Nice knowing you, kid."

"You think you can do something about Kinz." The kid shook her head, hard. "You can't."

"What d'you mean, I can't?"

"I mean, don't. I mean, if you go in there you'll never come out. I mean, if you do this, whatever it is, you're a *shalssiti* idiot, I don't care who you work for or what they pay you or what they hope to get out of it. Kinz is hell, that's all."

"Lainie—"

But the girl shook off Rayna's grip and fled down the corridor, leaving Rayna to wonder how a 17-year-old former street urchin could know so much about the Kinz weapons factory.

Sam hadn't been inclined to like this, and now he was sure.

Rayna had insisted on meeting her contact in the lowest dive down the dirtiest alley in LinHo's only settlement (a town so far undistinguished by any name). The place stank of sour synthohol, mushroom beer, sweat and urine. Drinkers shrank into the dark corners, shoulders hunched and eyes too aware.

The man was waiting for them at a corner table of his own, and when Rayna headed in his direction, Sam's pulse kicked up a notch. "Daniel's *Pataran*?"

Ray shot him a quelling glance. "Half. So?"

Sam shook his head. Just not what he'd expected. He'd thought maybe a pale, skinny type, full of the earnest fire of well-meaning righteousness. This guy looked like he could throw a punch. He looked like he *wanted* to throw a punch.

The man stood as they reached the table, distrust twisting the handsome features of his dark face. Not as tall as Mo, but tall enough.

"Who the hell is this?" The question was for Rayna, but his bright blue eyes never left Sam.

"Hello to you, too." Rayna sank into a chair. "This is Sam Murphy, captain of the *Shadowhawk*. Anything else is none of your business." She looked up at Daniel, who still towered over her. "You stand there any longer and you'll attract attention."

He sat, still staring. Sam did the same, giving no ground. He moved his chair close to Rayna's and watched as Daniel's gaze narrowed. *What the hell?*

Sam sought an answer from Rayna, but she refused to look at him.

"I assume you've been brought up to speed," she said to Daniel.

The man at last took his attention off Sam and turned to her. "The latest ion packet from HQ says some idiot fucked up half a circuit of planning by 'rescuing' your cover ship." He glared across the table. "This the idiot?"

Sam leaned forward. "Look—Daniel, is it? You may be Ray's friend, but I'm not feeling the love here. Your *cover* ship was a slaver. I don't tolerate slavers any more than you do."

"Oh, yeah? So where are those slaves, Captain—you sell 'em?"

Sam grabbed the man's shirt, and only Rayna's swift intercession stopped him from slamming Daniel's head into the table. "Sam, don't! He doesn't know. And we can't afford to cause a scene. Back off. Both of you."

Sam released the man and sat back, the adrenaline still running hot in his bloodstream. Daniel shrugged his collar back in place and turned back to Rayna.

"What don't I know? Since apparently it's a lot."

"Two Thrane agents were undercover with me on the *Fleeflek*. When Sam boarded the slaver, they took their own measures to try to get it back. When that didn't work, they contacted their friends on a Gray cruiser for pickup, sabotaged the *Shadowhawk* and escaped onto the Gray ship. The cruiser attacked the *'hawk*, and the *Fleeflek* was destroyed in the battle. All the slaves and 19 of Sam's crew were lost."

The Pataran was silent for a long moment, absorbing the story. Then he pinned Sam with his intense blue gaze once more.

"Forgive my ignorance, Captain. I'm sorry for your lost crew."

An olive branch. Sam gritted his teeth and accepted it with a nod.

Daniel turned back to Rayna. "Are you all right?" He touched her, a bare, light brush of fingertips on her forearm where it rested on the table next to him. And suddenly Sam knew—he knew why this guy rubbed him raw, why nothing the man said or did would ever be right enough. Sam's eyes flicked up to take in Rayna's reaction, his heart in his throat.

She moved her arm, frowning. "I'm fine. It was close, but Sam knows what he's doing."

Sam breathed again.

Daniel considered him for the briefest moment and moved on. "So what happened to the Gray ship?"

Sam shook his head. "We were lucky to escape with our lives. I wasn't tracking their ion trail. But I wouldn't be surprised to see them turn up here."

"Here? You're the only ship that's docked in the last tendays. Do they still have a reason to chase you?"

"Not me." Sam nodded at Rayna. "Our mutual friend here."

"The Thranes had a mission, just like I do," she said. "I say they've given up on it. Sam says otherwise."

"Anyone who'll go to the trouble to try to hijack one ship, then sabotage and attack another doesn't give up easy," Sam argued. "They'll convince that Gray captain to bring them here, and when they see you, you're dead."

"What?" Daniel whipped around to gawp at her. "They know what you look like?"

Rayna shot him a look that should have dropped him where he sat. "That's why I need to get into that factory ASAP. If I'm in place when they come in, there'll be nothing they can say without blowing their own covers."

"*Borz* shit!" Daniel's fist came down on the table, making the mugs jump. "There are dozens of ways they can expose you!"

Sam's estimation of the man rose a millimeter, but Rayna was having none of it. "And I them. I'll have had time to establish myself before they get there if you can get me in soon. You know how things work inside. That will give me the advantage. But I need to go *now*!"

"Rayna, it's too dangerous." Sam was pleading with her. He hadn't stopped pleading with her since last night on the ship.

Daniel's blue gaze slipped from Rayna to Sam and back again. "I have to agree with him, Ray. How about you go back to base, and we'll try this again in a few twentydays?"

"We won't have another chance, and you know it."

Rayna's tiny body was quivering with the need to move, but there was no place for her to go. She looked from Sam to Daniel with fire in her dark gaze; Sam had to control an urge to move back. "The Thranes are up to something. If they haven't gone home, they'll be here to finish it. And if not those two, then someone else. I don't know what they want, but I sure as hell won't find out by going back to base to sit on my ass for sixty days. I'm going in. Now, are you going to help me, or not?"

Of course, she gave him little choice, and in the end, Daniel caved. Just as Sam had caved eight hours earlier. They worked out the details of the plan while he sucked down the miserable mushroom beer by the mugful, with no hope of getting drunk and even less of drowning the ache in his chest.

Rayna nodded at the empties cluttering the table in front of him. "You still up for this?"

"My head's still clear if that's what you're asking."

Her jaw clenched. "Good to know."

Daniel stood. "There's a spacers' bar in dock dome—Alpha C. Meet me there in ten minutes. Make it look good." Then he was gone, weaving his way through the tables to the exit.

Rayna followed Daniel's movement through the crowd, but made no move to stand. She looked back at Sam, laid a hand on his arm.

"I wish . . ." She held his gaze for a second more,

then exhaled.

"I know. Me, too." He got up and pulled her with him. There was no use wishing for what couldn't be. She'd made up her mind. And any goodbyes they'd likely ever say to each other had been said last night.

They plowed their way through the drunken crowd to the alley. Outside, the recycled air of the envirodome stank of ozone and sewage and the faint off-gassing of the ion plant that powered the settlement, but it was fresher than the fetid swamp of the bar they had just left. Sam took a deep breath, trying without success to expand his chest beyond a tight band of heartache and dread.

He followed Rayna down the alley and out into a dimly-lit street, deserted at this hour and gritty with the fine sand that blew or was tracked in constantly from outside the dome. Filth lingered in the gutters, reeking and resistant to any efforts to flush it down the "storm" drains. Along the street a jumble of buildings leaned against each other for mutual support. Some had been constructed in the usual way from plasform bloc or durasteel framing. Most were just shipping containers with a hole cut here and there for entry and ventilation.

They ducked down into the entrance to the tunnel that would take them under 200 meters of blasted, lifeless surface to the dome housing the dock facilities. The tunnel wasn't empty—storage units lined the engineered walls, with guards posted at regular intervals to make sure no one found a home among the neatly stacked rectangles. Sam gripped Rayna's arm now—part of their plan—and led the way. They didn't linger, but emerged into the dock dome as quickly as they could get there.

It wasn't hard to find the block with the bar Daniel had mentioned. Bright neon seared the murk announcing "Alpha C—Ale and Syn." Sam drew Rayna deeper into the narrow alley across the street, away from the light. She sank into his arms, and he held her close while the last precious seconds ticked away. There was nothing to be said, except with the touch of skin on skin, of warmth on warmth, no comfort except knowing she felt the same pain he felt. He drew back to kiss her, and it was all he could do to let her go again.

But she was stronger than he was. When their brief time ran out, she turned from him and led him out of the alley.

From that moment on they played their roles. He gripped her arm as if she would escape him; she tugged at him and tested him like a shackled criminal. By the time they burst through the door to Alpha C, some of the anger and frustration they were showing was real—and everyone in the place could see it.

She snarled at him, and he threw her in front of him toward the table in the corner, where Daniel waited in full sight of most of the patrons. "I hope to hell you're ready to take this bitch off my hands," he announced when he got there.

Daniel stood and made a too-obvious attempt to shush him. "Shut the fuck up!"

Sam pulled out a chair for Rayna and forced her to sit. When she scrambled away, he grabbed her around the waist and planted her again, then reached for his stunner and stuck it in her ribs.

"Sit!" He looked at Daniel. "You have restraints?" When the Pataran passed the nerve cuffs over, he linked her wrists behind her back. "Should have done this myself back on the ship, but I thought she'd cooperate, given her circumstances. Not like there's any place to hide on this shithole." He huffed. "That's what I get for thinking." He glared at her. "You know those get tighter the more you struggle, right, sweetheart?"

She snapped at him with sharp, white teeth, then subsided into a sulk.

Daniel exhaled loudly. "Portal's balls! Are you done? You talk more than my mother! I'll give you 300 credits for her and our business is finished."

"Three hundred? You can't be serious. I hear the factory just lost a whole shipment of slaves. They must be desperate for labor, especially skilled labor. I'll need a thousand at least."

Daniel laughed. "Not in a million circuits. You think they're so desperate, you just march right up to the factory gates and try to offload your valuable merchandise directly. See how far you get."

"Maybe I will."

"And maybe they'll throw you both in the pit. I'm sure your XO is looking forward to taking over command of your ship."

Sam leaned forward. "They'd do that?"

Daniel met him halfway across the table. "In a heartbeat."

The *'hawk's* captain sat back. "I gotta show a profit on this. She's been a lot of trouble. And don't tell me they aren't looking for the help. Seven hundred fifty."

"Oh, they're looking, all right. But if I show up with this bright-and-shiny right now, suspicion falls on me. Plus, she's obviously either never been mindwiped, or she's *seriously* resistant."

Sam grinned. "Which is it, sweetheart?"

Rayna looked up from her supposed contemplation of a bleak future. "Fuck you."

"I'd say never been mindwiped *and* seriously resistant." Daniel crossed his arms over his chest. "That makes her a liability, not an asset. Four hundred."

"She's, uh, spunky. And strong! Six hundred."

"She's stubborn. And mean. Four-fifty."

A *sotto-voce* hiss finished the negotiations. "She's also sitting right here and can kick both your asses. Make it five hundred and shut up!"

Sam and Daniel exchanged a quick glance of amused kinship before the full weight of the moment descended. The scene played out and much show was made of the "payment" of credits. Daniel stood and drew Rayna up with him, her left bicep held firmly in one large hand. She held Sam's gaze as she rose to her feet. Then she turned and allowed her captor to pull her away.

She didn't look back.

Sam lifted a hand to the harried woman running ale from the bar to the tables and soon had a flagon of dark synthohol and a shot glass in front of him. He touched the commpiece in his ear to hail the ship.

Mo's voice answered. "It's done?"

"Yeah. I'm on to the drowning-my-guilt part now."

"This was her choice, not yours."

"Yeah, and I just stood back and let it happen. That'll be a great comfort when she winds up dead."

"Don't go there, Cap. She was doing this long before she met you. She knows how to take care of herself."

Sam nodded and downed a fistful of the bitter synthohol. "Right. You're right. She doesn't need me. She'll be fine. See? I feel better already."

Mo snorted. "I should come down."

"No. Somebody has to watch the ship."

"Kwan, then."

"Right." He drank again. "I owe him a drink. Where is he?"

"Dirtside. I'll send him over. Where are you?"

He wished he'd never heard of the place. "Alpha C. Near the docks. Tell him to get a move on. I'm drinking syn, and you know I hate that shit."

CHAPTER SIXTEEN

Lainie waited in the alley across from the Alpha C, melted into the shadows so she was indistinguishable from the darkness as she'd learned to do long ago. No one saw her there as they went in and out of the bar. She, on the other hand, had seen everyone since Cap had gone in shoving Rayna ahead of him like some kind of criminal.

The sight of it was like a lump of rancid meat in her stomach. What the hell was he doing?

There had been rumors on the ship. Rayna'd been seen coming out of Cap's cabin. People thought he'd taken a lover at last; they were happy for him. Lainie was secretly even happier it had been Rayna, someone who didn't suck. But now this? This didn't make sense.

She kicked the pitted corner of the plascrete wall beside her with a scuffed boot and paced a tight, angry pattern in her pool of shadows. *Fuck them both, anyway! What the hell is going on in there?*

Lainie still didn't know what kind of impulse had made her sweet talk her friend in the D-Mat room into allowing her onto the shore leave party. Why in hell follow Rayna and the Captain down from the ship? Curiosity, yeah. More like suspicion. Or fascination. She just couldn't help wondering what the woman was up to. And if Rayna got herself in another jam like the one she'd been in on the ship, Cap would have to pull her out of it this time. Might be entertaining.

Lainic'd peeled off from the boisterous gang of her shipmates and caught up with the two of them as they made their way through the alleys to the first bar in the residential dome, then back to this dump near the docks. She'd lost track of them once or twice, forced to drop back out of sight, but she didn't think she'd missed anything significant. If only she could make sense of what she was seeing.

The door to the bar swung open and Lainie stared, thinking, *Now, why would Cap pass her off to Mo?* But the Pataran holding Rayna unnaturally close wasn't nearly as tall as the *'hawk's* XO, and his skin was lighter. He was every bit as grim as Mo, though, his face drawn into a vicious snarl, his gaze alert for threats from any side.

Shalssiti pultafa! She didn't want to believe it, but there it was, as plain as the shit in the gutter at her feet. Cap had sold Rayna out. Maybe it was a deal gone wrong; maybe whatever Rayna had planned on LinHo got in Cap's way. *Perai*, maybe he just needed the fucking credits. She never would have thought her captain capable of it, but the two of them had gone in that bar and now the woman she'd started to think of as a friend was coming out the prisoner of a bounty hunter. Lainie's fists clenched in helpless rage at her sides. Her breath struggled to escape the band that tightened around her chest. And her heart—her heart wanted to break out of her ribcage and bleed all over the street.

Rayna and her captor were disappearing around the next corner. If Lainie had any chance of helping her, she had to act. She took off at a fast jog, hanging far enough back that they wouldn't see her, while still keeping them in sight. Street after street, turn after turn, she followed them, until it became horrifyingly clear what their destination was.

"Shit, no, Ray, you can't let him take you there!" The words came out in an angry, frightened hiss as she panted along in the shadows behind them. "Do something! You'll be there soon!"

She took a left through an alleyway and poured on speed, hoping to cut them off. The Pataran was big, but maybe with the two of them and the element of surprise, they could overcome him. He didn't have a weapon trained on Ray—that was good. She saw the alley entrance up ahead, knew she'd be there ahead of them. She grinned and palmed her *slith*. Maybe this would work out okay.

Then she heard the barest scrape of boots on pavement behind her, caught the flutter of movement in corner of her eye and before she could turn to see, felt the explosion of pain in the back of her head. Her knife slipped from her hand. And everything went dark.

"Well, ain't you in a sorry state. I'd offer to buy you a drink, but it looks like you've already had a few too many."

Sam raised his head from his hand and glared upwards. *Fuck.*

"Drew Vort. I suppose I can't avoid having you sit down."

"Don't mind if I do." Vort was human—mostly—but he'd had enhancements, both genetic and biomechanical, years ago when he'd competed on the underground fight circuit. The battles had taken their toll on the man, who moved slowly to sit. Still, Sam wasn't fooled. Vort was as dangerous as he'd ever been.

"What do you want, Vort?"

"What? I can't buy an old friend a drink?" He picked up the flagon from the table, found it empty, and signaled the bar girl with a massive hand. "You're here. I'm here. LinHo is a garbage pit with few distractions. Why not take advantage?"

Sam's mouth turned up in a bitter smile. "Take advantage. You do that so well."

"Aw, come on, Sammy boy! I thought my help getting you here made us square." The girl brought a fresh flagon of synthohol and a glass for Vort. He poured out two shots. "Let's drink to it, hmm? No more old scores to settle, no more past hurts? You forget about that little deal gone bad on Alberon, I forget about . . . well, so many things."

Sam's jaw went tight. The "deal" on Alberon had been a clusterfuck that cost him not only credits but two crew members. That was after too many business ventures with Vort had ended up with the profit heavy on the fighter's side.

Sam left his glass on the table. "I can't see where you'd have much to blame me for."

"No?" Vort's smile showed a jaw full of shark's teeth. "It seems we've become competitors, Sammy. Where once we were partners. We had a rendezvous planned in the Norian Sector. A business deal of mutual benefit. Looks like that won't be happening."

"Had to take a little detour thanks to the *shalssiti* Grays. Wasn't like I had a choice."

"Oh, we all have choices, my friend. How about I give you one now?"

"It's a free galaxy."

The big man laughed. "No, actually, it's not. There's a price on everything. The Rescue agent you smuggled onto LinHo, for example."

Sam's breath left his lungs. He reached for the full shot glass and tossed it down his throat.

When he'd recovered from the burn, he spoke. "What the hell are you talking about? I needed repairs to my ship. LinHo is the only dock within 50 parsecs."

"That's true, but it's not all the truth, Sammy." Vort watched him from behind a smirk. "I have this place locked up—every barkeep, every alleyrat, every mech/tech with a crank habit. They all talk to me, Sam. I know your *real* business. What I don't know— for sure—is whether you've still got your hands on the goods. If so, you're in luck. Give the woman to me and go on your way. The Grays will pay me a nice bounty for her ass. If she's already gone, I'll take you instead. ConSys Intel would be glad to give me a high stack of credits for you."

Sam tensed, gathering his legs under him to make a run for it. Through the buzz of the synthohol in his brain he heard the whine of a laze pistol on stun close to his right ribcage. He turned to see the man holding it sitting in the seat behind him. A glance around the room told him Vort had plenty of backup ready to make sure he wouldn't get out the door. He was just drunk enough to give one nanosecond's thought to fighting anyway. The tight press of the pistol in his side finally dissuaded him. Alcohol and a Level 1 stun made an ugly mix.

He exhaled and sat back in his chair. "Looks like you won the big prize, asshole. There's no one here but me."

Vort lifted a shoulder. "Well, I would have taken you both anyway, but I hate dealing with the *mulaak* Grays. ConSys, on the other hand, is easy pickings—like a vacation on the old home planet, eh, Sammy? Lots of sunshine and fresh air? Oh, but that's right, guess you wouldn't appreciate that much after you've spent 12 hours a day in the fields growing up."

Sam kept his expression carefully neutral. "What the hell are you blubbering about?"

"Oh, you know what I'm talking about." Vort wheezed out an unpleasant laugh. "I did some research on you, *Captain* Murphy. I know where you really come from. Maybe I should check into auctioning you off. ConSys has a fat bounty on you, but no doubt the Grays would be happy to get you back—the former slave who devils their trade routes."

Vort stood and gestured to the man who held the laze pistol. Sam was hauled roughly to his feet. His hands were pulled behind him and bound with nerve cuffs, as Rayna's had been such a short time earlier. Sam couldn't help but see the irony as he was frog-marched out of the Alpha-C behind the broad back of Drew Vort.

"I have two contacts on the women's side of the factory." Daniel had pulled her into an alley within sight of the Kinz gates for his final briefing. "Neko, a guard on the factory floor, can always get a message to me. He'll find you as soon as he can. Brilly works in the mess hall; you'll know her by the missing tooth. She'll get you extra food, utensils for weapons, supplies of all kinds. You'll be put on night-shift loading detail at first; new arrivals always get the heaviest work. It will be exhausting, so don't bother to try to do anything beyond your shift. While you're working, just keep your eyes open for where they keep the shipping data."

Rayna held up a hand. "Daniel. You don't have to tell me how to do my job."

He took a breath, nodded. "Yeah. Okay. But this place is different, all right, Ray? It's dangerous."

"Like Riza wasn't? I can do this."

"I know." His hand lifted toward her face, but dropped before he touched her. "What's with you and Blackbeard?"

"What?" She stilled, impatience warring with the feeling that she'd been caught doing something she shouldn't.

"You know who I mean. The pirate. Is it serious?"

"His name is Sam, and are you fucking kidding me?" She blew out a breath in exasperation. "We don't have time for a discussion of my love life. I have a job to do."

"So do I. Believe it or not, Rescue pays me to watch out for you. And even if they didn't I'd still think it was my responsibility."

"Your responsibility ends at my cabin door, Daniel." The look she gave him deliberately held no warmth, no hint of what they might once have shared. "Are we clear?"

He didn't look away. "We're clear so long as you know I've always got your back."

"As far as Sam is concerned, you can relax. I won't need your help." She turned and walked away, forcing Daniel to move quickly to catch up. She was done talking. She was done thinking about Sam or Daniel or anything else. Time to suck it up and go to work.

They came out of the alley and went to the end of the street. They turned the corner and found themselves outside the Kinz gates.

Daniel yanked on her arms, and she growled to put

on an appropriate show for the gate guards. She heard laughter as the window opened to reveal two tall Ninoctins in the guard house.

"That you, Xter? Finally got one?" The guard examined Daniel's captive with interest.

His friend hung over his shoulder. "Yeah, I figured you was all talk and no bounty after all this time, Pataran!"

"You don't know my business, Fowk. Slaves don't pay enough to keep me in 'shroom ale. I just picked this one up on the street. Heard you were short."

"That's true enough," the first guard agreed. "We've even had amateurs scrapin' the bilges for bodies, the bosses are so desperate. Just sent one up a few tics ago."

"This 'un don't look like much," Fowk said with an analytical scowl. "Kinda small, ain't it?"

"Oh, she's got special skills. Some you don't want to know about." Rayna could sense Daniel's tension. This conversation had gone on long enough. "And I'm anxious to get her off my hands. I'll just go up to the office, okay?"

"Right." The first guard waved him on. "You know the way."

"Mind it don't escape before you get there. Dangerous little thing, it looks." Fowk punctuated his warning with a nasty laugh that followed them as they entered a smaller walk-through in the four-meter-high titanium gates of the facility.

The smaller gate clanged shut behind them, leaving

them in a wide quadrangle surrounded by the dark fortress-like hulks of the factory buildings. Inside the quad the constant hum of the factory heard throughout the LinHo dome became a pounding felt in the bones, an ache in the teeth. Rayna couldn't imagine what it would be like inside the looming buildings. The quad, like the rest of the open areas of the facility, was artificially lit as bright as the surface of any planet and watched from both manned towers and strategically-placed cameras. The contrast with the rest of bleak, sunless LinHo made Rayna's eyes hurt.

Daniel led her across the wide, empty space and down a neat path between the larger factory buildings to find the office. It was set off by itself in a one-story block building distinguished by windows and white paint. Outside, a line of miserable beings sat on the ground, watched over by several guards. Rayna saw one of them lift her head and breathed out a curse. *What the hell is she doing here?*

Lainie looked at her, then looked away without acknowledging her.

Daniel whipped around to look at Rayna. "What the hell?"

"Somebody from the ship. Must've gotten scooped up."

"Would she blow your cover?"

Lainie was ignoring her. "No."

"Then her problem, not yours. Keep your head in the game."

Daniel dragged her inside as if she was resisting

and threw her against the cage that separated the staff from everyone else. With her face pressed up against the metal grill, Rayna scanned the interior, noting the location of passcards, alarms, communications and locking controls, before she moved back.

Daniel opened negotiations. "I hear you're looking for talent."

The Ninoctin inside the cage stood up to look at what he'd brought and grunted. "You call that talent? Should we put her to cleaning the ductwork?"

"She's got mech/tech skills and nimble fingers. Just what you need."

The clerk growled. "Everybody starts in loading. She couldn't load her own ass."

"She's stronger than she looks. And if you don't bust her up too much, she'll more than earn her way later. I'll let her go for 1500."

"Fifteen hundred!" The Ninoctin threw back his head and laughed. While he was distracted, Rayna checked out the security in the office—sensor-cams at the corners, simple bars and single line lasers on the windows and doors.

"I happen to know you're short of workers. Maybe you're short of your quota for the twentydays, too, huh? And training new ones is a bitch." Daniel waved at the beaten, dejected creatures hunkering in the dirt outside the window. "You may get one or two line workers out of that bunch. Everyone else will die in the loading bays. You need my girl. She's done this kind of work before."

The Ninoctin perked up at this. "Oh, yeah? Where?"

"The Orrin assembly complex on Matilla before they went bust. I got a bid on some of the assets. She's the last of the lot."

"I'll give you a thousand."

"Thirteen fifty."

"She's too *small*, Pataran." The Ninoctin peered into Rayna's face. She kept her eyes as blank as possible. "Has she even been wiped?"

"Of course!"

The guard folded his arms over his chest and frowned. "She's resistant, isn't she."

"If she was that resistant, would she be here?" Daniel spread his hands. "You know what happens to resistant slaves—they find their way out or they die."

"Eleven hundred."

"Thirteen."

"Twelve—and that's my last offer."

Daniel smiled. "You have a deal, my friend."

The transaction was completed and Daniel left without a backward glance. As she was uncuffed and taken out to join the others, Rayna knew she should be relieved, even happy, that things had gone so well. Instead, she didn't have to put on an act to fit in with her fellow prisoners. She was every bit as miserable as they were.

CHAPTER SEVENTEEN

The quality of the neighborhoods had been declining steadily since Stephen Kwan had left the bar he'd been drinking in for the one called Alpha C. The neon had made the place easy to find, but now that he'd found it, he almost wished he hadn't. He paused in the alley across from the bar and considered.

"You sure Cap is here? In this dump?" Javin Darto was a good fellow to have along in a place like this, but he wasn't what you might call tactful.

"Stow it, Javin. What he's doing here is Cap's business, understand? And what we see and hear stays between us. That's an order."

The big man nodded. "Aye, sir."

Kwan regretted he hadn't brought a few more of his drinking companions along with him on this trip. From the looks of the place, he and Darto could use the backup. Doc Berta had been with them—Cap would need her if he'd been here drinking synthohol for long. Kwan sighed.

"Come on," he said, and started out across the street.

He pushed open the door of the bar and wrinkled his nose at the blast of warm, sour air that rushed out. It smelled as if the beings inside had been caged there for half a circuit; as if the room were a prison with rations of 'shroom ale and synthohol. Kwan edged in to stand against the wall, Darto at his side, and scanned the crowded tables for his captain.

"Do you see him?" The crewman stood a head taller than Kwan, but apparently was having no better luck.

"No. Let's go." Kwan led the way through the maze of tables to the bar, where a surly bartender was pouring ale for a single harried bargirl. He nodded to the man, who simply stared in reply. "We're looking for someone."

"Ain't we all. You drinking or you leaving?"

"Two ales. The man we're looking for is human, tall, dark hair, square jaw. Might have come in with a short woman, dark skin."

The barkeep set up two ales, cloudy and frothy. Kwan sniffed, and when it didn't smell too offensive, drank. The earthy taste was tolerable. Beside him, Darto coughed once, then drank his down.

"I mighta seen him earlier."

"Not here now?"

"Does it look like it?"

Kwan held on to his patience. "No. That's why I'm asking."

The bartender's lips twitched. "Musta left then. Not sure I remember exactly."

Kwan drew his datapad out of his pocket and entered a figure. "Suppose we add a tip to the bill?" He turned the pad in the bartender's direction. "Now, memory a little clearer?"

The man smiled. "Yeah, but you ain't gonna like

what you hear." He got out his own pad and they accomplished the transfer, then he put his elbows on the bar and leaned in. "Your boy comes in with the girl, like you said. Meets a Pataran and makes some kinda deal for her. The Pataran leaves with the girl and your man starts in on the syn hot and heavy. Not too long after, a guy shows up you don't wanna know and before you can say *whatthefuck* your boy is trussed up like a Norian pig and hustled out the door." The barkeep straightened and spread his hands. "That's the story as I seen it."

Kwan glanced at Darto and saw the same look of horror plastered on the kid's broad face that he was struggling to keep from his own. "Who was this guy you say I don't want to know?"

The bartender started to turn away; Kwan grabbed his shirt at the throat and pulled him close. "Maybe you don't realize who you're dealing with here. My captain—Captain Solomon Armstrong Murphy of the *Shadowhawk*—is missing. You've heard of the *Shadowhawk*, haven't you? I'm tired of pissing around. Tell me who took him."

"Shit! Okay." The words came out in a strangled squeak. Kwan let go and the bartender fell back, rubbing his reddened throat. "But he owns this place. He owns half of LinHo. It can't get back to him that I told you."

"Who. Took. Him."

"Drew Vort."

Darto's eyes got wide and round. "Holy *perai*! The

fighter?"

Kwan shot him a look. "Ex-fighter. He's been a blackjack for years."

"Why's he want the captain?"

The bartender leaned forward to hear the answer, so Kwan didn't give it. Instead, he asked his own question.

"Where did he take him?"

"That I don't know." The man stepped back out of reach. "And I wouldn't tell you even if I knew. I don't want to end up dead, too."

Darto looked to him, but Kwan shook his head. He knew their captain was in little danger of being killed as long as there was a possibility Vort could claim the bounty on him. Sam Murphy was wanted alive, for his knowledge of the blackjack galaxy in which he was a rare shining light. Vort had no fear that knowledge would lead to his own arrest—the fighter paid protection credits in too many high places to be worried.

"How long ago did they leave?" Kwan made certain the barkeep could see the business end of his stun gun peeking through the fold in his jacket.

"Long enough to board a ship and be out of orbit. Why don't you follow him, and good fucking riddance." The man turned and ducked behind a curtain into the back room.

Kwan snatched at Darto's sleeve. "Come on." They started toward the exit.

"Do you think he meant it? Cap's on a ship heading

out?"

"Pretty likely. Vort's after that bounty." They had to find a way to get to the captain before Vort turned him over to ConSys. And that wouldn't be easy in a ship without a functioning jump matrix. What he had growing in Engineering would take too long to do Cap any good, even with the RES fluid he'd miraculously been able to score earlier using the ship's last credits.

He snagged the serving girl as she passed. "Where can I find a game of Slash on this godsforsaken rock?"

The muscles of Drew Vort's stomach and abdomen had long since been layered over with fat, the formidable structure of his chest and shoulders and back obscured by excess bulk. But his sheer size was intimidating, and stripped down to boxer's shorts his arms and legs showed nothing but lean power. Sure, there were scars at the vulnerable knees and elbows, but Sam wasn't laying any bets that those joints were particularly weak. With enough credits, you could buy servos on the black market that were stronger than real joints, if you were willing to take the risk of certain heavy metals leaking into your body. Vort had the credits, and gods knew he didn't give a fuck.

"Like my PT deck, Sammy?" Vort waved at the converted cargo bay from the center of a full-sized fighting ring. "It's got state-of-the-art equipment. Too bad you won't feel like using it after I get done with you."

The goons on each of Sam's arms gave him a shove toward the ring. "Aren't you a little old and out of shape for this sort of thing, Vort? You retired—no, scratch that—you lost your last fight five circuits ago. Got pretty busted up, if I recall."

Black rage washed across Vort's face before he wrestled himself under control. "I won that fight. The judges were paid off." He forced a feral smile. "Besides, I keep in shape. Don't I, boys?"

His goons laughed.

Sam laughed, too. "Oh, I get it. By beating up on punks and women. Maybe a few Grays here and there? Sure."

Vort loosened his shoulders. "Why don't we find out? Come on up."

"What, I don't get any wraps?" He was stalling, angling for any advantage. Vort was going to wipe the deck with him, so he needed all the help he could get. He took off his shirt and his boots and socks slowly, watching as Vort made up his mind.

"Sure, why not? Wouldn't want the captain to hurt his soft, white hands, would we, boys?" The fighter gestured to someone on the side, who came to wrap Sam's hands in canvas bands to protect the knuckles from the blows. Vort's hands were wrapped in *psoros* leather—soft, pliable and virtually indestructible. It was going to hurt like hell to get hit with those hands, and Vort wouldn't feel a thing.

"So I'm guessing we've left LinHo already." Sam

knew they had; he'd felt the vibrations as the dock clamps had disengaged and the engines had kicked in. "Want to tell me where we're headed?"

Vort growled a warning. "Enough with the chit-chat. You know full well there's only one place we could be going—to the ConSys Fleet station on Madras to turn you in." He grinned. "Fortunately, ConSys doesn't specify in what condition I have to deliver your ass. Now get up here."

Sam climbed into the ring and faced off with the fighter, guard up and vulnerable areas turned away from his opponent. There were no rules to this fight; no refs or timeouts or neutral corners. Sam knew he was just here to take a beating. He aimed only to give as good as he got, to make Vort hurt so much he quit, preferably sometime before Sam was seriously injured.

His mentor had taught him to be aggressive against a stronger opponent, so he struck first, moving to the outside and attacking the knee with a side kick. But Vort simply picked up the leg to avoid the kick and swiped at Sam's head with a vicious hook. Sam danced out of the way with no harm done on either side, but his test had given him valuable information. He'd heard the servos whine when Vort moved the leg; that joint was not a vulnerable target.

He tried a few hard jabs to test out Vort's blocks. The man was like a brick wall. Vort answered with a flurry of his own, but it was slow; Sam was able to throw up his forearms and move out of the way of blows. He stepped in with a left hook and was met with a block that nearly took his arm out of the socket. But Vort's chin was open! He switched feet and brought up the uppercut, then stepped back and kicked as hard as he could toward the man's balls. *Eat this, you sonofabitch!*

The old man wasn't going down that easy. He caught Sam's foot mid-kick and started to twist. Sam was forced to push off or lose the ankle; he flipped and landed hard face down on the mat. He had just enough time to get to his back and swing his legs around before Vort reached him. He scissored one leg in front of Vort's knees, one leg behind, and took him down, then he rolled until he had the man face down in a leg lock.

He punched Vort's head and ears and the back of his neck over and over, but it seemed to do no good; the fighter kept bucking and growling like a maddened bear. The man had a good 30 kilos on him, and eventually that and the servos began to tell. Sam lost his hold and was forced to scramble to his feet and away from a bloodied and enraged opponent.

"I was just going to fuck you up, Sam Murphy." Vort spat blood onto the mat. "You should have just taken your beating like a good boy. Now I have to fucking kill you, you *mulaak* cocksucker."

The goons on the side didn't laugh. In fact, Sam thought they looked a little alarmed. Vort stalked across the mat and opened a barrage of kicks—straight, then roundhouse, then a spinning hook that Sam couldn't move fast enough to avoid. Vort's heel caught him square in the ribs. *Portal's fucking balls!* He backed up, doubled over, trying to protect his side where the ribs were probably broken, but Vort was coming at him, so he got his hands up. The fighter knocked his blocks aside and hit him once, twice, three times in the face and, *perai*, didn't that wake you the fuck up!

He went to his knees, knowing it was death, but his legs just wouldn't hold him. He heard voices in the distance trying to call Vort off, something about the bounty. *Yeah, you fucker, they won't pay for a dead body.*

Looked like Drew Vort had decided that bounty credit just wasn't worth it. The *honto* was standing over him now like the Angel of fucking Death come to take him to Portal's Hell. But sometimes targets of opportunity present themselves, even from so humble a position as the floor. Sam saw one and took it, driving his fist through the protection between Vort's legs to smash into his balls. The man fell to the mat with a thud, clutching his damaged goods. Sam struggled to his feet, pulled back a wobbly leg and kicked him in the head.

Then a wave of black crashed over Sam's head and left him unconscious.

"Are you fucking crazy?" Waiting outside the office with the other slaves, Rayna had moved casually through the line until she reached Lainie. Now she stared into the distance and barely made a sound, but she knew the girl had heard the question. "What the hell are you doing here?"

Lainie didn't look at her, but she flushed red with embarrassment and anger. "This wasn't exactly my plan, okay? I was just trying to figure out what was going on with you and got scooped up."

There were no guards near them, and the slaves beside them were so sunk in despair they weren't listening, so Rayna let her have it. "For chrissake, Lainie! I told you this was none of your business." Guilt burned deep in Rayna's chest. "These people are so low on workers right now they're scouring the streets."

"Yeah. So I found out. But better than being sold out by your friends. Fucking Murphy. I never would have thought."

"No!" Rayna turned and hissed at the girl, "No, Lainie, it wasn't like that!" She wanted to say more, but this wasn't the place. The guards were coming down the line now, getting them to their feet, ready to move.

Rayna did her job, even as her gut roiled with worry for the young girl she was responsible for dragging into this mess. She counted the guards—one per five workers, all tall, long-faced Ninoctins. The guards wore armor and carried fully charged whipsticks in their hands. They carried their stun guns in holsters across their chests, where the weapons would be harder for a prisoner to snatch, and kept nothing on their backs or belts. When she was done with the guards,

Rayna lifted her eyes to note the placement of buildings in the yard; the distances between buildings, between buildings and the outer wall.

The laborers were moving now, and Rayna shuffled off after the man in front of her. She kept her eyes on his back, knowing the guards would be quick to spot any overt curiosity among the workers in the organized line. He was a young man, with broad shoulders and an easy walk that communicated athleticism. He was wearing a dark green ship's jumpsuit, one stripe on the sleeve. A merchant fleet officer, on his way up in command until he had one drink too many in the wrong bar on the wrong damn piece-of-shit rock in black space. Rayna's fists clenched at her sides. After processing, the workers would be segregated, male and female. Unless she was specifically assigned to rescue this lost spacer, she would never know what had happened to him.

Just before the line entered a building on the far side of the quad, she saw a shadow loom in the corner of her eye. A split-second later, the electrified tip of a whipstick hit her thigh and fire erupted along every nerve in her right leg. She stumbled and would have fallen if the guard who'd whipped her hadn't jerked her up by the arm

"Clumsy *vlitz*! Stay in line!" Then his lips were at her ear. "I'm Neko. I'm here to help."

"Yes, sir. I'm sorry!" She managed to stumble again, involving Lainie in the effort to steady her on her feet. She nodded minutely in the girl's direction. "My friend." She looked in the Ninoctin's eyes. "Please."

He shoved both of them back in line, hard. Then he pointed the stick at them in warning—and nodded once.

As the line approached the entrance to the building, the people at its head began to falter and the guards were forced to use the whipsticks to keep them moving. No one wanted to go through that door, one that read "PROCESSING" in big, red letters in both Galactic Standard and Ninoctin. Some of them might have been slaves before, but it was certain all of them had heard the stories of the mindwipe the Minertsans used on their slave labor. The technique removed all memory, higher emotion and sense of identity, leaving its victim docile and open to manipulation. It was, in effect, a closed-skull lobotomy.

No one had seen any of the little gray-skinned, black-eyed Minertsans during intake. But everyone knew who owned the Kinz factory. Processing would follow protocol. And the closer they got to PROCESSING, the more people were panicking.

The guards closed in and narrowed the line, pushing the struggling workers toward the entrance, where more guards waited to grab and propel them toward the cubicles where the procedure took place.

In the press of bodies, Rayna turned and grabbed Lainie's hand. "Keep your eyes on Neko and do whatever he says."

At the entrance it was a battle, people fighting for their lives as the guards dragged them away. Rayna saw the young ship's officer kick and punch his way through two guards and make a short run for it before he was brought down by whipsticks to the back of the neck. Guards on each arm hauled him off to an empty cubicle, where a technician strapped him to a table and swept a curtain closed on his life as he had known it.

Still gripping Lainie's hand, her heart pounding, Rayna hung back at the entrance, waiting for Neko's intervention. Others were pushed in front of them from the wailing crowd at the entrance and were dragged away by the guards. The two guards who'd handled the officer turned and headed in her direction.

"Where the fuck is he?" Lainie hissed, her body tense.

"There!"

He was striding toward them from the last cubicle in the row, his face a dark storm of determination. "You! Come with me, you mewling worms!"

They pretended to cower long enough for him to reach them. He grabbed each of them by the arm and pulled them nearly off their feet back to where he'd come from.

"The processor in Cubicle Ten has just had a 'malfunction.'" He spoke just loud enough for Rayna to hear. "The tech has gone for help. We have maybe sixty seconds. Go in, wait thirty seconds, go out the other side and do what they tell you. Make it look good." They arrived at the closed curtain outside the cubicle. "You first." He shoved Rayna inside. An exam table and tie-down straps took up most of the space in the square. The mindwipe equipment was no more than a comp interface and the electrodes that attached to the forehead. Rayna stuck them on above her cycbrows to ensure she'd have the tell-tale circles on her skin when she emerged.

On the other side of the curtain she heard Lainie putting up a sham fight as a cover for Neko's instructions. Then she heard, "Time!" and ripped off the electrodes. She slipped through the curtain, careful not to show there was no tech behind her in the cubicle.

On the other side, the chaos that had existed pre-processing had been transformed into an eerie calm. Workers stood without moving, staring blankly at the floor or into the middle distance. Guards—not so many, now, perhaps one for every ten workers—positioned the newly wiped laborers into two lines, men and women, where they simply waited for further instruction. Rayna let a guard lead her to her place and, once there, scanned the men's line for her merchant marine. He was there, a bruise forming over one eye, and no sign of discontent or self-awareness on his face. She wanted to weep.

Lainie came out and was led to the line. Rayna was careful not to make eye contact with her. No one in the line looked at her companions or her surroundings. No one spoke. No one cried. They simply waited. And after what seemed like an eternity, the silent lines were led away.

In the vast, noisy loading bay, Rayna and Lainie stood at the end of a slow-moving conveyor track. As each sealed plasform crate came off the track, the women each gripped two of the handholds molded into the corners and carried the heavy box four steps to stack it with the others on an auto-mule that would carry the load to a storage area. The crates came off the line at a steady, unbroken pace, forcing the pair to keep up without a break in the rhythm. There was no time for rest or hesitation. There could be no mistakes.

To Rayna's left was a red button that would stop the conveyor in an emergency—if a crate was dropped, for example, or a worker collapsed. The guard that had explained its use had said to push it meant a severe beating and no food for a day, no matter what the cause. Message: don't drop a crate, don't collapse, never push the button.

It was no wonder so many workers died in the loading bays, or at night in their bunks after a shift on the conveyors. Rayna wasn't planning to be one of them, though her back and arms were already aching and her legs felt like two bags of dominium slag. She wouldn't allow Lainie to be lost either, though to give the kid credit, she was holding her own.

"What's in these freakin' things anyway, rocks?" The one advantage of the loading bay was that the noise allowed for unobtrusive conversation, as long as the guards weren't looking. Lainie took frequent use of the advantage.

"In these?" Rayna took a quick glance around for guards, saw none nearby. "I'd say laze rifles, judging by the size of the crate."

They swung the crate onto the stack and returned to the line for another. "Yeah, well, I don't know why they're using slaves to move all this junk," Lainie complained. "You'd think robot loaders would be more efficient."

Rayna inclined her head toward the far side of the loading bay where a pair of tall robotic arms lifted much bigger containers off another set of conveyors. "They use them for the bigger stuff—the torpedoes and the ion cannon parts. Robots are expensive, you know. And delicate. Slaves are cheap."

"They have to feed us."

Rayna grunted in wry amusement as she hooked her cramping fingers under another handhold. "Not much they don't."

"You two!" The guard appeared from out of nowhere, a sparking whipstick at the ready. "Cut the chatter! Every one of these crates better be loaded by end of shift—" he raised the stick —"or do you need some of this to hurry you along?"

The two women lowered their eyes and sped up their work, hauling the crates in silence until the guard moved on. Rayna's back and arms were on fire, her head swimming with fatigue.

Lainie broke the silence. "That bastard Murphy.

I'd like to cut his balls off and watch him bleed to death."

"Stop it, Lainie." Rayna couldn't let the girl go on thinking that way about Sam, even if it meant revealing more of her own business than she might have wanted. "Murphy didn't sell me out; I asked him to help me. The Pataran was my contact on LinHo, my way inside Kinz. We had to make it look like a legitimate hand-off, and Sa—the captain—played along. Believe me, it wasn't his idea."

"*What*?" The girl stared at her over the top of the crate as they dropped it in place. "You let me think—"

"*Let* you think? When exactly did I have time to explain?" Rayna blew out a breath in exasperation. "You jumped to your own damn conclusions. Which, by the way, you wouldn't have done if you hadn't been following me in the first fucking place!"

"I wouldn't have been following you in the first fucking place if you'd told me what you were doing! I tried to warn you, but you wouldn't listen. *Nobody ever listens*!" The girl's expression went as dark as starless space.

The teenager's lament, Rayna thought, but she didn't say so. Instead she grabbed her end of the next crate and waited for Lainie to grip hers.

"This is my job, Lainie. I couldn't avoid it, even if I wanted to. And I couldn't talk about it. To anyone."

Lainie's blue eyes met hers. "I can help."

"You can help by keeping your head down. I'll get you out of here as soon as I can."

"No!" The girl shook her head. "I can help, Ray. I'm trying to tell you—I've been here before."

Rayna almost dropped her end of the crate. She forced herself to keep moving, to show no expression. They stacked the box with the others and went back for another.

Only then did she speak. "What do you mean? When?"

"I was a kid, living on the street in a city on Kotri. Slavers scooped up a bunch of us and brought us here to do the fine assembly work. It was an experiment. Turns out adults were better at it after all, so they sold us within a circuit. Not long after, Cap found me in the market on Barelius."

Rayna stared at the girl, who was struggling to lift her end of the next crate. "Tonight, after lights out, you're going to tell me everything you know."

Before Lainie could respond, a shrill whistle blew to signal the end of their shift. Rayna stopped and nearly dropped to her knees where she stood, suddenly unable to take another step. Lainie swayed across from her, and Rayna reached out to steady her.

"Come on. We get food now. And sleep."

"Thank the gods."

"Where do you think you're going?" Neko, the guard who'd helped them through processing, blocked their path. "You left a crate at the end of the line."

"Stick it up your ass," Lainie muttered as she turned.

"You say something, *vlitz*?" He towered over her,

huge and muscled, whipstick at the ready. Rayna tensed, the adrenaline shooting into her bloodstream. *Perai*, the kid was going to get them both killed.

Neko frowned down at the teenager. "For *mulaak's* sake, don't overplay it, girl." Then, louder. "Just stand over there. Your betters need to speak."

Lainie shot her companion a wary look and backed up to the conveyer line, watching. The big man turned and considered Rayna.

He flicked a glance in Lainie's direction. "We need to lose the kid."

"No, she's okay. She's a shipmate. She followed me and got grabbed."

The guard grunted. "So you feel responsible or some shit?"

"Something like that. But she might be useful. She's been here before, says she knows the place."

"Nobody gets out of here unless we help them. I don't remember her." Neko looked up and became aware they were attracting attention. He raised his voice. "I said you'll move those crates before you leave here. Now, get to it." The whipstick crackled near her shoulder.

She cried out and shied away as if the prod had hit its mark. Then she and Lainie picked up the last crate left on the line and struggled to haul it to the mule.

Neko shadowed them while Rayna panted out her argument. "She was only a kid, here for a circuit. A failed production experiment."

The guard thought about it. "Right. A while back."

He watched them stack the crate, then pushed them toward the exit. The next shift was coming in. No one was concerned with two slaves under guard on their way out.

"Okay." Neko followed Rayna closely across the vast factory floor and spoke so only she could hear. "Just be sure the kid keeps her mouth shut. She talks too much. You're supposed to be wiped, remember?" As they wove a path through a cordon of waiting empty mules, he reached inside his uniform for a one-read datacard. "Memorize this, then toss it in the nearest recycler. It's a map of the prison and the exit routes we use for getting people out—including you—if things go retrograde."

He grabbed her arm and pushed to hide the transfer of the datacard. Rayna stuffed the thing down the front of her prison jumpsuit in the midst of a stumble. She recovered her feet and looked back to reassure Lainie, who was trailing them with an expression of mixed confusion and resentment on her face.

"Have you seen two Thranes come in with the new workers?" she asked Neko. "A man and a woman?"

"No Thranes. Hardly anyone in the last twentydays except the ones that came in with you."

"They'll be undercover with a new batch of slaves. Soon. We need to take them out of play as soon as they get here."

"I'll do what I can." They arrived at the exit, and he gestured for Lainie to line up in front of them. "What are they here for?"

"Not sure. I only know they tried to kill me and blow up the ship I was on getting here."

"Okay. See any Thranes, take 'em out. Got it."

"Uh, you might want to pause in that sequence to ask a question or two, chief. If they fail, whoever sent them will send someone else. It would be good to know what the plan was."

Neko gave her a slow nod. "Understood."

"Oh, and Neko. I need a weapon, as soon as I can get one." Rayna shrugged as both Lainie and the guard turned to look at her. "I'm sure the Thranes aren't the only ones who'll try to kill me in the next few days."

CHAPTER EIGHTEEN

The bones had been rolling his way all night, but Kwan looked around the room and knew he was far from walking out a winner. Slash was a game of strategy and risk, of calculating the odds and taking bold chances. But those who played for big credits sometimes also played for blood. This was definitely that kind of crowd.

He and Darto had been stripped of their comms and weapons at the door. No surprise there. He still had the garrote he wore sewn into a tiny outside seam of his pants, though, if it came to that, and Darto—well, Javin was a walking wrecking ball. Even the hulking bouncers at the door had raised an eyebrow when he'd come in.

On the felt-covered table, the ivory tiles lay in their intricate patterns, a structure built as the players were dealt their hands and the emperor and empress tiles were rolled for each set. The bets were made at each roll and as each player placed tiles to add to the structure and/or block other players. Some said the game had come from Earth, with slaves taken from places with exotic names like Hong Kong or San Francisco. From Kwan's experience, the humans on Terrene mostly preferred card games.

Others swore it was Ninoctin in origin, and, true

enough, the Ninoctins loved to throw their pay away at the Slash tables. But strategic thinking was a bigger factor than luck in the game, which argued against the Ninoctin theory of origin. The tall aliens weren't known for their mental acuity, and they were big losers at Slash. There were several of them at the table with Kwan tonight, losing as usual.

The structure lay before him in sinuous intersecting lines, large and expanding nearly to the edge of the green bias, but Kwan could tell the patterns were shutting down. Opportunities were becoming limited, paths were being shunted into dead-ends. The game was entering its final phase.

Beside him, Darto was restless. "The other tables are closing up. Shouldn't we be going?"

"The game's almost over."

"Haven't you won enough?"

"You can't quit in the middle of the game, Javin."

Darto waved to indicate several empty seats. "Those guys did."

"They lost." In fact, Kwan had taken their chits to add to his substantial pile. "I'm still winning."

This was the high rollers' table. It had taken Kwan three games on the cheaper tables to earn the stake to play here. When the bets went forward it would cost him the minimum 1000 credits to stay in. That was until his only real opponent in the game, a hulking male with the heavy brow ridges of a Barelian, made his move, setting a Death tile where it would block Kwan's progression. The move lacked elegance; it simply condemned that line for anyone else's use. Kwan tried not to show his frustration.

One player saw the bet, two dropped out, before the Barelian grinned at him.

"We are almost done, are we not, Terrene? You and I, we have the biggest stakes here. We should finish it, I think. Ten thousand credits." He pushed his chits to the pot.

Kwan could see by the fright in the eyes of his fellow players that they would fold. He would be left alone with the Barelian to finish the game. That was an advantage in some ways; there were fewer variables with fewer players. But did he have the tiles to hold on?

He savagely repressed the urge to scan the structure for openings and opportunities. He knew the patterns; they were laid out in his mind in every detail, just as they had been placed on the green field of the table. Instead, he held the Barelian's feral yellow gaze while he counted his plays. A strategy formed in his mind. But if the Barelian had certain countering tiles in his hand, tiles that had yet to make an appearance in the game, everything that Kwan had spent the night accumulating would be gone in a single play.

Kwan glanced at his pile of chits. Respectable, but still not enough to do what he'd come to do. He needed that matrix, and he wasn't leaving until he had enough to buy one.

He threw the ten thousand into the pot. "See you."

The amount was enough to clear the field.

Everyone else dropped out. The Barelian bared his teeth in what passed for a smile.

Beside him, Darto said nothing. Refusing to look at Kwan, he poured himself a big slug of synthohol from the flask at his elbow. He tossed it to the back of his throat and grimaced as it went down. Kwan smiled. *Thanks for the vote of confidence, big guy.*

The dealer rolled the bones. The emperor and empress, ivory like the other tiles, but shaped more like dice, tumbled across the green felt and came to rest. The emperor, director of movement, came up North, indicating that the next tile would have to be placed to the north of any tiles already in play. The empress, controller of force, came up Red. The next tile would have to match Red to Red.

Kwan watched the face of his opponent. It was not an expressive face, full of nuance and subtlety. The Barelian wore a frown now that turned his mouth into an animalistic snarl. Was it the North he didn't like, or the Red? *Or does he just know that's a good combination for me?*

Kwan slid his tile into place. "Ten thousand."

His opponent saw the bet with little grace and they awaited the next roll of the bones.

East. Green. No help to Kwan, but he watched for the Barelian's reaction.

"Portal's balls!" He couldn't make a play and was forced to give up a tile. He threw it at the dealer's discard pile where it landed with an angry clink.

The dealer was at least part Savagnoir, and in

reaction to the lack of manners her green reptilian eyes closed to mere slits. She would be within her rights to have the Barelian removed, and, for a moment, movcmcnt around the table stilled.

Then she turned to Kwan. "Your move, sir."

He set a throwaway tile as a block on a secondary line. "Oh, let's not get greedy. Five thousand for now."

He could see the bet was enough to make the Barelian think, but not enough to humiliate him. He wanted to lure the man in, not put him in a killing mood. After all, if Kwan won, he still had to get out of the room in one piece.

The bet was matched and the game moved on. The bets ebbed and flowed, and the pot grew steadily while Kwan saved the best for last, waiting for the killers to come out.

The spot he was watching was still open as they went down to the last two tiles and the last rolls of the bones. He needed North or West, Black to place his master tile, the Crown Prince, and guarantee a win. The die tumbled and came to a stop. South, Yellow. The Barelian chuckled.

"Things are looking bad for you, my friend." He reached out and placed the Golden Dragon on the line. "Fifty thousand."

The Golden Dragon demanded a tile from him, either the game-winning Crown Prince, which required a specific roll of the bones, or the Magician, which could be used anywhere in the structure, regardless of the roll. Winning with the Magician would depend on the bets and careful placement of the tile to block his opponent's next move. He couldn't be certain of the tile the Barelian held, though the man's gaze kept returning to the yellow piece at the East end of Line Four.

"Or you could just fold," Darto offered in a harsh whisper.

"Not an option." Kwan took his last chits and counted them out. It took everything he'd made all night to see the bet. "I'm in." Then he gave up the Magician, handing it over facedown to the dealer.

The Savagnoir placed the royal couple in her cup and shook. The sound echoed in the silence that had fallen in the room. With a flick of her wrist, the die rolled out onto the table. Kwan stared, not believing what he saw until Darto grabbed his arm and began shaking.

The Emperor's Face. The Empress's Face.

"Wild! They're wild, Kwan! You *own* those bones! Holy shit!" Darto had him by the shoulders now, wanting to hug him, but Kwan put him off. The dealer was frowning, indicating the breach of decorum would soon mean eviction, win or no win.

He nodded to show he understood and settled himself to make the final move. He picked up the Crown Prince and placed it at the end of North, Line Six. The watching crowd gasped as the tile clicked into place.

The dealer bowed. "The Crown Prince is played. The game is ended. Congratulations, sir." She gestured at an assistant standing on her left, who gathered the chits into a polished wooden box and waited for Kwan to follow him to the cashier.

The Barelian intercepted them before they could take two steps. "You think I don't know what went on here?"

Kwan ignored him and tried to keep walking, but the stocky alien was having none of it and blocked the way. "Your pal was giving you a little help, no?"

"No. But if you'd like him to help me out now, keep standing right there."

Darto slid smoothly between Kwan and the Barelian, allowing Kwan to catch up to the assistant with his winnings. He found the man at the cashier's window, where an accountant was totaling his take.

"Two hundred twenty-eight thousand four hundred fifty. Your pad, please."

Kwan handed it over and watched while the transfer was made. When he got his device back, he ran his security scans and double-checked his accounts to make sure the credits—and nothing but the credits— were there.

When he turned away from the window, Darto was at his elbow. "Where's our friend?"

"He gathered up his boys and took off as soon as you headed over here." The big man was practically dancing in his excitement, a grin creasing his face. "Guess he could see there was no point in messing with you once you'd transferred *all those credits* to your pad, brother! Wooeee!"

"He'll be waiting outside in the nearest alley with all his boys to beat the shit out of us and take back all those credits, Javin." Kwan had counted at least three bodyguards with the Barelian, as overgrown and dense as their boss. Unless he and Darto shot them senseless with a stun gun in the first few seconds of the fight, they had no chance.

"Oh, well, I got that covered." Darto held up a finger. "Stay right there."

Kwan wandered over to the bar and ordered a drink. If he was going to take a beating, he should be well anesthetized.

Darto returned with a pair of blond giants in tow. "Meet the Thorson twins—Anders and Nils. We played bloodball together for the NuSouth Knucklers on Argent. They're newly arrived from Terrene on the *Eskehay*, hauling protein grow mix. Boys, this is Chief Engineer Kwan."

Kwan shook the hands that were held out to him since the men were wearing grins to match Darto's. They were as enthusiastic as two puppies. He lifted an eyebrow in Javin's direction.

"Well, you know, I got bored while you were playing those first games, so I was up at the bar and in walks these guys! We've been in a few scrapes together. Thought they might come in handy."

"We could use some exercise, Mister Kwan," said Anders (or was it Nils?).

"You know, to keep the skills up," added his brother.

Darto dipped his head close to Kwan's ear. "They're not asking, but I thought maybe we could give them a little something if they do well."

Kwan checked his pad for their ship's records and found the details matched. That made the decision an easy one. He'd prefer to use the stun guns if he could, but if it came to a beatdown, they could use the extra muscle.

"Okay, boys, you're with us. Keep your eyes open, get us safely through the next few hours, and we'll make it worth your while."

The *Shadowhawk*'s Executive Officer had been using every resource at his ship's disposal to search for her captain since Kwan had called hours ago with the news that Sam had been taken. Of course, Drew Vort would be smart enough to know about the transponder Sam wore under the skin of his left thigh. His people had disabled or removed it just outside the Alpha C, and it wasn't responding.

Mo's sensors gave him nothing; LinHo's security nets scrambled the signals so effectively it was as if a blanket had been thrown over the *mulaak* rock. The Pataran had been trying to break through the security blocks to get a view of the streets and buildings, or more importantly, of the docks, with no success. And now it was far too late.

Mo was inclined to agree with Kwan: Vort was long

gone with Sam, bound for Madras and the nearest ConSys station to claim the bounty. They *had* to get moving.

"I think I have something, XO." Patel turned toward him from the Communications station. "I just got into the Spacedock logs."

Crew members all over the bridge stopped what they were doing in anticipation of news—any news. "Tell me," Mo ordered.

"Request for departure from a commercial Raptor-class cruiser six hours ago. Registered as *Master of the Octagon II.*"

"That's him." Six hours ahead. And even if Kwan was successful, Vort would be in Madras at least a day before them. They needed help. "Stand by for a message, Patel."

He went to his comp and composed it:

PRIVATE COMMUNICATION
To: Gabriel Cruz, Access Code 569z24tY#8, Colony of Terrene
From: Morindarza Maatik, Access Code 223A57vu*6, M.S. *Shadowhawk*
Hope this finds you in time to do some good. Sam's been taken by Drew Vort from LinHo and is on his way to ConSys custody at the Fleet station on Madras. We are undergoing repairs and at least a day behind. Can you help?

Mo sent it to Patel's station, saw the Comm Officer

glance up at him and grin, then turn to send it. With the bounces the message would have between here and Terrene, they couldn't expect an answer before third watch. And there was no guarantee that the tracker would be within an easy jump of Madras or free to help them. The only thing Mo knew was that he could depend on Gabriel Cruz. He was a good friend and a half-Thrane with some frighteningly efficient extraction skills. If anyone could help them get Sam back, Gabriel could. If Vort didn't kill the captain first.

"Sam! Come over here and help me." His mother held out a hand to him, a smile creasing her face. "We have to pick some beans for supper."

He left off chasing the chicken around the barnyard and grabbed her hand. He didn't mind the helping so much—he'd grown up on the farm, after all, and chores were chores—but he'd have to make a stand on the hand-holding pretty soon. He was six now and getting too big for that kinda stuff; his brothers had already started teasing.

Mother and son strolled to the vegetable garden at the side of the modest wooden house and began at the end of one row. He held the basket for his mom while she picked the long, green pods and tossed them inside. The sun lay on his shoulders like a snuggly blanket, and the smell of warm earth and growing things rose up from the ground to fill his nose. He felt like laughing for no reason.

The basket he held was almost full when the dogs started barking. His mother looked up, a question on her face that instantly turned to something he'd never seen before. Her eyes grew big and round, and her mouth dropped open as she stared toward the place where the road emerged from the edge of the woods surrounding their little farm.

She took the basket from him and dropped it on the ground. She grabbed his hand and shouted, "Run, Sammy!" But then the big, bright light came, and his beautiful, peaceful world collapsed into ruin.

Sam awoke with the horror of that moment still clinging to him. For an instant of time he could almost smell the green fields of his home planet, and his heart, thumping within his chest, was wild with fear. Just like that boy, taken from everything and everyone he'd known, along with nearly a hundred others, the entire isolated agricultural colony of Ixta IV.

He had survived the next eleven years, resistant to the Grays' mindwipe, resilient in a way even he had never understood. He'd been alone, separated from his family at processing, but somehow others had stepped up to help him, other resistants, he supposed now. He had vowed to pay it forward when he escaped. He had done so for years.

But now it seemed his luck had finally run out. He was light years from his ship and his crew. And Rayna. If things went wrong on LinHo, Sam had no way of getting to her.

He was trapped here on Vort's *mulaak* ship, nothing but the thin pallet under his aching body, the cold plasteel walls of his cell, the dark and the unending silence. He had had little else for he didn't know how long. He had tried to judge the passage of time by keeping track of how often his guards brought him food and water—they fed him every shift change—but he'd soon realized he must have passed out from the pain of his injuries long enough to throw his calculations off by as much as a day. They would be close to Madras now, if that's where they were going.

Well, damned if I'll just lie here like some wounded targa. He rolled off the pallet and got to his feet, stumbling to the corner of the tiny cell where a bucket of water and a drain served as his only means of hygiene. He stripped and rinsed off the worst of the blood and sweat, shivering at the splash of frigid water on his skin. He dried off as best he could with the filthy remains of his old clothes and reached for one of the spare jumpsuits they'd left him—Vort's cosmetic effort to show the authorities he'd been well treated. Sam wondered how his captor would explain the cracked ribs and concussion, the bruises and scrapes. Resisting capture, no doubt.

Those injuries made him slow. He had barely managed to dress himself when the door to his cell banged open. Two guards armed with laze rifles flanked the entry.

"The captain wants to see you. Let's go."

His pulse began a frantic thumping in his veins, and

he swallowed against a throat suddenly gone dry. He was stiff and slow with pain, battered and broken and bruised all over. He couldn't raise his arms to protect his head, or move fast enough to protect anything else. One good shot to the ribs and they would cave on him, puncturing his lungs and drowning him in his own blood. Another round in the ring with Vort and he was a dead man.

He played for time. "Aw, *perai*, boys. I just took a shower."

One of them laughed. "Don't worry. If the boss was gonna kill you, he'd-a done it before we hit Paradon orbit."

He followed the guards out of the cell, and did his best to keep up as they hustled him out of his holding area in the darkened cargo bay, through the ship toward the bridge. "Paradon? What happened to Madras?"

"Above my pay grade," the answer came. "Shut up and walk."

Sam did as he was told, moving down the increasingly busy corridors to the lift. On the bridge deck they turned right and stopped in front of a cabin where his own would have been aboard the *Shadowhawk*—Vort's command room. This one was bigger, appointed like a conference room, with a fair-sized round table in the middle and Vort's large desk at one end.

His captor wasn't alone at the table. Waiting with him was a Ninoctin in the flowing colors of his traditional planetary dress, strapped across the chest with enough weaponry to blast Vort and half his bridge crew into the next galaxy. If Vort thought the single guard with the lase rifle he had trained on the Ninoctin would be enough to control this character when he decided to go off, the fighter was sadly mistaken. On the other hand, the denizens of Paradon *never* gave up their weapons, even in a negotiation. Which, Sam supposed, explained the standoff.

The guards came to a halt with Sam at the end of the table opposite the two men. Vort smirked at him and threw back a shot of something that smelled wonderful—real whiskey?—before he turned to speak to the Ninoctin.

"This, my lord Teliath, is Captain Samuel Armstrong Murphy, formerly of the *M.S. Shadowhawk.* You may have heard of him."

Teliath's long face could not have looked less impressed. "*This* is the pirate captain that strikes such fear into the hearts of the Minertsan fleet? I don't believe it." He waved a hand in Sam's direction. "I've been told he is as tall as a Ninoct', as big as an asteroid, as strong as a *pteryx*! You show me this shrunken human, beaten like a child?"

"Hey!" Sam stepped forward, but his guards held him back. *I'll show you shrunken, you overgrown* honto*!*

Vort laughed in dismissal. "Well, it's true he's been beaten. He and I played a little in the sparring ring a couple of days ago."

"Yeah, and who got the better of that one, Vort? How are the boys today, huh? You still walking with a limp?" The guard on his right smacked him in the head, hard enough to send him to his knees. His vision blacked for a moment, but he fought to stay conscious. This was important.

"As you can see, his mouth is still in working order, even if his judgment is not," Vort was saying. "There's been no brain damage, however. I'm sure he still remembers all the route and contact information that makes him so valuable to ConSys Intel. His bounty is currently offered at 50,000 credits, more than enough to erase my debt to you, my lord."

"You're proposing I take this petty thief in exchange for all that you owe me?" The Ninoctin frowned. "As I recall your ship repairs and your gambling debts totaled more than 35,000 credits—and there is the interest to consider. To claim this bounty I would have to deal with Confederated Systems authorities myself, which puts me at some risk."

Teliath appeared to be thinking, so Vort stayed quiet. Sam could see no advantage to himself either way, so he said nothing.

The Ninoctin tented his long fingers in front of his face. "Of course, if this is truly Captain Murphy—which I doubt—then I might get more for him from the Grays. He's just torn a big hole in their prize battle cruiser, the *Tifan*, and delayed their plan to blow up the weapons factory on LinHo. They'd probably pay big credits to get hold of him."

The blood roared in Sam's ears, drowning out Vort's protests. *Sonofabitch! Did he just say "blow up the weapons factory"?*

Sam shook his head to clear it. "How do you know?"

Vort lunged across the table. "Shut the fuck up! You're nothing but meat here, Murphy."

The Ninoctin considered him. "Know?"

"About the factory on LinHo. How do you know the Grays plan to blow it?"

"So you *are* Captain Murphy!" Teliath bared yellow teeth in a semblance of a grin.

"Tell me!"

"Shut him up!" At Vort's order, the guard on Sam's left punched him in the jaw, a blow that blinded him with pain and flooded his mouth with blood. Above the ringing in his head, he heard Vort plead, "My lord, do we have a deal or not?"

Teliath rose from his seat, a move that Sam could barely see through a haze of pain. "I didn't like that lizard captain of the *Tifan*, or his high-ass Thrane spies either, though they paid well enough for their repairs." Sam looked up from his knees to see the Ninoctin standing over him. "I wouldn't give you over to them, Captain, no matter what the price. I know what the Grays do with their captives. I think you'll hold your own with this one, yes?"

He turned to Vort. "No, we don't have a deal, Captain Vort. I don't trust ConSys. I'm not sure I trust you." His hands hovered near his holsters. "I'm leaving now. You still owe me 35,000 credits plus interest, due in the next twentydays. And if I don't return to my nest unharmed, my cohort will take it out of your hide."

"My lord!" Vort was on his feet, his hands spread in protest, but the Ninoctin had already swept through the hatch. His furious gaze landed on Sam. "This is your doing, you *mulaak* bastard!" He rounded the table, fist clenched, and raised his arm to deliver what would surely have been a killing blow.

Sam put everything he had into his voice. "You don't want to do that, old friend." When Vort hesitated a nanosecond, he went on. "You're going to need my bounty to pay Teliath what you owe him. Last I knew I was wanted *alive*."

The mountain of a man loomed over him, his muscled arm still upraised. "I don't have to kill you to make myself feel better. You'll live. You just won't feel like talking for a long, long time."

Sam had two thoughts before the beating began: So much for impressing ConSys with how well he'd been treated. And he had to survive this and get back to the *'hawk*; he had to get Rayna out of the Kinz factory before the Thranes blew it to hell.

Then that arm came down, and there was no more thinking at all.

CHAPTER NINETEEN

"We have a contact to make here." Rayna kept her voice low and her face blank as she and Lainie shuffled their way through the mess hall line toward the servers. "Keep your eyes open."

There was no other conversation among the prisoners in the line with them. The mindwipe left its victims without the impulse to communicate, without the normal human desire for interaction. These beings bereft of emotion stumbled through their truncated lives looking forward only to food and sleep and avoidance of pain. They paid no attention to Rayna and Lainie or to anything else around them, unless a guard came down the line, in which case they cowered in primitive fear.

Rayna noted the few exceptions to this rule, however. The ones who watched with wary eyes despite carefully composed expressions. The ones who pushed aggressively to the head of the line to get their food. These were the prisoners who were resistant to the mindwipe, both those she had come to save and those she would be forced to fight for control of her territory.

The intel Rescue had on Kinz was largely either outdated or wrong. Once you were on the inside, security at the factory was looser than many places she'd been. Rayna wasn't sure whether this was a recent development tied to the lack of workers, or due to something else. But the aggressive resistants didn't bother to hide their awareness, or the fact that they ruled as they liked. She watched as they openly took food from the others, attacked them or bullied them. The guards stepped in only when a beating threatened to damage a victim to the point where she wouldn't be able to work.

She'd have to fight somebody, probably tonight.

"Things are likely to get rough later." Rayna nodded at a table where a smirking woman had just stolen a bowl of food. "Stay out of it."

Lainie managed to look offended without changing her expression. "What? I got you if shit flows our way."

"You could get hurt."

"You've never seen me fight." Lainie's lip quirked.

Rayna thought of the advantages of having it known they were partners. There were drawbacks, too, but if the kid could throw a punch . . .

She sighed. "Try to stay out of it."

They reached the food at last, and Rayna's stomach clenched in gratitude. The women behind the line were serving nothing but the usual gray institutional stew and something like bread, but her nose and stomach acknowledged it as the nourishment it purported to be. As she reached for her plate, the woman handing it across touched her hand. Rayna looked up to see the server was missing a tooth.

"Mind you don't spill your plate, now," the woman said. Underneath the plate was something long and thin wrapped in a cloth.

"Brilly?" She mouthed the syllables, unwilling to say the woman's name out loud.

The woman nodded and waved her on without another word.

Lainie glanced at Rayna, but didn't speak. The kid was smarter than she seemed sometimes.

They found a spot at the end of a long table in one corner of the vast dim room, away from others, and Rayna slipped the package inside her jumpsuit. It lay there, hard and unyielding, against her ribs. She'd have to find a way to conceal it on her body, where she could get to it when she needed it.

"Was that what I think it was?" Lainie nodded at her midsection.

"It wasn't hot sauce." Rayna shoveled food into her mouth and swallowed quickly. "Though, come to think of it, I could use some of that." She pointed at Lainie's plate. "Don't waste time."

The girl didn't need to be told twice. She was a child of the streets—food of any kind was a precious resource.

They were nearly done when trouble found them. Rayna watched a hulking woman and two smaller followers get up from their seats a table over and come in their direction. The shiv she carried inside her jumpsuit was still wrapped in a towel, and in any case would probably be overkill. This was just a test.

"Here they come," Lainie said. "You gonna use that?" She mopped up the last of her food as she spoke.

"Not this time." Rayna finished her stew and looked up. "Oh, too bad, ladies. We'd share, but it's all gone."

The leader of the crew scowled at her. "Oh, yeah? Then I'll just have to take it out of your black *shalssiti* ass, bitch." She grabbed Rayna by the lapels and lifted her to her feet in preparation for a haymaker that would have sent her halfway across the room. But as Rayna felt her feet hit the floor she sank her weight and dropped onto her back, pulling the other woman over her head. The big woman flipped and landed hard on the floor. Before she could recover, Rayna was on her, straddling her chest and punching her in the face over and over. When it was clear the woman was unconscious, Rayna stopped and got to her feet, prepared to meet the leader's two sides.

But Lainie was already taking care of that. One lay moaning on the floor, while the other was looking nervously from Lainie to Rayna to the guard that had just noticed the commotion from the other end of the room. By unspoken agreement, the three left standing scattered to melt into the crowd of eerily silent prisoners surrounding the scene. The guard let them go and bent to deal with the injured bodies left behind.

A whistle blew to line the prisoners up for their return to the barracks. Rayna saw no challenge from her attacker's remaining sidekick, but she had no illusions that she'd established her position with this one fight. Several of the other resistants were watching her and Lainie with suspicion now, wondering what their next move would be. The tests would get harder, and she'd no longer be able to win by virtue of surprise. Rayna took a deep breath, and rolled out her neck to make herself relax.

"You okay?" Lainie's harsh whisper came from behind her in line.

"Fine," she growled. "Just watch your back from now on."

In the barracks the cots were stacked three deep in a room as cold and bare, as shadowy and forbidding as an ancient tomb. A strip of bluish lightcell ran along the base of each wall and down the center of the floor, concealing more than it revealed. Rayna shuffled to a halt just steps inside the room, waiting for her eyes to adjust to the gloom.

A guard shoved her in the back. "Move along! Find an empty bunk and get your ass in it!"

She grabbed Lainie by the hand. "Come on—all the way down!" They pushed past others in the line and dashed to the end of the line of bunks, where they found two bottom cots side by side.

Rayna felt along the thin mattress and discovered someone had stolen the blankets. She reached up to take the one from the bunk above hers—along with the pillow—and looked over to see that Lainie had done the same. She'd just begun to think this had been too easy when a shadow fell across the bunk.

"This is my place." The owner of the voice wasn't

overly tall, but as a Barelian she had to weigh 100 kilos. She wouldn't have many vulnerable spots either. It would be a punishing fight—one that Rayna might lose.

"Take the one on the other side of my friend and I'll give you my blanket."

The Barelian's eyes glittered in the dim glow from the lightcell. The creatures hated the cold. She glanced at the still-empty bunk on Lainie's right and grunted. Then she snatched the blanket from Rayna's hand and stalked away. The unfortunate soul who arrived at the chosen cot at the same time as the Barelian was shoved to the floor as the woman claimed the space. That prisoner climbed to the upper bunk.

Rayna scrambled to the third tier to find another blanket and made it back to the lower bunk just in time to fend off another weak attempt to claim it from a wasted skeleton of a woman with the blank look of a wiped mind.

"Not here," Rayna told her. "Try there." She pointed to the other side, where there might be some blankets.

Eventually even the stripped mattresses above her head were filled, and the workers succumbed to their exhaustion and despair. The guards retreated beyond the doors, and the barracks settled down for the night. Rayna hunkered down under her blanket and drew the two items from inside her jumpsuit that would be key to her survival in this hellhole.

She set the shiv aside and pressed the corner of the data card to activate it. The first page showed a simple two-dimensional schematic of the entire facility giving her the layout of the place. She zoomed in on the details of hallways and exits, storage areas and mechanical rooms, blind corridors and dead ends. Other pages gave her guard stations and comm connections, power junctions and weapons lockers and medical supplies. The next-to-last page showed the entrances to the hidden passages to the outside. This one she stared at the longest, making sure she understood where the sites fit in the map that now existed in detail in her mind. When she'd stored things away to her satisfaction she hit the corner to run through the three-dimensional test on the final page. The test walked her through the facility as she touched a wall here, a door there, to open and identify the resources she'd just memorized. She racked up a perfect score the second time through.

Rayna started to hit the opposite corner to destroy the card when Lainie grabbed her by the arm. "Let me see."

"I thought you said you knew the place."

"I'm guessing there are a few details I missed." She held out a hand. "It won't hurt for you to have some backup. Gimme."

Rayna handed it over. "Upper right corner turns the pages."

Lainie hunched over the card, her face lit softly by the screen, her eyes bright with excitement. "They've changed a few things since I was here. But I knew that was a way out!" She turned the card and pointed.

"That corridor leads down below the factory floor. I knew it! I got my ass kicked but good one time for going that way—and not by the guards."

Rayna huffed out a laugh. "You always were too smart for your own good, that what you're saying?"

"If I'd been smart I wouldn't have been here in the first place."

"That wasn't your fault, Lainie. You were a kid. Your parents should have taken care of you."

"Parents were in short supply where I came from." The words were like shards struck from the edge of a stone knife. She tossed the data card back in Rayna's lap and curled up under her blanket.

Rayna recognized the end of a conversation. It was better that way; she wasn't much for sharing either. She turned her attention to the shiv, careful as she pulled the blade from its thin protective sleeve in the dark. This was no machine-fashioned tool, with a shiny, new cutting edge and a smooth grip that molded to your hand. The six-centimeter blade was black and non-reflective. And sharp! It nicked her twice as she handled it. It was set in a rough, flat, wooden handle wrapped with a few strips of leather. This was a professional-grade piece created to look home-made. Smiling in satisfaction, Rayna slid the blade back into its sheath and set about finding a way to strap the thing to the inside of her forearm.

"I suppose you had the perfect childhood." Lainie's voice in the dark held both resentment and longing.

"No. But it was good enough." Rayna waited.

When the girl said nothing else, she went back to considering her problem. The tight undershirt she wore was the only thing suitable for tearing into strips to hold the shiv. She would lose half of one of the long sleeves—and warmth she could ill afford to miss—but just slipping the sheath up her sleeve wouldn't do; it was too heavy.

"What was it like?"

Rayna sighed; seemed like there was no avoiding this. "I grew up on Terrene. Both my parents had been taken from Earth. They were slaves until Rescue found them." She turned back her jumpsuit sleeve and yanked at the undershirt until she found a likely spot, then she used the knife to tear a hole in the thin fabric.

"Had they been wiped?"

"Everyone is wiped." She worked her fingers into the hole and ripped, her jaw clenched, not caring that the sound echoed in the dark like the tearing of thunder, until the bottom two-thirds of her sleeve jerked free. She tore the sleeve into two thick strips, wishing only that the cloth in her hands was a little Gray neck.

"Maybe that's a good thing." Anger tinged Lainie's voice in the dark. "Sucks seeing all this shit with open eyes."

"No." Rayna swallowed hard and focused on securing the shiv in its sheath against the skin of her left forearm, the handle snugged close to her wrist. Otherwise she would see the scars on her mother's face, the limp that made her father tight with agony, the evidence of scars in both of them that no one could see. "Rescue told me they'd been Taken together. The Grays punished them, wiped them until almost nothing was left. When Rescue finally found them and deprogrammed them, nothing could be recovered. They couldn't be returned to Earth so they ended up on Terrene. They were broken, never the same."

"But at least they had each other." Lainie sat up in the bunk, staring at her. "They had you."

Rayna snatched the knife from its nest with her right hand and held it up in front of her face, testing the ease of access to her weapon. "It wasn't enough."

A door clanged open at the far end of the barracks, flooding the first few bunks with light. The prisoners at that end groaned and tossed in protest. Rayna and Lainie disappeared under their blankets, hid themselves except for a tiny fold that allowed them to see what was happening.

Beneath the blanket, Rayna slid the knife back in its hiding place and slowly searched the mattress around her body for the other item she'd taken out to look at tonight. The data card had been in her lap as she worked on the shiv, but now her questing fingers could not find it. She began to sweat.

The guards came down the line, big, bright handheld lightcells swinging from side to side. Every third or fourth bunk they would stop, jerk the blanket off some poor, shivering soul and throw the light on her. That would be the prisoner's signal to stand up and turn around. The light would sweep over prisoner and mattress, blanket and pillow before she was allowed to go back to her interrupted sleep.

Shit, shit, shit! Rayna shifted as quietly as she could in her bunk, her hand sweeping first one side, then the other. *Where is the* mulaak *thing?* She reached out, her fingertip touched something, then she heard the tiniest *tick!* as the card hit the floor on the far side of her bunk. Her heart dropped into her stomach.

Lainie turned her head to stare, her eyes wide with panic. Rayna shook her head. The guards were halfway down the barracks now, well within sight, though the shadows were still thick at this end of the room. She had to pick up that card; there was no leaving it on the floor in hopes they wouldn't see it.

She ducked down under the blanket, pulling her pillow behind her to serve as cover. Rolled into a ball in the center of the bed, she and the pillow combined to form a single large person. She crawled on her belly under the blanket, keeping her arms and legs tucked in tight, and peeked over the side of the mattress. In the dark it was impossible to see the floor, much less where the data card might be in the gloom. The screen had gone dark; Lainie might even have deactivated it, but she couldn't take the chance the lightcells would pick it up.

She could hear the guards coming closer, see the light sweeping her way. She reached down, touched the cold, dusty floor, stretched. Nothing. Nothing. *Shit!* She shifted, reached again. *There!* Her fingers curled around the card and scooped it up into her palm.

She brought it under the blanket and stashed it inside her jumpsuit, in the waistband of her underwear, then zipped up and made sure all the evidence of her earlier work was tucked out of sight, too.

And then they were there. "You. Number A578. Up."

Rayna stood in the glare of the lightcells. Did her best to seem blank and disoriented.

"Turn around."

She did as she was told, praying she hadn't left any detail unattended. The light swept up, down.

Across the mattress.

Across the floor.

Nothing.

Thank God. Nothing.

The light moved on to the other side of the aisle and soon enough the guards left them alone. They'd found nothing in the barracks, but Rayna was on notice. Sleep wouldn't come easy in this place.

"*Perai*, that was close, huh?"

Rayna had to bite her tongue to hold back a groan. Just because she wasn't asleep didn't mean she wanted to talk. She grunted in response.

"Ray. You're wrong, you know."

Jesus. "Go to sleep."

"You said it wasn't enough. But your parents had more than most people have."

She couldn't see the girl's face in the huddle of thin cloth in the bunk across from her, but she could hear the intensity in her voice. The kid had grown up hard;

she yearned for something she'd never had. She couldn't know that was just a dream some mediamixer had spun to entertain the gullible.

"You never saw my parents," Rayna said at last. "What they had didn't help them—it hurt them. Badly. Be careful what you wish for."

The kid huffed. "You know what? I used to think like you. I used to think love made you weak. Being a part of the *Shadowhawk* changed my mind. Stick around long enough—maybe Cap will change your mind, too."

CHAPTER TWENTY

The Executive Officer of the *Shadowhawk* stood at the edge of the D-mat pad in Cargo Bay One and considered the ship's Chief Engineer. Kwan's lip was split and bleeding, his left eye blackened and swelling. His black hair was matted with blood, and his clothes were torn and dirty. But the engineer was grinning, his arm wrapped protectively around a tall thermocase the size of –

"A matrix?" Mo breathed. "How?"

Javin Darto and two massive blond strangers Mo didn't recognize helped Kwan move the case off the pad before he finally looked up to answer. "Won it in a Slash game."

Mo crossed his arms over his chest. "Say again?"

Kwan must have caught his expression, so he filled in the details. "Well, not exactly. I won the credits for it in a Slash game. The loser wasn't so happy." Which, Mo thought, explained the injuries and the two giants hovering like the Angels of Vantyr behind Kwan. "Then we hit up a tech/mech shop I know and got lucky." Kwan found his grin again and patted the case. "This little baby is fully grown and ready to roll. All I need to do is plug 'er in."

Mo suddenly realized he was no longer interested in how the Chief Engineer had managed it. He just knew that Kwan was here with a fully-functioning matrix and the 'hawk could be under way in a matter of hours to rescue her captain. For the first time since Sam had disappeared he took a decent breath.

"How long?"

Kwan shrugged. "Two-three hours."

"Do I have to remind you the captain is in Vort's hands, on his way to Madras?"

Kwan shoved a hand through his hair and winced as it came back bloody. "Two hours. But can I get a shower first?"

Mo felt a twinge of something that might have been conscience. "I'll send Doc Berta to your cabin to take a look at you."

The engineer grinned as he gestured at his companions to move the case. "Nah. She'll just waste my time. When I'm done I'll take some painkillers and sleep until we get to Madras."

Mo nodded in approval and headed back to the bridge to give the orders to make way for the C5 jump node. He still had received no confirmation from Gabriel that the extractor had received his first message, but he sent another one anyway, saying they were on their way. It should arrive a day or so ahead of them. And he could only hope they were all in time to help Sam before Vort turned him over to ConSys.

Sam.

You have to get up, Sam.

He didn't want to get up. He wanted to lie here, not moving, not breathing, until the pain stopped. He suspected the only way that would happen was if he died. He didn't mind.

Fuck that. Get up, Sam.

Funny. The voice urging him to save himself wasn't his own. It was in his head, like it was his, but it was *hers*. Rayna's. Right now, it was fucking annoying. 'Cause *he* just wanted to lie here. And die.

Get your ass UP. NOW!

Shit! He rolled from his side to his hands and knees, his head hanging between his shaking arms, and stayed there, swaying. He could not envision moving any further—even raising his head brought on a wave of dizzy nausea so severe he thought maybe his entire stomach might erupt out of his throat. He dry-heaved into the blood-stained tee-shirt lying next to the pallet, nothing left to bring up but his guts, and collapsed back down to the fetal position that seemed to be his only refuge.

Concussion, possible skull fracture and brain damage floated through his mind, along with *broken ribs* as pain stabbed through his torso and *possible internal injuries* as the dull ache in his kidneys and the burning in his lower abdomen indicated worsening problems. God, he wanted to stay down. But that voice in his head started up again.

If you don't get up, I'll never see you again. And I want to see you again. So get up, you stupid son of a bitch.

And now he wasn't sure who was talking, her or him.

After a long while, he tried again, agony in every movement. This time, he made it to his knees, his hands walking up the wall to keep his upper body upright. The room spun for a moment, then settled into place. Progress.

Still, he didn't trust himself to walk the distance to the far wall and water. So he crawled across the filthy floor, avoiding the areas where he'd puked his guts out over the last twenty-four hours—he hadn't always made it to the drain in time. He should have just stayed where the water was, chained to the wall by the drain, but it was cold, so cold on the plasteel deck, and he'd always found his way back to the pallet to curl up under what passed for a blanket. He hadn't had the strength or presence of mind to move the pallet.

He barked out a laugh. *Idiot.* Now that pounding in his head was not only a concussion but dehydration, too, possibly serious enough to kill him.

He was trembling all over by the time he reached the water bucket. There was maybe enough to fill the dipper sloshing around in the bottom of the metal container, slimy, cloudy stuff that smelled of mold. His throat ached with need at the sight of it. He drank every drop and still it wasn't enough. If they didn't come soon to give him more . . . He refused to finish the thought. They would come. They needed him alive.

Sam fell back against the wall—*perai*, that was

freezing!—to catch his breath. He eyed the return trip to the pallet. What was it—three meters? Four? The thought of crossing that distance exhausted him. *Just stand up*, he thought. *Walk. Like a man.*

"Portal's balls, it stinks in here! What a fucking animal!"

"Oh, for fuck's sake, he's puked everywhere!" A boot slammed into Sam's hip. "Get the hell up! We ought to make you clean this place up before we take you out, you *shalssiti pultafa*!"

Rough hands grabbed both arms and hauled him to his feet. He fought his stomach for control as the room swam around him.

"Stand up! You think we want to carry your stinking ass?"

"Can't." His voice was rusty with disuse. And he tried, but his legs wouldn't hold him.

The guard on his left pulled his arm over a burly shoulder and swore again. "We're wasting time. I'm going to throw him in the shower. Call the galley crew to clean this mess up, then find me. The boss is waiting."

The guard pulled Sam's arm tight around his shoulder, gripped him around the waist and took off through the cargo bay and into the ship's corridors. Sam was vaguely aware they were not headed toward the bridge this time, but into the bowels of the ship, toward the crew quarters. He willed himself to note his surroundings, to put strength into his legs, but his mind was obscured by fog and his body unresponsive to his call. He might be one-on-one with this guard, but escape was impossible. He needed water and food and days of healing. Or a hypo full of stims.

They made the head at last and Sam was dumped in the first of a line of shower tubes. He collapsed in a heap of black and blue skin and aching bones on the tile at the bottom of the tube and looked up at his captor.

"Well?" The man gestured at the controls. "You don't expect me to strip you and scrub you down, do ya? Portal's balls in a fucking vise!"

Okay. Okay, he could do this. He braced his heels and walked his hands up the wall behind him until he was standing, his backside on the wall supporting him. He stripped off what was left of his grimy clothes and threw them outside the tube. Then he shut the door to begin the sequence.

The lights and the heat went on. Oh, gods! He shivered as the warmth blanketed his skin. He used the depil first. No reason for it, except maybe he needed to feel civilized, and he'd always shaved first. The stubble on his cheeks had grown to a genuine beard. He wanted it gone.

Then he pumped the foam cleanser into his hand and raked it through his matted hair, reveling in the clean, citrusy smell. He repeated the process, cleaning carefully around the knots and gashes, watching his hands come away bloody. More foam, covering every centimeter of his battered body, his hands tallying every bruise, every cracked bone, every break in the skin, seeking to cleanse not only his body of blood and filth, but his mind of memory and pain.

At last he hit the pad for "rinse" and the water came down like a blessing, taking the blood and the filth, if not the memories and the pain, and washing them down the drain. He opened his mouth under the stream and gulped at the life-giving liquid, desperately thirsty, but the rinse sequence was limited and wouldn't repeat. He wanted to be clean above all, so he scrubbed until all trace of that cell he'd nearly died in was obliterated.

When the water stopped flowing, the dryer came on, the heated air blowing like the desert wind on Savagne. Sam was ready to step out of the tube in less than thirty seconds.

His guard tossed him clean clothes. "Cover that shit up."

"Yeah, you're going to meet your new masters at the Fleet station." The other man held a large water pak. "You want to look your best."

Sam dressed quickly, suddenly feeling vulnerable. His gaze kept returning to that plastic envelope of water.

He waved a hand at the liquid. "That for me?"

The guard lifted his chin. "What makes you think so, *pultafa*?"

"No reason," he said with a shrug. "But I could sure

use a drink. Do you mind?"

The guard considered him, a cruel smile teasing his lips. Sam swayed as he waited, barely able to stand, but he was damned if he would show any weakness in front of this pimple on the ass of the galaxy.

The guard who had carried him from the cell snatched the pak from the other's hand. "For fuck's sake, give it to him. He's ready to fall out. We don't have time for this shit, and I'm tired of carrying his ass."

Sam's hands shook as he held the straw to his cracked lips and drank. But he was careful; he made himself drink slowly so he didn't spill a drop. The cool liquid washed over his tongue and down his constricting throat like a healing balm, and he groaned with relief. As deliberate as he tried to be, the pak was gone in seconds, but so was the fog that had filled his head. The trembling in his legs had nearly stopped. And when the guards grabbed his arms to hustle him out into the corridor, he could almost keep up with them on his own.

They headed back the way they had come—at least as far as Sam could tell. He was clearer now, but he hadn't been able to focus enough earlier to be certain. The guess was confirmed when they passed back into the cargo bay. He tensed—damned if he would go back in that fucking cell!

"Relax!" The guard who had already shown him some sympathy continued to read him. "You're getting off this ship today. Not that it'll help you any."

They turned toward another section of the bay, toward where the lights indicated the loading hatches on the port side of the hold.

"We're on Madras?" The *Master of the Octagon* was smaller than the *'hawk*; she was an atmospheric lander. No dematerialization system. Vort would have to put her on the ground to hand him over.

His guard confirmed it. "Spacedock II."

"Why? You got a date?" The guard on his other arm growled in frustration and pushed him forward. "Shut the fuck up and walk."

As they approached the loading area, Sam could see Vort was waiting for him. The fighter was grinning in triumph, relishing the moment.

"Well, don't we clean up nice!" Vort reached out to touch his clean, beardless chin, and, gods help him, Sam flinched. Vort laughed. "Oh, don't worry, Sammy, I wouldn't want to mess with that pretty face now. ConSys Intelligence is just smart enough to ask questions. I suspect I'll have to concoct some sort of story about how vicious you are as it is."

"I don't care what lies you tell, Vort, just as long as I don't have to see you again."

Vort grinned. "Don't think that'll be a problem, my friend. They're going to put you away for the rest of your natural life. Which, given the number of your enemies in Hellsmouth Prison, shouldn't be too long."

Hellsmouth would be where they'd send him, of course. On a frozen planet at the bitter ass end of the inhabited galaxy. No parole. No escape. No end to the misery except in death. Sam hadn't given much thought to what would happen to him once the government in control of half of the organized systems owned him. Now the weight of it settled on him like so much living rock.

"Yes, I can see you finally understand how this is going to end." Vort stood toe-to-toe with him. "After all the grappling and the scrapping and the blood between us, Murphy, I'm going to win. Glory. Halleluieah."

Vort stood back and gestured to the man standing at the panel that controlled the cargo bay doors. The big hatch yawned open with a deep, metallic screech, revealing the dim outlines of the dock slip beyond. The ramp extended out and down to the slip and locked into place. Then the guards took up their positions on either side of Sam again and marched him down the ramp. Vort fell into step behind with two more men to watch his back.

This part of the 'dock was deserted and dark, except for the required yellow emergency lighting. Sam smiled. Vort was in such a hurry to get him off the ship and into ConSys hands he was hustling him out during third watch. Or maybe he thought the *Shadowhawk* crew would stage a rescue attempt. Little did he know the *'hawk* was crippled, maybe now for life. No rescue would come from that quarter.

They were at the base of the ramp, turning onto the narrow slip that led back toward the main part of the spacedock terminal when Sam heard the whine of a lase rifle. He turned to see one of Vort's men drop like a stunned *psoros* in a slaughterhouse. In their shock the guards loosened their hold on him, so he slugged the smallest one, the one who'd refused to help him. The man went down, surprise on his hateful face. The other looked at him and shook his head, as if to say he'd gone too far, and moved to take back control.

But the rifle whined again, the shot going over their heads. They hit the deck. Then again, and Vort's second man dropped in the act of firing toward the flash of light that had indicated where their attacker was hidden. The big fighter was alone now at the base of the ramp, and the guard with Sam saw he had a choice. Cursing, he jumped up and ran to his boss, grabbing him up and hauling him toward the safety of the ship.

"No, you *shalssiti* idiot, leave me alone and get that prisoner!" Vort fought the guard until the sniper put a smoking shot into the cloth of his right arm. Only then did he allow the man to cover him and drag him back up into the cargo bay.

Vort's curses rang in Sam's ears as he limped down the slip and into the shadows. He found a narrow slot between two shipping containers and wedged himself inside to wait. He had no strength left, and he knew whoever had wielded that rifle would be down to find him soon. Friend or foe, he wanted to meet the man standing on his own two legs.

CHAPTER TWENTY-ONE

The work in the loading bays was grueling, relentless, a constant ion storm beating against their depleted shields. Rayna ached in every muscle and bone, the weariness settling in for the long haul. She knew this kind of cell-deep fatigue, knew it was born of too much work and too little sleep, of barely-contained fear and constant vigilance. She knew the only way to survive it was to grit your teeth and bear it for as long as it took. And she could tell her companion knew that, too.

"They carted off another body this morning," Lainie said as she tugged her end of the crate off the line.

"I saw."

"But I heard they're bringing in fresh meat—maybe today." The kid grinned.

Rayna perked up. "Where'd you hear that?"

"Guards moving the body. Grays just showed up with a ship full of newbies. Emergency stock, they called 'em."

Shit. "You seen Neko around this morning?"

Lainie paused to look at her as they headed back for another crate. "No. Why?"

"I'd bet my last credit those Thranes who tried to blow up the *Shadowhawk* arrived with the *emergency stock*. They have business here."

Lainie stared, her hands on the crate handles. "What kind of business?"

"That's what I plan to find out." She nodded at her partner and they lifted the heavy box, moving it to the mule a few steps away.

As they turned back to the line, Lainie inclined her head. "Hey—look!"

Slaves emerged at the far end of the echoing warehouse in two neat rows, the men peeling off toward the more distant lines for the heavier ammunition crates, the women marching closer to fill in gaps in the lines near Lainie and Rayna. The men were too far away to identify, and as the women drew closer, Rayna could see her job wasn't going to be easy.

"*Perai*!" Lainie whispered. "There's a shitload of Thranes! Which one is she?"

Rayna scanned the passing newbies in disgust. "Fuck if I know." Not one of the workers passing by betrayed any sign of recognition or interest. They all looked like the good, little mindwiped slaves they purported to be. That was unusual in itself. Thranes were almost never used as slaves because specialized techniques were needed to successfully wipe their telepathic brains. It didn't pay for owners to use Thranes; so this was either a complete ruse or the Kinz owners were so desperate now they would truly take anything in a mixed lot of slaves.

"You don't know what she looks like?"

"She's seen me, but I haven't seen her—not her face, anyway." In body shape, the five Thrane women were enough alike to be sisters—any one of them as tall and athletic as the figure she'd seen fleetingly in the *Shadowhawk*'s Sickbay and shooting at her from a catwalk in the ship's cargo bay. Rayna cursed again.

"Damn, where did they get those girls—the Amazon gladiator store?" Lainie was staring open-mouthed. "You're going to need backup."

Rayna exhaled and went back to work. "The good thing is I only need to fight one of them." *I just need to figure out which one she is. Where the hell is Neko?*

--*You will never guess who I saw today on the factory floor*. Zetana didn't bother to shield her anger and frustration from her bondmate. She let it flow with her thoughts across their bond, joining them though they lay in different bunks in the separate men's and women's wings of the Kinz facility, far from each other.

--*Who could you have possibly recognized,* k'taama? Rex sounded tired after his first long shift on the floor. He was a strong male, but the only hard labor he had ever experienced was in combat training.

Zetana squelched her impatience and sent a mental slap his way to wake him up—an image of the small, dark-skinned figure she'd seen as she'd passed the work line.

Shock came back at her. *The ConSys agent? But the* Shadowhawk *was destroyed. She would have died with the others.*

--We have no confirmation of that. If they discovered the explosive in time—

--Impossible!

--Apparently not. The agent lives; I have seen her. And now we know what she was doing on the Fleeflek *with us.*

--Not so distracted by the captain after all.

Zetana allowed herself a smile. The woman was smarter than she appeared, then. That kind of intelligence could be dangerous.

--I have to find a way to get rid of her as soon as possible. My 'sisters' won't provide cover for long.

Amusement rippled through his mind. *Did I not tell the captain of the* Tifan *anything could be found on Paradon for the right price?*

--On Paradon. And among the Blood Legion. Pay that house of vipers enough and they will kill their own bondmates. Zetana usually tried to avoid the secret society of Thrane ultraminds. In truth, she feared them. For that reason, she would have refused their help with the mission, but Rex had insisted they would somehow prove useful. And so they had. *Now our little agent will waste time trying to discover which of five Thrane women is the assassin bent on killing her. And while she ponders that question, I will slip up behind her and quietly slit her pretty throat.*

Sam Murphy huddled on a narrow strip of cold

thermocrete between two shoulder-high shipping containers and tried to control the sound of his breathing. He was shivering, the effect of the drop in adrcnaline from his escape from Vort, the lack of adequate clothing in the vast, unheated space of the 'dock and his injuries. His teeth were clacking together in his jaw as he shook. But it was his breath, sawing in and out of his laboring lungs, that he feared would give him away to the one who'd shot two men and left them lying on the ramp outside the *Master of the Octagon*. Sam had no desire to be the next victim.

"Hey, *amigo*." The voice was a whisper of sound at the far end of the opening between the two containers. A familiar whisper. "If I show my face, will you promise not to shoot me?"

Sam got up and scrambled toward that end. "An easy promise since I'm not armed. I could maybe spit at you for scaring the shit out of me."

The man who met him at the end of the row was little more than a tall, muscular shadow, his black body armor and stealth paint obscuring everything but his mahogany eyes. Still, Sam could fill in the details of his friend's face from memory—the aristocratic angles, the strong jaw, the white smile flashing in tan skin. Gabriel Cruz, half-Cuban/Terrene, half-Thrane, all focused hardass. Cruz was the best extractor in the galaxy—as he'd now proved yet again.

"I just saved your ass and you're whining?" The man's lips curved just enough to be perceived in the dark. "You can walk, can't you?"

"Yes, no thanks to you." He just wasn't sure how far.

Cruz considered him. He pulled out a hypogun and punched it into Sam's shoulder. Warmth flooded through Sam's body, followed by a surge of energy.

Stim, thank the gods. Sam's vision cleared.

"Come on, *mi hermano.*" Cruz slipped a hand under Sam's elbow and guided him through the dark rows of silent containers.

They weren't headed toward another dockslip. "What, no ship?"

Cruz chuffed out a laugh. "I thought you had one."

"Not at present."

"Yeah, that's a problem." The extractor turned toward an exit at the end of the long row of stored goods. "The *Shadowhawk* is on its way, but it's not here yet. I'm taking you to a safe house."

But it wasn't going to be that easy. Just as they were crossing the open area between the cover of the last of the containers and the safety of the exit, the flash and whine of lase rifles lit up the thick, black space around them.

Gabriel pushed him. "Run!" The extractor turned to open up on their attackers, spraying blue lase fire in an arc from right to left.

Sam didn't wait to see if Gabriel had hit anyone. He just gathered what inner resources he had left and ran for the door. It couldn't have been more than ten or fifteen meters, but in his weakened state, his goal seemed to stretch out in front of him like distant mountains seen across a plain. He moved so slowly, expecting any second to feel the scorch and sear of the laser on his back.

But Gabriel kept up the covering fire and Sam's stubborn body kept moving and somehow they both made the exit doors. By another miracle, the doors were unlocked; they crashed through into an empty corridor. Gabriel found a chair in the passageway and jammed one of its plasteel legs through the door handles. They could hear their attackers rattling at the doors as they made their escape down the passage to the 'dock's outside exit.

By that time, spacedock security was streaming in the direction of all the noise, ignoring the two men walking through the facility at a calm pace. Despite the stim, Sam fought to keep his feet, to keep moving under his own power as a wave of weakness threatened to take him under.

"You okay?" Gabriel maneuvered closer and clamped a hand around his bicep.

"How far is this safe house?"

"In the city. We have to take the train, then a taxi."

Sam nodded, exhaustion blanking his vision for a moment. He let his friend guide him through the spacedock terminal to the maglev train and onto one of the cars, nearly deserted at this time of night. He faded out as the train left the station, headed for Amara, the capital city of Madras III.

When Gabriel woke him again at their station stop in an older part of Amara, he was even foggier and more disoriented than he'd been when they started out. He barely noticed the night streets they passed through in the taxi, or the low-lying housing clusters that seemed integral with the rock formations that made up the mountainous area around Amara. He felt the pull of gravity on his body as they climbed into the hills; he looked out and saw the lights of the city spread out below him. And at last the taxi left them in front of one of many round-roofed, dug-in dwellings in a complex like any other in that part of the city.

Sam stood and waited for Gabriel to open the door to his house. His gaze was drawn up, to the millions of stars overarching the city, in a deep, black sky still unsullied by the pollution of sentient habitation. He oriented himself and found the infinitesimal spot in that sky where his heart could be found. And he prayed that heart was somehow still beating, back on LinHo.

Gabriel caught him just as the sky began to tilt and wheel above his head. "Inside. You need to lie down." His friend steered him into a well-kept living/kitchen area and deposited him on the couch. He sank into the cushions and heaved a grateful sigh.

Gabriel left him there. "I'll get you something to eat."

Sam lay in a sort of warm, surreal haze while Gabriel clanked and shuffled around in the tiny kitchen. The sounds of cleaning and food preparation provided background to the formless thoughts running through his head—his imprisonment, his rescue, the *Shadowhawk*, Rayna. There was something important he needed to remember, but it would not come to mind; something that had grabbed at him when he thought of LinHo and Rayna. Rayna . . .

Gabriel appeared in front of him with a plate full of hot food in one hand and a big glass of water in another. He dragged a small table around with his foot and arranged his offerings on top. He pulled out the injector and jabbed Sam's shoulder again.

The stim took hold and lifted Sam out of his haze. "What the hell?"

"Need you awake enough to eat." Gabriel gestured at the food.

Sam sat up and sniffed. "Smells good. What is it?"

"Rice and beans, just like my mama used to make."

"You cook?"

"Hell, no. It's PrePak. But I add the spices. Now eat. If you're good, I'll give you a drink of rum for dessert." Gabriel went back to the kitchen for his own plate and was already helping himself to the rum.

Sam dug in. Either Gabriel was a better cook than he let on or Sam's starvation made the food taste exceptionally delicious. He had to make himself eat slowly. Even so the food disappeared at an impressive pace. One plate. Then two.

"This your place, *amigo*?"

Gabriel lifted a shoulder. "One of them." He glanced around. "Not the nicest one."

Sam grunted. "It's an improvement over my previous circumstances." He paused in mopping up the sauce on his plate with a piece of bread to look at his friend. "Thank you."

"*De nada*. I'm glad I was in a position to help." He gestured at Sam's plate. "You want more?"

Sam pushed back. "No. That was great."

Gabriel got up and took the plates to the kitchen. "Rum, then. You earned it." He brought back a short, fat glass and handed it to Sam. "Spit in Vort's eye."

"Thanks to you, brother." They touched glasses and drank, the fiery liquor warming Sam all the way to his belly and numbing some of the pain of his injuries. "Ah, the good stuff. Where the hell do you get it?"

Gabriel smiled. "You can find just about anything on Paradon, if you're willing to pay for it."

"Paradon, *shalssit*! You're just as likely to get your throat cut!" Sam started to laugh, then his amusement abruptly cut off. *Paradon! And Teliath!* "When did you say the *'hawk* was due in?"

Gabriel's brows met, puzzled at the change in subject. "Eighteen hours. Maybe more. They had to make repairs before they could get underway."

"Not soon enough!" Sam set his drink down and scrubbed at his face. "We have to get a message to Rayna in Kinz."

"What? Wait a minute." Gabriel held out a hand as though he could stop Sam's runaway train of thought. "Who the hell is Rayna? And did you say Kinz?"

"Rayna is . . ." Sam careened to a halt. It was complicated. He simplified. ". . . mine. She's a Rescue agent undercover at the Kinz factory. And two Thrane spies working for the Minertsan government plan to blow the place to bits any day now. I have to warn her."

Gabriel sat staring at him, his dark eyes round with shock, his rum glass halted halfway to his mouth.

Sam thrust his hands out. "Ideas?"

The rum glass continued its journey to Gabriel's mouth and delivered a healthy slug of liquor down the man's throat. "I hardly know where to start. With the information that one of the galaxy's most infamous lovers has suddenly decided to become possessive of one woman? Or that said woman is crazy enough to infiltrate the Kinz factory? You could be here all night explaining either one of those things."

Sam couldn't help himself; he started up off the couch, only to be brought down again by a wave of dizziness. He shook it off.

"We don't have time for all that. You'll just have to trust me that Ray and I know what we're doing."

"*Dios mio!*" Gabriel got up and headed for the kitchen. "I need more rum."

Inspiration hit Sam, almost bringing him to his feet despite everything. "Daniel! *He* has contacts inside Kinz!"

"Who the fuck is Daniel?" Gabriel had brought the liquor bottle back from the kitchen with him. He put it on the table and faced Sam. "Look. Calm down. Explain this to me and start making some kind of sense before I think maybe Vort screwed up your head."

Sam took a breath and one look at his friend's scowling face and realized he might seem more than a little out of orbit. He allowed Gabriel to pour him another drink. Then he gave the extractor a full debriefing, from the time he'd hauled in the *Fleeflek* to the minute Vort had sent him down the ramp at Madras spacedock.

Gabriel sipped at his rum as Sam finished his story. "The Thranes hadn't shown up by the time you'd left LinHo?"

"No. But I'm sure they must be there by now. And who knows what kind of timeline they're on?" Urgency rose in Sam's chest again. "I have to get a message to Daniel on LinHo."

"Rescue has an office in Amara. I can go there in the morning."

"I'll go with you."

Gabriel stared him down. "Do you have any idea how unpopular you are with Rescue? You walk into that office and everyone in the place will have a finger on a comm to ConSys Intel or city police to pick you up."

Sam wanted to laugh, but the look on Gabriel's face stopped him cold. "Why? I bring them boatloads of lucky ones on a regular basis." Granted, he never actually delivered them in person. Chen usually managed it, he never asked how. The *Shadowhawk* came and went in Spacedock with impunity thanks to liberal bribes, and he just kept his own, wanted head down.

"You're a loose cannon, Captain, that's why. They can't control you." Gabriel shook his head. "Just like this little operation you mucked up. Think your girlfriend was unhappy about her detour? Imagine how her bosses felt. Now you want to waltz in there and demand they do something to pull her out of a place they had so much trouble getting her into? Yeah, that'll go over like a pair of gravity boots."

Sam's jaw set. "They may not like me. They may not want to see me. They may even throw my ass in jail. But by gods and starshine I *will* get them to warn Rayna about what those Thranes are going to do at Kinz. If Daniel gets the message, he'll get it to Ray. So they will send that message to Daniel before they haul my ass out of that office—and you're going to see that they do."

CHAPTER TWENTY-TWO

The whistle blew and, with a groan, Rayna heaved the last crate into place on the mule and stepped back. She wasn't sure how much longer the bosses would keep them here in the loading docks; she refused to consider how much longer her body could tolerate the heavy loads and unending abuse. Until the pounding initiation of time on the lines was over she couldn't begin her real work of moving the likeliest survivors to the outside, of sabotaging the Kinz operation in the smallest, least detectable ways. She'd schooled herself to be patient in dozens of other jobs like this one, but her patience was running thin.

After the long shift, Lainie was done talking. The girl's shoulders slumped as she shuffled into the line. There were dark circles under her eyes now, too—she didn't sleep well. Rayna heard her reliving her childhood in her nightmares.

You'll be the first one out. I promise, little sister.

Rayna lined up behind Lainie as the shift prepared to file out of the loading area. The lines of workers lurched forward toward the exits, and her mind turned inward again, wandering aimlessly until it latched on to something warm and solid—Sam. Where would he be now? She hadn't thought to ask him where he'd be headed next. Did pirates even have destinations—or did they just go where their whims took them? So many things she'd never asked him.

A gap had opened in the line between herself and Lainie up ahead, and just as they passed the end of a conveyor, a woman turned and bumped into the girl. The woman was big—tall, athletic, *Thrane!*—but Lainie pushed her off, not giving an inch. The Thrane grinned, backed up and held up both hands in a show of surrender, then turned quickly back to her work.

The guards had ignored or missed the encounter. Rayna tried hard for a look at the woman's face, but she'd turned so that was impossible. The line moved on; Rayna was forced to give up and rush to join the others.

Just past the active conveyors, in the dark canyons of the storage platforms, Lainie abruptly peeled off to the right of the line and disappeared into the shadows. The guards took no notice.

What the hell? Rayna had no time to think; she had no idea why the girl would do such a thing. But there was no way in hell she was leaving her to her own devices. She waited a few more steps, then ducked into the dark passageway between the two ceiling-high scaffolds that held the packed crates she spent her days moving off the line. She ran down the aisle, peering through the open platforms for a glimpse of Lainie. *There!* Walking in no great hurry toward the end of the line of platforms a few aisles over.

She got to the end of her passage and turned right, catching the girl as she got to the end of her aisle.

"What the hell are you doing?"

Lainie said nothing. She frowned, and sat down.

"That's a good girl." The voice came out of the dark behind Rayna.

She turned, just in time to deflect the blow that would have smashed the back of her skull. The Thrane wielded a piece of plasteel as long as her forearm—some part of a lase rifle filched from one of the crates?—and Rayna's shoulder where she'd taken the strike burned deep into the muscle. She grabbed at the hand that held the weapon and punched at the Thrane's throat, but the woman was too strong; she found herself flying through the air to land with a bone-jarring crash on her back.

Before she could roll to her feet, hands caught her and held her down. She struggled, but without effect. Two hulking Thrane males grinned down at her and would not let her up. *Males? How can they be males? And where the hell did they come from?*

"Let her go. It's me you want."

Sam emerged from the shadows not three meters away. Another Thrane held a shiv to his throat.

"What? No!" Rayna fought to get up. "What in Portal's Hell are you doing here?"

"I came back for you." His voice was flat; his expression was blank. What had they done to him? He looked at the Thrane woman. "Let her go, Zetana. Fair trade—me for her."

Now he knows her name? "No! What is *wrong* with you?" The hands holding her slammed her back to the floor.

He turned his blank stare on Rayna. "I love you."

Zetana laughed. "How sweet. And such a lovely offer! But I don't need you, Captain. I need your ship." She gestured to the man holding the shiv, who pulled a comm out of his pocket and held it to Sam's mouth. "Call your XO and order him to prepare for boarding. Tell your crew not to resist."

Sam's jaw clenched, the only sign that there was anything left of him inside.

"Do it, or I will kill her."

A cold blade appeared against Rayna's throat. She felt the trickle of warm blood run down her throat before she felt the sting where the sharp edge had nicked her.

Sam opened his mouth to speak.

"Sam Murphy, so help me. If you do this, I will never forgive you." *Or myself.*

But he did it anyway. He called the *Shadowhawk* and ordered his crew to stand down. And then he looked at her with nothing in his eyes and said, "I had to. I love you more than anything."

Zetana smiled, a smile as wicked and cold as the vast, black vacuum of space. Then she stepped up, took the shiv from her man, and swiped it across the right side of Sam's throat. Blood sprayed onto her hand and arm as Sam, his face a mask of shock, dropped onto the floor.

Rayna heard someone screaming. It couldn't be her, because she didn't believe this. She refused to believe this. This could not be her Sam, dead on the floor with his throat ripped out. Her Sam was safe and warm and alive all the way to his eyes, somewhere on the other side of this sector of space.

And suddenly she knew: she was not being held down by two male Thranes, because the males in this prison were housed in a separate wing and worked in a different section of the factory floor. This fight was just between her and a Thrane woman named Zetana, who, like all her kind, could manipulate the minds of her enemies.

Just as Zetana turned from Sam's "body" to come in for the kill, Rayna jumped up from her prone position on the floor, slapped at her left arm to put her own shiv in her right hand and stepped in. She thrust the shiv deep into the Thrane's abdomen and jerked upward, opening a fatal gash. Blood slicked the knife as Zetana folded over the wound. Rayna pulled out the shiv and struck again, this time at the carotid. When she stepped back, the bigger woman crumpled to the floor in a bloody heap.

"Holy shit!" Lainie scrambled to her feet, eyes wide. "Who the hell is that?"

"This is half of the team I've been waiting for." Rayna glanced at the shiv in her hand, then reluctantly dropped it on the floor. Her bloody jumpsuit was another matter. No way she'd be able to hide that.

But it didn't look like she'd even have a chance; someone was coming up the aisle, with a lightcell and a squawking comm—a guard, and probably not alone.

"Don't move! Stay right where you are!"

Oh, thank God! "Neko?"

"Shut up!" His whisper was urgent as he found them. "Portal's balls! What the fuck did you do?"

"Nothing I didn't ask you to take care of before it came to this."

Neko scowled at her. "How was I supposed to figure out which of five Thrane bitches was the spy?"

"Well, now we know." Rayna couldn't repress a shudder. "She lured us back here to take me out."

He looked over his shoulder as the comm at his waist issued a string of garbled sounds. "The others will be here any minute. I'm taking you into custody— for your own protection. Strip off that jumpsuit."

When Lainie stared at him, he growled back at her. "Even I can't explain that much blood."

Neko took the bloody clothing, wrapped it into a tight ball and stuffed it inside his uniform. Then he escorted his two charges out through the darkest part of the warehouse section, his ear to the comm to avoid his fellow guards, who were still searching for the source of the screaming someone had reported earlier. When he got to the corridor, he parked the two women in a storage closet.

"I'll be back as soon as I can," the guard told them. "Don't move. Don't talk. Don't even breathe."

They waited in the dark while the scene of Rayna's encounter with the Thrane assassin replayed over and over again in her mind. Every detail had seemed so real—the weight of hands on her, holding her down; the color of Sam's skin; the dark scruff of beard along his jaw, as if he hadn't shaved today; the way his chest had risen and fallen with his breath—too fast, like hers; and his blood, deep red and . . . everywhere. The power of that illusion held her still; she was shaking so hard she thought her bones might break.

Lainie watched her. "Are you okay?"

"Not really."

"C'mon." Lainie pushed her gently on the shoulder. "A big, tough Rescue agent like you?"

Rayna inhaled an uneven breath and let it go. "Yeah. Right. You're right. Just don't like all that mess, you know?"

"Yeah, I got you. Lase weapons are much cleaner." The kid was looking at her like she understood it was more than that, but she didn't call her out.

"Have to say I was glad to have the shiv, though." Rayna forced a laugh and rubbed her arms to cover the shaking. "Damn, it's cold in here."

"Ray, I'm sorry. It was my fault you ended up alone with that woman." The girl sat on the floor, her gaze directed between her hands to her feet, struggling for words. "It was strange. I thought I was back on the ship." She glanced up, laughed a little. "I was headed to the galley for chow."

Rayna huddled down on the floor beside her. "Some Thranes are powerful enough to project illusions without touch. That bitch had me thinking I was fighting her and two males. She even threw Sam into the mix."

Lainie gawked. "Cap? How . . .?"

"She tried to use what was in my mind against me." Rayna smiled. "Guess he was on my mind."

Lainie grinned. "But it didn't work, huh?"

"No. Something you said broke the illusion."

"Something *I* said?"

Sam Murphy would never have let his love make him weak. His love for her would have only made him stronger.

"Yeah. I do pay attention sometimes."

Half an hour later, Neko came back and threw a clean jumpsuit in her direction. "Here, put this on quick. The boss is going crazy trying to figure out what went on. I put you on report for some minor infraction, so I'm gonna lock you up 'til this blows over." He pointed at Lainie. "You, I gotta get back to the barracks ASAP."

"What? No! Put me on report, too!" Lainie was frantic, panic in her eyes. She grabbed Neko's arm.

"Hey! Calm down!" Neko put her off. "Trust me, you don't want to go where she's going. It ain't no fun and games. But it's only for a day or two, until I can plant this on some sucker." He held up something wrapped in a bloody handkerchief.

Rayna grinned. "You picked up the shiv!"

"Somebody's gotta do the thinking around here."

Lainie turned away from the guard and spoke in a

whisper. "Ray, let me go with you. I don't trust myself not to kill somebody while you're gone."

"He's taking me to Solitary. You'd go crazy in there. And, besides, I need your eyes and ears on the outside."

"I need to know where you are, at least."

Rayna looked at Neko for agreement. Heaving a big sigh, he waved them in front of him.

He led them quickly down the corridors away from the factory and the barracks. At the end of a poorly-lit hallway stood a tritanium door protected by its own electronic security check. Neko put his thumb to the scanner and was allowed entry with his prisoners. On the other side, six cells lined the corridor, three on each side, with a tiny reinforced amberglas window in each door. All appeared to be empty at the moment; the cellblock was as quiet as death.

"*Perai*. You have to stay *here*?" Lainie's whisper echoed in the void.

Neko unlocked the first cell and ushered Rayna in. Inside was a cot, a toilet and sink, and nothing else. She knew the lights would go out when Neko left, depriving her of any kind of stimulation.

"Neko, it's even more imperative that you find the male half of this couple," she said before the guard could leave. "Now that his bondmate is dead, he'll be out for revenge. Whatever he's here to do, he'll do fast. Do you have that information I asked you for?"

The guard pulled his comm from his breast pocket. He tapped a few times, then passed the device to her.

He pointed. "Those are the new men who came in

with the last shipment. There were four male Thranes. Do you see him?"

She recognized him right away. "That's him. The one who looks like a mediamix star."

"Really? You think so?" Neko frowned at the image.

Lainie leaned in. "Oh, yeah. How can such an evil sonofabitch look so fine?"

Neko humphed. "I still don't think I can convince my boss he's a threat without some kind of evidence. Maybe I could frame him for his mate's murder?"

Rayna heart dropped into her stomach. "No! He'll kill you, Neko. Stay away from him. Just talk to your boss; explain that this man is a spy for the Minertsan government. That should be enough to have him searched and isolated, at least. Then we can both take him on."

Neko appeared to consider it. "I'll see what I can do."

Rayna sat on her cot and prepared to wait out her sentence. "Whatever you do, do it fast. I have a feeling we don't have much time."

Rexus Kor awoke from a black hell of tortured dreams into a world of pain. At first he didn't recognize his surroundings—blank walls of some faint color, punctuated with electronic monitors and harsh lighting panels; a sharp, metallic smell of blood and disinfectant; the beep and murmur of equipment.

The infirmary.

His senses were dulled, muffled, as if he were wrapped in cloth, but the drugs they had given him did nothing to blunt his awareness of the hole in his being, as deep and wide as any canyon on his mountainous home of Thrane.

Zetana.

For the first time in more than a hundred circuits, he called out to her and she did not answer. She was gone, departed forever from this plane. Taken from him, *murdered*, ripping his soul in two. From his place at the machine on the factory floor he'd monitored every step, every word. His Zetana's performance had been flawless, her mind perfectly focused on the illusion she'd created to entrap the bitch and her little shadow. It had worked—he had seen it! The young one had led the agent into the stacks; she had sat down quietly without protest. The agent had responded just as planned, behaving as if her lover, the captain, was there betraying her, as if she herself was being held down by two strong men.

But then it had all fallen apart. The cursed *pultafa* sprang to her feet and thrust a knife . . . He'd collapsed into screaming pain at the moment of his *k'taama's* death. When people came to his aid, he fought them, raging and cursing, blind to his surroundings. Guards came to subdue him, he didn't remember how many. He only remembered he wanted to kill them; he wished they would kill him.

Zetana!

Rex writhed in agony on the hospital cot, sending the monitors into a frenzy of alarms, and noticed for the first time that he was shackled to the bed at his wrists and ankles. He cursed and fought until he felt a sting on the inside of his wrist where the cuffs he was wearing clamped down tight.

Just as the sedative began to take effect, he understood: he would have to hide his grief from the world. He would have to lie to explain his sudden "seizure" on the factory floor as the knife had slashed into his bondmate's body and her life's blood had spilled out over her murderer's hands. He would blame his violent spasms of rage on a relapse of Vargellan fever. The symptoms matched, and a prison infirmary would be unlikely to have the tests to confirm the diagnosis. He would be "fine" after a day or two of rest. He could return to work.

And he would plant this cursed place with enough explosive to blow it to Portal's Hell in less time than it would take for his sweet Zetana's soul to find its way to the Blessed Lands. Then he could join her there forever.

But first, he would find the *shalssiti vlitz* who had killed his *k'taama* and make her scream for hours until she died. This he vowed on the bond of his heart.

CHAPTER TWENTY-THREE

"You realize this is a fundamentally bad idea." Gabriel scanned the street before he glanced at his companion for confirmation of his opinion. "You'll either wind up in custody or shot in the back trying to escape capture."

Sam grinned at him as they crossed to the other side of the nearly-empty sidestreet. "Actually, I believe Rescue will be just as anxious to save the life of their agent as I am. That should give me a pass, don't you think?"

Gabriel looked grim. "Maybe. But just in case, there's a side alley that exits near a maglev station. We'll make for that if things go nova."

"Ever the optimist."

"Just part of my sunny disposition."

Partway down the block, next to the alley Gabriel had identified, was the storefront that housed the Rescue office. The space wasn't large, but the front window showcased a holo-display highlighting the appalling conditions under which slaves were transported and kept. The images weren't nearly as shocking as they could be, Sam knew. They were sanitized for public consumption. No donor or potential volunteer would want to see what conditions were really like. To see what he had seen, what he knew Rayna had seen, was to have those images seared into your consciousness forever.

"Cheerful bastards, aren't they," Sam said as he reached for the door.

Gabriel huffed out a laugh. "Brother, you ain't seen nothing yet."

The hour was still early, but to the organization's credit, the office hours etched on the window glass showed Rescue opened early and closed late—and the staff this morning hadn't slacked. Two young people were at their posts in the outer office, so bright and shiny Sam's eyes hurt. Along the back wall, doorways led to the offices and meeting rooms at the heart of the organization. Sam wanted beyond those doorways. But he clamped down on his impatience and let Gabriel, who knew the place, take the lead.

The tracker was already leaning on one of the front desks, smiling at the young girl who worked behind it. "Is Sophia Oksana in this morning, agent?"

The girl blushed. "Oh, I'm not an agent. I just volunteer here."

"Uh-huh. Well, I think that's admirable." Gabriel flashed her a grin.

Sam noticed the young man who worked with the girl wasn't so happy about the conversation. He signaled Gabriel to hurry it up.

"So. The director?"

"Oh!" The girl looked like she'd just woken up from a dream. "Yes, she's here. And your name, sir?"

"Gabriel Cruz. Tell her I have some information

about one of her field agents."

The girl knew her job; her back straightened and the smile dropped off her face as she hit the comm. "Ms. Oksana, there's a Gabriel Cruz here to see you. He says he has information about one of our field agents . . . Yes, ma'am."

She looked up, her eyes gone suddenly cold. "She'll be right out, Mr. Cruz."

Gabriel just smiled and nodded as he moved back from her desk, but Sam could feel the drop in temperature as both the young volunteers glared icily at them. Even office workers were aware if someone had "information" about a field agent, chances were they came bearing bad news. Sam didn't blame them for wanting to kill the messengers.

A center door in the back wall banged open and the director of the Madras Rescue station emerged, but she wasn't alone. Three husky men backed her up—Sam could only assume they were field agents—and none of them looked happy. Too late he noticed the tiny sensor over the door they'd come through. Security was better than expected in the Rescue office. He and Gabriel stood shoulder to shoulder, and again he waited to see what the tracker's move would be.

Gabriel merely nodded. "Sophia. Nice to see you again."

Oksana, tall, dark and unfathomably exotic, favored him with the merest glance. "Under different circumstances I would say the same." She gestured to the men beside her, who surrounded and put Sam in an armlock. "As it is, you show up in my office with a criminal who has caused my office no end of grief. Are you asking for some kind of reward?"

Sam, struggling against the men who had hold of his arms, missed how it happened. One second Gabriel was standing beside him, the next he was behind the young girl with a stunner to her head. The girl's eyes were as big as plates.

"Sophia, *mi amor*. I regret that I'm here for business, not pleasure, today." Gabriel seemed so relaxed and off-hand that one of the agents took a step in his direction. The tracker shot him and returned the weapon to the girl's head in a motion so fluid and quick Sam could hardly follow it. The agent writhed on the floor, his nerves on fire.

Gabriel went on. "My friend has information vital to the safety of a Rescue agent active in the field. He'll share it with you if you guarantee his continued freedom from incarceration. Otherwise we'll leave this place and your agent will likely die, her mission a failure."

Sam fought against his captors. What the hell was Gabriel doing? He *had* to tell Oksana what he knew. She *had* to believe him. They couldn't afford to walk out of here without doing what they'd come to do.

"Gabriel!" The man on Sam's left smashed him in the mouth. He sagged to his knees; the guy had a punch. Somewhere in the air above him he heard Gabriel's voice: "Trust me, *amigo*."

Sam looked up and saw Oksana capitulate. "All

right. I'll listen to what you have to say. Let the girl go—you know you're not going to hurt her."

Gabriel loosed his grip—and took an elbow right in the sternum. The girl might have missed his solar plexus by a centimeter.

He backed up, rubbing his chest, a grin creasing his face. "Ouch, little *targa*." The girl just scowled at him and adjusted her clothing.

"Let's go." Oksana ushered Gabriel, Sam and one of the agents through into the back offices. The other agent stayed behind to tend to their stunned companion. "She wants to be an agent, you know."

Gabriel rotated his shoulders, working out the soreness in his chest. "She'll do fine."

Okasana glanced back at him, and Sam saw a hint of what must have once been between them. "Big baby."

Gabriel smiled, but said nothing.

The Director led them to a conference room, with a table that took up most of the room and a set of mismatched chairs. A media-projector took up space at one end of the table, a model not unlike the one Sam had onboard the *Shadowhawk*, meaning it was ancient, but serviceable and projected both flatscreen and holos. Otherwise the room was bare and could use a coat of paint.

They settled in, the agents took up a post at the door, and Okasana got to the point. "Okay—what is it you have to tell me?"

"You're aware I picked up your agent Rayna Carver

while she was undercover aboard the slaver *Fleeflek*." Sam's chest constricted around his heart; this cold recitation of facts made it seem like she was already gone somehow.

Oksana frowned. "Yes, I received a message from onboard your ship. We thought she'd have to give up the mission, thanks to you. But a few days later I heard from my agent on LinHo that she'd made it there and was going to go through with it."

"She did go through with it." Sam refused to think about what that meant for Ray. It had been her job, her choice. "We made the contact with Daniel, and he took her in to the Kinz facility. Then I ran into someone who wanted to settle an old score. Before Gabriel saved my ass I learned that the two Thrane spies who tried to sabotage my ship while Ray was aboard—the ones who had also been undercover on the *Fleeflek*—were working for the Minertsan government. They're planning to blow up the Kinz factory. Personally I don't care what the fucking Grays do to each other. But we have to get Rayna out of that factory before they do it."

Oksana folded her arms over her chest. "And how, exactly, did you pick up this unlikely information? Seems like we're missing a few details from your account, Captain."

"Look, I don't have the time to walk you through this." In his frustration, Sam got up out of his seat; the agents at the door reached for the stunners inside their jackets. Oksana waved them off, but Sam stayed on his feet. "I heard this directly from Teliath of Paradon, during . . . negotiations . . . of which I was an unwilling part. The negotiations failed, and we came on to Madras, where Gabriel found me."

"Teliath." The Director spat out the name like it tasted bad. "Did he say how he'd come by what otherwise would be knowledge of a highly classified nature?"

Sam grinned in satisfaction. "My *Shadowhawk* beat the hell out of that Gray ship before we parted ways. The Grays were forced to seek repairs on Paradon."

"Where, apparently, the Thranes made no secret of their mission?" Oksana's face was a picture of skepticism. "Why do I find this hard to believe?"

"Teliath is a very persuasive host, *querida*," Gabriel explained. "Drugs, alcohol, sex, food, gambling. He finds his guests' weaknesses and exploits them ruthlessly. No doubt he found a way to loosen the Thranes' tongues like everyone else's."

Oksana turned her deep brown eyes on the tracker. "You think this is a credible threat?"

"I wouldn't be here—risking my friend's life— otherwise."

Seconds ticked by in the silent room while the Director considered her next move. Then, "Very well." She reached for one of several datapads scattered on the table. "I'm sending our agent on LinHo a message to shut down the Kinz operation immediately. He'll extract our agents in the facility, and we'll find a way to warn the factory operators to avoid loss of life. Damn it!" She pinched the bridge of her nose with two delicate fingers. "Do you know how long we've worked to set up this operation?"

Anger flared in Sam's chest, and he took a step in her direction. The boys at the door jumped. He saw Gabriel tense, ready to back him up, but he wasn't going to make that play. He'd gotten what he wanted.

Still, he had a thing or two to say to Ms. Sophia Oksana, Director of the Interstellar Council for Abolition and Rescue/Madras. "Do you know how close you've come to losing Rayna in the last tendays? You've worked together for years, maybe you've been friends—does she not matter to you at all? I tell you she could be blown to pieces any day—literally any moment—and all you can think about is the mission?" Beautiful or not, the woman was an unfeeling bitch. "You can care for the millions out there, but you can't care for your own. My girl needs another job."

Oksana humphed up at him. "What, playmate to a blackjack?"

"If I didn't need you to send that message right now, I'd show you how a blackjack treats someone who disrespects his woman." Sam's hands curled into fists at his side; his voice dropped into a growl. "Send it. And tell Daniel the *Shadowhawk* will be there in two days to pick Rayna up. It'll be her decision where we go after that."

All around them the crew of the Shadowhawk celebrated with wild abandon, dancing to what passed for music in this mishmash of young, multicultural men and women, drinking to excess, hunting for partners for the night. Rayna and Sam stood off to the side of the surging mob. Even they had had a little too much to drink. Rayna figured they all deserved it.

"We really kicked some Gray ass today, huh, Cap?" It was Javin Darto, with a huge, grog-fueled grin on his face and a sturdy young woman—she was new to the crew—tucked protectively under one arm.

"That was mostly you doing the kicking, Javin." Sam grinned back at him. "If pirate ships had commendations . . ."

"You'd give me one! Heard that one before, Cap! I'll settle for my share of the loot."

"Should be a big haul this time," Rayna told him. "Rescue's letting us keep whatever we can carry from the liberated estate."

"Gods bless 'em! Who knew going legit could pay so well?" He lifted his mug in the direction of his captain and wandered back into the crowd.

"I've had about enough of all this public celebration." Sam's words washed across her ear on a whisper of warm breath. Rayna shivered. "Let's go back to the cabin."

She turned to see the light in his eyes and smiled.

It wasn't in her to resist.

They made their way back to the captain's cabin through empty corridors, the occasional cat or security crew member the only soul they met. Rayna tried to think back to a time when every centimeter of the 'hawk had not been familiar to her, when the man at her side had been a stranger, when she'd been so lost and alone she hadn't even known it. But the memory was distant, dim. This was home now. Here, with Sam.

The cabin door slid open for them, and Sam pulled her inside. The hatch had barely closed behind them before he picked her up, grasping the backs of her thighs in warm hands. Rayna wrapped her legs around his waist and her arms around his neck and brought her lips to his. His kiss tasted of drunken cherries, his tongue tangling with hers, his heat igniting hers. He pulled her into his body, and the hard length of his erection found the swelling flesh between her legs. She ground against him with a moan.

When he broke off to trail fiery kisses down her throat, she finally found her voice. "Do you think maybe we could take our clothes off and do this on the bed, sweets?"

The room abruptly tilted, and she found herself on her back on the bunk. With a grin, Sam straddled her hips and stripped off his shirt. She laughed back at him in delight, her heart thumping as she spread her hands to caress the broad chest with its sprinkling of dark hair in the center, the flat, rippling stomach, the bulge just below the waistline where other treasures lay still hidden. While she explored, he unzipped her top to expose her breasts, wrapped in a lacy red bra she'd chosen just for him. She smiled at his growl of appreciation. Some purchases were worth the trouble.

She sat up to slip out of her top and let him do the honors with the bra. He took his time, lowering the straps and bestowing kisses to the collarbones underneath, removing the scrap of lace and cupping her breasts one after the other to bring them to his mouth. Her nipples peaked under his attention, and the ache between her legs became a throb of need. Her hands reached for his zipper and released him from his confinement. She squeezed the broad head and stroked down the hard shaft until Sam groaned in sweet agony. Desire burned in her body in response.

She lay back and pulled him with her, wanting only to feel him deep inside. He kissed her, hungry and hot, his tongue bringing the taste of passion and unquenchable love. His hand slipped inside her pants, to a core that had become molten with need. His fingers drew circles around a clit swollen tight with want.

She broke off the kiss, impatient for him, moaned his name, unable to wait. He rose over her and tugged the rest of her clothes, and his, off. And, at last, he settled between her thighs and pushed inside, slowly, one delicious centimeter at a time, until he was seated deep, so deep, in her throbbing heart. She couldn't breathe. Oh, God! *She couldn't move. Every cell in her body waited for him to give her what she needed so desperately.*

And when he began to move, withdrawing his length to thrust deep inside again, over and over again, she felt the wave building, building. From her burning core to her heated skin she felt it overtake her until there was no escaping it. The pleasure crashed over her, core spasming, muscles clenching, heart hammering. She screamed, clinging to him, begging for more even as the sensations tore her apart and he pounded into her hard, harder for an endless time.

But he was only human; they were only human. She heard the rumbling groan that was his alone, felt him tense and the hot, pulsing release of his seed as he came, felt the aftershock of tenderness for him as she held him. She felt everything so deeply and yet she knew . . .

. . . it wasn't real. Rayna woke from the dream of a life she knew she could never have to the reality of a cold, dark cell. At this hour the only light came from the window in the door, 15 centimeters on a side, which let a hint of the outside world into the cell. It would be some time yet before "daylight" in the domes of LinHo, when the lights inside the cell would come on, a routine that spared prisoners' eyes and made them fit for work when they came out of Solitary. Rayna preferred this time, these hours in the dark, when she could hide inside herself and dream.

"Ray!" The urgent whisper came not from outside

the window, which was solid amberglas, but from the food slot at the base of the door. A quick knock followed.

She scrambled off the cot to the floor. "Is that you, Lainie?"

The slot shot back and a face appeared in the small space. "Yeah. We have to talk."

"How the hell did you get in here?" Okay, the systems were computer-run, but someone was monitoring them. And just thinking of all the security checks the girl would have had to go through to get here made Rayna's heart pound.

"When we left you here, Neko gave me a bypass code for the thumbprint access—you know, in case it's not working, which apparently happens all the time. The rest was too easy. I should have been sneaking out of the barracks all this time—for extra food and stuff. I'm definitely gonna do that from now on."

Rayna blew out a breath in exasperation. "No, you're not. Why are you here, Lainie?"

"Because Neko's disappeared. I haven't seen him since he put you in here. Wasn't this supposed to be temporary?"

Apprehension clutched at Rayna's chest. The guard could have extra duties in the aftermath of Zetana's death. He could be avoiding making contact with Lainie. There could be any number of reasons why she hadn't seen him, other than the most likely one—that Zetana's mate had found him and slit his throat.

"What are people saying about the murder? Guards

still looking for the killer?"

"No. Neko planted the knife on a lowlife who'd already killed a few other people. They executed him this afternoon—uh, that would be yesterday afternoon."

So I should be out of here. "You've heard nothing about the Thrane."

"He went crazy on the factory floor and was taken to the infirmary. I haven't heard anything since then."

"But that makes no sense." Until suddenly it did. The pieces of the puzzle fell into place with a deadening thud. "Shit."

Lainie stared through the slot at her. "What?"

"Neko was supposed to tell his boss that the Thrane was a spy. It would have been cake to remove him from the infirmary—they would probably have locked him up here." Rayna ground her teeth. "But I don't see him here, and Neko has disappeared. That means someone at the top is working with the Thrane, and we can assume Neko is dead."

"Fuck." Lainie's face showed only determination. "I'm going to pick the lock and get you out of here."

"No! The locks are alarmed, keyed to comp sensors." And the cameras. *Fuck!* "Lainie, what did you do to disable the security cams when you came in?"

Lainie let out a long-suffering sigh. "What do you think? I hacked the comp at the entrance to put them on continuous loop for a few minutes. Think I'm stupid? So I can just hack in again and disable the lock sensors."

"Yeah? And how would we explain my sudden

reappearance in the barracks? No. We need help."

"Help, from where?"

"You'll have to contact Brilly. In the mess hall, you remember?"

"The one missing a tooth."

"She'll find a way to get me out of here." Rayna took a breath. "In the meantime, I think I've figured out why the Thrane is here. And if I'm right, we only have a matter of hours to keep this place from being blown into black space."

CHAPTER TWENTY-FOUR

Sam stepped off the D-mat pad into the familiar blue-lit embrace of home. He took a deep breath and inhaled the welcoming smell of ozone, warm electronics, clean surfaces, people. His people. Some part of the tension inside him uncoiled; with the *Shadowhawk* around him the impossible had just become possible.

Mo was waiting for him and snatched him into a bear-hug as soon as he got within reach. "You *mulaak* fool!" His voice was just loud enough for Sam to hear it. "I didn't think I'd get you back this time."

Sam pulled back and grinned at him. "Neither did I. Thanks for sending the cavalry."

Mo turned to shake Gabriel's hand. "Good to see you again, my friend."

"Worth it just to hear you set your captain straight." Gabriel looked at Sam. "And what the hell is 'cavalry'?"

Sam waved a hand in dismissal. "Old Earth reference. Forget it."

"Yeah, he's full of 'em." Mo led the way into the corridor. "He watches too many holovids. I don't understand half of what he says."

Sam acknowledged the smiles and nods of his crew members as he made his way to the bridge with the others. It was clear they were happy to have him back.

He was more than happy to be here.

"Ship's status, XO?"

"We took on as many supplies as we could while we were in port; we were running low after so long at LinHo, where there was nothing to buy. This took twice the usual number of bribes, of course, since we needed everything fast. And I'm not sure our usual contacts in port are going to hold after this visit. Everyone had heard Vort had you ready for delivery to ConSys."

Sam grunted. "Sorry to disappoint. Continue."

"All ship's systems are operational, but we are only at nominal efficiency, especially in life support and weapons. We really need more time for repairs, but that will have to wait. Crew is present and accounted for onboard. We have clearance to leave orbit when you're ready, Cap."

The back of his neck prickled at the report of nominal efficiencies in crucial areas, but there was little to be done about that now. Time was against them.

Still, Sam couldn't help grinning as they swept onto the bridge. "Crew!"

"Cap!" All turned in their places to grin back at him—Sipritz at Navigation, Dartha at the helm, Ot at Weapons, Patel on Communications, Ordman monitoring status boards.

His chest tightened, and for the briefest moment, he couldn't find any words. He cleared his throat.

"Well, I see we're all in our places, with bright, shiny faces. Let's not waste any more time. Helm, prepare to leave orbit."

"Aye, Cap!"

"Navigation, lay in a course for the C5 jump, maximum ion drive."

Sipritz smiled—or at least he thought she did. "Already calculated, Cap. Laying it in now."

"Estimated time of travel?"

"Eleven hours, thirty-two minutes, at three-quarter ion speed."

Sam looked at Mo. "Three-quarter is the best we can do?"

"If we hope to sustain it." The Pataran's usual grim expression grew even darker. "Kwan has things cobbled together like a hoocher's still. Don't push it."

Gabriel, now sprawled in one of the "observation" seats, raised an eyebrow.

"Understood. Three-quarter it is. Mark course and speed once we're out of orbit, Sip."

"Aye, Cap."

"Ready to leave orbit, Cap. Spacedock Central is standing by." Dartha looked at him expectantly.

"Let's get the hell out of here, helm."

"Leaving orbit, Cap."

He paced the Cap's walk above the horseshoe-shaped conn and watched as they scribed a graceful arc out of Madras orbit. The two companion planets in Madras's solar system were well off his flight path. Once away from the gravity well of the planet he'd just left, his ship found her highest possible speed, and they raced for the jump node at C5, which would chute them to the C4 node and LinHo.

Mo put a stop to Sam's pacing near Gabriel's chair. "We need to talk."

Sam took note of the strain in his First Officer's long face. "Tell me."

Mo shook his head. "Your command room."

Sam recognized that tone of voice and felt his heart drop into his stomach. He glanced at Gabriel to indicate he should join them, and inclined his head in the direction of the tiny cabin just off the bridge.

He put a hand on his helm officer's shoulder as he passed. "Dartha, you have the conn."

In the cabin, Sam slid behind his desk. This would be an official report, he knew. He would have to be the captain. Might as well take the position.

Mo stood before him. "I reported that all crew members were onboard and accounted for. That was not entirely accurate." He waited a beat while Gabriel sank into the seat behind him. "We're missing Lainie Butaar."

"The kid we picked up on Belarius?" Sam absorbed a sudden, gripping pain in his chest. "Since when?"

"Since LinHo. I had a party go out and look for her while we installed the new jump matrix, but word on the rock was that work details from Kinz were picking up anything that moved on the streets."

He'd arrived once just in time to save her from a life of degradation and misery on Belarius. Now his XO was telling him she'd been dragged back into it on LinHo? The pain morphed into anger.

"How the hell did she get off the ship? A kid like that—"

Mo held up a hand. "You'd ordered limited shore leave—senior crew only. And I held to that. In fact, the only people down on that planet were yourself, Chen, Doc Berta, Kwan and Javin Darto—and Darto was only there because Kwan needed him. Lainie took herself off this ship. She ran."

"Why would she run? To a garbage pit like LinHo?" Sam raked a hand through his hair in frustration.

Gabriel stirred. "How long had she been aboard?"

Sam thought back. She'd only been a slip of a thing when they'd found her on that auction block—maybe thirteen or fourteen? But tough as the hull of his ship; it had taken a circuit at least before she let her guard down.

"I don't know. Maybe three circuits." He shook his head.

"Was she usually a rebel? Breaking rules, coming in late off shore leave, that sort of thing?"

"Never." Mo spoke up in her defense. It was his job to know, after all. "Her only problem was a smart mouth."

Gabriel's lips quirked. "It's a pirate ship." He looked at Sam. "Doesn't sound like she's the kind of kid who would go AWOL without a reason."

Sam blew out a breath in exasperation. "What possible reason could she—oh, shit. She was Rayna's cabinmate for the first few days she was here."

From long habit, Mo caught his line of reasoning.

"You think Lainie followed Rayna off the ship?"

"I think she suspected something was up that night and followed us all the way to the bar where I made the hand-off to Daniel." He clenched his fists to keep from hitting something. "Gods, what she must think of me."

"She probably tried to follow Daniel and Rayna to Kinz and got picked up somewhere on the way." Gabriel looked up at him. "You can see this one of two ways. Either you've got a second person to find and rescue from that hellhole, or by a freaking miracle Ray has someone to watch her back in what has become a giant clusterfuck." He shrugged. "Me, I'm an optimist. From what you tell me of these two women, I choose to believe they found each other. Now all we have to do is get our asses to LinHo and get them out of there."

"I need more freedom of movement. Returning me to the barracks is unacceptable."

From behind his desk the Minertsan regarded Rexus Kor with opaque black eyes, his normally silver-gray aura tinged dark green with fear. "But how am I to explain giving a slave free access to the facility? Surely you can see that would be suspicious."

Rex had nothing but disgust for the little slime lizard, but he restrained his worst emotions. After all, the factory manager was a patriot, working against the private Minertsan owners who were selling the Kinz factory output to the Grays rebeling against their own government. But he was a coward, too, afraid to do all that was necessary. Not for the first time, Rex thought to touch the Gray's mind and force him to his will. Only impatience stayed him. Overcoming the manager's natural resistance would take time he did not have.

"You would not have to 'free' me," Rex explained. "Simply leave me in the infirmary. It should be easy to make some excuse in the official record. Provide me with a security access card; I'll do the rest."

"What about the infirmary staff?"

Rex waved a hand. "I can control them."

The Gray opened a drawer and reached for the access card, his aura dark and swirling with doubt. "You will be cautious?"

"I know my business."

Deep red and black now marked the creature's aura. "Your business has already been a bloody one."

Anger flared in Rex's chest, and he slammed both fists on the manager's desk. "Not nearly bloody enough. My mate is dead! And her killer has yet to be found. Where is that *shalssiti* bitch? Tell me that!"

The manager shrank back into his chair, his aura flashing deep yellow and green in terror. "We've searched the whole compound! She must have found a way out. Surely you've had your revenge on the guard you said was helping her?"

"That guard had nothing to do with Zetana's murder. I killed him because he came to you about me." Rex backed away from the desk and started to pace. "He must have been allied with Carver, though. And it makes me wonder—how many other agents of the enemy hide among your staff? How many will I have to eliminate before I can complete my task?"

"If you do your work quickly and quietly, perhaps no one."

Rex turned to look at the little Gray. "But where would be the fun in that?" He held out his hand for the access card. The manager handed it over, and Rex secreted it inside his jumpsuit. Then he left the manager's office without another word, picking up his escort outside the office door to return to the infirmary. He walked meekly behind the guard through the passageways and into the medical wing to his cot, his mind busy.

After lights out tonight he would begin his task of setting the charges throughout the facility, planting his packages in all the places guaranteed to cause the greatest devastation, the maximum amount of suffering. Rex calculated the work would take no more than two nights, by which time, by previous arrangement, the *Tifan* would be waiting for him in LinHo orbit.

Only now he had nowhere for the *Tifan* to take him. He had no home to return to, no future ahead. The life he had envisioned with Zetana was nothing but ashes and dust, its memory a bitter taste in his mouth. All because of that bitch. *That shalssiti pultafa vlitz!*

She was still here, he could feel it. He was connected to her—through pain, through blood. He didn't believe she had escaped this maximum security facility. Yes, inside Kinz it was easy to get away with almost anything—including murder. But to get in or out of Kinz? That was nearly impossible. And despite what he'd said to the manager, he didn't think there were that many others working with the agent on the inside. Otherwise why bring her in?

No. She was here, and he would find her. A simple death in the fire and crushing weight of shattered thermocrete and durasteel that he had planned for the Kinz factory was not good enough for that bitch. She must have something more elaborate and protracted, something more intimate, just between the two of them. Rex smiled in the isolation of his cot in the infirmary, and the comp monitors set into the mattress noted his anticipation with indications of elevated heartbeat, respiration, blood pressure.

He would find that bitch Rayna Carver and take her with him when he left this place. That would be his future—to torture his enemy until she died, in sweet revenge of his beloved mate. Then perhaps he could finally have peace.

Doc Berta had insisted he waste several hours under the healing light. And there were the interminable files full of facts that he had to get through to reacquaint himself with the *Shadowhawk*'s current status. By the time Sam was in his command room with a drink in his hand, he was heavy with fatigue. Maybe a few minutes in his bunk . . .

Gabriel examined the amber liquid in his glass. "Have you given any thought to what might happen after LinHo?"

"We connect with Daniel, he makes contact with his people on the inside of Kinz. We pray that Ray has already found Lainie so we don't have to wait long for them to come out." Sam re-crossed his feet on top of his desk in the command room. He poured himself another two fingers of the good stuff, which he drank only three or four times a circuit, when Gabriel was aboard. "Then we hightail it out of orbit as fast as this beautiful bucket of bolts will take us."

The corners of Gabriel's mouth ticked upward. "Not a bad plan, but that's not what I meant. I meant, when this is all over and you have Rayna safe and sound aboard your ship—what are you going to do then?"

"I haven't figured that out yet." Something with claws scraped through Sam's chest. At best he'd be lucky to be with Rayna as often as he savored the taste of real alcohol. He tossed back the liquor and anything else he might have said.

"Oh, *m'hijo*, you are in deep shit." Gabriel leaned forward to look him in the eye. "You're a pirate, for God's sake. And this woman—she works for Rescue. As an *agent*. You don't get any more committed to a cause than that. Has she ever said why?"

"Her parents were slaves."

"And Rescue got them out—like most of the families on Terrene, including mine. There's more to it than that."

Sam swung his feet to the floor with a growl. "What are you, her psych counselor, now? I'm going to the bridge; it's almost time for the jump."

Gabriel rose to let him pass. "Figure out why she needs to do this, Sam. Then you might have a chance of changing her mind."

Sam turned to look at the man who had been his friend since the day he'd rolled off the 'hawk for his first shore leave. "Maybe she's already changed mine. Wouldn't that be a kick in the teeth."

He stepped out to the bridge, where the chorus of voices greeted him. "Cap."

"Crew." Sam tamped down the worry and confusion that still burned in his gut over his future with Rayna and focused on the here and now. "Status, Mo?"

His XO turned from the sensors. "Approaching Jump Node C5 at just under three-quarter ion power. We'll encounter the outer limits of the Ming Ra asteroid field in approximately ten minutes, thirty seconds at this speed."

"Very good. Give me a schematic of C5, showing Ming Ra, would you, Sip?"

"Aye, Cap."

"And prepare to slow to half speed on my mark, Dartha."

"Whenever you're ready, Cap."

The detailed three-dimensional rendering of the area around the C5 jump node filled the main viewscreen, showing the small spatial distortion that was the node itself in front of a spray of asteroids the size of half a solar system. The space approaching the node was relatively clear of rocks, the gravitational cone of the node itself having captured whatever may have orbited within range and sent it through the wormhole to the other side. But nothing was ever guaranteed around C5; it was a minefield, one that changed every hour.

"Slow to half ID, helm; ready on weapons, Ot. I'm sure we'll have one or two rogues to pick up before we go in." Just because the random asteroids weren't yet visible on the screen didn't mean they weren't there.

Both helm and weapons officers acknowledged the orders; he gave a few more. "Shields up. Give us the best approach, Sip."

"Aye, Cap. Approaching at 100,000 kilometers now."

"You seeing those rogues yet, Mo?"

"I have one within sight now, Cap, 130 mark 7, maximum range."

A light appeared on the viewscreen, indicating the presence of the rogue along their course. Then another. And one more. Mo called out the coordinates as he saw them.

"Navigation, maintain a position on those things. Helm, keep us clear of them. As soon as we get within weapons range, we may have to take one or two of them out just to make sure."

Sam paced the upper walkway, apprehension twisting the back of his neck. He tried to shrug it off.

"What's our weapons status, Mo? Still no forward transducers?"

Mo straightened from his post and gave him a look that would have withered a lesser man. "When last I checked, credits did not fall from the stars. The only reason we aren't still stuck in LinHo orbit is that your Chief Engineer is an extremely talented gambler. We spent all of his winnings at Slash on a new jump matrix. He didn't win enough for new transducers."

"Okay, I get it." Shame burned Sam's cheeks. How long had it been since they'd taken a profitable haul? "I haven't been doing my job. You'd be right to toss me over."

Mo crossed his arms over his chest. "Oh, I doubt it would come to that, Cap." He allowed the barest of smiles as he met his captain's gaze.

"Thanks, my brother." Sam clapped the Pataran on the shoulder. "I will make it up to you. Somehow."

"Captain!"

He heard something in his navigator's voice and turned to the viewscreen. A blip, larger than those indicating the asteroids, had separated itself from the asteroid field.

"Sipritz?"

"A ship, coming at us straight out of the Ming Ra, bearing 10 mark 18."

"Identification."

Mo checked his own sensors and shook his head. "No beam. And she's too far away yet to get her size."

Sam felt his gut clench. He didn't need to see the ship to know who had just appeared to fuck up his day.

"It's Vort. He knew we'd have to use the C5 to go anywhere from Madras and he waited for us." His own blood had built the *Master of the Octagon II*; he knew her inside and out. "He's armed to the teeth—heavy plasma cannons fore and aft; concussion torpedoes port and starboard."

"And we won't be able to outrun her," Sipritz pointed out. "She'll be between us and the jump before we can get there."

"Battlestations, Ordman."

"Aye, Cap. Battlestations." The kid didn't quite look so pale this time out. He'd be okay.

The alarms sounded, the lights flashed red and the various ship's stations reported ready. Sam stepped down to his seat in the center of the horseshoe-shaped conn between and just behind navigation and helm and waited for Kwan to call from Engineering.

Within seconds the pad lit up. "Captain."

"Kwan here, Cap. Are you seriously considering taking this ship into battle?"

"Nice to hear your voice again, too, Stephen. Good job getting us a new matrix. And, yes, I'm afraid we have no choice. It's either that or let ourselves be blown into stardust."

"The jump is right there!"

"And the enemy is in front of the node. Would you

like to come up to the bridge and play captain while I take over Engineering?"

Silence. "No, Cap. We'll do the best we can down here."

"You always do, Stephen. Bridge out."

At the observer's station, Gabriel shook his head. "Is it always so calm around here when you're rushing to your destruction?"

Sam glanced back at him. "No. We've had a lot of practice lately."

"Should I be somewhere else?"

"Stay where you are. You'd only worry if you were in your cabin."

The captain could have known the closing distance by the instruments on the console below him, but he asked anyway so everyone on the bridge could hear. "Range, Sipritz?"

"Eighty-five thousand kilometers and closing fast, Cap. Bearing now 15 mark 21."

On the screen, he watched the approach of Vort's ship, like some gathering storm about to break over their heads. They were still several minutes out of weapons range; he had time to use his brain, rather than his raw instincts, to find a way out of what was sure to be a sweaty, bloody death for the men and women who trusted him. This was his fault, after all. Vort was coming after *him*. It wasn't right that his ship and his crew should have to pay their captain's debts to a lowlife, cheating scum like Drew Vort.

He would have offered himself up as tribute, but it

was too late for that. Vort was out for blood, and he wanted every drop. If they fought head-to-head, the 'hawk would lose. She was missing too many pieces, her speed too slow, her weapons crippled, her reserves hovering close to zero.

Sam stared at the viewscreen. The three asteroids hung in the vast space between his ship and Vort's, too small and too few to afford any real protection along the route to the jump node.

But what if their destination wasn't the node at all?

"Sipritz, give me a course that will put those asteroids between us and the *Octagon* as quickly as possible."

The Mper looked back at him. "But, Cap, that course will take us wide of the jump node. We'd have to circle back to make the jump—through the Ming Ra."

"The Ming Ra is where I want to go right now, Sip. As fast as you can get me there."

There was an audible gasp from half a dozen throats on the bridge, then silence. "Uh, aye, Cap," the navigator finally acknowledged.

His second-in-command stepped down to stand by his elbow and spoke quietly. "Are you out of your mind?"

"Vort won't have the patience to wait me out. He'll follow me into the Ming Ra, but his crew won't be able to handle it. We'll have the advantage of skill and experience in there. And before you even ask, yes, I got this from an old Earth media mix."

Mo stood and stared at the viewscreen.

Sam looked up at him. "Aren't you going to argue with me?"

"I would if I had any alternative to offer. We're clearly no match for the *Octagon*. Guerrilla warfare in an asteroid field seems almost sane."

"Course laid in, Cap," Sipritz said. "Ready on your mark."

"Helm, full—er, three-quarter ID. Ot, you'll have a shot at them from the starboard cannons before we pass to port of those three rogues. Be ready. And give me split viewscreen."

He got acknowledgment from Dartha and Ot and the screen split to show both the comp simulation and a sensor compilation of what was going on outside his ship. Sam studied the screen and gripped the arms of his seat as he waited for the *Octagon* to come into range. It didn't take long.

"Sixty thousand klicks and closing."

"All hands brace for incoming fire."

Lines of blue laze fire spit from the enemy ship, rocking the *Shadowhawk* like a succession of violent waves on a stormy sea. Anyone standing on the bridge was tossed to his knees. Alarms blared and the familiar battleship smell of smoking electronics and overloaded ventilation systems filled the air.

"Evasive maneuvers, Dartha. Keep us out of their sights as much as you can without reducing speed."

"I'll do my best, Cap."

The next series of shots glanced harmlessly off the aft and starboard shields.

Ot danced in his seat. "If we could turn another 15 degrees to port, Cap, I could fire back from the starboard cannons."

"Not yet." Sam knew they were taking a beating, but they needed speed. Deviating from their course now would cost them the chance to make the Ming Ra.

"Concussion torpedoes incoming." Mo's voice was without emotion. It always was when the news was dire.

"Brace for impact!"

The *'hawk* shook from stem to stern as the torpedoes, two of them, struck her amidships. Sam knew her shields would have taken most of the impact, but from the feel of it, the shields had collapsed under the assault. They were vulnerable now, her belly exposed.

"Mo! Shields!"

The XO shook his head. "Down to 20 percent on the starboard aft quarter. Still have 40 percent on the starboard fore quarter."

"Dartha, show them our asses long enough to fire rear cannons."

His helm was turning the ship even as he spoke. "Aye, Cap!"

"Ot, fire as we bear."

"Aye, Cap!"

Sam felt the thud of the cannons firing through his bones and watched on the screen as the *Octagon* was forced to take evasive action. "That should keep them off us for a minute. Resume course and get around those asteroids. Keep up the pressure, Ot."

"Aye, Cap, firing as we bear."

The cannon laid out fire as Dartha took them in a tight outer loop back to their course; the *Octagon* veered off its forward trajectory to intercept them. But the rogue asteroids loomed ahead and to starboard. Vort was impatient, his crew inexperienced, but he wasn't stupid. If he wanted to keep the *Shadowhawk* from taking that jump, he would have to stay between the rogues and the node. That would give Sam the protected route he needed to the Ming Ra.

But he had to reach the shelter of the asteroid cluster first. "Hit him again, Ot! We're almost there!"

Laze fire from the *'hawk*'s starboard cannons lit up the *Octagon*'s port shields. Return fire shattered what was left of the fore starboard shields, rocking the bridge, nearly knocking Sam out of his seat. He pulled himself back into place and looked up at the screen. The big rocks of the rogue asteroids loomed into view, filling the sensor half of the screen.

"Reduce magnification, Mo. I've lost him."

"Magnification 200, Cap."

"I have him at 89 point five mark seven, Cap."

"Good. Fast as you can on that course to the Ming Ra, helm."

Dartha allowed herself the tiniest shift in gaze in his direction. "Aye, Cap."

Mo was at his side again. "These rocks are orbiting in a flat plane, you know. They'll only protect us as long as he doesn't come over or under them."

Sam reached down to his own console and switched the screen to aft view as they began to pass the rogues. "He won't have time. He'll want to protect that jump node, and we'll be gone before he comes after us."

But Vort had other ideas. Just as they began to gain distance from the shelter of the rogues, a stream of laze fire splashed against the largest of the rocks and blasted it into fragments.

Sam had time to shout "Aft shields!" mere seconds before the first of the pieces hit them. The ship bucked and shuddered under the assault of dozens of projectiles, large and small, the aft shields flaring like a supernova.

"Dartha, get us the hell out of here!"

"Trying, Cap!"

"Aft shields are down forty percent, Cap," Mo reported. "Make that fifty percent."

"Ot! Use the aft laze cannon. Target the largest fragments and fire at will."

"Aye, Cap. Firing."

Sam watched rock after rock explode just before it reached his shields. The *Octagon* had backed off, closer to the jump node, waiting for them to make a break for it. At least that part of his plan was still working.

"We're outrunning the worst of it now, Cap," Sipritz told him. "Passing point of no return for approach to jump node. Approaching the Ming Ra." The navigator sounded as if even now she expected a reprieve.

"Continue on present course. All possible speed,

helm."

"Aye, Cap. Steady as she goes. Three-quarter ID."

Sam ignored the false cheer in Dartha's voice. Instead he increased magnification again and watched his aft sensors to see if Vort would take the bait.

"Encountering outriders in sixty seconds, Cap." Sipritz looked up at him. "Orders once we're inside the Ming Ra?"

On his sensor screen the *Octagon* remained motionless, hanging in space just outside the jump as if Vort had decided simply to wait out his foolishness. On the computer sim-screen, blinking lights clustered like Ordian phosfer flies, indicating thousands of asteroids milling in destructive paths around them.

"Find a large rock a few hundred klicks in and get in tight. We're going to play a little hide-and-seek."

The sounds of his bridge crew identifying a likely asteroid behind which to hide and delicately weaving a path through the tumbling chunks of iron and ice faded into the background. Sam Murphy had eyes and ears for only one thing now. And after what felt like an eternity of waiting, he finally saw what he'd been looking for: the *Octagon* left her post at Jump Node C5 and came seeking him in the Ming Ra.

CHAPTER TWENTY-FIVE

Lainie shuffled slowly along in the serving line, so nervous her recycled-fiber tray clacked against the metal sliders where it rested. She studied the gap-toothed woman ladling out the slop that passed for food in the prisoners' mess. The server was the woman who had given Ray the shiv—wasn't she? What if she wouldn't agree to help them again? Lainie had no choice but to risk asking her. Rayna couldn't stay in that hole any longer. The Thrane had already had too much time to do his work.

Her heart threatened to break out of her chest as she drew even with the woman and held her tray up for the food. "B-brilly."

The woman's eyes narrowed and her hand paused mid-ladle.

Lainie kept her voice low and tried to make it look as if she was still moving. "Rayna's in trouble. We need your help."

Without a word of warning the server poured the full ladle of stew over Lainie's hand. The hot, gelatinous mess shocked Lainie into dropping her tray with explosive impact. Those near her jumped back, the guard at the end of the line came running and Brilly came out from behind the line, brandishing the empty ladle.

"You clumsy *vlitz*! What in the name of Portal's balls is wrong with you?" She reached Lainie before the guard and cuffed her hard enough to make her ears ring. Then, while Lainie cowered at her feet, unsure of what she would do next, Brilly reached back over the line to exchange her ladle for a towel from one of her co-workers. "Get the line going. I'll take care of this." She turned to address the guard. "I'll deal with her. Just make sure this wasn't a distraction for anything else."

The guard looked as if he hadn't thought of that and scurried back to his post. Lainie would have smiled if her arm hadn't still been burning where the hot stew had scalded her skin.

Brilly tossed the cloth at her. "Clean up that mess, you clod. And there'll be no supper for you tonight."

Lainie's stomach growled. She supposed there had to be a price to pay for getting Brilly's help—if she was going to get any help.

"Who the hell are you?" Brilly's voice was so low, Lainie could barely make out the words.

The question was unexpected; Lainie said the first thing that came to mind. "I'm the bitch you just maimed for life." But when she realized the woman might actually slit her throat because she didn't recognize her she straightened up fast. "I'm Lainie, Rayna's friend from the *Shadowhawk*. I've been with her every day. Don't you remember?"

For a long moment, Brilly stared darkly with no sign of recognition. Then, "What's happened?"

"Neko put Ray in Solitary until he could pin the Thrane woman's murder on someone else. He's done that, but now he's disappeared. We need to get her out of there. Ray thinks the male half of the Thrane team is here to blow up the factory."

Brilly grunted. "That will be a little difficult for him to do from the infirmary. He's still recovering from his little fit on the factory floor—Vagellan's fever or some shit."

"Oh." Relief flooded Lainie's chest. "That's good then. And Neko?"

"Gone. Or dead." She gestured at her charge and raised her voice. "Hurry it up, girl! I have work to do."

Lainie made a show of cleaning the floor, though there was not much left to clean. "What about Rayna?"

"I'll meet you at the Solitary block two hours after lights out." She grabbed Lainie's collar and hauled her to her feet. "Now get out of my sight before I decide to kill you!"

"Kwan, I need power to those starboard shields."

"And as my sainted mother used to say, people in Portal's Hell need to cool their burning feet."

Sam scrubbed a hand down his face. "Are you telling me there's no chance of getting them back at all?"

There was an extended silence on the other end of the comm. Sam waited while his Chief Engineer sorted his priorities.

"Our power reserves are below critical, Cap. If we can remain at stationkeeping for ten minutes, or find a way to avoid using weapons altogether for even longer, then, yes, I can get the starboard shields back. Otherwise, keep your port side to him."

"Understood. Captain out." Sam stood up and found his pathway on the Cap walk. Ten minutes would be an eternity; even Vort could find them before then.

Gabriel watched him with dark eyes and a somber expression. "Time is not on our side, *amigo*."

"No."

"But surely Vort will run out of patience soon?"

Sam shook his head. "Depends on how good his sensors are." The *Shadowhawk* sat in near darkness, emergency lights only providing the barest glimmer of ambient light, the lights of panels and displays dimmed down to a minimum, voices hushed and comms blocked to prevent giving away their position. "But he won't go home without me. He'll start blasting rock at random before he does that."

Gabriel might have smiled. "That I believe."

Long, slow minutes ticked by as the sensors tracked the progress of the *Octagon*'s search on the viewscreen, now nearer and every muscle on the bridge tensed, now farther and every breath was exhaled in relief. Four minutes. Five. Sam began to think that perhaps they had a chance.

"Power reserves are coming back up, Cap," Mo

reported. "We're at 60 percent and rising slowly."

"Thank you, XO." Once the power reserves were at 75 percent, the damaged shields could be re-engaged without endangering engines or life support. Of course, full reserves would be ideal, but what was that about people in hell wanting what they couldn't have? Though Sam wasn't a religious man, he was praying now: *Just a few minutes more.*

"Cap, we're starting to drift away from this rock." Dartha, at the helm of his ship, looked to him for orders. "Should I risk a burst of the thrusters to keep us behind it?"

Sam's hand curled into a fist. The screen showed the *Octagon* was headed away from them. Still, she was close, too close. She would be on them in a blink if they used the thrusters.

"No. Let us drift. We'll just hope the *Octagon* gets a little further out before we're forced to use the engines to avoid slamming into a *mulaak* rock."

"Aye, Cap."

Six minutes. Seven. And now they were fully exposed in the space between hunks of eternally rolling rock. The shields would hold off the smaller rocks—at least, the functional shields would. But the only way to avoid being smashed to bits by the larger asteroids was to navigate using the thrusters. His helm was sweating just looking at the screen. Sam would have to engage the engines soon.

"Mo. Reserve status."

"Seventy-two percent."

Perai.

"Permission to fire thrusters, Cap?" The pitch of Dartha's voice had gone up half an octave.

"Not yet."

Now every face on the bridge was turned in his direction. He ignored them and watched the screen, willing the *Octagon* to continue its fruitless snuffling behind the stones in another section of the field. He imagined the scene on that ship's bridge. Vort would be nearing the end of his patience by now, likely screaming at his crew to *Find him! Find him!*

Eight minutes.

The *Octagon* continued its zig-zag path deeper into the Ming Ra. Vort was surely not aware he'd left the way open for the *Shadowhawk* to make a run for the jump node.

Nine minutes.

Mo looked up from his sensors. "Reserves at 75 percent, Cap."

Thank the gods! "Sip, we need a course back to the node, one that allows for us to drift part of the way at first. Dartha, put us on that course with a short burst of thruster power. I want them to miss it if they're not paying attention."

There was a heartbeat of stunned silence before both crew members acknowledged the extraordinary orders and reported ready. "Now. Go thrusters."

"Aye, Cap. Firing thrusters."

He felt the engines thrum briefly and watched the orientation change on the viewscreen as the *'hawk* took her course out of the Ming Ra. For a moment he thought perhaps Vort had missed the burst of thruster power; the *Octagon* sailed on without pause. Surely they couldn't be that lucky?

Ten minutes.

"Power reserves are at 80 percent, Cap." Mo turned to raise an eyebrow at him. "Should I try raising the starboard shields?"

"Yes, I think we're going to need those, XO." Sam turned back to the screen, where the *Octagon* had made a course correction. "Sooner, rather than later."

He felt the thrusters growl again and a dark slab of rock looming in the sensor screen fell harmlessly to port. On the comp-sim side of the screen, the *Octagon* had completed her turn. Their time was up. Vort was on to them.

"All possible speed now, Dartha. Get us out of here as fast as you can."

"Aye, Cap! Three-quarter ID."

The engines now hummed full-time in his bones, and the asteroids shrank in the sensor screen, a function of the reduced magnification that was automatic at this speed. "Ot, stand by on aft cannons." Sam wouldn't waste anything on Vort until he had to, but he'd bet that wouldn't be long.

"Aye, Cap. Standing by."

"She's in weapons range, Cap," Mo said. "Coming in hot."

Sam hit the comm. "All hands brace for incoming fire."

The first streams of laze fire shot out from the nose of the *Octagon* and sheared off the face of a nearby asteroid. Dust and bits of rock bloomed into a cloud that obscured ships, asteroids and anything beyond on the sensor screen. The second shot fared better, striking the *'hawk*'s aft shields and shaking the ship to her core.

"Evasive maneuvers, Dartha! Ot, time to use those cannons."

"Aye, Cap, firing now!"

Laze fire splashed against the *Octagon*'s forward shields, lighting up the dust cloud.

Ot turned to his captain with a grin. "Got him, Cap! Direct hit!"

"Dartha, give him our port side for half a minute."

Both crew members acknowledged and the maneuver brought them broadside as the *Octagon* raced closer. "Fire port cannons!"

Twin arcs of blue laze fire raked across the enemy's flank, pounding her shields until they flared and collapsed. Sam saw it and gripped the arms of his seat.

"Come about, Dartha. Now, now! Aft cannons, Ot. Hit him amidships. We've got the sonofabitch!"

"Coming about, Cap."

But not fast enough. Sam felt it in his gut; his *'hawk* was not her graceful self and fought to make the turn. Ot bounced with impatience waiting for his target to line up in his sensors.

Concussion torpedoes erupted in a swarm from the *Octagon*, slamming into the port shields, knocking Sam and everyone else standing to their knees. The *'hawk* bucked and yawed with the impact. Connections snapped in the bridge control panels, throwing sparks and smoke into the air. Outside the ship, a few torpedoes found targets in nearby asteroids, exploding them into dust. The sensors picked up little but a swirl of multicolored gas and tiny fragments.

On his knees on the deck, Sam wiped something warm and wet from his brow; his hand came away bloody. "Ot! Tell me you're lined up!"

"Firing aft cannons."

Even in the chaos of the bridge under attack, Sam could feel the rhythmic thud of the cannons as they let go. He pulled himself to his feet and watched the comp-sim as the two lines of blue-white laze fire hit their mark.

"Got him dead center, Cap!" Triumph lifted Ot's voice.

The sensor screen flared as the *Octagon*'s damaged engines became critically unbalanced and swallowed what was left of the ship, her crew and her oxygen in a brief, fiery explosion. On the computer simulation, the light that had indicated the enemy ship winked out, leaving nothing in its place. Sam knew, even if the sensors were clear of dust and gas, there would be little more than debris to show that the *Master of the Octagon II* had occupied space and time seconds earlier. His nemesis had been erased, as neatly as if he had never been. Only the scars on Sam's own body now existed to show that Drew Vort had ever lived in this universe.

His crew was cheering, but Sam didn't join in. As the adrenalin rush of battle drained from his body, his mind returned to its one true focus. Vort was part of his past. If Sam was to have a future, he had to get through that jump and make it to LinHo in time to save the only thing that mattered.

CHAPTER TWENTY-SIX

It was dark again. In her jailors' parody of night and day, the lights had been turned off for the hours meant for sleeping and resetting of the body's circadian rhythms. But Rayna was not asleep. Her mind wouldn't allow it, regardless of whether her body might want to respond to the dark as it should.

She'd spent the long "day" exercising in the tiny cell—pushups, situps, squats, every *ahx zun* martial arts routine she could remember from her training days. She'd pushed herself to the point of exhaustion, rested, then started up again. And still, when the lights went out, she'd stared into the blackness and waited for a sleep that would not come while the walls closed in on her.

No matter which direction her thoughts took, frustration followed. From Lainie, out there on her own, possibly in trouble. To the Thrane, setting his charges all over the factory, maybe even this minute sending the signals to rip the place apart. To herself, stuck in here, unable to do anything to stop him. And, finally, always, to Sam. Sam, who she would never see again.

Rayna turned over and punched the flat, lifeless pillow. She would give a significant body part to be able to punch a living being right now. A shot at the main target of her anger—the Thrane—would be too much to ask for. But a guard or two? Yeah, that would be very satisfying.

A whisper of sound wafted through the slot at the base of her cell door—someone was accessing the security system to enter the cell block. Adrenalin surged through Rayna's veins, kicking up her pulse, tightening her chest. She fought it with deep breaths. If they were coming to kill her she would only have one chance, a very slim one. But she'd be damned if she'd go out without a fight.

As she slipped behind the door, the corners of her mouth curled up. *Remember, you asked for a fight, you dumb ass.*

Light flooded the cell, and Rayna could hear voices now as the guards approached—low murmurs, as if they were trying not to disturb the sleeping cell block. Why bother? This place was far removed from the dormitories; guards never worried about who heard them. Then another thing struck her—the voices were feminine.

She waited.

"Ray! It's me, Lainie! We're here to get you out."

"Oh, for chrissake!" Rayna exhaled the breath she'd been holding and stood back from the opening door. "I came this close to breaking your neck."

"*Perai*! Touchy much? We're here to rescue you!"

Rayna noted the storm clouds of righteous anger gathering around the teenager and shook her head. "Never mind. I am very glad to see you." She extended her welcome to the older woman with Lainie. "You, too, Brilly."

Brilly responded with a terse nod. "If the meet-and-greet is over, can we get our asses out of here? I was only able to program the camera malfunction to last for 90 seconds." She led the way out of the cell and down the corridor. "It's on continuous loop, but the security comps have programs that scan for things like that. A loop goes on too long and an alarm is triggered."

Rayna nodded. Kinz was not the solid, impenetrable bastion of security it was reputed to be on the outside, but it was secure enough where it counted, and Brilly's help had been essential. She offered up a prayer, too, for the departed Neko.

The trio exited the Solitary block and sealed the doors behind them. Brilly spent several precious seconds with the security comp to delete all evidence of this latest visit and to make sure there was no record of Rayna's having been there at all. When she was done they turned and moved back toward the main hub of the factory building, away from the cameras watching Solitary.

In a darkened corridor away from any prying eyes, Rayna called a halt. Not much distinguished this section of hallway; it was flanked with large storage lockers. Up ahead, a little-used passageway led into a mechanical room, at the rear of which was a tiny ventilation grate. The vent led directly to the outside, but though it was hidden and covered with a heavy perforated-metal plate, some clever children had still found it during their brief time in the factory. They'd never had a chance to use it before their "experiment" ended and they were sold. Or so Rayna had been told.

Lainie's gaze flicked from the lightless passage to the mech room back to Rayna's face, her jaw tightening as she recognized the place. "No. No, Ray. I'm not leaving you here."

"I'm not giving you a choice. You weren't meant to be here in the first place."

The girl clenched her fists and took a step forward. "Really? Well, it's a fucking good thing I was here, wasn't it, or you'd still be stuck in that *mulaak* cell. You need me."

Rayna flushed, and she just caught herself from meeting the teenager's anger with her own exasperation. As an agent of Rescue she had a job to do, and not much time in which to do it. Lives were at stake. The girl would only be in the way. But that's not why Rayna was sending her away.

She made herself back off. "You're right, I do need you, Lainie. I don't have too many friends, and I can't afford to lose one."

"Friends don't leave friends behind. I can help. You know I can."

"It's too dangerous!" Rayna couldn't keep the note of desperation from her voice. "This guy, this Thrane, he may already have us sitting on a ton of explosives. They could blow any second."

"No, Ray, that's just it!" Lainie rattled off her argument with breathless excitement. "That Thrane has been laid up in the infirmary since you killed his *shalssiti* mate. He hasn't had a chance to place any bombs, and he's too weak to fight us. He's a drifting freighter in an asteroid field! We go, we get him, *then* we leave. Together."

Rayna shot a glance at Brilly. "This true?"

"He took a beating on the factory floor." She shrugged. "But Thranes are mightily attached to their mates. Maybe he just doesn't want to get up."

"Yeah, and maybe he just likes working from the infirmary."

Brilly raised an eyebrow and nodded, but Lainie's face showed only confusion. "What does that mean?"

"It means he may not be as injured as he seems. It means I may have to use every bit of the training and experience I have to kill a wounded fang-eel." Rayna put all of her authority as an agent of the Interstellar Council of Abolition and Rescue into her voice. "It means I have to do this alone."

Lainie's expression grew dark. "And what if you can't do it alone? What if he kills you instead because no one was there to help you?"

"Then I'd like to know you were safe. I'd like to know you were out there with Sam and the *Shadowhawk*, even if I can't be. You understand?"

The girl seemed caught between defiance and despair. "No," she said, but her body had given up the fight, standing with shoulders slumped and head lowered, as if she'd been sentenced to life in the prison around them instead of freedom in the wide galaxy outside.

Rayna knew she had won; she didn't hesitate. "Brilly, you know this way out, right?"

The woman nodded. "We use it sometimes. She'll fit through the opening just fine. I won't be able to go with her, though."

Lainie lifted her chin. "I'll manage."

"Don't linger on the streets," Rayna told her. "Go to the bar where you saw Sam make the handoff to the Pataran. His name is Daniel."

Brilly handed the girl a comm. "Call him as soon as you get there. If anyone else picks you up, smash this and it'll send out an emergency signal." Brilly turned to Rayna. "Should I meet you back at the infirmary?"

"No. I do this on my own."

"Then you'll need this. Knocks out the cams for ten seconds while you access the security comp." The woman handed her a package. "Little something extra, too."

Lainie couldn't seem to help a last appeal. "This is fucked up."

Rayna pulled her into a hug. "You have to go. I'm gonna kill that bastard, then I'll be right behind you." She'd never noticed how thin the girl was, how frail. Lainie resisted the contact, her body stiff in Rayna's arms.

Rayna pulled back and met Lainie's vulnerable gaze with a lift of her chin. "Go. See you on the other side."

"Standard orbit established, Cap. Maintaining as ordered."

In Sam's chest a curious mix of relief and fevered anticipation greeted those words. His heart boomed against a ribcage tight with impatience. He couldn't wait to get down on that stinking piece of rock.

He kept ruthless control over his voice. "Thank you, helm."

"LinHo Central is hailing, Cap." Patel raised an eyebrow at him. "They're not happy."

"Put 'em through." He waited while the connection was made and the pinched features of the dark-skinned human in charge appeared on his screen. "I'm Solomon Armstrong Murphy, Captain of the *Shadowhawk*. I am requesting full port privileges for my ship and crew for five planetary days. What's the delay?"

The man in charge scowled. "No delay, Captain. Just *no*. No privileges for your ship or your crew." An oily smile slid across his face. "Seems you've made a few enemies."

"That right? And what if I told you I'd taken care of those enemies—permanently?"

LinHo Central's unconcern was profound. "My boss was alive and well at dinnertime."

"I'm not talking about your boss. I'm talking about *his* boss."

The man's head tilted under the weight of a disbelieving grin. "You trying to tell me you've eliminated Drew Vort?"

"Blew him into space dust at the C5 jump node. Guess that makes me the new boss, huh? I'd show a little respect if I were you."

"Where's the proof?" His voice was steady enough, but the man's grin had faded now. His face said he had started to think this crazy story might just be true.

Sam turned to his XO. "Send him the ship's log." Then he watched as the Spacedock official's face blanched and his knees gave out beneath him. "And, no, the log wasn't faked. Vort is dead. At the time, I was still technically his partner. What was his is now mine. Set up a meeting with Vort's Number One on LinHo in two days."

The man found his feet and his voice. "Yes, sir. But what are you going to be doing in the meantime?"

"That's my business. Now, are we good?"

"Absolutely. Full port privileges for five days. Done. Enjoy your time on LinHo, Captain Murphy, sir!"

Sam gestured to cut off the connection. "Little *veer*. But at least the message will be all over that rock by the end of first watch today."

"You better hope it doesn't touch off a turf war before you have a chance to establish your own leadership." Gabriel had appeared at his elbow in that silent way of his.

"You think I really want the smuggling rights to a

cesspool built on slave labor?" Sam's voice was little more than a growl.

Gabriel shrugged. "Your crew might think differently. There's profit in it. What's *your* plan?"

"I'm going to get Ray and Lainie and the LO's out of that factory. Then for all I care that *mulaak* Thrane sonofabitch can blow LinHo to Portal's Hell."

Brilly had left her the gift of another shiv and a security access card that would allow her to enter the infirmary. But Rayna refused to believe it would be that easy to get to her target. He was Thrane, after all, with the ability to manipulate her view of reality. She'd experienced Zetana's grip on her mind, felt that helplessness in the face of a world that suddenly made no sense. Her enemy could make her think she was anywhere, doing anything. He could strip the weapon from her hand with a thought and leave her open to the attack that would kill her.

Thranes varied in their natural talent, in their level of skill, in their training. Some were limited to touch telepathy; some could project their control over great distances. Zetana had been able to project a short distance, at least. Rayna expected no less from her mate.

But Rayna had some defenses of her own. She had her own natural resistance to mind control—the resistance that had made it possible for her to be a

Rescue agent in the first place. Her Rescue training had reinforced that resistance. Her shields were respectable—for a human. Given adequate warning, she could stave off an incursion. For how long, she didn't know.

All of this weighing of accounts left Rayna's mouth dry as an airlock and the shiv shaking in her hand. Fuck it. The *mulaak* bastard had to die before he had a chance to do any damage. With that thought she silenced all her doubts. She flexed her fingers around the hilt of the shiv and slipped through the shadows of the empty corridors toward the infirmary entrance.

Like Solitary, the infirmary doors stood at the end of a separate hallway, the unmanned security comp standing guard outside. Cameras above the entrance monitored who entered and exited. At this hour, deep in the night, there was no movement in and out of the hospital wing—no visitors, no injuries or illnesses to deal with (aside from the rare emergency created by a fight in the barracks or a collapse from life in this hellhole), no deliveries. The staff inside would likely be dozing, the patients, including her target, sleeping.

Rayna took another quick look up and down the hall from her hiding place in the shadow of a doorway and aimed the device she carried at the security cams. The green lights on the cams winked out. Rayna sprinted for the security computer, keeping the time count in her head while she entered the code. She'd just counted "nine" when she ducked through the doors and pushed them closed behind her. Now the cameras would be safely back on, showing the corridor empty once again.

Ahead, through a small lobby, a wide hallway separated two examining rooms on the left from the walled-in reception desk on the right. The tall counter at reception faced the hallway, not the door; Rayna couldn't see if anyone was there. She slipped around to the right and waited.

Seconds later someone woke up and stuck a head across the counter. "Anybody there?"

Rayna hit the anti-cam device just in case and rushed the woman, slamming her head into the plasteel counter before she had a chance to move back or protect herself. The nurse was a big girl, but she went down in a boneless heap. Rayna knew she wouldn't stay out long; she hadn't hit her head that hard. She found some gauze bandaging in an exam room and tied the nurse to her desk with a gag across her mouth. She murmured an apology to the unconscious woman and turned to survey the patient monitors.

Empty. All the rooms were empty. Where the fuck was the Thrane? Her mind raced with the possibilities—he was dead; he'd been transferred back to the barracks; he was out somewhere in the factory leaving his packages; he'd heard the ruckus she'd made dispatching the nurse and was lying in wait for her. The last possibility chilled her bones and raised the hairs on the back of her neck. She gripped the shiv tighter in her fist and studied the monitors again.

One bed in the eight-bed infirmary barracks had

been made with less than military precision. The pillow at its head was rumpled, and there was an extra blanket at its foot. Someone was using it, someone who was absent at the moment. Not a patient—there were no IV tubes snaking from the wall or medications on the nearby table. If the Thrane had been injured or ill when he was taken from the factory floor, he'd long since healed. The infirmary bed was just a base of operations. Rayna's search for him would have to start there.

She aimed her device at the two cameras covering the hallway and watched the operating lights blink out, then jogged down the floor toward the Thrane's room. She paused at his door and peeked through the small, square observation window. The monitoring camera was mounted high in the corner. She took it out and confirmed the room was otherwise unoccupied, then ducked inside before the hall cams switched back on. Knowing she'd need more time in the room, she climbed on a chair and turned the room cam toward the wall. By the time Central Monitoring was alerted, she'd be gone.

Rayna jumped down from the chair and scanned the room for the bed she'd seen on the monitor. It was the last one in the row, furthest from the door, and as she approached it, every instinct told her she was descending into a pit of vipers. The Thrane hadn't bothered to hide the tools of his trade or the base materials of mass destruction. Was his mind really that powerful that he could keep the infirmary staff blind to all this? Stored neatly under the bed he slept in were thin plastic bags of explosive strips, packs of the delicate vials of chemical accelerant, lines of inactive nanoprocessor links, these in black, gray and white. A shallow tray held cases to contain his packages, simple black or gray plastic boxes that would attach to the back of a pillar or the underside of a girder.

There was an extra laser knife, too. Rayna stuck it deep in the side of her boot.

There was little else in the area of the bed to tell her what she needed to know: where was the Thrane now? She could wait for him here and risk discovery as the watch turned and the day staff came on, or she could seek him out in the little time she had left tonight. She blew out a curse and headed for the door.

At the reception desk, the big nurse was just beginning to rouse. Rayna stepped behind her and put an arm around her throat and her hands at her carotid arteries. The nurse promptly went back to sleep. Rayna untied her hands, but left the gag on and her feet tied, just to slow her down. She turned for the exit—

--and felt flames rocket up her spine and explode in her brain. She crumpled to her knees, the shiv loose in her grip, a scream gathering in the back of her throat. She was blind with the pain, deaf with it, unable to move or to think.

Until she heard a voice somewhere in the air above her head. "I wondered when you would come. You owe me a debt of pain, Rayna Carver. And, believe me, you will pay before you die."

CHAPTER TWENTY-SEVEN

Daniel Chang leapt off the D-mat platform wearing a glower as dark as unending space. Security Chief Chen and Javin Darto, who'd been sent to fetch him from the planet surface, followed at a slower pace, rolling their eyes at their captain.

"What the hell is this, Murphy? You know being seen visiting your ship can blow my cover, right?"

"After we've done what I've come to do, it won't matter." Sam turned and swept through the hatch into the corridor, dismissing his crew and leaving the Rescue agent no choice but to follow him.

"What are you talking about?" Words spilled out of the agent in a strained whisper as he struggled to keep up. "I got no details from headquarters on Madras— just that the mission was compromised and I was to wait to hear from you. What's going on? Is Ray in danger? *Perai*! Murphy! Stop!"

Sam pulled up in front of the lift. "Of course she's in danger, you *mulaak* sonofabitch. You put her there. We *both* put her there, when we allowed her to take this *shalssiti* mission." His teeth were clenched so tight he could barely open his mouth to speak. "Not that she gave us any choice."

"Are you going to tell me, or am I supposed to guess?"

The lift arrived, and they crammed into a space that

Sam thought was much too small for the two of them and all their anger, too. "Those Thranes that were aboard my ship? They're in the factory. She's an assassin; he's a munitions expert given the mission of blowing up Kinz on behalf of the Minertsan government."

Light dawned in Daniel's expression. "Because Kinz has been producing weapons for the Gray rebels. How do you know all this?"

The lift arrived at the bridge level, and Sam led the way to his command room. "It's a long story that I'm tired of telling. What's important is that we need to get Ray out of there—*now*."

Inside the cabin, Gabriel looked up from the data pad he'd been studying and nodded. "Gentlemen."

Sam let Daniel and Gabriel make their own introductions. He slipped behind his desk and called up the data he'd asked Mo to put together on Kinz on his desk screen. It didn't amount to much—yet.

He looked up and called the meeting to order. "Well?"

Daniel shrugged. "Normally, I'd say getting Rayna out of Kinz would be easy. There's no dematerializing in or out of the compound, of course, due to the security shield, but I have people on the inside. I contact them with the pull order, and they send her out. I pick her up. Done."

Gabriel shifted in his seat. "I'm hearing a big 'but.'"

"But she's not going to want to leave without eliminating those operatives." Daniel caught Sam's gaze and held it. "We couldn't keep her from going in. I don't think we'll get her to come out without a fight."

Sam cursed, his body itching for the physical release of pacing, but unable to move in the cramped space. "Damn stubborn little hellcat."

"And there's the question of what to do with the workers. We have a guard on the inside, but he's nowhere near command level. I doubt he'd be believed if he said there was a saboteur planting bombs in the factory."

"We have to risk it anyway," Sam said. "We have to evacuate that factory. And once we get the LO's on the outside, they're mine."

Daniel stared at him. "You're planning to liberate the factory, too? You're insane! What would you do with 1500 slaves—spirit them away on the *Shadowhawk*?"

"Your boss is sending a ship." Sam crossed his arms, realizing all at once what he had to do. "If Ray won't come to us, we'll have to go to her."

"Now I know you're crazy!" Daniel's head swiveled from Sam to Gabriel. "You! You tell him! This is a high-security labor facility. It's a prison. You don't just walk around inside and chat with whomever you please!"

"Oh, for fuck's sake, stop whining. It's not like I'm planning to take a tour." Sam put the confidence of his command in his voice. "You have people on the inside. You have ways to get people in and out. Get a message to Ray to meet us at the exit. I'll talk to her."

Daniel snorted, and even Gabriel, lips lifting in a skeptical grin, had to ask, "And when she won't come with?"

"Maybe she can use some help taking out a couple of Thranes," Sam suggested. "Once the evacuation begins, the place will be chaos. Think the guards will be keeping track with 1500 workers in the yard?"

"More like 1500 targets for a madman like this Thrane," Daniel shot back. "Have you thought about that?"

"Mo's working on it. Hacking the security network at one of the most secure facilities in the quadrant hasn't been easy." He grinned as he turned his desk comp in their direction. Red panels were turning to green all over the screen, giving his XO control of the gates of Hell. "But I think he's almost got it."

The Thrane's handsome face was twisted by a dark, furious hatred, his eyes alight with an eager fire. He stared down at her as the Devil must stare down at lost souls in their perdition, enjoying her suffering, anticipating what was to come.

"My name is Rexus Kor of the House of Kor of Thrane. My mate was Zetana, but you know that. You are the one who ended her life."

Flames licked at the base of her skull; smoke obscured her vision. "Not before she tried to end mine. And if anyone owes a debt, it's you. All those lives aboard the *Shadowhawk*? And the *Fleeflek*?"

"Worthless! Collateral! They were nothing compared to my Zetana!" His face contorted with grief and rage, and he took a step closer to her, but, unaccountably, the pain in her head dropped.

Rayna gathered what strength she had and lunged at him. He stepped aside and kicked her savagely in the ribs, crushing them on that side and launching her entire body into a bank of cabinets as easily as if she'd been a child's ball. She rolled inward, trying to protect herself.

The shiv. Where is the shiv?

He bent close to her and held the precious thing up where she could see it. "Looking for this?" He snatched it back out of her reach before she could grab it, then he yanked on her arm. "Up. We can't stay here. I need privacy for what I mean to do to you, little agent."

Rayna gasped as he pulled her up. *Shit!* For sure at least one of those ribs was broken. She could be grateful that the debilitating pain he'd hit her with earlier was gone. Maybe he could only maintain that kind of control for short periods. Then again, he only needed it for a second to put her on the floor.

He gestured at the nurse. "Untie her. And get rid of the bandages."

She did as she was told; no reason to argue. She could only hope the woman would call in an alarm when she woke up.

But the Thrane had other ideas. He put a hand to

the nurse's forehead.

Rayna didn't bother to ask what he was doing. The woman would be lucky to remember her name when she regained consciousness now. But if Rexus's mind was engaged in wiping the woman's memory, he might lose focus elsewhere. Rayna didn't hesitate. She kicked out at his knee, hoping to break it. He buckled, bringing her next target to hand. She was poised to strike his temple and end it when the inside of her head went white-hot with searing pain, her heart exploded in her chest and her world went red, then gray, then deepest, darkest black.

"You hacked the Kinz security net?" Daniel stared at Sam, his mouth agog. "Everything? Even the D-mat shields?"

"No. Those are solid. But everything else is ours."

Daniel shook his head. "Our best people have never managed anything like that."

"You don't have Mo." Sam couldn't help the note of pride in his voice.

Gabriel's lips quirked. "I told Sophia a long time ago that 'the best people' were not inclined to work for next to nothing."

Daniel grunted. "And I suppose you pay top credit on this bucket of bolts?"

"Nobody's complaining." Sam had had enough talk, especially from the Pataran. He shot to his feet. "Time to get moving."

Daniel looked like he might protest the abrupt dash to the exit, but the sound of a call alert stopped him. He pulled out his comm.

Sam felt a thrill of anticipation. "Is that your people inside?"

The Pataran looked up at him in surprise. "No. It's an emergency code we only use when something's gone wrong." He punched a pad on the unit. "Chang. You're who? Okay. Yes, we can, but you should talk to your captain first. Hold on." He held out the comm to Sam. "Your girl Lainie."

Sam's throat closed up on him; he had to clear it before he spoke or the rasp in his voice would have given his emotions away to everyone in the room. "Lainie! Where are you?"

"Cap? I'm in an alleyway not far from Kinz. Shore leave sucks. Permission to come aboard?"

There was that choking sensation again. Sam swallowed.

"You better get your tail aboard this ship, sister. I've got some questions for you. I'll meet you in the D-mat room. Captain out." He exhaled. "She sounds okay." Fragments of information began to shift and coalesce into a pattern. "Daniel—how the hell could she have access to your comm?"

"Obviously she's been inside Kinz with Rayna. Looks like Ray's managed to get her out." The Pataran explained this as though Sam were mentally challenged. "That's her job after all."

Sam's emotions careened between relief and renewed worry. And he wanted to punch Daniel all over again, just for the hell of it.

Gabriel clapped him on the back. "She should be able to tell us something."

"Let's find out." Sam started across the bridge toward the exit to the corridor. He paused to give final orders to his XO. "We found Lainie. Make sure she stays on this ship. In fact, she's confined to quarters until further notice."

Mo's jaw tightened. "She won't follow anybody this time."

"Nice job on the Kinz security net, by the way."

The XO shrugged. "The locking systems are the simplest part of the system. It's going to be a lot harder to get all those LO's into the yard."

"Let me worry about that. Just be ready for my signal. Any word from Rescue?"

"They should be at the C5 jump within a couple of hours."

His space buoys were lining up in a nice little row. A sizzle of anticipation ran through Sam's chest and down his arms to his fingers. He recognized it—his body preparing for battle.

He laid a hand on Mo's shoulder and turned to leave. "Good. You have the conn. We'll check in every hour."

"And if you don't?"

The captain paused at the hatch and held his friend's gaze. "If we miss two check-ins, take this ship and get the hell out of here before the Grays show up to finish us."

Mo nodded, his expression unreadable. "Understood, Cap. See you on the other side."

The captain led his team of companions through the ship to the D-mat room. They stopped at the weapons lockers in the armory first to suit up.

Sam reached for a laze rifle, but Daniel stopped him. "No sense in taking anything bigger than a stunner. We find ourselves in a pitched battle, we've already lost."

Sam regretted that, but he had to admit the Pataran was right. He put the rifle back and chose two stunners and a pair of thigh holsters. Meanwhile, Gabriel had found an extra stunner to supplement the one he already carried on his right thigh and a lethal, black-bladed knife.

He grinned at Sam. "Quick and quiet."

"I thought you didn't need anything more than that mind of yours," Sam drawled.

"Mind control is too much work."

Sam knew better than to think his friend was lazy or lacking in any way. Gabriel might be only half-Thrane, but he'd spent a brutal childhood at the Academy on his father's home planet honing his mental talents. He could turn your mind inside out with a thought and leave you a quivering heap of flesh and bone.

"I hope you weren't planning this mission without a Security detail, Cap."

Sam turned to see Mae Chen standing in the hatch, dressed in black fatigues and boots and already outfitted with a pair of stunners. In the corridor behind her, he could see a small squad of his people similarly attired and standing at attention. The captain of the *Shadowhawk* had to swallow his shock. The most uniform clothing he'd ever seen his crew wear was a tee-shirt with "Security" stamped across the front.

Sam squared his shoulders. "What's this about, Mae?"

"Mo tells me you're going dirtside, Cap—a little covert action? I was thinking you could use some help."

Daniel was shaking his head—NO! But Sam was already ahead of him.

"You were right about one thing. This is *covert* action. I don't need a freaking herd of *psoros* at my heels. Stand down, Chief."

"Okay, you may not need *them*, but, respectfully, Cap, you do need me." She stared up at him, her expression set.

Sam's eyebrows came together. "Does this have something to do with that brawl on the PT deck? Because that wasn't your fault."

Chen tilted her head. "That brawl. Murder, sabotage, general bullshit aboard my ship, Cap. I might be a little pissed. Think I need to work off some aggression. Sir."

The corners of his mouth curved upward. "Understood. Just you, then." He looked over the squad in the corridor. "Nice uniforms, crew. Maybe next time. You're dismissed."

There was a groan as the squad members realized they were all dressed up with nowhere to go, but they dispersed quietly enough.

In the D-mat room, Lainie Butaar waited for him, her expression as woeful as her dirty, bedraggled clothing. Her heart-shaped face was as pale as bone, and her eyes flitted back and forth between him and Security Chief Chen. She looked for all the worlds like he might strike her. *Perai*, did she distrust him that much?

She drew to something like attention when he came near. "I—you can throw me in the brig, Cap, but you have to listen first! Please!"

All right, so she realized she was on the hook for jumping ship. That was a promising start. Sam wanted to hug her, but he was the captain, and he figured he'd play this for what it was worth.

"First, tell me Ray's okay." He didn't want to hear anything else until he knew.

Lainie bobbed her head. "She's fine. At least she was when I left."

He folded his arms across his chest and tried not to let the relief he felt show on his face. "Okay, then. From the beginning, and don't leave anything out."

Lainie told her tale, and Sam sent up a quick prayer of gratitude to whatever gods existed in the universe for keeping Rayna safe so far. Then he implored them to hold her in their hands a little longer. Just until he could get to her.

The girl finished her story. "Ray wouldn't let me help. She's gone to find the Thrane in the infirmary—alone."

Sam shook his head. "She was right to send you out, Lainie. Who knows how far that madman has gotten in placing his explosives."

"Hand-held sensor equipment can be modified to detect nanoprocessor links if that's the kind of device he's using," Gabriel said.

"That's what he used on the *'hawk*," Chen confirmed, "and we tried hand-helds on the ship. They work, but searching with them is slow. We'd never cover a territory as large as Kinz in time."

"And the only reason to do it would be to save lives. Get the people out and let him blow it to hell, I say." Sam's fists tightened at his sides. "This is an arms factory that uses slave labor. I want to see it reduced to a pile of rubble."

"Cap, please don't make me stay on the ship." Lainie leaned forward, her entire body pleading with him. "You want to take Kinz down, and I can help. I can get you in and out twice as fast as anybody else. And I can fight, you know I can."

Sam put his hand on her shoulder and tried to smile. "Do you know what Rayna would do to me if I let you go back there with us? *Perai*, I'll probably never hear the end of it for putting *my* ass in danger, and I'm a grown man. *If* I survive. Ray wanted you safe. I want you safe. Stay here. That's an order."

"But—"

"And don't make me enforce it by ordering you to the brig—which is what I ought to do for the offense of jumping ship. You're lucky I'm only confining you to quarters for the rest of your life."

The girl stood tall, her lips a thin line, but at last she accepted the reprimand. "Aye, Cap."

He turned, dismissing her. His mind was on only one thing now.

He nodded at his team. "Let's go."

CHAPTER TWENTY-EIGHT

Near Crystal Lake, Illinois, Earth, Sector Three, 1987

Over the cornfield the sky was a vast, black bowl full of bright stars, the air as clear and cold as only February in Illinois could make it. She snuggled into Tom's shoulder, seeking warmth, and reassurance. Shirley knew she was acting like a silly teenager, but she couldn't seem to help herself. It had, after all, been her first time.

Her boyfriend wasn't any older, but he seemed happy to provide what she needed. The two of them leaned on the hood of his ancient Chevy Nova and stared up with mouths open, breaths mingling.

"I told you this was a good spot," he said.

She snorted. "It's the middle of nowhere."

"Nobody bothered us."

She laughed, warm with memory. "True. But, damn, boy, we drove miles from home to get here. You're gonna have to book it to get me back before curfew. Mama'll kill both of us."

"It took twenty minutes to get here from the city limits. I timed it."

She turned to face him, her arms linked around his back. "Really. Well, aren't you smart!"

He leaned in to kiss her, humor, maybe even love, gleaming in his dark eyes, but his head snapped up before his lips reached hers.

Light—blinding, searing, shattering light—exploded all around them and obliterated every other sense. She screamed and latched onto him, even as she heard him shout—"Shirley!"—over and over again, as if he couldn't find her, even though he held her in his arms.

The ground shook beneath her feet. Then her whole body rose above the earth, and Tom was ripped out of her clutching hands. The light filled her head so she couldn't see; a high-pitched sound pierced her ears, making her want to scream. She did scream, in terror and in rage. What the hell was happening? She couldn't see Tom now, or feel him, and she was being carried up, up . . . and *oh, God, help me!*

Helpless!

Helpless! The emotion overwhelmed her, sapping her will to fight. Rayna lay on the cold concrete, unable to move, overtaken by the vision of two familiar teenagers in another time and place. In a flash of awareness she saw her real surroundings: a mechanical room, deep in the heart of Kinz. The machinery hummed around her. And across from her, Rexus Kor, his face contorted with hate. His eyes bored into her and pain smashed into her head once more.

Shirley wanted to fight against the shackles that bound her arms and legs in place tight against the cold, metal table. She wanted to scream in outrage and pain, to curse at the nightmare beings that had put her here and surrounded her now, like so many veterinarians putting down a stray dog. She longed to reach out to Tom, who lay still and unseeing on the table next to hers. But she could do nothing, say nothing. She waited like a piece of meat on the table for carving—awake, aware, alive to all the pain and humiliation. And when they began, she could only scream in silence in the echoing darkness of her mind.

Helpless.

No! Rayna shook off the vision once again. "No, you sonofabitch!"

She struggled to sit up, her head heavy, her limbs like durasteel. Sharp metal cut into her wrists and ankles and held her in place, but when she looked down, nothing was there. She fought the phantom pain, her muscles clenching and twisting against restraints that didn't exist, a cry of rage erupting out of her chest. Then her entire body went rigid in agony as the Thrane exerted his control over her again. Her shields were no protection. She was swallowed by darkness.

She didn't know how long she had been on the table. The cold, the pain, the intolerable light had gone on forever, were still going on. The creatures, with their big, black, nightmare eyes, their gray skin, their tiny, shrunken bodies and oversized heads, still hovered. Around her, around . . . the other. She could no longer remember his name. Or hers. She knew he was important, but she no longer knew why.

The creatures milled about, more of them now than before. They huddled over something that looked like a . . . a television screen. She could only be grateful that the thing drew their attention away from her. She could stop screaming now. The other could stop filling her ears with his screams, too. She no longer cared what was going to happen next. She only wanted to sleep. Her eyes drifted closed.

And snapped open again as a tall, hulking creature of an entirely different sort grabbed her arm and jerked her to her feet. Her heart gave a mild *thump-thump* in response to being roughly handled, but she did not scream; she no longer felt terror or anger or any urge to fight back. She would simply go with this .

. . creature . . . wherever he wanted her to go. It was easier that way.

She turned to look. The other, the boy (he wasn't yet a man, she noticed, not quite) had his own giant guard and was coming with them. Something deep inside her was reassured by that. He had been given a jumpsuit with a number on the front and back—5411. She looked down in some surprise to see she'd been dressed in the same kind of loose, white clothing. Her number was 3390.

The guards pulled them out of the examination room and through a maze of shiny equipment. Her image reflected back at her—a young girl with dark skin and wide eyes, small, lost, surrounded by monsters. It took her a moment to realize that they had shaved her head.

They emerged into a dim corridor crowded with people. Men and women of all colors and descriptions stood waiting in long, densely-packed lines, their faces blank, their eyes staring straight ahead. A tiny spark of fear and revulsion blossomed in her chest. *Where am I? What is going on here?* But a wave of pain rose up and washed through her head, nearly bringing her to her knees. Her guard jerked her back up and dragged her forward, cursing at her in some language that didn't make sense.

"Another fucking resistant. That's the third one this tendays," the other guard said, his voice a low, grating growl. In some distant part of her mind she recognized that she shouldn't be able to understand him. The syllables spilling from his mouth were nothing she'd ever heard before.

"Maybe we should just turn around and take her back for another wipe." Her guard started back.

His partner stopped him. "You know we can't. They'll just say it's too early. Somebody'll figure it out soon enough and drag her back through the program."

"Yeah? They don't have to deal with the consequences every *mulaak* day." This time he nearly yanked her off her feet to pull her down the corridor. The whole time the boy, 5411, had said nothing. He'd barely moved, even to follow the action with his eyes.

Wake up! she wanted to yell at him. *What is wrong with you? What is wrong with everybody here? Everybody except me!*

Rayna came to herself again with a jolt. Again, she was bound hand and foot, thick metal wire wound around her wrists and ankles. She cleared her mind and tested her bonds. Sharp pain lanced through her body from her extremities, and blood slicked the wire where it had cut into her skin.

Rexus Kor laughed from several meters away. "Oh, yes, the bonds are real. I need to leave you for a while, my pet. Can't have you running off while I'm working, can I?"

Time. Distraction. She knew what kind of work he would be up to while he was away.

"You could be breaking my fingers one by one. Pulling out my teeth." She fought to keep her voice steady. "You could fill my mind with thoughts of pain and suicide. Instead you give me this worn-out holovid of teenagers in the hands of the nasty aliens? Why?"

Something black and repugnant slithered behind Rex's eyes. "Because this is your darkest nightmare—the night your parents were taken. I can read it in your mind."

"But it's not real. You don't know what happened that night, because I don't know." Her parents had never told her anything about it.

He shrugged. "What does it matter? We both know what happens in the Grays' processing centers. And you have imagined your parents there over and over."

Damn him, it was true. As a child. As a teenager, their age. Even now, she wanted to be the one that pulled them out of there. She'd always seen herself as their rescuer. And here she was, in need of rescue herself. She hurled a glob of spit across the floor at the Thrane.

He leapt back and laughed. "You see? Those shields Rescue taught you to build are no match for me, and we have not even begun to find those things that will most terrify and degrade you. You are slippery, it's true, but that's the fun of it." He came closer again, and a vague, terrible grin curved his lips. "Once your mind is completely open, the physical pain will be so much worse. The breaking fingers. The lost teeth. The . . . other things."

Rayna was so captured by the feverish glint of obsession in his eyes, she almost missed the flash of the bright blade in his hand. She tried to roll, but was too slow, and the short knife caught her just below the last left rib. Agony bloomed behind it, and blood spread in a growing red stain.

"Don't move too much and that won't kill you for quite some time." Rex's grin was like Death itself. "We have lots more to explore together before the end."

Rayna drew a breath to curse him, but rampaging pain kicked her in the gut and darkness roared up out of nowhere to steal her sight, her hearing and, in the end, her tether to the world.

The team huddled against the thermocrete wall, out of reach now of the lights and sensors sweeping the cluttered loading area behind the Kinz factory. This was not one of the main loading docks, where materials went in and weapons went out. Those were heavily guarded at all hours of every shift. This was little more than a kitchen delivery door, crowded with noxious garbage disposal units and discarded containers, and it appeared unlit and unmanned as the third watch waned.

Sam waited with the others, muscles twitching in anticipation. He threw an unhappy glance at Daniel Chang. Until they got inside, this was the Pataran's show. That didn't mean Sam had to like it.

The door clanged open and a woman stepped out. She caught sight of Daniel and gestured at him. They all followed him inside.

The woman closed the door behind them and peered up at Daniel. "You're really going to do this?"

"We don't have a choice. The Thrane is planning to blow this place to Portal's Hell. Where is Rayna?"

Her gaze flicked over at Sam and the others. "She went looking for him in the infirmary. That was an hour ago. Haven't heard from her since. This the captain?"

Daniel nodded. "Sam Murphy of the *Shadowhawk*. He's here for Rayna. Captain, this is Brilly Zan."

Sam inclined his head. "Lainie made it back to the ship without a scratch. Thanks for your help."

She shrugged. "My job. But your people were worth taking a risk for. Both of them. So what's the plan?"

Sam looked at Daniel, and the Pataran nodded back at him. He acknowledged the hand-off with a lift of his chin.

He turned to Brilly. "You need to take Daniel and Chen, here, to the nearest auxiliary security office. Someplace where they can access the internal security comps. They're going to trigger the fire alarms and make it hard to find the source, so everyone will be sent to the yard. Gabriel and I will find Rayna and the Thrane—kill him and bring her out. Once that's done, we'll open the gates and let the lucky ones out of here. We have a ship coming to pick them up."

"Lucky ones? You mean the slaves?" Brilly looked horrified. "But they'll be shot! The guards won't let them just walk out of the gates!"

Daniel laughed. "No. But they will obey the Director's orders. Provided we can get to him in all the chaos."

Brilly exhaled in relief. "Oh, you leave that to me. I know how to get to that little slime lizard."

"Okay, two hours until the beginning of the first shift. We need to have alarms blaring and people scrambling long before then." Personally, Sam wanted to see Thrane blood spilled *now*. Everything in him was humming like the engines of his ship, primed for it.

He dismissed the others with a terse nod, then looked to Gabriel. "You have the layout?"

Gabriel tapped his temple. The wetware encoded in the man's incredible brain made him a walking computer—no comps, datacards or pads needed for him to access any downloaded or networked information. Daniel had given him the layout of the facility on the ship; he'd simply stored it up there.

The two men moved out of the kitchen area and into an adjoining storage room stocked with cleaning equipment. There were no security cameras to track their movements in the room—or at its exit into a corridor on the other side. That corridor was one of several shortcuts used by staff in the facility—poorly lit, poorly secured and little traveled. Brilly and Daniel had highlighted those in the layout, and Sam used them now to find a route to the infirmary without encountering either people or cameras.

The double doors to the infirmary, however, were covered by an active security camera and required a comp code to pass through. A focused electromagnetic pulse took care of the cam, and they had the code from Brilly, but Sam knew better than to just waltz through the doors without recon. Had Rayna accomplished what she came to do? Or had the Thrane gotten the better of her? Were there others—guards? Innocents? He took a deep breath, trying to control his racing heart. This close-in shit was more Gabriel's line of work.

As if he could hear him, the tracker stepped in front of him to the door, stunner at the ready. With a few signs, he indicated Sam should key in the code and follow him through.

Sam hit the pads. Gabriel slipped through an opening in the doors no bigger than his body and ran silently to a doorway leading to the reception desk on the right of a short hallway. Sam saw no one else in the facility as he followed the tracker inside and took out the interior cams with the pulse. But what he saw when he joined Gabriel inside the little reception office was bad news.

"She's not sleeping on the job," Gabriel said as he stood up from the nurse's body sprawled on the floor. "The Thrane wiped her mind and left her unconscious. She's barely got a pulse."

All Sam could think was that the bastard had Rayna, but he tried for a second to have some compassion for the woman at his feet. "Will she be okay?"

The shake of Gabriel's head was almost imperceptible. "He was in a hurry. We need to find your girl."

Sam clamped down hard on his frustration. "Where?" The infirmary had been their only lead.

The tracker headed for the exit. "If he has Rayna, he'll want time to work. He'll be in the deepest, darkest, least-accessible area he can find. There's a sump pump and plumbing cleanout in the southwest corner of the lowest level—a room about four meters square. That's where I would go, if it were me."

CHAPTER TWENTY-NINE

Cold, like the metal tables of the examination room. And *hard*, like the stone floor of a prison. *Weak*, unable to summon the will to fight, like so many others before her. *Dying*, the life flowing out of her minute by minute.

Rayna swam her way back to consciousness, cataloguing the physical sensations of her body and the rough floor where she lay curled around her leaking belly. The details of her surroundings gradually came into focus: the wire cutting into her wrists and ankles; the dust and grime covering every surface in the small room; the whirr and gurgle of a massive pump coming on at intervals and pushing water through the pipes that ran along one wall; the smell of sewage. And behind it all, the coppery tang of blood and the punch of pain that lit up her belly with every breath.

The bleeding was a slow seep of misery, not the frantic gush that would kill her in minutes. The Thrane had been precise. He'd wanted more time with her.

"Fucking bastard," she panted. "How 'bout I just rip this hole open and ruin your fun? Bleed all over the floor nice and quiet and go out on *my* terms?"

The thought was followed by a streak of curses in all the languages Rayna knew. Like she'd ever take the easy way out. No, this would be a fight to the ugly ass end. And if she wanted to keep her strength a few minutes longer, she needed to find a way to slow the flow of blood.

The long strip of cloth that had held her home-made knife in place was still wrapped around her forearm. Rexus Kor had been arrogant enough to think he didn't need to bind her hands *behind* her; she could reach the wrappings with her teeth. She attacked them, picking at them to find an edge, her mind focused on nothing but the task. Until suddenly her head jerked up, sending a flare of pain through her belly.

"Portal's balls in a fucking vise!" *The laser knife!* Kor couldn't have been stupid enough to leave it in her boot. She drew up her feet, ignoring the agony in her gut, and reached down the inside of her boot. *There!* The arrogant ass hadn't thought it necessary to search her. He thought he'd disarmed her by taking the shiv. She huffed out a thin laugh. "Joke's on you, asshole."

Not that it was going to be cake to cut through her bonds with that laser. It was a precision tool, all right, but it wasn't designed for surgery, and her skin was swelling around the wire.

"Oh, for fuck's sake, suck it up." She settled herself on the floor, put her wrists on her knees to brace them and flipped on the tiny switch. The barely perceptible blue line lanced out from the tip of the knife; she pointed it at the wire crossing the back of her left wrist and gritted her teeth as the laser hit flesh and metal at once. In seconds she'd severed the band of wire, leaving a line of fresh scorching across the bruise the metal had cut into her wrist. The rush of blood—and feeling—to her hand made her want to scream.

When she could move her left hand again, she unwound what wire she could from her right wrist and cut away the rest. There was some slack on this side, so she avoided the burns she'd experienced earlier. When she'd finished with her wrists, she did the same for her ankles.

But time was running out. Her lap was cold and sticky now with blood from the wound in her belly, and her head swam with every movement. She unwrapped the cloth from her arm and did what she could to fold the material into the slick gash below her ribs. It hurt like a sonofabitch, and by the time she was finished an inky black fog had reached up to claim her once again.

Nothing much had changed when she woke an unknown time later. She was weaker, much weaker. And thirsty, her tongue thick and clinging to the roof of her mouth. Her arms and legs were like thermocrete, and moving only brought agony to her belly, so she soon gave up.

It would be so easy to let go. Part of her really wanted to. She wondered again why she couldn't do it. The image of her parents flashed into her head. Not as she had known them—old, worn-out, damaged by their ordeal—but as she had seen them in the Thrane's torturous vision—impossibly young, afraid, but strong, so strong. And her mother's face, even glimpsed as a wavering reflection in glass or metal, was so like her own it was like watching herself go through the processing center.

Rayna's parents had never told her anything about their abduction or their escape, other than to say Rescue was responsible for their salvation. They had said almost nothing about her birth. Could she have been conceived before they were Taken? If that was true the Grays would have postponed her parents' removal to a labor camp, preferring to keep them for breeding at the processing center. But if they had discovered her mother was resistant, they would have battered at her mind over and over, determined to break her.

Rescue must have gotten to her parents before their baby was born. But not soon enough to save Shirley Carver's mind. Tom might have retained enough to be sent back home, but if Rayna knew her dad, he wouldn't have gone without Shirley. So the couple ended up on Terrene, where little Rayna was born, and made a new life.

It hadn't been such a bad life, as Rayna remembered it now. No one had it easy in the polyglot colony. There were shortages of the basics—food, water, housing, energy—but virtually anything could be had on the black market if you had the credits or something to barter. Tom Carver worked in the recycling center, an unglamorous job, to be sure, but he was a skillful picker and trader. The family lived decently on what he could barter for in the market. He was quiet, protective of his wife and daughter. And devastated when Rayna decided to join Rescue.

Rayna had always seen her parents as victims in need of saving. She saw everything differently now. They'd had to be so much stronger than she'd imagined to survive the Grays. But they *had* survived—for her sake. And her father had refused to go home to Earth out of love for his wife and child. Rayna had always believed their love had made them targets at the hands of the Grays. Instead it had protected them, both during their captivity and after.

A rusty, grating laugh escaped from her throat. "You stupid child!" *How could you live almost thirty years and not see such a thing? And Sam was right. You're afraid to love him.*

She supposed she should thank Kor for these insights before she killed him—she glanced down at the cloth under her hand, soaked now with bright red—or he killed her.

"Fuck that." She struggled to her knees and swung her head from side to side, looking for the laser knife. The tool was not far; she clutched it in one fist and lurched to her feet.

She found the door, durasteel and locked, of course. But the knife . . . her head floated like a body in zero-G. She braced herself against the wall with one shoulder and raised the laser to the lock. Her eyes refused to focus. This was delicate work, finding and melting the correct part of the mechanism without fusing the entire lock. Black spots threatened to steal her sight. Maybe she should wait.

"No!" She shook her head to clear it. "Just do this

and get the fuck out of here." She hit the switch on the knife, gently inserted the thin, blue line into the lock, heard a sizzle and a pop. She had time to smile before the black swept up to cover her like a thick blanket and she slid unconscious to the floor.

"Are you sure you know where we're going?" Sam couldn't see two meters in front of him in the murk, a close, hot dark filled with the smell of grease and metal, thermocrete and dust. Functioning machinery surrounded them, though Sam had no idea what the big, enclosed things powered or moved. Were they part of the plumbing system or the power grid? The recycling system or the ventilation? All he knew was that they ran loud and they ran hot. At the moment no one was here to monitor or service them, but the Thrane could be hiding anywhere in or around them. He and Gabriel hadn't found Rayna, and the alarms should be going off any minute.

Gabriel's gaze shot in his direction. "We're almost there. And relax. I don't sense him anywhere near here."

Sam had to admit the tracker was a useful sonofabitch, though his skills were enough to raise the hairs on the back of your neck. In this case, especially, it was necessary to fight fire with fire. Their enemy, too, would be able to sense them with more than just eyes and ears.

Gabriel jogged ahead as the space opened up in the large, underground chamber. The only lights illuminated gauges and panels on the equipment in the room; Sam was forced to keep close behind his friend or lose his way, even though the floor was smooth under his feet and nothing rose up to bark his shins. They crossed nearly the entire length of the space before Gabriel finally slowed, turned and inclined his head in the direction of a durasteel door.

—*This is it. No sign he's inside, but he might be well shielded.*

Sam had experienced Gabriel's telepathy before in combat situations, but it still shook him. No one liked to have another person in his head, and those *mulaak* Gray slime lizards had given him even more reason to want to keep his thoughts to himself. He shivered, and nodded.

They lined up on either side of the door, stunners at the ready, and Sam counted them down on his fingers. *Three . . . two . . .*

—*WAIT!* Gabriel held up a hand, then pointed. *The door is unlocked.*

In fact, it was slightly ajar. Did that mean the Thrane was here? Or had he left, with Rayna? They waited, listening. Nothing.

Gabriel pushed at the door, opening it a crack. Sam saw a room just as the tracker had described it: maybe four meters on a side, ringed with large-gauge piping, a big sump pump in one corner and a plumbing cleanout in another. No Thrane. But, there, thank the gods! Huddled off to the side. It was his Rayna.

Sam swung open the door and fell to his knees beside her. Then he saw the blood and his heart ripped open in his chest.

"Ray! Look at me! Ah, fuck, what happened? Let me see. C'mon, let me look." He was babbling, he knew it, but he couldn't seem to stop. He just kept up a stream of talk as his hands scanned her body for the source of all that red. "*Shalssiti pultafa*! What has he done to you?"

Gabriel knelt beside him. "Here. I have some supplies in my pack. Let me help."

Sam moved over to give the tracker room to work. As Gabriel cleaned the wound, sealed it with sprayskin and stuck a thick pad over it, Rayna finally opened her eyes.

"Sam?" She frowned at him, gaze not quite in focus. "You're not real."

"Oh, yeah, baby, I am." He touched her face. "I'm here to take you home."

"All right, then who the hell is that, and why does he have his hands all over me?" She looked like she'd take a swing at him just as soon as she got her strength back.

"My friend, Gabriel. But he's done now, right, Gabriel?"

The tracker's lips curved upward. "Lift her up so I can wrap this around her middle." He held a length of bandage in his hands, waiting for Sam to bring Rayna to a sitting position so he could secure the pad in place over her wound.

Sam gathered her in his arms. The tension in her body told him she was trying to sit up on her own, but a quick glance at her face showed him the effort it cost her. He would have let her have her pride, knowing how stubborn she was, but at that moment red lights started flashing in the equipment room outside the door and alarms blared behind them.

"Shit! The fire alarms!"

Gabriel caught his gaze. "The Thrane will be coming back here to get his prize. We have to get out *now*."

Sam hauled Rayna to her feet and let the tracker wrap the bandage around her wound. Then he started to pick her up.

"No!" She shook him off. "I'll make it for a little while on my own. Give me that much, at least."

He picked her up anyway. "Point taken. You're a scrapper, Little Bit. But you weigh less than a week's rations. I'm packing you out of here. Otherwise you'll slow us down."

He'd have laughed at the stream of curses that filled his right ear if they hadn't been issued in such a shaky voice.

Gabriel left the room ahead of them, surveying the larger mechanical chamber outside for any sign of the Thrane. He waved them on, and the three of them pounded through the cavernous space, their ears ringing with the echoing scream of the alarms, their vision distorted by the hellish red glare of the emergency lights.

The exit was in sight, Gabriel framed in the light shining in from the hallway. Sam put on speed, ready to be free of the dark and the oppressive clank and pulse of the heavy machinery. The blast came from ahead to his right, tearing a hole in the world and filling it with white-hot light and searing heat. His feet left the floor and he flew, losing his grip on Rayna. He landed the gods knew how far away. Broken. Deaf. And alone.

What the fuck happened? Rayna lay sprawled at the edge of a pile of rubble, covered with dust and small bits of debris. She could hear almost nothing; her ears seemed to be stuffed with foam. Her side hurt like a bastard—but that wasn't from whatever had sent her to the floor. Then it all came back in a rush: Kor and the knife thrust and Sam and Gabriel and the bomb blast. Sam. *Sam!*

She rolled over and managed to drag herself to her knees. "Sam!" She couldn't see him. It was completely dark now, except for a few faint, fragmented rays of light, the source of which she couldn't determine.

She crawled, the twisted metal and jagged edges of the wrecked thermocrete shredding her hands and knees. "Sam, goddammit, answer me! Where the fuck are you?"

She heard a moan, and though every movement tore at the wound in her belly and shot hot pain deep into her side, she scrambled over the debris toward the sound. "I hear you! I'm coming."

When the sound came again it was closer, and she soon found him, lying pinned under a slab of thermocrete the size of a bridge console. There was no hope of moving it without help. *Where the hell was Gabriel?*

"Jesus God, sweets. How am I supposed to fix this?"

He looked up at her and tried out a grin. "Unless you've got an AG lift or about ten guys, I don't think you'll be fixing this, Little Bit." His breath was constricted, wheezing.

She refused to believe there was nothing she could do. "What's underneath you? If there's enough debris holding you up, we could dig—"

"No. Except for a few *really* uncomfortable pieces of slag, there's just the floor."

She shouted for Gabriel, not caring if Kor could hear her. If the Thrane showed up, she would rip out his throat with her bare hands for this. Nothing answered her but the hiss of settling dust.

"Rayna."

No. She wouldn't lose him. Not like this, the breath squeezed out of him second by second.

"Lie still. I'll look for Gabriel and get this thing off you."

He grabbed her hand. "Ray. Stay with me. It won't

be long."

"Goddammit, Sam Murphy, don't say that! Don't you say that!"

His face, pale against the shadows of the rubble at her knees, showed no pain, no emotion to match the desperation in her heart. "It's okay. I'm a blackjack, remember? Short life span is part of the job description."

Blackjack. That's when she knew. She wasn't talking to Sam Murphy.

Sam had no idea how long he lay amid the crumbled thermocrete and twisted metal, fighting for breath, wavering in and out of consciousness. Now, as his eyes regained their focus, they could tell him little in the dark and the swirling dust. He tried to move, but everything felt loose and slushy inside his torso, and ragged coughs brought up hot blood. His right side, from the ribs to the ankle, seemed broken into a thousand pieces of sharp glass. *Fucking hell.*

He lifted his head, then struggled to his left elbow, though crushing pain sought to drive him back down again. "Rayna?" He couldn't see her, and there was no sign of Gabriel, either. The configuration of the room they'd been in was unrecognizable after the blast, machinery and structure reduced to piles of rubble. *Please, gods, tell me she's not in there.*

"Looking for someone?"

Sam dropped off his elbow and twisted his head to the other side to see the owner of the voice, and a curse escaped his lips. He could make out a tall, well-muscled male in the dim light—the Thrane, it must be. And he had Rayna clutched tight in his grip.

"Ray!"

"I'm fine, Sam. Don't bother getting up for this asshole."

He wanted to, gods knew he did, but that was impossible. He could only growl in frustrated fury.

The Thrane laughed. "Get up? Oh, yes, by all means. Rescue your woman before I slice her eyeballs. And take her ears for souvenirs. And do other things. Until I finally decide to put her out of her misery."

Sam was in agony, but the pain had nothing to do with his injuries. He saw the fear on Rayna's face, though she tried to hide it. Saw her struggle against the Thrane's hold, with as little effect as a ten-year-old girl might have. *Fight,* he wanted to tell her. *Fight harder!*

The Thrane pulled her closer, and Sam could see the glint of madness in the man's black eyes. "You begin to understand now, don't you." His boot lifted and came down on Sam's hip, crushing, crushing. "You've lost everything—your woman, your crew, your ship. You're going to end just like you started. A slave."

Desperation washed over him in a choking wave, the pounding of his heart drowning out the sound of his enemy's venomous words. But cutting through everything he suddenly heard Rayna's voice. He looked up and realized it didn't come from her lips. *It was inside his head.*

Sam! Wake up, Sam! This isn't real!

Sam opened his eyes at last, and Rayna exhaled the breath she hadn't known she'd been holding. He sat up so fast his head almost clipped her chin. Then she was in his arms, and she was holding on to him like she would never let go. Remembering the way he smelled, the way it felt to have him hold her, she almost forgot everything else.

But it couldn't last. They had no time.

He pulled back. "Where is he?"

She nodded. "There. With Gabriel."

The two men stood facing each other on the factory floor, feet braced and eyes closed. Their muscles tensed and rippled as if they ran in their dreams, and their faces grimaced in effort. Sweat ran from Gabriel's temple and stained his shirt, and his hands were balled into fists, his forearms taut with steel. With robotic steps he lurched forward. Kor slowly backed up a step.

Sam leaned closer, his weapon trained on the Thrane. "What's happening?"

"I'm not sure." Rayna watched them, fascinated. She'd heard about the Thrane ability to engage completely on the mental plane, to fight entire battles with their minds, but she'd never seen such a thing. Surely Kor was vulnerable on this plane, though?

"Shoot him."

"Right." Sam lifted his stunner and fired. The energy from the weapon hit some form of shield around the two men and fragmented in a flash of sparking light. Some of it bounced back in their direction. Sam shoved Rayna behind a control panel and shielded her with his big body.

"What the hell was that?" He stared at her, his eyes round with shock.

She just shook her head, too busy trying to stay conscious while the deep, grinding pain in her gut threatened to drag her under. Moving was becoming more and more an act of courage.

"What kind of mind can he have to maintain that shield, fight Gabriel and keep us under all at once? Portal's balls!"

"Well, he did lose us." She considered Sam. "You're resistant."

His jaw tightened. "Yes. I wouldn't be here if I weren't."

"You'll have to tell me about that some time."

There was a long pause before Sam finally nodded. "Everything, Little Bit. I swear. If we make it out of this hellhole."

That appeared to depend on Gabriel now. He was trembling, every muscle locked with tension. Still he advanced, step after step. And Kor was crumbling, sinking to his knees, his face contorting in pain. At last he collapsed, and Gabriel fell in front of him.

The tracker turned his head. "Now, Sam! Fire!

The shield is down."

Sam scrambled to his feet and positioned himself over the fallen body of his enemy. Rayna forced herself to go after him. He was standing there, not shooting. Why wasn't he shooting?

He kicked at the motionless Thrane. "Get up, you piece of shit."

Gabriel, sweat pouring off him like he'd run ten kilometers in jungle heat, lifted his head to growl at him. "For the gods' sake, Murphy, shoot the *mulaak* bastard. I can't hold him much longer."

"Keep the shield down, but let him go." Sam's face showed nothing of his intention.

His friend slowly got to his feet. "You are the craziest sonofabitch I have ever had the misfortune to know."

"What the fuck are you doing?" Rayna tried to get him to look at her, but his attention never wavered from where Kor lay. "Shoot him, and let's get out of here."

"I want him to know who's killing him. And for what. Hold this." He handed his stunner to Rayna.

He bent down and grabbed a handful of the Thrane's uniform, hauling him to his feet with one hand. As soon as he was in contact with the man, Sam staggered and seemed to falter. God knew what he was seeing now, what terrors Kor was showing him. Rayna glanced at Gabriel, but he shook his head. He was out of this fight.

Kor grinned. "Will you never learn, Captain? You

don't have what it takes to defeat me."

"It's true you've won a few battles." Sam's voice grated with the strain of this latest bout. "But I'm about to win this war, Thrane. This is for my crew. And for all the pain you've caused my woman. And just in case you put a scratch on my ship." He didn't even bother to look behind him. "Go ahead, Ray. And make sure the stunner is set on Kill."

She didn't hesitate. She put the targeting beam dead center in Kor's chest and squeezed the trigger. The Thrane crumpled, a look of incredulous shock on his face.

Sam turned to her—and caught her just as she fell.

CHAPTER THIRTY

Sam lowered Rayna to the floor and put a shaking hand to her throat. Her pulse was weak, but steady under his fingers. The bandage around her belly was secure and still dry; she was likely just dehydrated and suffering from shock. He had to get her back to the ship.

Gabriel joined him, holding a tiny comp pad. "We have to move."

"What's that?"

"The Thrane's cheat sheet. It's encrypted, but there's a map indicating where the nanolinks are." He pointed to blinking red lights on a tiny grid. "The problem is, I can't tell how long we have, and I can't deprogram the links. The only thing I can tell for sure is that they're set to auto-detonate. Those things will go off without him. We have to get out of here."

Sam scooped Rayna into his arms and stood, then followed Gabriel out through the long rows of machinery and into the corridor. Alarms blared in the dim hallway, and a string of green emergency lights snaked along the base of the wall, meant to guide survivors through smoke and dark in a crisis. The "crisis" in this case had done its job; they encountered no one until they'd almost reached the corridor outside the kitchens.

"You, there! Stop!"

Sam kept walking. *How many?*

Two. Let me handle them.

Gabriel slowed and faced the guards that had emerged from a side hallway. "Gentlemen, please. My friend is helping the girl. She's been overcome by smoke in the factory fire. We've been ordered to evacuate to the yard."

Sam kept walking, not looking back, not slowing down. He knew the tracker was quite capable of killing both guards if he had to. But he had other ways of defusing the situation.

The guard repeated his order. "You're not workers! I said *Stop!*"

Sam risked a look back and saw Gabriel take both men by the arm and turn them in the opposite direction, speaking in a low voice as if he was explaining a difficult situation to them. In the end, they both nodded and walked back the way they'd come.

"Really? It was that easy." Sam waited for the tracker to catch up.

Gabriel shrugged. "Some minds are simpler than others."

They made for the kitchens now and the exit beyond, Sam's heart thudding with every step. The heavy double doors that led to the food prep area were in sight, not five meters away, when the hallway before them shattered in an explosion of white fire and deafening sound. The kitchen walls blasted outward, then the ceiling fell in to fill the hole, leaving nothing but a mass of saw-edged metal and pulverized thermocrete, choking dust and flaring heat.

Sam found himself on the floor again, his head spinning. The Thrane was dead—he was *dead*, dammit!—so this could be no dream, no vision.

"Rayna!" The sound came out as little more than a gasp. He coughed and tried again. "Ray!"

"What the hell?" Weak, but he heard her, just to his right.

He reached out and found her. "Are you okay?"

"Fuck, no. I've been kidnapped, stabbed, almost murdered by mind control and now almost blown up for real. I'm definitely not okay. You?"

"I'm . . . in one piece. Gabriel!"

"I'm good." The tracker staggered over and held out a hand to help Sam up. The two of them got Rayna up. "But you remember the little red dots on that map I showed you? They're going green. This place is coming down around our ears."

Going out through the kitchen was no longer an option. "The yard. Now."

They ran back through the corridors, Rayna again in Sam's arms. Though she protested, it was faster that way. The hallways were increasingly crowded, with lines of workers herded through by panicky guards, the alarms making it impossible to hear their shouted orders, and individual members of the factory staff running for the exits without a thought for anyone but themselves.

No one challenged Sam and the others as they maneuvered through the chaos; the guards had too much to do to avoid a full-scale riot from the resistants in the crowd. With every deep shuddering boom! within the bowels of the factory, panic grew. And not only in the mob around them. Sam's chest was so tight he could barely breathe; his heart squeezed with fear. Not for himself, but for the woman he held in his arms. What if he failed to get her out of this stinking hellhole? Shalssiti pultafa, *can't these bastards move?*

They were within sight of the door when the fight started, resistants pushing their way through the few guards trying to keep the exit from the prison "orderly." The guards tried to force the mob back with whipsticks, but they were too few against too many. The workers overwhelmed them, punching and kicking and eventually stomping them into the ground. The crowd behind the vanguard surged forward, carrying Sam, Rayna and even Gabriel with it. Sam put Rayna's feet on the ground, and he and Gabriel formed a protective cage around her, bulling through the smaller people in front of them, fending off attacks with fists and elbows and, in Gabriel's case, a slap to the forehead.

Even so, it was like riding a wild, unpredictable wave in the oceans of Praetorix, something many a man had died trying. When the three of them finally broke free and stumbled out into an open area of the yard, Sam felt as if he'd been saved from drowning.

"Jesus, Murphy, when you break into a prison, you don't do it quietly, do you?" Rayna gasped for breath, her face pale, but she kept her feet, one hand clutching his sleeve.

"This is just a little more distraction than I bargained for." The yard was a heaving, shouting free-for-all, made violent and dangerous by the resistants who saw an opportunity and the guards fighting to maintain some semblance of control. Individuals were making a break for the walls or the gates, which were still locked, and were being shot for their trouble. The mindwiped unlucky ones hunkered down in miserable clumps or circled like flocks of stampeded sheep. And all the while the explosions were growing louder and closer, blowing away walls, collapsing roofs, raising wails among the workers in the yard.

"Gabriel, is the shield down yet? Can you get a signal to the ship?" He fended off two men in mid-fistfight with a shove and turned Rayna into his body to protect her.

"I have Mo." Gabriel looked up at Sam. "He says a Gray destroyer just came through the jump. Less than two hours until contact."

"*Perai*! Where's the Rescue ship?"

"In orbit. Mo's ready on the gates when you are."

Rayna shook her head. "You can't just open those gates now. We have to get a handle on this first or people will die."

"Where the hell is Daniel?" Sam looked up at the sheer amberglas-encased office tower that overlooked the yard. "You know he can see what's going on out here. He should have had that slime lizard on the loudspeaker by now."

"I can't raise him on the comm." Gabriel's face was grim. "Maybe we underestimated the Director."

"Daniel knows what he's doing." Rayna may have jumped to the Pataran's defense, but her eyes reflected her worry.

Whatever hope they might have had in Chang's skills was lost in the next second as the top of the tower erupted in a fiery ball of flame and smoke. Shards of glas and metal, chunks of thermocrete rained down on the naked crowd below, causing a mad scramble for cover. Sam took Rayna down to the ground with him, tucking her under his body, covering his head with his arms. He felt Gabriel's heavy body land on top of his. He could only hope it was deliberate.

In seconds, the deadly hail had passed. Gabriel rolled off and let him up. The tracker was bleeding in a half-dozen places, but otherwise seemed okay. He shook his head at Sam. No signal from Daniel. A hole opened up in Sam's chest as he remembered Mae Chen had been with Daniel in that office. Chen, who'd been part of his crew since he'd taken over the 'hawk.

Rayna, shaky with shock, grabbed his arm. "If Daniel was in there—" She stopped, swallowed, started again. "We have to think of something else to stop this riot. Every labor camp I've been in has kept sleeper gas on hand."

Perai! "Why haven't they used it?"

Gabriel gestured at the chaos. "Do you see anyone in charge? They're waiting for orders."

"Well, I say we give 'em some." Sam took quick stock of the immediate vicinity. A group of five guards battled hand-to-hand with a larger band of resistants—and looked to be losing. Too dangerous to step into. Several guards and more unlucky ones lay motionless in scattered heaps on the ground. And, there, not too far from them, one terrified guard hardly old enough to shave watched over a huddled mass of mindwiped UO's, sitting together with their backs to a tool shed. *Perfect*.

"Gabriel." He inclined his head to the youngster.

The tracker nodded and circled around behind the guard.

Sam and Rayna approached him from the front. "Help! Please, help! She's been hurt!"

The kid raised his stunner. "Stay back!"

"But she's hurt, can't you see? We need help!"

The guard had time to take one step before Gabriel had his hand on his shoulder and he went slack. The tracker took the stunner from his limp hands.

"Now, you can leave these people where they are," Gabriel said, his voice low and soothing. "You're going to show us how to deploy the sleeper gas."

"We're going to use the sleeper gas?"

"Yes, son. Don't you think that's a good idea?"

The boy nodded. "I wondered why no one was using it. This is a riot."

"Yes. Yes, it is." Gabriel squeezed his shoulder. "And we're supposed to use sleeper gas in riots, aren't we."

"Yes!"

"Okay, now. Do you know where the controls are?"

"Security shack." He pointed to a low building not twenty meters across the yard.

"Let's go," Sam said, and led the way through the mob.

Five meters from the door, the right half of the building blew apart. The little group was knocked flat. Sam rolled to his knees, ears ringing.

With a curse, he staggered to his feet and gestured to the others. "Stay here!" *Gabriel, tell Mo to have a Security squad standing by outside those gates.* He ran for the shack and forced his way through the mangled door into the former office, now filled with smoke and dust and fragments of what had been furniture. He pushed into the inner office and looked for the control panels on the outer wall. Still intact! But they were locked and passcode protected. Still, cops were cops. They always thought they were secure in their own house. His head swiveled, scanning the space. *There!* The passcodes were tacked to a dust-covered bulletin board next to the door where he'd come in.

He entered the codes and the panel cracked open. Inside the pads and settings were clearly marked; these were emergency controls, meant to be used by anyone at any time. No one in a place like Kinz had time or use for complicated instructions. The sleeper gas controls had settings for Yard, Factory, Dormitories or Mess Hall and for time in increments of ten minutes. He hit

"Yard" and "ten minutes". If the people in the yard were asleep any longer, his crew would be removing bodies from the rubble of what was left of the Kinz arms works.

Before he hit "SET" he searched the equipment lockers for breather masks. He grabbed a pack of the little filters, hit the pad to start the gas and scrambled out the door to his people. They slipped on the masks just as the gas hissed out over the battling crowd from nozzles hidden in posts and eaves surrounding the yard. Guards and resistants dropped in mid-punch. Huddled UO's fell over in heaps, their guardians slumped next to them. Escapees trying to climb the walls lost their grip and crashed to the ground; since most of them hadn't made it more than a few feet, Sam assumed they'd be okay.

In a few seconds, the yard was eerily quiet, bodies sprawled everywhere now that the battle was over. The gas dissipated, the yellowish cloud lifting and becoming indistinguishable from the dingy LinHo airmix.

Sam shifted his mask and took a tentative sniff. When he didn't feel like taking a nap, he removed the mask altogether. Rayna and Gabriel followed his lead.

"Your people are standing by outside the gate," the tracker told him. "Mo wants to know if you're ready?"

Sam nodded. "Open the gates. Have the Rescue ship stand by to receive the lucky ones in ten minutes plus one."

The gates swung open and his uniformed Security squad marched in, most of its members grinning ear-to-ear. He gave orders to the squad leader to disarm all the guards and ring the yard in preparation for the time when its occupants would awaken. The team rushed to get its job done in the remaining time.

Sam turned to Rayna. "We need to get you back to the ship."

"I want to see this through." She had a stubborn set to her jaw.

Gabriel raised an eyebrow. "I'll, uh, go help with the disarming." And he walked off.

"Rescue all the way, huh?" Sam crossed his arms over his chest.

Her mouth quirked. "Why should I let a pirate get all the glory?"

Something warmed deep inside him when she said that word "pirate" now. It wasn't quite the insult it had once been on her lips.

He grinned back at her. "Well, I might let you take some of the credit. You did kill the bad guy, after all."

She tilted her head, might have said something, but instead her eyes got wide and her mouth dropped open. He turned to follow her gaze. A tall, dark male, a short, trim female and a stockier older female, all of them covered head-to-foot in thermocrete dust, escorted a tiny Gray out of the ruins of the Kinz interior at stunner point.

"Daniel," she breathed.

"And Chen," he added, his voice no louder. He swallowed.

"Is that Brilly with them?"

"Yeah. And they've got the little slime lizard. Holy shit."

The team limped to a halt in front of them. "Captain." Daniel gave him a tired salute.

Sam hardly knew what to do with the gesture, so he gave it back. "We thought you were up there." He pointed at the blasted office tower. "Chen?"

She grinned, but blood streaked down her arm, which hung loose at her right side. "Well, you're right, Cap, it was close. This little devil was not being cooperative, so we'd just decided to bring him to Gabriel for a sitdown when the bomb went off. Had we hesitated another minute we'd be soyburger."

"You're injured."

She shrugged. "Might need a sealant."

Brilly snorted. "And an hour in the regen tank for that broken bone!"

"Everybody else okay?" Sam thought they all looked a little shell-shocked, and the Gray had likely been smacked around some.

"I don't recommend trying to go back in *there*." Brilly had a look of horror on her face. "We barely made it through. The place is collapsing."

Daniel brushed the worst of the dust off his jumpsuit. "We're fine, Captain." He surveyed the yard. "Sleeper gas?"

"We have about five minutes left. Then we'll get everybody up and to the ship." He squinted at the former director of one of the most notorious slave factories in the quadrant. "What are we doing with him?"

Rayna spoke up. "Rescue will want to talk to him. Then I guess they'll send him home."

"He'll be a fucking Loyalist hero." Daniel spat in the dust at the Minertsan's feet. The Gray shrank into himself as if he thought the giant Pataran might follow the insult with a death blow.

Sam stood over the meter-high creature and wondered, not for the first time, how something that looked so insignificant could be the source of so much misery in the galaxy. "You're one of the lucky ones, today, Minertsan. If I had found you, I'd have thrown you back into that flaming pit and left you to burn."

He grabbed the nearest Security uniform and gave orders to have the Gray and his captors sent back up to the *Shadowhawk*. All around them now, "bodies" were starting to come to life, waking to find their world had changed. Sam and Rayna watched as the *'hawk*'s Security team sorted through the groaning, confused people in the yard, determining which of the lucky ones were resistants and which were still under the full influence of the mindwipe, sending batches of LO's up to the waiting Rescue ship, sending guards and staff home to their dwellings in LinHo.

Sam suddenly realized he had a responsibility for those people, too. "You know, technically I own most of LinHo now."

"What?" Rayna looked at him like he'd sprouted an extra head.

"I was still Drew Vort's partner when I killed him.

He owned most of LinHo, so now I own most of LinHo."

"What the hell would you want with this godforsaken rock?"

"Good question. And I better figure it out fast. LinHo's major place of employment will be a pile of shit in another ten minutes."

Rayna looked around. "This place always was a pile of shit."

"You're right. And you know what? You've had enough of it. Come on." He wanted to sweep her off her feet, to feel her warmth and negligible weight in his arms, but he held himself back. She had wrapped a fragile dignity around her tiny body now and was holding onto it with grim purpose. He wouldn't interfere. She needed to leave this place under her own power.

But she wasn't moving. She was just looking up at him, tiny frown lines between her brows.

"I would have died in there if it hadn't been for you." There was none of her usual snap behind the words.

He couldn't tell her he would never have let that happen. "You were practically out the door already. You just needed a little help with the walking thing."

"Still." Her gaze locked on to his. "I should've known you'd be there when I needed you."

"Always. You can count on that, Little Bit." He almost scooped her up despite his vow to resist it, but they were suddenly jostled by Security crew trying to round up a gaggle of LO's. He took Rayna by the arm instead. "Let's go."

He led the way through the quad until they found Gabriel and the head of the Security detail, a freshly promoted Javin Darto. "Things seem well in hand here." Sam grinned at the big man in his new uniform. "We're going back to the ship."

Darto stood a little straighter. "Aye, Cap. Glad to see you're all right, ma'am."

"Thanks for the help." Rayna smiled at him. "Again."

The squad leader seemed at a loss for words, but the huge grin on his face spoke volumes.

Gabriel joined them as Sam and Rayna stepped into a clear space in the yard. A few seconds later the beam enveloped them and they reformed in the 'hawk's D-mat room.

Mo was waiting for them. "We have a problem, Cap."

CHAPTER THIRTY-ONE

Sam turned to his XO, but before he could open his mouth Rayna collapsed at his side. He gathered her in before she could hit the floor and took off for Sickbay at the end of the corridor, Gabriel and his XO on his heels.

Mo tried for his attention. "Cap?"

"Save it!" In his arms, Rayna was nearly as white as he was, the blood drained from her face. Under his hand he could feel the bandage had begun to soak through. He ran into Sickbay and bellowed for Doc Berta. The startled medic met him at the exam table in the first open bay.

The table scanned Rayna's vital signs while Doc Berta made her own exam and in seconds looked up to nod. "She'll be fine. She's lost some blood is all. Get out and let me do my job."

Sam exhaled a shaky breath. He finally let go of Rayna's hand and stepped back, giving the doctor room to do her work.

When his heart returned to its normal rhythm, he looked to Gabriel. "Stay with her."

Gabriel nodded and found a place in an out-of-the-way corner.

Sam followed his XO into the corridor. "Now. You were saying?"

"The Gray destroyer. The ship entered orbit ten minutes ago."

"What?" Sam punched the lift panel for the bridge. "Why didn't you say so? And who the hell is on the bridge?"

"I did say so, and Sipritz has the conn."

Sipritz could hold command as well as anyone, but a primal possessiveness roiled in his guts. Something threatened *his* ship. *He* needed to be on the bridge.

The lift doors slid open and he swept onto his bridge, tension tightening his greeting. "Crew!"

"Cap!" They were worried, all right. Maybe they thought he wouldn't make it back from Kinz. Maybe they thought the Gray destroyer taking up most of the viewscreen would end it for them this time.

"Report, Sipritz!"

"The Minertsan destroyer, the *Tifan*, took up orbit approximately eleven minutes, fifteen seconds ago. We are on battlestations. Shields are up. Her captain is demanding our surrender. The only reason he hasn't blown us out of space is the non-aggression rule in force in LinHo orbit. Obviously, he's not yet aware of the change in ownership of LinHo, or of what's happening down below."

"Okay. Status of the transfer of LO's?"

Patel at Communications had an answer for him. "Rescue ship *Harriet Tubman* reports transfers are seventy percent complete, Cap. They're nearly full, though. We'll have to pitch in."

Mo groaned. "Why am I not surprised?"

"Right. Put me through to the *Tifan*. And, Mo, have the former director of the Kinz facility brought to the bridge."

Patel looked over his shoulder. "Onscreen, Cap."

Sam stood on the Cap walk with arms crossed over his chest and scowled at the image of the *Tifan*'s captain resolving on his viewscreen. The Gray's aura showed no subtlety through EM communication; the colors were muted and difficult to distinguish. The dark gray that billowed around the captain's form could have meant a neutral emotional tone shading into anger, or a fault of the color translation in the comm system. At any rate, Sam was no expert at decoding the Grays' emotional projections. He had seen only the basest of emotions in his time with them.

"Surrender, *Shadowhawk*. You are an enemy of the Minertsan Consortium. Your ship and your cargo are forfeit. Your captain and crew are subject to the justice of the Consortium." What came through the comm was an electronic simulation. The Gray's "lips" didn't move; he had no "voice."

All of it was an offense to Sam's ears. "I've had a taste of the 'justice' of the Consortium before, Captain. I won't yield to it again. And before you go making threats, you might want to know the situation on LinHo. Kinz has been destroyed. I take it that was your goal, though the Thrane mercenaries you sent to do the job failed to survive. The workers in the factory, however, *did* survive. They'll be returned to their own lives. I assume that's the cargo you were referring to?"

The aura around the Gray captain swirled with what was clearly bright red and black now. "Those slaves are property of the Minertsan government!"

"No. They are free people, as of this moment."

Mo stood behind him. "Cap. The Kinz director is here."

"Ah! Feel like taking a shot at us, do you? You might want to reconsider. We have a hero of the Consortium aboard." He grabbed the Gray by the arm and brought him forward. "If not for Arek, Director of Arms Facility Number Four Seven Nine Three, your Thrane bomber might not have completed his mission. Isn't that right, Arek?"

The Director's aura was a sickly shade of yellow and green, but he nodded.

"Speak up. Tell the captain."

"I cooperated with Lord Kor, sir. I . . . did everything he told me to do."

"And yet he is dead, and you are not."

"I . . . regret that I was taken prisoner before I could die in service to the Consortium."

Sam feigned surprise. "Die? A hero like Arek here? This was a facility given over to the production of weapons for the rebels, you realize, Captain. Without his cooperation, Kor would never have been able to do his job. You need to take him back to Minertsa for his reward."

The Gray was shivering under his hand. "I deserve no recognition for doing my work."

On the screen the captain of the *Tifan* showed an

aura tinged with triumphant gold and bloodthirsty red. Sam had seen that combination many times. Things might not go so well for Arek back on the home planet. The term *scapegoat* came to mind.

Sam smiled at the screen. "Of course, if you attack my ship, I'll just kill him. Then you can explain to your superiors what happened to him. I don't think I have to remind you we've beaten you once already. No reason to think we won't do it again."

The captain of the *Tifan* considered, his aura fading from blood red to a more unreadable mix of colors. "If you turn Arek over to me, I will leave the system and return to Minertsa directly. You have my word."

Sam wanted to laugh, but he managed a straight face. "And just how much is your word worth, Captain?"

"I might ask a pirate the same thing. But that might insult you."

Sam did laugh then, and so did his crew. A Gray with a sense of humor? You had to like that. And what choice did he have, really? Take the thing's word or start blasting. With D-mats underway the latter wouldn't be an option.

"Okay. Take him and be gone with my blessing."

The Gray captain's aura shone with an obvious gold. He nodded in farewell as his image winked out.

As soon as the light moved past her abdomen,

Rayna pushed the call button. Things were busy in Sickbay, so she had to push it for a while before a medic appeared to see what was wrong.

"Get me Doc Berta."

The medic, veteran of many a ward war, with the no-nonsense demeanor to prove it, crossed her arms over her chest. "What for?"

"She needs to sign me out."

The woman laughed. "Not today, hon. You just got out of surgery."

Maybe. But I'm not staying here another hour. She'd spent all the time she was going to spend locked down. "That's right, *out* of surgery. The light's done its job, too. See?" She pointed to the pink line running just under her ribs on the left side.

"Uh huh. But you still need rest and rehydration. Just try sitting up. You'll see."

Rayna put her hands on the mattress and pushed. Her upper body levered to a sitting position, where she wavered, her vision washing in and out. The medic grabbed her arm to stabilize her, and Rayna felt the bed come up to meet her back. She was still halfway sitting up; the medic must have raised the mattress for her.

But the woman had the look of I-told-you-so all over her face. "Now. Any more outta you and I'll sedate you. The doc will be here in the morning to take a look at you."

Fuck. She waited for the room to stop spinning and considered her options. Maybe if she hijacked an assist-chair . . .

"You're supposed to be recovering." He filled most of the open side of her cubicle, his grin lighting the space. "Why do you look like you're planning Rescue's next mission?"

Her heart thumped in her chest, a fact that the monitor duly recorded. Sam's grin grew wider at the sound of it. No hiding how she felt for him.

"I was trying to plot my own escape. Please tell me you're here to rescue me."

He sat at the edge of her bed and took her hand. "Restless already?"

"I feel fine. I'm tired of being cooped up. Can't you do something? You're the captain."

His finger traced the line of her scar, a frown wrinkling his brow. "Doc Berta rules in here, you know that. You need time to heal."

"I can heal anywhere. I can heal in my cabin."

Sam lifted an eyebrow. "Your cabin? And where might that be, Little Bit? We're full up with LO's heading back to Madras. Even Lainie has four other bunkmates."

The monitor registered the acceleration of her heartbeat into a dangerously high zone. An alarm sounded and the screen turned yellow. Had she made too many assumptions? Had they been through too much to just pick up where they'd left off? His face gave her no answers.

The medic showed up before Rayna could say anything. "Cap?" She looked from her captain to her patient and back. "Everything okay?"

"Fine, Jenson. Carry on."

"Aye, Cap. Not too long, now."

"Understood."

Rayna tried to regain control of the conversation. "I thought we might . . . I mean—"

"You'll be staying in *our* cabin, Little Bit. Yours and mine. For as long as we're together. Unless you've changed your mind?"

Relief flooded through her, causing the damn alarm to whoop again. "No! Hell, no, I haven't changed my mind!" She threw her arms around his neck and pulled him close. He smelled like fresh air and warm earth. "We may not have much time, but I want to spend every second with you, Sam. God, I love you. Take me out of here. I can't stay here another minute."

Doc Berta rushed into the cubicle and spoiled the moment. "What the hell are you doing to my patient?" The medic hovered behind the doctor, if a woman of her girth could be said to hover. From her smug expression, it was clear she'd tattled.

The captain of the *Shadowhawk* stood to his full height and faced the wrath of his med department. "I'm removing her from your care."

"Like hell. I just closed her up a few hours ago. Jenson here just turned the light off on her. She needs rest."

"And rehydration," Sam added. "I know. I can be sure she gets that. In my cabin."

The doctor gaped. "*Your* cabin? Am I missing something here?"

Rayna had to smile. "If you are, you're probably the last person on this ship to know."

"If you insist on keeping Agent Carver here, she'll only find a way to escape that bed before she's ready." Sam didn't look at her as he said this. He kept his gaze on the doctor. "I take full responsibility for my fiancée."

Three voices joined the chorus. "Your *what*?"

Before Doc Berta could recover, Sam had unhooked Rayna from her monitor and IV and lifted her into his arms. "Sign the pad. I'm taking her." The doctor was still protesting—loudly—as he strode from Sickbay into the corridor.

Rayna squirmed in his grasp. "I never agreed to a marriage contract. You know we can't do that."

"Stay still. Do you want to be rescued or not?"

She didn't think he'd take her back to Sickbay, but she didn't have the strength to fight him. She'd save her breath for the real argument when they got to his— their—cabin.

Besides, it was embarrassing enough to be carried like a baby through the ship, with his crew grinning at them like schoolkids. Some of them even cheered and applauded. And her erstwhile "fiancé" was eating it up, prouder than a Melbax arborian who'd just won a mate challenge.

"I am going to slap that grin clean off your face, Captain Snark!" she hissed at him.

He drew back to look at her, his grin growing. "Oh, so it's back to Captain Snark, is it? You must be feeling better."

They reached his cabin at last, and he carried her inside, the hatch sliding closed behind them. It was dimly lit, but, as always, it was neat and clean and smelled like Sam. Suddenly she didn't feel much like fighting anymore.

"Put me down, you evil *ptark*!" But she was laughing now, warmth glowing in her chest for this man who had rescued her in so many ways.

He laid her on the bunk and followed her down, entwining his big body with hers so she could feel his strength, his heat held in reserve. His hands cupped her face, and without a word, he took her mouth, his tongue bringing that taste of drunken cherries. He was gentle, his hunger leashed, but still her body responded to him with a familiar ache. She had been too long without him.

He broke off with a moan. "You need rest."

"I need you." So damn much. More than he could ever know.

He wanted her, too. She could feel his hard length pressing against her thigh. But the expression in his deep, green gaze was more than sexual. That gaze spoke of protection, loyalty, love. Everything about him promised forever.

"And you'll have me, Rayna. For the rest of our lives. We have time now. Rest and heal." He dropped a lighter kiss on her lips.

He was right, of course. She was still a little woozy from the surgery. She could wait a day, as long as it was here in his arms. But how much time did they really have? That was a question that could break her heart.

Sam cleared his throat. "I've had a proposition from Rescue. Daniel brought it to me."

Rayna brought her head around to look at him. He seemed . . . hesitant. Were they firing her and afraid to tell her?

"This wasn't my finest moment, was it."

Now he looked confused. "What? No. I mean, yes. I mean, you killed two enemy operatives and saved 1500 LO's. What more could you want?"

"You did most of that. Saving the LO's, killing Kor."

"You pulled the trigger, as I recall."

She grinned. "Yeah. I guess we make a pretty good team."

"Well, that's sort of what Daniel talked to me about." Sam shifted beside her, as if he was uncomfortable. "He wants to recruit me."

She sat up, though it sent a sharp stab of pain through her side and made her head spin. "For Rescue? As an agent?"

He laughed. "No! Never as an agent. Rescue wants me *and* my ship."

She stared at him, mouth hanging open. It was perfect. He would just keep doing what he'd always done, only now he'd do it for Rescue—and with their help. But her Sam, the pirate . . .

"Are you considering it?" Her heart crashed against her ribs.

"I'd have to take it to my crew." He stared at the ceiling.

"They'd follow where you lead." She didn't want to push him, but, God, she wanted this.

"It doesn't sound too bad. You. Me. The 'hawk doing a job for Rescue."

She took a breath; let it out. "You think so?"

He finally looked at her. "Marry me, and let's find out."

No was there on her lips, despite all the reasons to say yes. She loved this man, but to open the bay doors and leap into black, unending space with him was something else. Did she have that faith? Did she have that courage? And to make this commitment, when she might have to leave him behind and take up her work in a labor camp or a mine far from his loving arms? Wouldn't it just be easier to end this now?

But she thought of her parents, dedicated to each other though the Grays tried to break them. Loving each other millions of miles away from everything and everyone they knew. They had only each other. And love. Her love for Sam was that kind of love. Could she do any less?

She pulled him down with her onto the bunk, her arms circling his neck. "Yeah. Little Bit Snark. I kinda like the sound of that."

THE END

ACKNOWLEDGEMENTS

Right up front I'd like to acknowledge a debt to Gene Roddenberry, the creator of STAR TREK, and Ridley Scott and the team who turned author Philip K. Dick's short story into the SF masterpiece BLADE RUNNER. Without them, Sam and Rayna might have met in a very different way, rather than in this space opera noir homage.

My beta reader and critique partner Laurie A. Green was even more crucial to this project than usual, given her talents in the more starship-driven side of SFR. I really needed her help with this one!

As always, intrepid editor Deborah Kreiser went wherever the story took her, come laser blast or ion storm. And, as always, the book came out the better for it. Thanks to Deborah for all her special skills.

My agent and friend Michelle Johnson continues to provide encouragement, advice, promotion and unending support. I can't thank Michelle enough for all she does.

I have the amazingly talented Jessica Hildreth to thank for the bright, shiny new cover designs which grace not only *Fools Rush In*, but also *Unchained Memory* and *Trouble in Mind*, too, now.

And finally, you, my small, but mighty Rescue Squad of devoted readers. Thank YOU for seeking my stories out, whether they're set in Nashville or Arizona or the deep black of space. No matter where the battle is fought to save Earth, I promise love will always be the ultimate weapon.